Empire and Honor

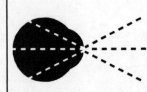

This Large Print Book carries the
Seal of Approval of N.A.V.H.

EMPIRE AND HONOR

W.E.B. GRIFFIN AND WILLIAM E. BUTTERWORTH IV

THORNDIKE PRESS
A part of Gale, Cengage Learning

GALE
CENGAGE Learning®

Detroit • New York • San Francisco • New Haven, Conn • Waterville, Maine • London

GALE
CENGAGE Learning®

LIBRARY OF CONGRESS CATALOGING-IN-PUBLICATION DATA

Griffin, W.E.B.
   Empire and honor / by W.E.B. Griffin and William E.
Butterworth IV.
      pages ; cm. — (Thorndike press large print core) (An honor
   bound novel series)
   ISBN-13: 978-1-4104-5409-6 (hardcover)
   ISBN-10: 1-4104-5409-6 (hardcover)
   1. United States. Office of Strategic Services—Fiction. 2.
Intelligence officers—United States—Fiction. 3. World War,
1939–1945—Fiction. 4. Large type books. I. Butterworth,
William E. (William Edmund) II. Title.
PS3557.R489137E47 2013
813'.54—dc23   2012043586

Published in 2013 by arrangement with G.P. Putnam's Sons, a member of Penguin Group (USA) Inc.

Printed in the United States of America
1 2 3 4 5 6 7 17 16 15 14 13

IN LOVING MEMORY OF

Colonel José Manuel Menéndez

Cavalry, Argentine Army, Retired.
He spent his life fighting Communism
and Juan Domingo Perón

PROLOGUE

When the Edificio Libertador was built (1935–38) to house the headquarters of the Argentine army, known as the "Ejército Argentino," the twenty-story structure was the largest building ever constructed in Argentina. It had been commissioned by President Agustín Justo, a retired general who had been minister of War before moving into the Casa Rosada, Argentina's pink equivalent of the United States' White House.

Justo's directions to architect Carlos Pibernat had been essentially to "do it properly" — which Pibernat interpreted to mean that cost was not to be a consideration. Argentina was prosperous; it had the world's largest gold reserves and liked to think of itself as a world power.

Argentines took a smug pride when they heard the phrase "As rich as an Argentine."

This was not a new state of mind. For example, when at the turn of the century Argentina decided it needed a new opera house, the government's instructions to the architects were essentially "make it bigger, better, and more grandiose than the Paris Opera, the Vienna Opera, and any other opera house in the world."

When the Edificio Libertador was completed on an eight-acre plot east of the Casa Rosada, it was what today would be called state of the art. It had high-speed Siemens elevators, and a communications system installed by Siemens and other German firms to the high standards of the German army.

The Ejército Argentino had a close, admiring relationship with the German Wehrmacht and the leader of the German people, Adolf Hitler, who was in the process — nearly finished in 1938 — of bringing Germany out of the disaster caused by the Weimar Republic and the Versailles Treaty. Argentine officers were sent to the Kriegsschule in Germany, and the Wehrmacht sent officers to train the Ejército, whose uniforms closely resembled those of the Wehrmacht.

There was also a great admiration among Ejército Argentino officers for "Il Duce," Benito Mussolini, the Italian dictator and founder of Fascism, who, it was said, made the trains run on time. Argentina, like the United States, was a nation of immigrants. There were more Argentines of Italian ancestry than of Spanish or any other nationality.

In 1938, Fascism and its cousin, Nazism, were clearly on the rise, and war was as clearly on the horizon. Nevertheless, it took five years, until 1943, to settle the differences between various factors of the Ejército vis-à-vis who got which wings and floors of the Edificio Libertador.

By then, it appeared almost certain that Fascism was to be the New World Order. The Wehrmacht, using a new tactic of fast-moving armored formations called "Blitzkrieg," had brought France — and the rest of Continental Europe — to its knees in just over a month, May 10 to June 14, 1940. Britain was isolated.

On June 22, 1941, Germany launched OPERATION BARBAROSSA against Russia, and by August 20 the Wehrmacht was on the outskirts of Leningrad.

On December 7, 1941, the Japanese bombed Pearl Harbor, Territory of Hawaii, sinking most of the U.S. Pacific fleet, and quickly turned their attention to the Philippine Islands. Germany declared war on the United States, and the conflict became the Allies — Britain and the U.S. — versus the Axis — Germany, Japan, and Italy.

The British bastion in the Far East, Singapore, fell to the Japanese on February 15, 1942, the largest capitulation in British history.

And on May 6, 1942, Lieutenant General Jonathan M. Wainwright unconditionally surrendered the Philippines to the Japanese. It was the worst defeat in American history.

Although Argentina was neutral, most of the Ejército Argentino — but not all — cheered the

Axis triumphs.

The Argentine navy, which had been trained by the Royal Navy, was disheartened.

The British had been in Argentina for a long time in such numbers that they tended to think of it as almost a British colony. The Brits had built — and owned — the Argentine railway system. There was an Argentine branch of Harrods, the famed London department store, in downtown Buenos Aires, and many members of the upper class had been educated and continued to educate their children in Argentine versions — Saint Paul's, for example — of British "public" — actually private — schools.

Anglo-Argentines volunteered for service in the British armed forces, as did Germano-Argentines for service to the Third Reich. There were daily English- and German-language newspapers in Buenos Aires. The government permitted them to continue publishing but forbade their reporting of war news.

Both the Germans and the British, as in the First World War, turned to Argentina for foodstuffs. This was a very profitable business for Argentina.

One of Argentina's neighbors to the north, Brazil, had declared war on the Axis shortly after Pearl Harbor. This was to give the United States airbases in Brazil from which specially equipped B-24 bombers could be used against German submarines. The Nazi *Unterseeboots* — U-boats — had been interdicting British merchant ships carrying Argentine beef and other foodstuffs to England.

On April 18, 1942, sixteen B-25 bombers took off from the aircraft carrier USS *Hornet* and bombed Tokyo. Not much physical damage was done, but the raid destroyed the notion of Japanese invincibility.

On November 8, 1942, American forces staged a successful invasion of North Africa, and many historians consider this the turning point of World War II. Certainly, things went, slowly but inexorably, downhill for the Axis after that date.

On November 19, 1942, the Russians at Stalingrad were in a position whereby they could launch a counteroffensive — and did so. They quickly surrounded the German Sixth Army, which Hitler had ordered to fight until the last man and the last round.

On January 31, 1943, Field Marshal von Paulus surrendered the southern sector, and on February 2, 1943, General Schreck surrendered the northern group. Ninety thousand German soldiers became prisoners and perhaps at least that number were in unmarked graves.

The Russian march to Berlin began.

On September 3, 1943, Anglo-American forces landed in Italy. The same day, Italy surrendered unconditionally to the Allies.

On June 6, 1944, the Allies landed in France. The Germans surrendered Paris on August 25.

On October 20, 1944, MacArthur made good his promise — "I shall return" — by landing his Sixth Army on Leyte Island in the Philippines.

The U.S. and Royal Air Forces began day-and-night one-thousand-bomber raids on the German homeland, as Allied forces fought their way to Germany.

On January 16, 1945, the Red Army breached the German front and marched — as much as twenty-five miles a day — through East Prussia, Lower Silesia, East Pomerania, and Upper Silesia, to a line forty miles east of Berlin along the Oder River.

On March 27, 1945, Argentina, finally realizing that defeat was imminent, declared war on Germany.

On April 30, 1945, Adolf Hitler committed suicide as Russian tanks rolled through the streets of Berlin. A week later, on May 7, 1945, Germany surrendered unconditionally.

On August 6, 1945, the United States obliterated Hiroshima, Japan, with an atomic bomb. Three days later, a second atomic bomb obliterated Nagasaki.

On September 2, 1945, a formal surrender ceremony was performed in Tokyo Bay, Japan, aboard the battleship USS *Missouri*.

World War II was over.

Not a single Argentine soldier or sailor had died in the war.

Not one bomb or artillery shell had landed on Argentine soil.

And, as a result of supplying foodstuffs to both sides, Argentina was richer than ever.

Argentina's role in World War II, however, was by no means over.

When — as early as 1942 — the most senior members of the Nazi hierarchy, as high as Martin Bormann, generally regarded as second in power only to Hitler, and Reichsführer-SS Heinrich Himmler, realized the Ultimate Victory was not nearly as certain as Propaganda Minister Joseph Goebbels had been telling the German people, they began in great secrecy to implement OPERATION PHOENIX.

Should the Thousand-Year Reich have a life shorter than they hoped, by establishing refuges in South America — primarily in Argentina and Paraguay — to which senior Nazis could flee, National Socialism could rise, phoenix-like, from the ashes.

Vast sums were sent to Argentina, some through normal banking channels but most in great secrecy by submarine. The U-boats also carried crates of currency, gold, and diamonds and other precious stones. Senior SS officers were sent to Argentina — some of them legally, accredited as diplomats, but again most of them secretly infiltrated by submarine — to purchase property where senior Nazis would be safe from Allied retribution.

The Allies learned of OPERATION PHOENIX and tried, without much success, to stop it. Their concern heightened as the war drew to a close.

13

They learned that when Grand Admiral Doenitz issued the cease hostilities order on May 4, sixty-three U-boats were at sea.

Five of them were known to have complied with their orders to hoist a black flag and proceed to an Allied port to surrender, or to a neutral port to be interned. There was reliable intelligence that an additional forty-one U-boats had been scuttled by their crews, to prevent the capture of whatever may have been on board.

That left between seventeen and twenty U-boats unaccounted for. Of particular concern were U-234, U-405, and U-977. They were Type XB U-boats — minelayers, which meant that with no mines aboard they could carry a great deal of cargo and many passengers for great distances.

There was credible intelligence that when U-234 sailed from Narvik on April 16 — two weeks before the German capitulation — she had aboard a varied cargo, some of which was either not listed on the manifest at all or listed under a false description. This included a ton of mail — which of course almost certainly hid currency and diamonds being smuggled. It also included Nazi and Japanese officers and German scientists as passengers. And something even more worrisome: 560 kilograms of uranium oxide from the German not-quite-completed atomic bomb project.

It was only logical to presume that U-405 and U-977 were carrying similar cargoes.

A massive search by ship and air for all submarines — but especially for U-234, U-405, and U-977 — was launched from France, England, and Africa, and by the specially configured U.S. Army Air Forces B-24 "Liberator" bombers, which had searched for submarines since 1942 from bases in Brazil.

The searches, of course, were limited by the range of the aircraft involved and, as far as the ships also involved in the searches, by the size of the South Atlantic Ocean once the submarines had entered it.

There were some successes. Submarines were sighted and then attacked with depth charges and/or aircraft bombs. While it was mathematically probable that several of the submarines were sunk, there was no telling which ones.

The concern that the U-boats that — either certainly or probably — had uranium oxide aboard and were headed for Japan was reduced of course when the Japanese surrendered on September 2, 1945.

But that left Argentina as a very possible destination.

I

[ONE]

"Let me have a look, please," SS-Brigadeführer Ludwig Hoffmann said to Fregattenkapitän Wilhelm von Dattenberg, captain of U-405, who was looking through the periscope.

Hoffmann's tone suggested it was less a request than an order. Hoffmann, a diminutive, intense forty-five-year-old, was superior in rank to von Dattenberg. If they had been in the Kriegsmarine, Hoffmann would have been a *vizeadmiral.*

Von Dattenberg, a slim, somewhat hawk-faced thirty-four-year-old, stepped away from the periscope eyepiece and indicated to Hoffmann that it was his.

Five months earlier, SS-Brigadeführer Hoffmann and fifteen other SS officers —

19

two SS-*standartenführers,* a rank equivalent to *kapitän zur see;* six SS-*obersturmbannführers,* a rank equivalent to von Dattenberg's; and seven SS-*sturmbannführers,* a rank equivalent to *korvettenkapitän* — had come aboard U-405 at Narvik, Denmark, with five heavy wooden crates.

And at least once a day since then, Fregattenkapitän von Dattenberg had very seriously considered how he might kill all of the Nazis, who carried orders signed by Reichsführer-SS Heinrich Himmler himself.

Right now, he genuinely regretted having missed all of his opportunities to do so because each time he had come up with a plan, he realized that it would have endangered his crew. After all he'd been through with his sailors, he had no intention of doing that.

"I can't see a goddamn thing," Hoffmann snapped.

"The sun hasn't come up, Herr Brigadeführer," von Dattenberg said. "And there's not much to see. As you know, this location was chosen because of its isolation."

Hoffmann did not directly respond.

"But I can make out the shoreline," he said. "Why are we so far offshore?"

"If we move any closer to the shore, Herr Brigadeführer, we would run the risk of going aground and tearing our bottom."

"Then how are we going to get ashore?" Hoffmann asked.

What you mean, you sonofabitch, is: "How am I going to get ashore without getting my shoes wet? Or drowning?"

Von Dattenberg resisted the temptation to reply with what popped into his mind — *I don't really give a damn how you do, just as long as you bastards get off my U-boat* — and instead said, "Perhaps we'll get lucky, Herr Brigadeführer, and the people we're trying to establish contact with will have a boat of some kind. Otherwise, I'm afraid it will have to be in our rubber boats."

"Don't you mean, von Dattenberg, the people we're *going* to contact?" Hoffmann asked.

"I think we have to consider, Herr Brigade-führer, the changed circumstances."

Hoffmann took von Dattenberg's meaning: *Germany has surrendered and the war is over — there may not be anyone waiting for us to arrive.*

"The people who will meet us are SS. They will comply with their orders," Hoffmann said.

"Of course," von Dattenberg said.

He thought: *And if there is no flashing light from the shore, then what do I do?*

Comply with that last official order from the Kriegsmarine to hoist a black flag and proceed to the nearest enemy port and surrender?

Himmler's order told me to ignore that Kriegs-marine order when it came and place myself at the orders of Hoffmann.

Hoffmann and the other SS swine are not go-ing to go docilely into internment. That would carry with it the threat of being repatriated to Germany to face whatever it is the Allies have in mind for people like them.

So what do I do? Kill them all?

I could wait until they're in the rubber boats and then machine-gun them, "leaving no survi-vors," as I was ordered to leave no survivors of the British and American merchantmen I sank and who had made it into their lifeboats.

Nice thought, Willi, but you're pissing into the wind.

I could not order the machine-gunning of these swine in my rubber boats any more than I could order the machine-gunning of those sailors in their lifeboats.

The dichotomy here is that while Hoffmann and the other SS slime aboard deserve to be shot out of hand, I simply cannot do that.

I still am an officer bound by the Code of Honor.

"So what do we do now?" Hoffmann asked, as he put his eyes back on the periscope.

"The protocol, Herr Brigadeführer, is for us to come to periscope depth at oh-four-thirty for a period of thirty minutes, flashing the signal at sixty-second intervals during that period of time, while proceeding at dead slow speed along the coast . . ."

As you should goddamn well know, Hoffmann. You've nearly worn out the protocol folder reading it over and over with all the attention the Pope would pay to the original version of the Gospel according to Saint Peter.

". . . and, in the event contact is not made, to submerge and wait until twenty-one-thirty, at which time we are to come again to periscope depth and repeat the process for another thirty-minute period."

Hoffmann grunted.

"Would you like to look for a signal from the shore, Herr Brigadeführer? Or . . ."

Hoffmann stepped back from the periscope.

"Schröder," von Dattenberg said, and gestured for Korvettenkapitän Erik Schröder, U-405's executive officer, to take the periscope.

"Maintain signaling," von Dattenberg ordered. "Proceed dead slow at this depth for twenty-five minutes."

"Maintain signaling. Dead slow for twenty-five minutes, aye, Kapitän," von Dattenberg's Number One answered.

"You have the helm, Schröder. I'll be in my cabin."

"I have the helm, aye, Kapitän."

"Why are you going to your cabin?" Hoffmann demanded.

"For my daily cup of coffee," von Dattenberg answered. "Would you care to join me, Herr Brigadeführer?"

"I'll stay here," Hoffmann said.

"Very well."

Von Dattenberg made his way through the boat to his cabin. It was crowded, but not nearly as crowded as it had been when they left Narvik, or after they had been replenished at sea from a Spanish merchantman just about in the center of the South Atlantic.

All the supplies with which they had sailed and with which they had augmented from the replenishment vessel — including fuel — were just about gone.

And the odds are that the SS men in Argentina aren't going to be on the beach looking for a signal from a submarine.

Despite Hoffmann's pissing-in-the-wind belief that they will "comply with their orders," they will have decided that no U-boat is coming.

What they are doing is desperately trying to hide themselves in Argentina.

So, what do I do?

Von Dattenberg pushed aside the curtain that served as the door to his cabin and stepped inside. He shared his cabin with Brigadeführer Hoffmann, which meant von Dattenberg slept on a mattress on the deck, his bunk being one of the privileges that went with Brigadeführer Hoffmann's rank.

He saw the steward had already stowed the

24

mattress atop the bunk.

He sat at his desk, opened a drawer, and took from it a small jar of Nescafé. Just as soon as the Swiss had developed the powdered coffee, which didn't spoil and took up very little space, it had been enthusiastically adopted by the submarine service. That was in 1936, when von Dattenberg had been a twenty-three-year-old *oberleutnant zur see* in submarine training at a secret base in Russia.

Von Dattenberg unscrewed the cap and peered inside the jar. He had enough coffee left for maybe a week, at a one-cup-a-day consumption rate. He wondered why Hoffmann had not stolen his coffee, and decided that Hoffmann, not wanting to unnecessarily antagonize him, had stolen Nescafé from one or more of his brother officers.

Von Dattenberg put a scanty teaspoon of Nescafé into a china mug. As he then put water into a small electric pot and plugged it in, he decided that there was a silver lining in the black cloud that was his mission: Whatever happened, this would be the last time he would ever be off the coast of Argentina looking for a signal from shore.

He had made eleven successful similar voyages. He had even smuggled other senior SS officers into Argentina, including SS-Brigadeführer Ritter Manfred von Deitzberg, who was Himmler's first deputy adjutant.

He was certain that that was the reason —

no good deed ever goes unpunished — he had been selected to make this voyage, too. He didn't know specifically what the swine he had aboard had done for the SS to earn themselves a place on U-405, but in addition to OPERATION PHOENIX, there was no question in his mind that it had a good deal to do with another operation — a nameless, shameful one — run by senior SS officers.

By the time he learned of this operation, von Dattenberg thought he knew all there was to know about the despicable behavior of the SS and its senior officers. He had known, for example, that before joining the SS, SS-Obergruppenführer Reinhard Heydrich, Himmler's deputy, had been a naval officer whom Admiral Erich Raeder had forced to resign for unspecified "conduct unbecoming to an officer and a gentleman."

And von Dattenberg had known all about the SS's role in the "Final Solution" and their administration of the extermination camps. But he had been shocked to learn that for a stiff ransom, Jews outside Germany could buy their relatives and friends out of certain death in the *konzentrationslager* and have them sent to Argentina and Paraguay. The only thing he didn't know was whether Himmler himself was involved in this obscene trade or whether it had personally enriched only such high-ranking officers as Hoffmann and von Deitzberg and their immediately subordinate swine.

The water in the electric pot finally came to a boil. Von Dattenberg was carefully pouring it into his mug when a voice called through the curtain.

"Herr Kapitän, we have a signal from the shore."

I'll be goddamned!

"I'll be right there," von Dattenberg said.

After I finish my coffee . . .

The landing protocol went smoothly. Kapitän von Dattenberg was not surprised. It had been rehearsed dozens of times at sea, as much to give the men a chance to come on deck as because the relatively simple procedure needed practice to make its execution perfect.

When the cabin cruiser — it looked to von Dattenberg to be an American-made Chris-Craft — approached U-405, everything was in place. A line of his men, securely attached to a cable running from the conning tower to the saw-like anti-submarine net cutter on her bow, were prepared to carry out their roles. They had already opened the number three hatch and taken the crane from it. The crane would be used to hoist the five heavy crates and load them onto the cabin cruiser.

Others had already dropped cushions over the port side to protect the hull of the Chris-Craft from that of U-405. Still others were prepared to put a ladder between the submarine and the cabin cruiser. When von Dattenberg looked down from the conning tower, he saw his passengers, all wearing life jackets and civilian clothing, waiting to cross the ladder.

SS-Brigadeführer Hoffmann came onto the bridge.

Without asking permission, of course.

"Presumably everything is in order?" Hoffmann said.

"Yes, Herr Brigadeführer, it is. Would you prefer to transfer to the boat before or after we move the cargo?"

"Before."

"Very well."

"I wanted a final word with you, von Dattenberg."

Is the sonofabitch actually going to say "thank you"?

"Yes, sir?"

"I think you should wait twenty-four hours before you scuttle your ship."

It's a boat, a U-boat.

"The protocol, Herr Brigadeführer, calls for the immediate scuttling of U-boat 405 once I am satisfied that you have made it safely ashore."

"I don't give a damn about the protocol, von Dattenberg. I'm telling you I want you to be twenty-four hours' sailing time away from here before you scuttle it."

Scuttle her.

"Whatever you wish, of course, Herr Brigade-führer."

Fuck you, Herr Brigadeführer.

Von Dattenberg looked down to the deck again.

"They are ready to move the cargo at your order, Herr Brigadeführer, and the ladder should be in place by the time you get below."

Hoffmann offered his hand. After von Dattenberg shook it, Hoffmann then shot his arm out in the Nazi salute.

"Heil Hitler!"

Do you really believe that, you asshole? Der Führer is dead.

"Heil Hitler," von Dattenberg parroted as he casually returned the salute.

Hoffmann returned to the hatch and dropped through it.

Von Dattenberg picked up a megaphone.

"Commence cargo transfer," he ordered. "Men first, then crates." Fregattenkapitän von Dattenberg waited until he could no longer make out faces aboard the Chris-Craft before issuing his next orders.

"Secure from off-loading procedures," he said. "And then take us to sea."

"This is the *kapitän,*" he said to the micro-phone, his voice filling the submarine. "We have just completed our orders to land our passengers and cargo safely and secretly in

29

Argentina. Accordingly, we no longer are under the orders of Reichsführer-SS Himmler, and are now going to comply with our last order from the Kriegsmarine.

"We are, therefore, going to hoist a black flag and make for the nearest enemy port, where I then will surrender U-405. The nearest enemy port is the Port Belgrano Navy Base at Punta Alta near Bahía Blanca, about seven hundred kilometers south of Buenos Aires.

"On our surrender, we will of course be interrogated by our captors. After some thought, I have decided the honorable thing for me to do as an officer of the Kriegsmarine is to forget who our passengers were and what our cargo was. Because I will no longer be in command, I can only ask all of you to go along with my decision.

"As you know, Admiral Canaris was a prisoner of the Argentines in the First World War, and the crew of the Panzerschiff *Graf Spee* has been interned here since December of 1939. Both the admiral and the crew of the *Graf Spee* have stated that the Argentines are gracious captors, and that the food and women of Argentina are spectacular."

There then came the sound of the microphone clicking, and for a long moment the speakers — and the crew — were silent. Then the mic clicked again.

"Korvettenkapitän Schröder," von Dattenberg ordered. "Hoist a black flag. Set course for Mar del Plata. All ahead full."

[Two]

The Lafayette Room
The Hay-Adams Hotel
800 Sixteenth Street, N.W.
Washington, D.C.
1335 6 October 1945

Cletus Marcus Howell — a tall, sharp-featured, elegantly tailored septuagenarian — walked briskly across the lobby of the hotel and into the Lafayette Room. He stopped before the headwaiter's lectern.

"Well?" he demanded.

"Around the corner, behind a screen, Mr. Howell."

"How long has he been there?"

"About ten minutes."

Howell reached in his pocket and came out with a thick wad of cash secured by a gold money clip shaped like an oil well drilling rig.

"I said to tell me within five minutes, but that's close enough," he said, extracting a one-hundred-dollar bill from the clip. He handed it to the headwaiter.

"Thank you, sir."

Howell marched into the dining room, found the screen, and stepped behind it.

A well-tailored, barrel-chested, bald-headed fifty-year-old with a pencil-line mustache was sitting alone at a table.

"Well, if it isn't my old friend Alejandro Graham. What a pleasant surprise!"

The man looked up from his menu.

"Marcus, I knew damned well if I came in here, you would show up and ruin my lunch."

Howell pulled out the chair opposite Graham and began sliding into it.

"Yes, thank you, I will join you. Very kind of you."

A waiter appeared almost immediately with a tray holding a pinch bottle of Haig & Haig scotch whisky, glasses, a bowl of ice, and a pitcher of water. Howell for years had maintained an apartment in the exclusive hotel across from the White House and delivering his tray was a ritual approaching a sacred custom.

"Put his lunch on my tab, Charles," Howell said. "I always try to assist the unemployed in our midst however I can."

Graham shook his head resignedly.

"Been across the street, have you, Alejandro?" Howell said, nodding toward the White House. "Seeking employment?"

The waiter prepared the drinks — hefty doses of whisky, equal amount of water, two ice cubes. Graham was no stranger to the Lafayette Room.

They tapped glasses and took a swallow.

32

"Well?" the old man asked.

"Actually, I was talking about Howard Hughes," Graham said.

"Don't change the subject, Alex."

"I must have missed something. What subject was that?"

"You know goddamn well! The subject is my grandson: When do I get Cletus back?"

"Well, actually, we were talking about Howard and Clete."

"I think you're trying to weasel out of answering me, but go ahead."

"The President wanted to know the story behind the Constellations. In other words, how come, in the middle of a war, Howard got away with selling thirteen of the fastest transport airplanes in the world to Argentina."

"He didn't sell them to Argentina. He sold them to Clete, who is not only an American but a Marine Corps lieutenant colonel with the Navy Cross."

"Really?" Graham said sarcastically. "I never knew that."

"I'm not surprised," the old man said. "But the story I got was that Howard was just about ordered to sell — at least strongly encouraged to sell — them to Clete."

"Because Franklin Roosevelt thought he had been crossed by Juan Trippe and wanted to pay him back," Graham said. "Harry Truman hadn't heard that story."

"And you're surprised? Roosevelt never told his Vice President about the atomic bomb either. How did the subject come up?"

"Just before Truman went to Berlin, Howard offered him one, a specially configured VIP version intended for some general. The general suddenly remembered that Truman had made his reputation as a senator going after the brass taking care of themselves at taxpayers' expense. So he canceled the order. There being virtually no market for a VIP-configured Constellation — Truman told me the inside of this one looks like a flying brothel — and wanting his money, Howard talked Admiral Souers into taking it."

"Who?"

"Rear Admiral Sidney W. Souers. He's a reservist, and Harry's buddy. Good man. We went to the Naval War College in 1938 together. Anyway, he's close to the President, duties a little vague. Truman flew to Berlin in the *Sacred Cow* and Sid, after picking up Clete, by the way, in New Orleans, flew there in the Constellation."

"Stop there and tell me about 'picking up Clete in New Orleans.' "

"Clete had business with the President."

"What kind of business?"

"I can't tell you, Marcus. Sorry."

"I'm not accepting that, but go on about Berlin."

Graham took a sip of his scotch, then said,

"When Sid got to Berlin, he bubbled over with enthusiasm for the Constellation, which is really a much better airplane than the *Sacred Cow,* which is a converted Douglas C-54. Truman heard that Clete was flying back to Buenos Aires in an SAA Connie. He had other things on his mind — this was the day he told George Marshall to immediately shut off all aid to Russia — and he didn't say anything. But he didn't forget either. So today he asked me about SAA having Connies, and I told him what I knew."

"Tell me what you know about Clete and Truman."

Graham ignored the question.

"Truman made Sid give the Flying Brothel back to Howard. You could probably buy it cheap, if you're interested."

"Tell me what you know about Clete and Truman," the old man repeated.

"Marcus, I really can't."

The old man then sipped his scotch and said, "I understand. The war's over. Hitler and Hirohito are gone, but Uncle Joe Stalin's still around. And I'm a well-known Communist sympathizer and obviously can't be trusted. Right?"

Graham didn't answer.

"Consider this, Alex. All it would have taken when you were recruiting Clete for the OSS so that he could go to Argentina and make a Christian out of his goddamn father was a telephone call to Clete from me. Following which, he would have told you to go piss up a rope."

Graham met Howell's eyes for a moment. He shrugged.

"Okay, Marcus. A moment ago, you said Stalin's still around. That situation is going from bad to worse. What Clete is doing —"

"Goddamn it, Alex! Wouldn't you say he's done enough already? Get someone else to do what you think has to be done."

Graham didn't reply.

"I need him, Alex. My son Jim's gone. I'm seventy-seven goddamn years old. Someone has to take over Howell Petroleum, take over the family."

"Marcus, if I could send Clete home, if I could even tell you what he's doing, I would. I just can't. I just can't."

"Fuck you, Alex!" the old man said, furiously.

He stood up, looked down at Graham for a moment, and then walked out of the Lafayette Room.

In the lobby, he looked at the doorman and mimed steering a car.

The doorman gave him a *thumbs-up* gesture and signaled his car was outside.

Howell started for the door, and then changed his mind.

He walked to the bank of elevators and took one to his penthouse apartment. There, he

36

sat down angrily in a red leather armchair and picked up the telephone.

"Person-to-person, Mr. Howard Hughes, the Lockheed Aircraft Corporation in Los Angeles, California."

There was a response, to which he responded: "If I had the goddamned number, I would have given it to you. I'm old but not completely senile."

He slammed the receiver into its cradle and looked out the window that provided a marvelous view across Pennsylvania Avenue of the White House.

Ninety seconds later, the telephone rang. He picked it up before it could ring a second time.

"Howard?" he said. "In which movie star's boudoir did they find you?"

"How are you, Mr. Howell?" Howard Hughes said sincerely.

"A fat Mexican half-breed of our mutual acquaintance just told me you have a flying brothel for sale, cheap. True?"

"I understand that's what Truman called it," Hughes chuckled.

"Yes or no?"

"Yeah. You're interested?"

"That depends on how much you want for this piece of fire sale merchandise."

Hughes told him.

"Is that your best price, Howard? Or are you trying to take advantage of someone in his dotage?"

"For you — God, I think you're serious. What the hell would you do with it?"

"What does anyone do with a flying brothel? Take fifty thousand off that price and you've got a deal. I'll need somebody to fly it. I presume you can handle that?"

"Mr. Howell, I have to tell you, if you're thinking of Clete and SAA, so was Juan Trippe. He got to his senator, and all Constellations are embargoed from sale outside the U.S."

"That sonofabitch strikes again. But not a problem. How soon can you paint 'Howell Petroleum' on it and deliver it to Washington? No. New Orleans. I'm getting out of this goddamn town this afternoon."

"Three days, tops. I'll bring it myself. But I'll want the crew I bring with it back as soon as you can get your own."

"I don't care what all those people are saying about you, Howard, I really don't think you're an unmitigated bastard."

Hughes laughed and hung up.

Cletus Marcus Howell reached for a humidor, selected a long, thin brown cigar, and went carefully through a ritual of rolling it between his fingers, cutting the end of it, and lighting it with a wooden match.

Then he went to a cabinet, opened it, and took out a bottle of Collier and McKeel Tennessee sour mash whiskey. He poured an inch

38

and a half of it into a squat glass.

Chimes announced that someone was at his door.

When he opened it, three men were standing there. Two were tall, muscular, and young. The third, who stood in front, was shorter, trim, and in his fifties.

"I understand you don't talk to Democrats," the older man said, "but I was hoping you'd make an exception for me."

"Please come in, Mr. President," Howell said.

"You fellows wait out here, please," Harry S Truman said. "I know Mr. Howell doesn't like me, but I don't think he'll try to kill me."

The President walked into the suite and closed the hall door behind him.

The two men looked at each other without speaking. Finally, Howell raised his glass.

"May I offer you —"

"If that came out of that Collier and McKeel bottle, you certainly may," Truman said.

"How do you take it?"

"The same way you do, straight."

Howell poured the whiskey and handed Truman the glass.

Truman raised it, touched it to Howell's, and said, "The United States of America."

"The United States of America," Howell parroted.

The two sipped the whiskey.

"You ever hear, Mr. President," Howell

then asked, "that patriotism is the last refuge of the scoundrel?"

"In this case, it's my last refuge to . . . how do I say this? . . . turn you off."

"Is that so?"

"I just spoke with our mutual friend Colonel Graham," the President said.

"He told me."

"I mean he called me after you talked to him," Truman said. "He said he thought he should tell me you were entirely capable of buying that flying brothel Howard Hughes built and flying down to Buenos Aires in it."

"I'm a little old for brothels, flying or otherwise, but yes, I just spoke to Howard. I told him to paint Howell Petroleum on that airplane and deliver it to me in New Orleans."

"And then you're going to fly to Buenos Aires in it? You do move fast, don't you?"

"I've learned that's the way you stay ahead of the pack," Howell said.

"And I've learned over the years that there are some men who don't take orders, or even suggestions, from anyone."

"I suppose that's true."

"That puts me on the spot," Truman said. "I realize I can't keep you from going down there to see your grandson."

"No, you can't."

"So I have no choice but to tell you something — what your grandson is doing down there — that is absolutely none of your business, and then rely on your good judgment — and, okay, your patriotism — that what you do with that information won't hurt the United States and a good number of other people."

"You can tell me, or not tell me, anything you want, Mr. President. But if it's your intention to tell me something and then imply that I am now silenced by patriotism, that, I'm sorry, just won't work. The war is over."

"No, Mr. Howell, the war just started."

"Is that so?"

"That's so. And Cletus is right now up to his ears in that war."

"I'm listening, Mr. President. As long as you understand what I just said."

"I understand. Cletus was in Berlin the day I told Joe Stalin we had the atom bomb, and the day I told George Marshall I wanted all aid to the Soviet Union shut off immediately. Were you aware of that?"

Howell nodded.

"Do you know why he was there?"

Howell shook his head and said, "No."

"Shortly before the Germans surrendered, a German general named Gehlen, who was in charge of German intelligence vis-à-vis the Soviets, met and struck a deal with Allen Dulles, the OSS man in charge of Europe . . ."

[THREE]

There were two armed soldiers in field uniforms virtually indistinguishable from that of the defeated Wehrmacht — their helmets and leather accoutrements were German, and their rifles Mausers from the Waffenfabrik in Berlin — standing at what an American soldier would call Parade Rest before the heavy iron gate at the Edificio Libertador when the Mercedes-Benz turned off Avenida Paseo Colón.

The soldiers popped to Present Arms as the Mercedes approached and then was passed inside the gate. The Mercedes was an Ejército Argentino vehicle, a convertible sedan painted olive drab. A sergeant was driving and a corporal sat beside him.

In the rear seat was General de Brigada (Brigadier General) Eduardo Ramos, commandant of Campo de Mayo, the huge army base and site of the Military Academy north of Buenos Aires. Ramos was a tall, trim, and erect officer with a full, neatly trimmed mustache beneath a rather prominent nose. Beside Ramos was his aide-de-camp, Capitán Ricardo Montenegro, who looked like a

younger version of General Ramos.

The Mercedes rolled up to the main entrance and stopped. The corporal in the front seat jumped out and opened the rear door, and then stood at attention as General Ramos and Capitán Montenegro got out. The two officers climbed a wide, shallow flight of stairs to the huge double doors to the building.

Two more soldiers stood on either side of the doors. They were dressed in uniforms of the late eighteenth century, closely patterned on those of Hungarian Hussars, except for their headgear, silk top hats with a large black plume rising from them. They were members of the Húsares de Pueyrredón, Argentina's oldest and most prestigious regiment.

When the British occupied Buenos Aires in 1810, Juan Martín de Pueyrredón, a large *estancia* owner, recruited a cavalry force from the gauchos — cowboys — on his estancia and marched on Buenos Aires. They had no uniforms. Pueyrredón seized a British merchantman in the harbor, found in its cargo a large supply of silk top hats, and issued them to his men, whom he then somewhat immodestly decreed to be the Húsares de Pueyrredón.

The Húsares saluted with their drawn sabers as Ramos and Montenegro passed them and entered the long, wide, high-ceilinged foyer and marched toward the bank

of elevators.

A flag officer of the Argentine navy, trailed by his aide, came down the foyer toward the door.

"*Hola,* Eduardo," Vicealmirante Guillermo Crater called cheerfully, putting out his hand. "Up early this morning, are you?"

"Admiral," Ramos replied curtly, and kept walking without taking the outstretched hand.

Ramos had not forgiven Vice Admiral Crater for what had happened outside a downtown motion picture theater five days after the Japanese capitulation. They were standing on the sidewalk, waiting for their cars after watching newsreels of the Japanese surrender in Tokyo Bay. That sequence had begun with an aerial view of the U.S. Pacific fleet at anchor, which was what was on Crater's mind.

"Well, Eduardo, we were lucky, weren't we?" Crater had begun the conversation.

"Excuse me?"

"To be on the right side," Crater had said. "I would really have hated to see all those ships, even *half* of all those battleships and aircraft carriers, sitting out there" — he had gestured toward the River Plate — "and thinking of us as the enemy. Wouldn't you?"

You sonofabitch! General Ramos had thought.

You've been cheering for the goddamn Americans all along!

He had not responded. Instead, he had given Crater a cold smile and turned his back on him.

At the elevator bank, a *teniente* (lieutenant) sat at a small desk beside the last elevator door. A sergeant, a Schmeisser submachine gun slung in front of him, stood beside him. The lieutenant got to his feet as Ramos and Montenegro approached.

"Mi General?" he asked politely.

"The general is here to see el Colonel Perón," Montenegro answered for Ramos.

The lieutenant consulted a list, and then politely announced, "*Mi General,* you're not on the minister of War's schedule."

"I know," Ramos snapped. "Open the damned door!"

As a general rule of thumb, lieutenants do not challenge generals. And, in this case, the lieutenant knew that General Ramos was both a member of the clique at the top of the Ejército Argentino and one of Perón's oldest and closest friends.

The bronze elevator door whooshed open, and Ramos and Montenegro got on. The elevator rose quickly and smoothly to the twentieth floor, where the doors opened onto the foyer of the offices of the minister for War of the Argentine Republic.

Ramos marched to the minister's outer office.

A major, seeing Ramos, rose to his feet

behind a large, ornately carved desk.

"Be so good as to tell el Coronel Perón that I am here," Ramos ordered, and then, as if anticipating the question, added, "He does not expect me."

The major walked quickly to ceiling-high bronze double doors, opened the left one, and entered. The door closed automatically behind him.

Fifteen seconds later, he reappeared, now holding the door open.

"*Mi General,* the minister will see you."

Ramos announced, "Capitán Montenegro will see that we are not disturbed. You will see that the telephone doesn't ring unless General Farrell is calling."

He then walked into Perón's office.

General Edelmiro Julián Farrell had been the dictator — or, more kindly, the *de facto* president — of Argentina since February 24, 1944. He had made no secret of his sympathies for the Axis during the war, but most people believed they were rooted in the ancestral hate of the Irish for all things British rather than admiration for the Nazis and Adolf Hitler.

The vice president, secretary of War, and secretary of Labor and Welfare of the Argentine Republic, el Coronel Juan Domingo Perón, was a tall, olive-skinned man with a luxurious head of black hair. He came out from behind his enormous desk to greet

46

General Ramos. He opened his arms to Ramos, and they patted one another's back.

"And to what do I owe this unexpected pleasure, Eduardo?" Perón asked.

"Unexpected, to be sure. But pleasure? I don't think you're going to take much pleasure in my being here when you learn why."

"That sounds ominous," Perón said.

"How long have we known each other, Juan Domingo? Been friends?"

Perón considered the question for a moment as he waved Ramos into one of the chairs facing his desk.

"From our first day at the academy, I would say," Perón said. "When they lined us up — me, then Jorge, then you — according to size." He made a gesture with his hands. "Just before they started screaming at us."

"I thought of Jorge on my way over here," Ramos said. "If he were still here, I think he'd agree with my coming to say what I have to say."

"If Jorge was still here, he'd be over there." Perón gestured out the windows, which looked down on the Casa Rosada and the Plaza de Mayo.

"He would have made a good, even a great, president."

"Yes, he would have. Are you finished beating around the bush, Eduardo?"

Ramos nodded.

"There is a plot to assassinate you, Juan

47

Domingo," he said.

"As you well know," Perón replied, "every afternoon, after their third martini at the Circulo Militar, a dozen senior officers with nothing better to do sit around deciding which of us should be assassinated."

"This isn't like that, Juan Domingo. This threat is bona fide. Even Farrell takes this seriously. You will shortly be arrested for your own protection."

Perón considered that for a moment.

"What are they upset about now?" he finally asked.

"There's a long list."

"And what's on that long list?"

"Aside from Señorita Evita Duarte, you mean?"

"Aside from my personal life is what I mean."

"Shall I start with your relations with the Nazis?"

"Which Nazis? The ones we're supposed to have here in Argentina?"

"Them, too. But what they're concerned about is the ones in Germany who want to come here."

"What am I supposed to have done in that regard?"

"Let me back up a little. These people have always been more than a little upset that you didn't sever your relationship with Rudy Nulder when the rest of us did."

El Señor Rodolfo Nulder was the director of security at the Secretariat of Labor and Retirement Plans.

"And I was a little upset with people, including you, for your treatment of Rudy after his resignation —"

"He didn't resign, Juan Domingo. He was cashiered."

"Rudy is a classmate of ours, Eduardo."

"And of Jorge Frade's, who said that if Rudy ever put foot on Estancia San Pedro y San Pablo again he'd kill him. Your loyalty to your friends may be commendable, but the fact is Rudy is a pervert and a cashiered officer."

"I think we had better drop this subject," Perón said icily.

Ramos met Perón's eyes for a long moment before going on.

"It has come to their attention that Rudy Nulder, when you sent him to get our diplomats out of Berlin —"

"You mean when President Farrell sent him?"

"— carried with him one thousand blank passports," Ramos finished.

"How could they possibly know that? Did Cletus Frade tell them?"

"How could Cletus possibly know about it?"

"Then Martín," Perón said.

General de Brigada Alejandro Bernardo

Martín was chief of the Ethical Standards Office of the Argentine Ministry of Defense's Bureau of Internal Security, the official euphemism for the Argentine intelligence and counterintelligence service.

"Bernardo is very good at what he does," Ramos said. "I wouldn't be at all surprised if he knew about the passports. But do I know he told the people at the Circulo Militar? No, I don't."

"And what is Nulder alleged to have done with a thousand blank passports?"

"Made them available to Germans whom the Allies — and, if I have to point this out, Argentina is now one of the Allies — are looking for."

"Anyone who went to the Kriegsschule has friends in the German officer corps. Or have you turned your back on them, too, Eduardo?"

"I turned my back on the Nazis, the SS, among my former Kriegsschule friends once I learned what they had done to the Jews and the Russian prisoners and the Gypsies, et cetera. Even before the SS murdered Jorge."

"How self-righteous of you."

"What these people believe, Juan Domingo, is that your man Nulder is not trying to rescue decent German officers from the Allies with these passports, but selling them a way to escape the righteous wrath of the Allies. For his personal enrichment, and possibly yours."

"And you're accusing me of that?"

"If I believed you were capable of that, I would be in the Circulo Militar planning when and where you were to be shot, not here trying to save your life. But they believe it."

"Just who are 'they'? Do you know who's involved in this plot to assassinate me?"

"I — we — have our suspicions, but no proof."

"I presume that Martín is keeping an eye on those you and Farrell — and presumably Martín — suspect?"

"Of course."

"Isn't that a case of the fox protecting the chicken coop?"

"I don't think so," Ramos said. "More important, Farrell doesn't think so. Martín is an honorable officer."

Perón snorted.

"Farrell is sometimes naïve," he said. "I wouldn't be at all surprised if Martín knows full well who wants to get me out of the way, and hasn't arrested them because he hopes they succeed."

"That's nonsense, Juan Domingo."

"Well, what's your advice, Eduardo? What do I do, sit here waiting to be shot? Or for Farrell to arrest me?"

"The latter. And, in the meantime, try to make peace with these officers."

"I thought nobody knew who they are?"

"You know who they are," Ramos said.

"And how am I to make peace with them?"

"For a beginning — you're not going to like this . . ."

"If it has to do with what I think you're going to say, I won't."

"Get rid of Rudy. Distance yourself from him. Publicly."

"I don't turn my back on my friends, Eduardo. You should know that."

"And of course there is that other problem of yours," Ramos went on. "I heard this myself from a general officer I'm sure is part of this —"

"If you're sure he's part of this, why don't you tell Martín, and have Martín arrest him for treason?"

"I'm sure General Martín heard what I heard. I'm sure General Martín reported what he heard to the president — and since the officer in question has not been arrested, I think it's obvious that the president doesn't think arresting him at this time is wise."

"Why not?"

"General Farrell does not want the officer corps split in two, and believes that arresting this officer — or any of the officers close to him — would do exactly that. How many times have you heard Edelmiro say that the one thing Argentina cannot afford is a civil war? He saw what happened in Spain, and it really affected him."

Perón considered that a moment, and then asked, thickly sarcastic, "Just what else did you hear this general officer whose arrest would likely plunge us into civil war say?"

" 'If he'd only get rid of the blonde,' " Ramos quoted.

"Presumably he was referring to Señorita Duarte?" Perón asked sarcastically.

"Yes, I think he probably was," Ramos said, also sarcastically. "For God's sake, Juan Domingo, she's twenty-five years younger than you are!"

"Actually, twenty-four," Perón corrected him. "And my relationship with the lady is none of anybody's business."

"They think it is. They think it reflects badly on the honor and prestige of the officer corps. They think it is conduct unbecoming an officer and a gentleman."

"And you, Eduardo, do you think my relationship with Señorita Duarte is conduct unbecoming?"

"What I think isn't germane. What they think is the point here."

" 'Judge not, lest ye be judged'?"

"Something like that," Ramos agreed. "Juan Domingo . . ."

"What?"

"They have also heard that young Frade threw you out of his house on Libertador when he found you there with an even younger female."

"Cletus is going to these officers with tales like that?" Perón asked furiously.

"I'm sure he didn't. But you must have known that story would come out."

"Why should it come out? What happened between Cletus Frade and me — my God, I'm his godfather! — is personal, a family matter."

"And I'm sure your godson feels the same way."

"Then how did it reach these people if he didn't run off at the mouth?"

"When Jorge was murdered, Sergeant Major Rodríguez was driving his Horch. Rodríguez was badly wounded —"

"I know that. What's your point?"

"— but survived. He took this to be divine intervention — that he was spared because God wanted him to protect Cletus. Rodríguez has never been far from Cletus since he was released from hospital. Cletus even takes him with him when he flies to Europe."

"So?"

"Was Rodríguez there when Cletus asked you to leave the house on Libertador?"

Perón's expression answered for him.

"What is it we say about *suboficial mayors,* Juan Domingo?" Ramos went on. "That 'they gossip more than women at the village well'?"

"Goddamn that old sonofabitch!"

"You can't condemn a dog for barking, Juan Domingo. It's the nature of the beast."

"I have known Rodríguez since he was Teniente Frade's batman!"

"He didn't even think he was doing anything wrong. He was having a glass of wine with some other old soldiers, and he knew what happened would be of interest to them. An hour later, that story was all over the barracks, two hours later all over Campo de Mayo, and within two days all over Argentina. It was not Rodríguez's intention to harm you, Juan Domingo."

"You're a good deal more forgiving than I am," Perón snapped.

"I hope that's contagious, when you start asking yourself, 'How dare Eduardo come here and talk to me the way he did?' "

Perón looked at him for a long moment.

"You were never very bright, Eduardo," he said with a smile. "But you have been a good and loyal friend since our first day at the academy."

"Thank you, and please remember that."

"Is there anything else you have to say, Eduardo?"

"Get rid of both Rudy Nulder and the blonde, Juan Domingo, and make sure that everybody in this building, the Circulo Militar, and at Campo de Mayo knows you have."

Perón's face tightened.

"What is it we said as children? 'Don't hold your breath'?"

Ramos rose to his feet.

They less-than-enthusiastically patted one another on the back, and then Ramos went to the office door and through it.

[FOUR]

Highway 252
Three Kilometers North of Marburg an der Lahn
The American Zone of Occupation, Germany
1300 6 October 1945

The roadblock had been established primarily to look for former members of the Schutzstaffel — the infamous SS — and other Nazis in the long lines of Germans fleeing what was now the Russian Zone of Occupation. The border between the two zones was about fifty kilometers northeast of the roadblock.

The roadblock was operated by U.S. Army military policemen, twenty-four men supervised by a captain and a lieutenant. Three checkpoints had been established, each under an MP sergeant. A long line of refugees led to each.

Each refugee was asked by an MP — whose proficiency in the German language ranged from fluent to almost nonexistent — for his or her *Personalausweis* — identity card — which was then carefully scrutinized.

If the ID appeared genuine, the refugee was asked where he or she had come from, and where he or she was bound.

In the case of females, especially women with children, the document check was perfunctory. The names were checked against a Wanted List. If there was no match, the women were permitted to continue down the highway — actually a two-lane cobblestone road — toward Marburg an der Lahn.

Males of any age, but especially those of military age, were scrutinized far more carefully. Most of the MPs who spoke fluent German were Jewish, and some of them had barely escaped Nazi Germany with their lives. Many — perhaps most — had family members who had perished in the concentration camps. They were motivated to find Nazis trying to escape retribution.

Any refugee who could not produce a *Personalausweis,* or whose identity seemed questionable, or whose name matched one on the Wanted List, was taken to a U.S. Army six-by-six truck and loaded aboard for further investigation by the CIC, the Army's Counterintelligence Corps.

A representative of the CIC sat in a jeep watching the proceedings. James D. Cronley Jr. was blond and blue-eyed, an enormous — six-one, two-twelve — twenty-one-year-old whose sole qualification for the CIC was that he spoke German fluently.

Cronley had been commissioned into the Army of the United States as a second lieutenant of Cavalry seven months before, on his graduation from Texas A&M.

Just about as soon as the outcome of the war had been clear, there was concern in the Army about dealing with the capture and trial of Nazis as war criminals in a defeated Germany. It became obvious that the CIC was the best-qualified agency to deal with the problem. It was equally obvious that the CIC was not large enough to deal with their to-be-expanded duties. Further compounding — indeed, greatly compounding — the problem was the awareness on the part of senior officers that as soon as the war was over there would be a great hue and cry to "bring the boys home."

The chief of staff of the U.S. Army told the assistant chief of staff for Intelligence to take whatever steps necessary to deal with the problem.

The result of this was that in his third week of the Basic Armor Officers Course at Fort Knox, Kentucky, Second Lieutenant James D. Cronley Jr. was summoned from a course in Track & Bogie Maintenance to the Orderly Room of the Student Officer Company.

He was told to report to the colonel now ensconced in the company commander's office. Following the protocol, he knocked at the frame of the open door and was told to come in.

He was already inside the office and saluting before he realized the order to come in had been issued in German.

"How well do you speak German, Lieutenant?" a major standing beside and behind the full colonel asked, in German.

"Pretty well, sir."

"Learned it from your mother, did you, son?" the colonel asked in German.

"Yes, sir."

"From now on, speak German."

"Jawohl, Herr Oberst."

"Your mother is Wilhelmina Stauffer Cronley? And your father James D. Cronley Senior?"

"Ja, das ist richtig, Herr Oberst."

"Who is A&M '16, and president of Cronley Petroleum Company?" the colonel asked, now in English.

"Ja, das ist richtig, Herr Oberst."

"Who won the Distinguished Service Cross with the Big Red One in France, and then volunteered for the Army of Occupation after the Armistice?" the major asked, in German.

"Ja, das ist richtig, Herr Major."

"Where he met, wooed, and won over the lady who would become your mother?" the colonel asked.

"Ja, das ist richtig, Herr Oberst."

"Tell me, Lieutenant, what do you know about the Counterintelligence Corps, the CIC?"

"I don't know anything about it, sir," Cron-

59

ley confessed in English.

"Try saying that in German," the colonel snapped, in German.

Cronley did so.

"Well, they'll tell you all about it in Baltimore," the colonel said, now in English.

"Entschuldigen Sie, bitte, Herr Oberst?"

"Congratulations, Lieutenant Cronley," the colonel went on, in English. "Your application for transfer to the Counterintelligence Corps has been approved. Go pack your gear. And hurry up. We have a five-fifteen flight to Washington."

Cronley was about halfway through the six-month Basic Course at the Counterintelligence Corps Center at Camp Holabird in Maryland when he was again summoned to an orderly room. There he was handed the credentials of a CIC special agent, issued a snub-nosed .38 Special Smith & Wesson revolver, and told, "Pack your gear, Cronley, you're on the 1900 MATS flight to Frankfurt."

The major from the XXIInd CIC Detachment who met his plane was visibly disgusted when Jim Cronley outlined his military intelligence experience for him, but said, "Well, we'll find something for you to do where you can cause only minimal damage."

Cronley was shocked at the near-total destruction of Frankfurt am Main, and just

60

about as shocked when, after an hour's drive in a requisitioned Opel Admiral sedan, they arrived in Marburg an der Lahn. The city seemed absolutely untouched — except for the population, which was incredibly drab and visibly malnourished — by the war.

He was quickly given the explanation.

Philipps University in Marburg an der Lahn was famed as the site of Roentgen's discovery of the X-ray, but it owed its survival to something else few people knew and even fewer talked about. Since before the Civil War, it had been where the War Department had sent intelligence officers for training.

One such alumnus had been a brigadier general of the Eighth Air Force charged with selecting targets for aerial bombardment. When the time came to take out the Marburg railroad marshaling yards, the general had personally delivered the pre-raid briefing, ending it with the announcement that if one bomb fell anywhere but in the marshaling yards, the entire wing could expect to be transferred to the Aleutian Islands, where they could expect to remain literally on ice until after every other last swinging dick in the Air Forces had gone home.

Another alumnus, this one a full colonel, had been the G-3 (Plans and Operations Officer) when the Ninth Army approached Marburg on its way to Kassel. He issued much the same threat. Anyone shooting at his university while taking Marburg would regret it.

A third alumnus, another colonel, was named the first military governor of Marburg. He summoned the citizenry to the market square and began his speech in fluent Hessian German. *"Meine Damen und Herren,* while I regret the circumstances, it is wonderful to be back in the city of my university."

Cronley was at first nothing more than a translator. But he was smart, and an officer, so he was quickly given greater responsibilities. Keeping an eye on the MPs as they searched for fleeing Nazis seemed to be an ideal duty for him.

He also quickly learned there were certain privileges associated with being in the CIC.

He had the choice of wearing his uniform and insignia of rank or "civilian clothing." This was defined as a rank-insignia-less uniform. Not only did he no longer have to display his gold second lieutenant's bar — second lieutenants were a standing joke in the Army — but he could put away what the Army called "Shoes, low quarter" or "Boots, combat" and replace them with something more appropriate for a civilian from Texas: pointed-toe Western boots.

And he had a choice of weapon. He had grown up in Midland, Texas, around guns. He had a low opinion of the snub-nosed S&W .38 Special he had been issued. He replaced it with the standard Model 1911-A1 .45 ACP pistol, which he elected to carry in a holster slung low on a web belt across his hip.

The first time Elsa von Wachtstein saw Lieutenant Jim Cronley, he was sitting slumped down in his jeep, his Western-booted left foot resting on the left fender extension. He had an overseas hat cocked on his head, and his .45 and holster were dangling from the jeep's windshield. He was puffing on a long, black cigar.

The first time Jim Cronley saw Elsa von Wachtstein, who was standing in line waiting to undergo MP scrutiny, he was uncomfortable. Her face was gray and her hair unkempt. She was wearing a fur-collared overcoat and had a battered suitcase strapped to her back. Her shoes were literally worn out. She was, he thought, probably fifty.

Sonofabitch! That was once, when she was young, a damned good-looking woman.

Occupied Germany was known to be a cornucopia of sexual pleasure for the victors. Women were literally available for a few cigarettes or a Hershey's bar.

Jim Cronley had not availed himself of the opportunity. He had wondered why, and decided it was because of his mother. She had been an impoverished German woman when she met his father.

Still, he felt a little sorry for himself: *I got*

laid a hell of a lot more often in Midland and College Station, by maybe a factor of 100-to-0, than I am getting laid here.

Elsa von Wachtstein, aware that Cronley's eyes were on her, and wondering idly who he was and what he was doing — he was obviously not a military policeman — handed her *Personalausweis* to an MP.

"Coming from where, fräulein?" the MP asked in halting German.

"I came from Pomerania," she replied in English.

The MP, surprised, looked at her closely.

"Going where?" he asked.

"Marburg," Elsa said. "I have — at least, used to have — friends there."

"And if your friends ain't there?" the MP asked, as he handed her *Personalausweis* to the sergeant who had the Wanted List.

"Then on to Wetzlar or Giessen," Elsa said. "I once had friends in both places."

"You speak English pretty good," the MP said.

"Thank you," Elsa said.

"Got a fucking hit!" the sergeant with the Wanted List cried in surprised elation.

"Oh, shit," the MP said. He sounded genuinely sorry.

"Is something wrong?" Elsa asked.

"Put your suitcase on the ground and open it," the MP said.

"May I ask why?"

64

"Because I'm going to search it, and then you're going to carry it over to that truck, put it on the truck, and then get on with it."

The sergeant with the Wanted List was now standing with his hands on his hips beside the MP.

The young man who had been slumped in his jeep walked up.

"What have we got, Sergeant?"

"What's it look like? We got a hit," the sergeant said.

"Try that answer again, and this time preface your answer with 'sir,' " the young man said.

Elsa tried not to stare as she thought, *My God, he's enormous! A perfect blue-eyed Aryan!*

He looks like a recruiting poster for the SS.

And he's an officer — he made the sergeant call him "sir."

But he doesn't have any officer's insignia?

"Sir, this fräulein's name is on the Wanted List," the sergeant said.

Cronley gestured for the sergeant to hand him the list, and then again to get Elsa's *Personalausweis.*

"Is this you, fräulein?" Cronley asked in German, showing her the Wanted List.

Elsa looked. "Yes, it is. But it's 'Frau,' not 'Fräulein.' "

"I told you," the sergeant said, belatedly adding "sir."

The MP captain walked over.

"What have we got?" he asked.

"We got a hit, sir," the sergeant said. "I've been trying to tell this guy —"

"You have a problem, Mr. Cronley?" the MP captain said.

"Well, somebody obviously didn't explain this list to your sergeant," Cronley said.

"Meaning what?"

"After Frau von Wachtstein's name is the number four. On the bottom of the list is an explanation of the numbers. Four says 'Personnel in this category are to be courteously detained, and Colonel Robert Mattingly will be immediately contacted by the most expeditious means at Frankfurt Military 4033.' "

Cronley then handed the Wanted List to the captain.

"Jesus, Cronley, that went right over my head," the captain said.

"Yeah," Cronley said. And then, switching to German: "Frau von Wachtstein, will you come with me, please?"

"Is something wrong?" Elsa asked.

"I don't think so," Cronley said.

"Where are we going?" Elsa asked.

"To Marburg, so I can get on the horn and call this Colonel Mattingly, whoever the hell he is."

Elsa went to her suitcase and reached to pick it up. Cronley beat her to it, and effortlessly carried it to his jeep and tossed it in

66

the backseat.

He gestured for Elsa to get in the jeep, and then got in himself. He started the engine and started to move the jeep. Then he fished in his tunic pocket and came out with a Hershey's bar and handed it to her.

She looked at him as if he had just offered to meet her price.

He read her mind.

"My mother is German," he said. "Okay?"

Then he revved the jeep and started off.

They were quiet for the first ten minutes or so of the trip to Marburg. Then he said, "Your *Personalausweis* says you're thirty-two. Is that correct?"

"And I look fifty. Is that why you ask?"

He didn't reply.

"I'm thirty-two," she said after a moment. "How old are you?"

"Twenty-one," Cronley said.

A boy, Elsa thought. *He's just a boy.*

[FIVE]

Alte Post Hotel
Stadt Mitte
Marburg an der Lahn, Germany
1355 6 October 1945

The XXIInd CIC Detachment had requisitioned Marburg's Alte Post Hotel, including the staff, for its headquarters and living quarters. It was in what the Americans thought of as the Old Town, on Steinweg, the ancient cobblestone road that led to the fortress on top of the hill.

Cronley parked in front of the hotel and led Elsa into the lobby, then to the door of the office of Major John Connell, the executive officer.

"What have you got there, Cronley?" Connell asked, looking askance at the German woman.

"This is Frau von Wachtstein, Major. She's a Four on the Wanted List."

Major Connell had been born in Philadelphia, as his parents had been, but he was Jewish, and he didn't like people whose name appeared on the Wanted List.

"Why the hell did you bring her here? You should have taken her directly to the POW enclosure."

"She's a Four, Major," Cronley said.

"What the hell does that mean?"

"She is supposed to be 'detained with courtesy' and we're supposed to notify some Colonel . . . a Colonel Mattingly . . . in Frankfurt."

"What the hell? You said 'Mattingly'?"

"Yes, sir."

"You have the Wanted List? Let me see it."

"I don't have one, sir."

"Damn! Well, I've got one here somewhere."

Connell rooted through the papers on his desk until he found it. He read it, and learned what the number four after Frau von Wachtstein's name required.

He picked up his telephone.

"Get me Frankfurt Military 4033," he said.

The reply could be heard metallically but faintly.

"Four Oh Three Three."

"Colonel Mattingly, please."

"Who's calling?"

"Major Connell, Twenty-second CIC."

"Hold one."

It took a full minute to locate Colonel Mattingly.

"Mattingly."

"Sir, this is Major Connell of the Twenty-second CIC. The MPs picked up a German woman on the Wanted List. It said to notify you."

"Who? What's her name?"

"Frau . . ." Connell looked at Cronley for help.

"Elsa von Wachtstein," Cronley furnished, and Connell repeated it.

"Where is she?"

"Here in my office, sir."

"Put her on."

John Connell handed Frau von Wachtstein the telephone.

"Hello," she said.

"*Guten tag,* Frau von Wachtstein," Mattingly said in fluent German. "May I ask what your relationship is to Generalleutnant Graf Karl-Friedrich von Wachtstein?"

"He was my father-in-law," Elsa said immediately.

"And Generalmajor Ludwig Holz?"

"He was my father."

"And Major Karl von Wachtstein?"

There was a moment's hesitation, then in a quiet tone she replied, "He was my husband."

"And one more, if you please, Frau von Wachtstein. Major Hans-Peter von Wachtstein?"

"He was my brother-in-law — my late husband's brother."

"*Is* your brother-in-law, Frau von Wachtstein," Mattingly said.

"Hansel survived?" Elsa said after another moment's hesitation. With the back of her hand, she began wiping away the tears starting to roll down her cheeks.

"I saw Hansel last week," Mattingly said. "I'll explain everything when I see you, Frau von Wachtstein, which will be in the next three or four days."

Elsa was now sobbing.

Without realizing that he was doing it, Cronley put his arm around her shoulder. She leaned against him, now dabbing at her eyes with a rag of a handkerchief.

"Put the major back on the phone, please, Frau von Wachtstein," Mattingly said.

70

Elsa wasn't listening.

Cronley gently pried the handset from her fingers and handed it to Major Connell.

"Yes, sir?"

"What was your name?"

"Connell, sir. Major John Connell. I'm the Twenty-second's exec."

"Is the commanding officer there?"

"No, sir. The colonel's in Kassel."

"Okay, then, you're elected," Mattingly said. "Listen carefully to me, Connell."

"Yes, sir."

"Frau von Wachtstein is not a prisoner, but an honored guest."

"Excuse me?"

"Her father and father-in-law were brutally exterminated for their role in the July 1944 attempt to assassinate Hitler at Wolfsschanze — Wolf's Lair, his headquarters — in East Prussia. Getting the picture?"

"Yes, sir."

"If the SS had been able to find her, she would now be dead," Mattingly went on. "God only knows how she managed to stay out of their hands."

"I understand, sir."

"As much as I would like to drive up there right now, that's out of the question. It'll be three, four days before I can get away."

"Yes, sir."

"In the meantime, you are to provide her with whatever she needs."

"Yes, sir."

"I mean whatever she wishes, Major. Put her in the BOQ. If she needs clothing, get it for her. See that she has every creature comfort within your means to provide. Make sure she is not left alone. Got that?"

"Yes, sir."

"Good. Any problems, call me. If I'm not here, speak with Colonel Jim Born."

"Colonel Jim Born. Yes, sir."

"Don't fuck this up, Major," Colonel Mattingly concluded, and broke the connection.

John Connell hung up.

The action seemed to remind Elsa that she was leaning against the boy who looked like an SS recruiting poster, and when she straightened, Cronley was reminded that he had his arm around the soft, warm back of a woman who looked fifty and was in fact thirty-two. He withdrew it as if it was burning him.

"Major, can I ask who Colonel Mattingly is?" Cronley asked.

"You certainly can," Connell said. "It is important, Lieutenant, that you know."

So the boy is an officer, Elsa thought. *So he's not a boy?*

And why isn't he wearing officer's insignia?

"Colonel Robert Mattingly is the commanding officer of OSS Forward," Connell explained. "Know what that means? The OSS?"

"I've heard of the OSS, sir, but I really don't know what it is," Cronley said.

"The Office of Strategic Services," Connell clarified, "is our super-secret intelligence organization. In the European Theater of Operations it is directly under General Eisenhower. OSS Forward is the OSS in Germany. In the last Intelligence Conference — two weeks ago at U.S. Forces European Theater headquarters in the I.G. Farben Building in Frankfurt — the USFET intelligence officer, Major General Seidel, told us that we were to cooperate fully with OSS Forward, and if we were unable to comply with any of their requests, he was to be personally notified. Getting the picture?"

"Yes, sir."

"When we first met, Cronley, I said something to the effect that we would find something for you to do, where, despite your somewhat rudimentary — strike that — your *nonexistent* intelligence background, you could cause only minimal damage. Do you remember that?"

"Yes, sir."

"That opportunity seems to have been dropped in our laps, doesn't it? Except for your ability to cause only minimal damage."

Cronley didn't reply.

"I'm throwing you to the wolves, Cronley," Connell said. "For the good of the service, so to speak. I could assign one of the other officers — one of my few remaining competent officers — to care for Frau von Wachtstein. But if I did, and the performance of that officer failed to meet Colonel Mattingly's expectations — and he has the reputation for being impossible to satisfy — that would result in the loss to the Twenty-second of an officer whose services the Twenty-second desperately needs. Still with me?"

"I think so, sir."

"On the other hand, if your caring for Frau von Wachtstein until Colonel Mattingly shows up here to take her off our hands failed to meet Colonel Mattingly's expectations, and you were transferred to duties counting snowballs in Alaska, the loss to the Twenty-second would not be so devastating."

"I understand, sir."

"You are relieved of all other duties, Lieutenant, except those of caring for Frau von Wachtstein, until relieved by Colonel Mattingly."

"Yes, sir. Sir, I don't have any idea how to do that."

"I suspected that might be the case. So let's consider what has to be done. For one thing, you'll need a place for her to stay. I will call the Kurhotel and order that she be placed in their best accommodations, and you in an adjacent room."

The Kurhotel, on Marburg's south side, had a natural spring that allegedly offered health-giving properties. The large, fairly modern hotel had been requisitioned to house field grade officers in the Marburg area.

"Yes, sir."

"You will require transportation. Take my car — I'll use your jeep until I can get something from the motor pool."

Major Connell drove a requisitioned Opel Kapitän, a GM-produced car about the size of a Chevrolet.

"Yes, sir. Clothing, sir?"

"Good question. It shows you're thinking, son. Take her to the Officers' Sales Store. I'll call ahead and tell them they are to sell you two complete WAC officer's uniforms, including the appropriate undergarments. As an honored guest, I see no reason Frau von Wachtstein cannot be attired in an officer-equivalent civilian uniform, can you?"

"No, sir. And the PX, sir, to provide Frau von Wachtstein with toiletries?"

"I'll call them and authorize the sale to you of whatever Frau von Wachtstein requires."

"Yes, sir."

"I will do what I can to protect you, Cronley," Connell then said. "But it probably won't be much."

"Thank you, sir."

"Carry on, Lieutenant Cronley," Connell said, and then switched to German and told Frau von Wachtstein that Lieutenant Cronley was going to take care of her and that if there were any problems, she should not hesitate to bring them to his attention.

Before leading Elsa from the office, Cronley wondered how the hell Frau von Wachtstein was supposed to bring any problems to Connell's attention, and they were in the Kapitän before he realized that Connell had not addressed the subject of who was going to pay for the Officers' Sales Store and the PX items.

What the hell, it's not a problem.

After not getting his pay at either Fort Knox or Camp Holabird, it had caught up with him a week before. He had been carrying around thick wads of scrip twenty-dollar bills — the Army-issued currency designed to keep real dollars out of the economy — totaling a little over a thousand dollars.

I'll worry about getting repaid later.

"Your call, Frau von Wachtstein, what would you like to do first? Go to the hotel? Or the clothing store? Or the PX?"

"Or the what?"

"The PX. It stands for Post Exchange. It's a store where you can buy soap and shampoo, and other stuff."

Elsa considered the question before replying.

"If I was asked what I want most in the world right now, it would be a long, hot bath."

Cronley had a quick shaming moment, wondering what she would look like climbing naked into a bathtub. Or standing in a shower.

"To the hotel then?" he asked.

"But eventually, I would have to get out of the tub," Elsa continued, "and then I would be standing there in the nude, with nothing to put on but these dirty rags."

He had another shaming mental picture of Elsa standing there in the nude pondering her choices.

"First things first," she said. "Soap and shampoo. Then clothing. Then the hotel and a long, hot bath."

"Yes, ma'am," Cronley said.

[SIX]

The PX was not far from the Alte Post Hotel.

When Elsa was finished selecting what she needed — including a bottle of Chanel No. 5, which she said was the first she'd seen since her husband had brought her a bottle back from Paris in 1940 — it made quite a stack on the checkout counter, the movement of which was solved by the purchase of a Valve Pak canvas suitcase.

It also substantially thinned one of the wads of twenty-dollar bills after Cronley retrieved it from where he had been carrying it — inside the calf of his Western boots.

The Officers' Sales Store was on the other side of town, in the Quartermaster Depot.

On the way, Elsa volunteered, "We had a Kapitän like this."

"You and your husband?"

She nodded.

"You said he . . . had died."

"He gave his life for the fatherland on the Eastern Front in 1941," she said with no expression in her voice.

"I'm sorry."

"At least he died a soldier's death."

"As opposed to what?" Cronley blurted.

"The way his father died — strangled to death hanging from a butcher's hook."

"Jesus Christ!"

"Yes," Elsa said, and mockingly parroted, "Jesus Christ!"

Then she reached over and touched his shoulder.

"I'm sorry," she said. "I guess it was being in here. I shouldn't have said that."

"Why not?"

"It's not your concern," Elsa said.

At the Officers' Sales Store in the Quartermaster Depot, a German clerk showed her what was available: Uniform, Class A, Female Officer's — which consisted of a brown tunic and a pink skirt, a khaki shirt and necktie, silk stockings, and a pair of Shoes, Female Officer's, Brown, w/2-Inch Heel.

"These are the first silk stockings I've seen in years," Elsa said.

There was a dressing room into which Elsa disappeared to try on everything.

Cronley had a mental image of her stripping down to her underwear.

He shook his head.

What the fuck is the matter with me?

She came out wearing her old clothes with the new shoes.

"I'll change into this," Elsa said, holding up the uniform on a hanger, "after I've had my bath."

He had a mental image of the absolutely worn-out shoes she had been wearing when he first saw her.

"Where did you come from, Frau von Wachtstein?"

"Pomerania," she said. "Do you know where that is?"

"Yes, I do. You walked all the way?"

"Most of the way. The usual price for a woman's transportation is one I didn't want to pay."

He nodded.

"I shouldn't have said that either," she said.

"Why not?"

"I wasn't thinking of our current situation."

What the hell does she mean by that?

That with me, she'd be willing to pay the usual price?

You are out of your fucking mind, Jimmy Cronley!

Paying for the two uniforms wiped out the last of the stack of scrip twenty-dollar bills and he had to take a second stack from his other boot.

[SEVEN]

In the Kapitän on the way to the Kurhotel Marburg, the smell of Chanel No. 5 told him she had decided not to wait until she had her bath before applying that.

"This is the Goethe Suite," the manager of the Kurhotel Marburg said, "normally reserved for colonels and general officers. But Major Connell explained the situation. I hope you will be comfortable, Frau von Wachtstein. If you need anything, just pick up the telephone."

"Thank you," Elsa said.

"And per Major Connell's request, Lieutenant," the manager went on, handing him a key, "I've put you near to Frau von Wachtstein — in 408a, next door. It's usually where aides-de-camp are placed. There is a connecting door to 408, the Goethe Suite. It's locked."

"I'll be next door when you need me, Frau von Wachtstein," Cronley said.

Cronley went to 408a and let himself in.

Compared to the rooms in the suite in which Frau von Wachtstein had been installed, 408a was small. But compared to his room in the Alte Post Hotel, it was almost luxurious.

He saw the door connecting 408a with 408, noting that it seemed substantial and that the locking mechanism could be operated only from within the Goethe Suite.

Which is a good thing, otherwise I might go completely bananas and "accidentally" burst in there to get a look at that woman in her bathtub.

A woman who is thirty-two fucking years old, looks older, and, as another consideration, is under the personal protection of a bird colonel who has Major Connell, a ruthless bastard himself, scared shitless. . . .

What the fuck am I thinking?

If I get two inches — hell, a half inch — out of line with Frau von Wachtstein, then it's auf Wiedersehen, *good life in the good ol' Twenty-second.*

I'll wind up changing tracks and bogie wheels in the mud in some tank company in Grafen-wöhr.

Cronley sat in an armchair, lit a cigar, found a copy of the Army newspaper *Stars & Stripes,* and started to read it.

And, when he had finished going through it, fell asleep.

"Well, Mr. Cronley, how do I look?" Frau von Wachtstein asked.

Startled awake, he stood up.

She was standing in front of him, wearing the Uniform, Class A, Female Officer's.

How the hell did she get in here?

She unlocked the connecting door, Stupid, and came through it, that's how.

"Very nice," he said.

You don't look fifty anymore. You don't even look thirty-two.

And you smell good. You must have used half of that bottle of Chanel No. 5.

"Do you have a knife?" she asked.

"Excuse me?"

"A knife," she said. "To cut things."

He searched in his pocket and came out with a pocketknife adorned with the insignia of the Boy Scouts of America. It had been a present on his promotion to Star rank in BSA Troop 36, Midland, Texas.

He extended it in the palm of his hand. She took it.

"That should do nicely," she said. "Thank you."

"What are you going to do with it?"

"Can you keep a secret?"

"That's what you do in the CIC," he said. "Protect secrets."

"The CIC? I saw that on the door of the Alte Post Hotel. What does it mean?"

"It stands for Counterintelligence Corps."

"Like the German Sicherheitsdienst? Secret police?"

"Something like that."

"You don't look to be old enough for duties like that."

"I get the least important duties."

"Like taking care of someone like me?"

"I didn't mean that," he said.

"Major Connell said he was throwing you to the wolves," she said. "That you were sort of expendable."

"I think Major Connell forgot — or never knew — that you speak English. I can't imagine him saying what he did otherwise."

"That's what I thought. Well, I will try to do nothing that will get you in trouble."

"Thank you."

She met his eyes. Hers were blue, and they made him uncomfortable.

"What are you going to do with the knife?" he asked, looking at it.

"I don't want to keep calling you Mr. Cronley," Elsa said. "What's your name?"

"You can call me Jimmy or Jim."

"What's the difference?"

"In Texas you can call a man Jimmy and it's all right. Other places — up north, in the Army — you hear a man called Jimmy, you suspect he's a little funny."

He made a waving gesture with his hand.

"I take it you're not a little funny," she said, smiling as she mimicked the waving gesture.

"No, ma'am."

"Jimmy, do you think it's all right for someone to hide something . . . something of value? Something that's yours?"

"Hide it from whom?"

"Right now, Major Connell. Maybe, probably, later from this Colonel Mattingly he's so afraid of."

"No. If it's yours, you should have the right to hide it from anybody you please. But I really don't know what you're talking about."

"When I took off my clothing to take my bath, I looked at it, and realized I never would have to wear it again."

Cronley had a quick mental image of her standing naked beside the bathtub, looking down at her discarded clothing.

Picture changing bogies and tracks in the mud, Stupid!

"No reason that you would have to," he said.

"What I wanted to do was burn it, burn it all."

"No problem, Frau von Wachtstein. Give it to me and I'll burn it."

"If I'm to call you Jimmy, why don't you call me Elsa?"

"All right, give me your old clothes, Elsa, and I'll burn them."

"Come with me," she said, and led him through the connecting door to the Goethe Suite.

When they had been shown the Goethe Suite by the manager, Cronley was shown only the sitting room. Elsa now led him into the bedroom, and through that into the bathroom.

She pointed at a pile of discarded clothing — her overcoat, blouse, skirt, and sweater — on the floor. On top were a gray and well-worn brassiere and a pair of gray baggy underpants. He saw that the elastic waistband of the underpants had been replaced with what looked like two shoelaces tied together.

No wonder she wanted to get rid of this crap and burn it!

"I'll get it," he said.

"I forgot to ask for underwear when we were at the clothing place, or the PX," Elsa said. "Could you . . . ?"

"I don't know about the PX. But I'm sure they have it at the clothing store. We'll just have to go back."

The first thing Cronley thought was that the underwear in the clothing store was probably going to be olive drab.

Well, maybe white.

Then he suddenly thought: *Jesus Christ! If she didn't have any underwear to put on, that means she's not wearing anything under her uniform.*

"Could we?" Elsa asked.

"Certainly," Jimmy said. "We can go back there right now if you'd like."

Of course she'd like, Stupid.
She's naked under her uniform.

He bent over, intending to scoop up her discarded clothing.

"Wait," she said. "There's a problem there."

He straightened up and looked at her.

"What I started to talk about before," Elsa said.

"You're hiding something in there?" Cronley guessed. "What?"

She opened his pocketknife and dropped to her knees beside the pile of clothing. She separated the skirt from the pile, then attacked the waistband seam with the blade, sawing her way through the stitching.

The first thing she retrieved was a ring, a square-cut diamond set in gold. She handed it to him.

It looks like my mother's engagement ring.
Three karats at least. Maybe four.

"That's the ring Karl — my husband — gave me when we became engaged," Elsa said, as she moved his knife to another part of the waistband.

This time she came out with another square-cut diamond, this one larger than the one in the ring — *Jesus Christ, it's enormous!* — and suspended from a necklace studded for most of its length with diamonds.

She handed this to him.

"This was my father's gift to my mother on their twenty-fifth anniversary."

She met his eyes again.

"I would rather that Major Connell and Colonel Mattingly not know I have these," she said. "Are you going to have to tell them?"

Of course I'm going to have to tell them.

For all I know, your husband — or for that matter, your boyfriend — took them away from a rich Jew just before she was marched into the gas chamber!

And if they're really yours, and Connell will know how to find that out, no problem.

"That's all that's left," she said, almost as if to herself, "of everything."

And then she spoke directly to him.

"Everything the traitors owned — after July '44 — was forfeited to the Reich. Everything. And if the SS had found me, they would have gotten this, too."

She's probably lying through her teeth.

But how could she look at me with those blue eyes and lie to me?

"I was never in your bathroom," Jimmy then said. "You never showed me either the ring or the necklace."

"Thank you," Elsa said.

"Give me ten minutes to find some way to burn this stuff. Then we'll go back to the clothing sales store."

"I'll go with you to burn them," Elsa said, adding, "please."

The manager of the Kurhotel was very cooperative and asked no questions when Cronley told him what he wanted to do.

Probably because Connell told him to give me whatever I asked for, and he's afraid of Connell and/or the CIC.

The manager led them to a furnace in the basement.

Cronley fed Elsa's clothing onto the glowing coals and watched as they finally burst into flame.

When there was nothing left of the clothing but gray ash, Cronley closed the furnace door.

"So ends my old life," Elsa said, "and begins my new one."

"Yeah," Cronley said.

The manager waved them onto the stairs. Cronley waved Elsa ahead of him.

Her buttocks moved under the pink skirt of the uniform, and his imagination went to work.

They went to the clothing sales store in the Quartermaster Depot, where the same German clerk from earlier now told Elsa that while they stocked underwear, it was "GI." The PX, the clerk said, had a much nicer and larger selection.

At the PX, Elsa selected a mixed bag of black and red and pink brassieres and underpants. Paying for them exhausted Stack Two of Jimmy's back pay, requiring him to take a third wad of twenties from his boot top.

"Thank you again," Elsa said, touching his arm.

Cronley now wondered if he was going to get any of what he had spent back from Connell — never mind all of it — and decided that he wouldn't.

The only place Connell could get the money was from the XXIInd, and Cronley doubted the XXIInd had funds to pay for clothing for a German national. And Cronley understood that Connell was not at all likely to pay those expenses from his own pocket.

When they were back in the Kapitän, Cronley told her, "I'm going to have to stop by my quarters and pick up stuff — my toilet kit, a clean shirt, et cetera — if I'm going to spend the night in the Kurhotel."

"All right," she said. "And then do you think we could get something to eat?"

Jesus, I didn't even think about feeding her!

He looked at his watch. It was quarter to seven.

"When was the last time you had something to eat?" he asked.

"I had the last of my bread and sausage this morning. All I've had since then is that chocolate bar you gave me."

"The Mess in the Kurhotel —"

" 'The Mess'?"

"The dining room," he clarified, "opens at

89

seven. It's pretty good. Can you wait that long?"

"Of course."

[EIGHT]

Major Connell was leaving his office when Cronley and Frau von Wachtstein walked into the lobby.

"Well, look at you," he said in German. "Permit me to say you look very nice, Frau von Wachtstein."

"Thank you," she replied. "All of these things, plus what we bought in the PX, cost a great deal of money, Herr Major."

"Well, don't you worry about that. We're under orders to take care of your every need," Connell said, then thought, *Which means I'm going to get stuck for everything.* "Is there anything else you need?" he added.

"No, thank you."

"Don't be hesitant to ask," he said, then looked at Cronley. "Why are you back here?"

"I came to pick up my toilet kit and a clean shirt, sir," Cronley said.

"Oh, that's right, you'll be staying at the Kurhotel, won't you?"

"Yes, sir."

"You might take Frau von Wachtstein to the Mess there, Cronley. It's really very good."

"Yes, sir."

"If you need anything, you know where to find me," Connell said.

"Yes, sir. Thank you."

On the way to the Kurhotel, Cronley's mind turned to Frau von Wachtstein's intimate undergarments.

She's still naked under that uniform; she hasn't had a chance to put on any of the stuff she bought.

Well, she can do that as soon as we get to the hotel. Maybe that black brassiere and the matching see-through underpants . . .

Damn it! Get your filthy mind off her underwear, pervert!

In the hotel lobby, Elsa pointed to the sign that read DINING ROOM.

"In there?" she asked.

"Yes, ma'am."

They were shown to a table next to windows that overlooked the Lahn River.

"The river, the Lahn, is out there," he said, pointing. "But you can't see it in the dark."

Brilliant conversation, Jimmy!

"I saw it earlier from my room," she said.

A waiter appeared and asked in English with a thick Hessian accent, "May I bring you a cocktail before dinner?"

"I really would like a glass of wine," Elsa said, in German, looking at Cronley.

"I will bring the wine list," the waiter said.

"I don't know anything about wine," Cronley said.

"Would you like a cocktail instead?" Elsa said.

"What I would really like to have is a double Jack Daniel's on the rocks."

"What is that?"

"Whiskey. Bourbon whiskey. They make it out of corn."

Elsa looked at the waiter. "Bring two. And the menu."

"If you want wine, have wine," Cronley said.

"I probably wouldn't know anything on an American list. And besides, beggars can't be choosers."

"You're not a beggar."

"How about a charity case?"

"Not that either."

A menu was produced.

She opened it, studied the selections, then closed it.

"Would you order for me? A piece of meat and a potato, please."

"I'm going to have a medium-rare Porterhouse and a baked potato and corn on the cob. Would that be all right?"

"May your charity case ask questions?"

"You're not a charity case!"

"I had the feeling that Major Connell is not going to reimburse you for what you've spent — and are spending — on me. Doesn't that make me a charity case?"

"What you are is a very beautiful woman with whom I'm having dinner."

She started to reply but was interrupted by the delivery of the Jack Daniel's.

"This is what we call 'sipping whiskey,' " Cronley said. "You take small sips. Not big swallows, I mean."

He demonstrated.

She picked up her glass and took a tiny sip.

"Well?" he said.

"If I took a big swallow of this, I'd be on the floor."

"Then don't drink it. Order some wine."

"Tell me what a Porterhouse is," she said, and took another tiny sip of the Jack Daniel's.

"It's a beefsteak. A big one. With the bone. On one side of the bone is a small tender part, the filet mignon, and on the other, a larger steak, called — depending on where you are — a Kansas City filet or a New York strip."

"That sounds wonderful. You know about meat, I see."

"I was raised on a cattle ranch in Texas."

"You were a cowboy?"

"Until I was fourteen. Then I became a roughneck."

"A what?"

"Someone who works on oil rigs. Drilling for oil. Midland sits on what they call the Permian Basin. A very large oil deposit."

This is where I should skillfully and subtly work into the conversation that the F-Bar-Z ranch, which cattle ranch has been in the family for three generations — four, counting mine — extends over four sections, and the last time I looked there were two hundred and thirteen horsehead pumps on it extracting oil from the Permian Basin.

Then I should modestly make sure she understands that I am the heir apparent to what is known as an oil fortune. Which is true.

But I don't think she'd believe me, for one thing. And if she did, she'd think I was telling her that to get into her pants.

I would happily trade my left nut to get into her pants, but I don't want to do it that way.

Not that there's any chance of my getting into her pants under any circumstance.

Think changing muddy tank tracks and bogie wheels, Stupid!

"Corn on the cob," Elsa said. "What's that?"

"It's what it says — corn, which comes out of the field, on the cob."

He mimed eating from a corncob.

"I tried that twice," she said. "Both times on my honeymoon. First in Vienna and then again in Budapest. It was terrible. Tough."

"Well, this corn on the cob comes from the States. Frozen. It's tender and delicious."

She looked him in the eyes and nodded.

"All right, I'll trust you," Elsa said, and took

94

another tiny sip of her Jack Daniel's.

"That's enormous," she said, when her medium-rare Porterhouse steak was placed before her.

As hungry as she has to be, it'll probably be gone in two minutes.

Fifteen minutes later, by which time Cronley had devoured all of the filet mignon, three-quarters of the Kansas City filet, most of the baked potato, two ears of corn on the cob, and enough of his Jack Daniel's to permit him to raise it over his head as a signal he wanted a refill, Elsa had eaten only a tiny portion of her filet mignon, and maybe two small mouthfuls of kernels from her corncob.

"You don't like the steak?" he asked. "Or the corn?"

"Oh, it's wonderful," she said, and then understood why he had asked.

"Jimmy," she said, meeting his eyes, "have you ever been hungry, very hungry, for days at a time?"

"No," he said, shaking his head. "No, I haven't."

"Well, when that happens, and then you suddenly come upon all the food you want to eat, and you eat your fill, then you suddenly become very ill."

"I didn't think about that," Jimmy said, visibly embarrassed.

"It's okay. It's just that what you learn to

do when you've been very hungry for a week or ten days, and then a feast like this is put before you, is to take tiny bites, and chew them slowly and very well."

"I guess I'm stupid."

"Naïve. Not stupid. There's a big difference."

The waiter delivered two Jack Daniel's doubles on the rocks.

He looked at her glass. It wasn't empty — but close.

She must have been sipping steadily and I didn't notice.

She looked at the new drinks.

"Well, I guess I better finish the first one, hadn't I?" Elsa said.

Before he could object, she did so.

"Elsa, watch it. That was a double. It'll —"

"Thank you. I appreciate your concern."

Thirty minutes later, she had finished all of the filet mignon, eaten most of one ear of corn, perhaps a quarter of the baked potato, and all of her second Jack Daniel's double on the rocks.

"And now if you would be so kind, I think my knight in shining armor should escort me to my room."

"Would you like some dessert?" he asked.

"I would love some dessert, but I think it would be ill-advised."

In the elevator, she took his arm, and continued to hold it as he led her down the corridor to the door of the Goethe Suite.

She couldn't find the key.

"I must have left it," she said. "But we can get in through your room, can't we?"

"If you'll be all right here, I'll go around and let you in."

"Whatever," she said.

He went to 408a, and then into the Goethe Suite and opened the door for her.

"Thank you," she said.

"You're welcome," he said.

She closed the door behind her.

"Good night, Elsa. Thank you for your company."

She chuckled.

He started back for the door connecting 408a and the Goethe Suite. She followed him.

"Jimmy," she said, catching up with him as he started to pull open the door, "do you want to know what I was thinking at dinner and just now in the corridor?"

"That American corn on the cob is better than the Viennese variety?"

"That when this Colonel Mattingly shows up to take me wherever he's going to take me, we'll never see one another again."

"I guess that's so. It's a pity."

"I was also thinking that I haven't been with a man since the night before I put Karl on the train that took him to the Eastern Front."

Where the hell is this going?

"I never wanted to be with another man," Elsa said.

"I understand."

"Until now," she said, and moved closer to him.

He was frozen.

"Don't I appeal to you? I'm too old?"

"I don't want to take —"

"Take advantage of me? Believe me, my sweet naïve Jimmy, that shoe is on the other foot."

Elsa raised her hand to his neck and pulled his face to hers.

■ ■ ■ ■

II

■ ■ ■ ■

II

[ONE]

The Goethe Suite
Kurhotel Marburg
Marburg an der Lahn, Germany
0715 7 October 1945

Counterintelligence Corps Special Agent James D. Cronley Jr. put his hands under his head and tried to reconstruct exactly what had happened the night before.

It had not been an exceedingly clear erotic dream ending in a nocturnal emission. The proof of that was the naked woman in bed beside him.

One moment he had been standing by the door between the Goethe Suite and Room 408a with Frau von Wachtstein — with whom he had been absolutely determined not to get a half inch out of line even if she had had a good deal more Jack Daniel's than was good for her — and the next moment they were on her bed, with her uniform skirt above her waist and his trousers at his ankles.

They had subsequently divested themselves

of their clothing and had at it again.

And then again.

Was it three times total — or four?

He looked down at her again. She was more beautiful, he decided, than she had been in the wildest of his fantasies about her. And she was sound asleep.

Not surprising.

After what happened — it was four times! No, five! — she would probably sleep all day.

Moving as carefully as he could, he eased out of the bed and walked on his toes toward the connecting door.

"Jimmy," Elsa said, her voice soft and sleepy, "where are you going?"

"To muss my bed, so the chambermaid doesn't get any ideas."

"Then come back . . ."

I will come back if I have to crawl through the fires of hell on my hands and knees.

"Sixty seconds," he said, and went through the door.

He jerked the cover from his bed, tried to muss the sheets, didn't like the result, and then jumped on the bed with both feet, marched around it, and then finally punched the pillows until they appeared to have been used.

When he went back to the bedroom of the Goethe Suite, Elsa lifted the sheet so that he could slide in beside her.

■ ■ ■ ■

"Well, what should we do now?" Jimmy said, when he had regained his breath.

"After we have a shower, you mean?" Elsa asked.

"After *we* have a shower?"

She smiled. "That might be interesting. And after *we* have a shower, how does breakfast sound?"

"I think ham and eggs seems like a very good idea," he said. "And after that?"

"I came to Marburg because I had friends here. A girl I went to school with, and her family. I'd like to see if I can find them. Would you help me?"

"Of course," he said.

"Then let's have our shower," Elsa said, and got quickly out of bed and walked naked to the bathroom.

Jimmy quickly followed.

Jimmy lay on the bed and watched as she took the lingerie from the PX out of its bag and cut the labels off the black brassiere and the see-through matching panties. She dropped the towel she had wound around herself in the bathroom and started to pull the panties on. Then she sensed his eyes on her.

"Stop looking," she ordered. "You're embarrassing me."

"No, I'm not. You want me to look."

She met his eyes.

"Otherwise," he said, "you wouldn't have flipped the sheet off you" — he demonstrated with his sheet — "when I came back in here from the other room."

"Guilty," she said, after a moment, finished pulling the panties on, and then reached for the black brassiere.

"If I told you I loved you, what would you say?" Jimmy asked.

"That you're very sweet and very young and that you weren't paying attention to what I said last night."

"What you said *when* last night?"

"That when this Colonel Mattingly shows up to take me wherever he's going to take me, we'll never see one another again."

"That was before what happened last night happened," Jimmy argued. "I gather you don't believe in love at first sight?"

She walked to the bed and sat beside him.

"I believe in lust at first sight," she said. "And that you shouldn't do anything about it unless you know that it's only going to be for a day, or two, and then you will never see the man ever again."

He didn't reply.

"And I also believe that you can't count, sweet Jimmy. I'm thirty-two, and that's much too old for you."

Again he didn't reply.

"Jimmy, please don't ruin what we have."

"I don't want it to end," he said, finally.

"There's nothing either of us can do about that."

She ran her fingertips down his cheeks.

"Can we change the subject?" she asked.

"Why not?"

"What do you know, or think, is going to happen when this Colonel Mattingly comes and takes me wherever he's going to take me?"

"I don't know what I'm talking about," he said. "But it seems pretty obvious my government is grateful for what your father and the other general —"

"Generalleutnant Graf Karl-Friedrich von Wachtstein," she furnished. "My husband's father."

"What's a Graf?"

"A title of nobility. A count — or an earl, as the English rank their nobility."

"Does it come with a crown? Or a castle?"

"No crown, Jimmy, at least in recent times. But there is a castle, Schloss Wachtstein."

"What about you? Were you a princess in a castle?"

"No. My father was a simple soldier."

"I thought he was a general."

"He was."

"Generals are not simple soldiers."

"What does Colonel Mattingly have in

mind for me?" she said, changing the subject.

"I'm crushed. I've been lying here thinking, 'Jimmy Boy, here you are sitting with a *princess* in her see-through underwear. You're a long way from the ol' F-Bar-Z.' And now you tell all you are is an Army brat."

"You're making me blush."

"I like it when you blush."

"Even though I didn't understand half of what you said."

"The see-through underwear part?"

"What's the F-Bar-Z?"

"The name of the ranch, outside Midland, Texas."

"An 'Army brat'?"

"An officer's daughter. There were a lot of them around A&M."

"And what's A&M?"

"My university. Texas Agricultural and Mechanical University."

"If it makes you feel any better, when I married Karl, I became a *Baronin,* a baroness."

"So, at least, here I am, sitting around with a baroness in her see-through underwear."

She shook her head. But she smiled as she touched her fingertips to his face.

"You're not going to tell me, are you?" she then said, pulling back her hand.

"Tell you what?"

"What Colonel Mattingly is going to do with me."

"All I can do is guess, Baroness. I think the government, my government, is grateful for what your father and the count tried to do with Hitler, and are going to try somehow to show that gratitude. Let you go to the States. Something like that."

"I'd like that, to go to the States," Elsa said softly.

"There's an easy way to have that happen, without Mattingly. Let me arrange it."

"How in the world could you do that?"

"You ever hear that money is grease?"

"No. And I have no idea what it means."

"With money, anything is possible."

"I've heard that."

"I've got a lot of money."

She looked at him.

He went on: "There are four sections of land on the F-Bar-Z. A section is a square mile, or six hundred forty acres. One of the sections is mine — my grandfather put it in my name when I was born. When I came here, I was curious about how that would match up with your land measurement. I found out. Six hundred forty acres is two hundred fifty-eight point nine nine eight eight hectares. Call it two hundred fifty-nine hectares."

"That's enormous. I don't think there was that much land around Schloss Wachtstein. And your family owns four of these sections?"

She believes me. So far.

107

"Yeah, and I'm an only child, so presumably one day all four sections will be mine. But right now, I own just the one."

He let that sink in, then added: "But what's important, Elsa, is that on the section I own there are fifty-one horsehead pumps sucking West Texas sweet crude oil out of the ground and, after the Texas Railroad Board takes its cut, into my bank account."

"What are you saying, Jimmy?"

"That you're sitting here in your transparent underwear with a rich guy who's in love with you. You don't need this Colonel Mattingly. I can take care of you. I *will* take care of you."

"Oh, Jimmy!" she said, and touched her fingertips to his face again.

"Okay?"

"I want you to promise me something."

"Anything."

"I want you to promise me you'll never tell what you just told me to another German girl, German woman, after I'm gone."

"Why should I? And what do you mean, after you're gone?"

"I'm going with Colonel Mattingly, wherever he takes me. Understand that. And after I've gone, the next time you're with a German girl, or a German woman, I don't want you to say one word about your ranch. My God, my sweet Jimmy, don't you have any idea how many thousands of women there are in Germany even worse off than I am? I at least have my engagement ring and the necklace. And my brother-in-law survived, and apparently has some connection with Colonel Mattingly.

"These women have nothing. No husbands. No families. Many of them have children to support. If they'll go to bed with an American soldier for a Hershey bar, to stay alive, what do you think they'd do to get an American officer to take care of them? A rich, young, foolish American officer?"

"I'm not a fool, Elsa!"

"Oh, my sweet Jimmy, you are! My God, what have I done to you?"

"Aside from making me fall in love with you, you mean?"

She took a deep breath.

"Now listen to me very carefully, Jimmy. Unless you promise me right now — and mean it — that you stop this nonsense about being in love with me, and never bring it up again, I'm going to call Major Connell and tell him that you're making unwanted advances to me."

"You wouldn't do that."

Oh, shit — yes, she would!

"Yes, I would, sweet Jimmy. And I want you to promise what I said before, never to tell the next German girl you get into your bed anything about being in love or your ranch."

"Fuck you," he said, without thinking about it.

Elsa pushed herself off the bed and walked around to the other side of it. She picked up the telephone on the bedside table.

"Okay, okay," Jimmy said.

She put the handset back in its cradle.

"Have I your promise?" she asked. "Your word as an officer and a gentleman?"

"I'm not an officer and a gentleman. I got my commission from A&M."

She shook her head and smiled.

"Yes or no?" she asked.

"Okay."

"Not good enough, sweet Jimmy. Say it."

"*I promise.* Okay?"

"Say, 'You have my word, Frau von Wachtstein.' "

"Damn it! Okay. You have my word, Elsa."

"Thank you."

"Why did you . . ."

"Take you into my bed?"

He nodded.

"I told you," she said. "I hadn't been with a man since the night before I sent my husband off to die for the fatherland on the Eastern Front. And I knew the young American who looks like an SS recruiting poster would be out of my life in two or three days."

"It meant nothing to you?"

She considered her response and then walked back around the bed and sat down next to him before giving it.

"I probably shouldn't tell you this," she said, "but I'll never forget you, sweet Jimmy."

She ran her fingertips tenderly over his face, then softly kissed him on the lips.

"Now get up, get dressed, and then feed me breakfast before we see if we can find my friends."

She got up and walked to the closet where her uniform was hung.

Jimmy wondered if he would ever see her in her underwear again.

[Two]

233 Heinrichstein Strasse
Marburg an der Lahn, Germany
1030 7 October 1945

The house was large and in good shape, and the first thing Lieutenant Jim Cronley thought when he saw it was that it had most likely been requisitioned by the Army.

He told Elsa this, and added, "Maybe I better go with you."

She nodded.

A middle-aged German woman answered their knock. She had a worried look when she saw what she understandably mistook for two Americans. The look was replaced by one of surprise and confusion when Elsa told her, in German, that she was looking for Family

Hofstadter.

"They are no longer here," the woman said.

"Where are they?" Elsa asked.

"How would I know?" the woman replied, unpleasantly.

"This was their house?" Cronley asked.

"It was forfeited," the woman said.

"Why was it forfeited?" Cronley asked. "Forfeited to whom?"

"To the state," the woman said. "After the attempt to murder Adolf Hitler, Oberst Hofstadter was arrested. On his conviction for treason, all of his property was forfeited to the Reich."

"And you, being a good Nazi," Cronley said sarcastically, "got to buy it for next to nothing?"

"Jimmy!" Elsa said warningly.

The woman's face whitened, but she said nothing.

Elsa turned and stepped quickly down the walk to the Kapitän.

Cronley followed, then got behind the wheel.

"I can probably find these people for you," he said.

She looked at him. He thought he could see tears forming.

"Can you?"

"I think so," he said, and started the engine.

There was a thirty-five-year-old military

112

police captain on duty in the offices of the Polizeidistrikt fur Kreis Marburg.

Relations between the MP and the CIC were usually frosty, and icicles quickly formed when the young CIC special agent — who the captain knew was probably a sergeant and certainly no more than a lieutenant — told the MP captain that he was sorry but the captain did not have the need to know why he wanted to know where the Hofstadter family, formerly of 233 Heinrichstein Strasse, could now be found.

If he calls Connell, Jimmy thought, *I'm fucked.*

"I'll see what I can do, Sergeant . . . excuse me . . . *Mister* Cronley," the captain said sarcastically. "It's always a pleasure to co-operate with the CIC. When do you need it?"

Cronley remembered something from A&M: *The best defense is the attack.*

"Major Connell told me to get that information now."

Ten minutes later, in the Kapitän, Jimmy handed Elsa a slip of paper on which was written: 4-E, 73 Obtierstrasse.

Elsa smiled her gratitude.

73 Obtierstrasse turned out to be a shabby apartment block.

"I think it would be best if I went in here alone, Jimmy."

"You're sure?"

She nodded. "Please."

When he saw her enter the building, Cronley settled down for what he was sure would be a long wait by lighting a cigar.

Elsa was back in the car before there was enough ash on the cigar to knock off.

"Not there?" he said.

"Frau Hofstadter was there. Jimmy, please take me back to the hotel. Now."

"Is there something I can do?"

"Just take me back to the hotel."

At the corridor door to the Goethe Suite, she smiled quickly at him, said, "Thank you," and went inside.

It was obvious that he was no longer welcome in the Goethe Suite.

"I'll be next door," he said to the closed corridor door.

He had been in the armchair with his cigar and the new *Stars & Stripes* perhaps five minutes when the connecting door opened and Elsa came in.

"Do you mind?" she asked. "I don't want to be alone."

There were tear tracks running down her cheeks.

He stood up and put his arms around her.

You are not going to make a pass at a crying woman.

Just comfort her.

Nature overrode that noble determination. Her breasts were soft against him, and the smell of the Chanel No. 5 intoxicating.

He felt the stirring at his groin and pulled his midsection modestly away from hers.

Not quickly enough.

She pulled her head back and smiled up at him through her tears.

"Oh, sweet Jimmy, you never get enough, do you? You remind me of a bull in a field."

"What would you like me to do with it?"

"What you did with it the last time," she said, and pulled his face down to hers.

"So much for firm resolve," she said three minutes later.

"To hell with firm resolve."

"Look at me. At us."

They were lying on the cover of his bed. Her skirt was again up above her waist and his trousers again around his ankles.

"God, I love you," Jimmy said.

"If you start that again, I'll pull my skirt down and leave. Once and for all. I mean it, Jimmy."

"And if I don't start that again, then what?"

"I told you, I don't want to be alone," she said. "I want to be held."

"Naked or clothed?"

She sat up and started to unbutton her uniform shirt.

Jimmy ran his fingers up her backbone.

She was lying on him. He could feel the

warmth of her breasts against his chest, and the bristle of her crotch against his leg.

"You want to tell me what happened in the apartment house?" he asked.

"I don't want to. It's not your concern."

"Tell me, Elsa."

She exhaled audibly.

"Tell me," Jimmy repeated.

"Frau Hofstadter said that I had my nerve, showing up in an American uniform at her door, and that she really had nothing to say to me."

"Why?"

"She said that if it wasn't for the treason of my father and Graf von Wachtstein, her husband would still be alive and she wouldn't be living in a two-room apartment struggling to find enough to eat. She said she wasn't surprised that I was a whore . . . and fucking Americans . . . and hoped I would burn in hell."

"Jesus Christ!"

"And she's right, Jimmy. Oberst Hofstadter was never involved with Claus von Stauffenberg and the others. He was a loyal officer to the end."

"Then what happened?"

"Hitler arrested everybody who even knew anybody involved. There were eight thousand trials and executions, and at least half, maybe three-quarters, of them were of innocent people."

"Why is she holding you responsible?"

"Because I'm my father's daughter. And I showed up at her door in an American uniform."

"Baby, I'm sorry."

"In there," Elsa said, gesturing toward the Goethe Suite, "before I came in here, I realized she was right. I am a whore. I'm sorry, but I can't find any shame in what happened between us. It was stupid of me, but it wasn't wrong."

"Well, you're not a whore. What you are is a fool."

"I know."

"For not letting a man who loves you take care of you."

"Stop! Not one more word!"

She started to sob then, and he held her, stroking her back and her arms until he realized that she had both stopped sobbing and fallen asleep.

What the hell am I going to do?

[THREE]

Rhine-Main Airfield
Frankfurt am Main, Germany
0755 8 October 1945

"Rhine-Main," the pilot of South American Airways *Ciudad de Rosario,* a Lockheed Constellation aircraft, announced, "South

117

American Double Zero Five on the ground at five to the hour. Please close us out."

The "Connie" was arguably — perhaps inarguably — the best transport aircraft flying. Designed by the legendary aviator Howard Hughes, it carried forty passengers in a pressurized cabin as high as thirty-five thousand feet at a cruising speed of three hundred knots, and could do so for 4,300 miles. Its wing design was nearly identical to that of the single-seat Lockheed "Lightning" P-38 fighter, which Hughes had also designed.

"Roger, Double Zero Five. You are closed out."

Immediately, there was a fresh voice: "South American Double Zero Five, Rhine-Main ground control."

"Good morning, ground control," the pilot replied cheerfully, even unctuously. "And how may South American Airways be of service to you this morning?"

It was not the response the ground control operator expected. This was, after all, a U.S. Army Air Forces base. There were rules, a protocol, to be followed.

The pilot of SAA 005 knew this. In another life, he had been a Naval Aviator, and was still carried on a Classified Top Secret "Roster of Personnel on Duty with the Office of Strategic Services" as "Frade, Cletus H., Lt. Col., USMCR."

Once a Marine . . . as the saying goes.

This was not the first time he had tweaked the tail of control tower operators. In his sealed records at Headquarters, USMC, there was a copy of a Letter of Reprimand alleging that First Lieutenant Frade, of Marine Fighter Squadron VMF-211, in an act prejudicial to good order and discipline, had buzzed the tower at Fighter One on Guadalcanal in his Grumman F4F Wildcat fighter, causing the occupants to jump therefrom.

The ground control operator regained his aplomb.

"South American Double Zero Five, Rhine-Main ground control. Take taxiway two and stop. A Follow-Me will meet you. Acknowledge."

"Roger, ground control. It will be my pleasure," Frade said to his microphone, and then switched it to INTERCOM.

"You get that, Hansel?" he asked.

The co-pilot, a trim blond twenty-seven-year-old who in another life had been Major Freiherr Hans-Peter von Wachtstein of the Luftwaffe, nodded.

"Try not to run over the Follow-Me," Frade said.

Von Wachtstein shook his head resignedly.

Both were wearing the uniforms prescribed for pilots of South American Airways. Frade was a captain. There were four inch-wide golden stripes sewn to his dark blue, double-breasted, brass-buttoned tunic. Von Wacht-stein, a first officer, had three such stripes. The trousers of both were a powder blue and had an inch-and-a-half-wide gold stripe down the leg seams. Both wore SAA pilot's wings, about twice the size of Frade's Naval Aviator's Wings of Gold, and which had what looked like a sunburst in their centers. It had actually been taken from the flag of the Argentine Republic. SAA was an Argentine airline.

Frade had once confided to his wife that the uniforms reminded him of those worn by bandmasters of a traveling circus, except the SAA uniforms were a bit more flamboyant.

The Follow-Me, a ton-and-a-half weapons carrier painted in a black-and-yellow checkerboard pattern and flying two checkerboard flags, appeared. The Constellation began to follow it far across the airfield.

"Where the hell are they taking us? Italy?" Frade asked.

Von Wachtstein did not reply.

Eventually they were led to a remote corner of the airfield, where a collection of vehicles were waiting for them. There were two Mercedes-Benz buses; two fuel trucks; five jeeps (each carrying a pair of MPs); two Ford pickup trucks with stairways built on their beds; and two German passenger cars, now bearing U.S. Army markings. One was an Opel Admiral, a GM vehicle about the size of a Buick that was produced in Germany. The other was a Horch.

Frade knew that the Horch was the car of Colonel Robert Mattingly, who commanded OSS Forward. He had taught him how to get it out of low gear.

Every time Frade saw the Horch, he was painfully reminded of his father, el Coronel Jorge Frade, Cavalry, Ejército Argentino, who had brought one of the cars to Argentina before the war, loved it, and had died in it on his estancia, assassinated at the orders of the SS.

As soon as the aircraft engines had been stopped, one of the pickup trucks moved its stairs to the passenger door while the second pickup went to the smaller crew door behind the cockpit.

Colonel Mattingly rose from the Horch and walked — more accurately marched — toward the stairs leading to the crew door.

Mattingly was a tall, startlingly handsome, nattily uniformed officer. He had a yellow scarf around his neck. His sharply creased trousers were tucked into a pair of highly shined "tanker" boots. He carried a Model 1911-A1 Colt .45 ACP semiautomatic pistol in a shoulder holster. The eagles of a full colonel were pinned to his epaulets, and the triangular insignia of the Second Armored Division was sewn on his sleeve.

On the aircraft, a stocky, middle-aged man

in a business suit entered the area behind the pilots' seats and opened the crew door. He was Suboficial Mayor Enrico Rodríguez, Cavalry, Ejército Argentino, Retired. He had served the late el Coronel Frade most of their lives, had been gravely wounded and left for dead when el Coronel Frade had been assassinated, and now regarded his mission in life as protecting el Coronel Frade's only son, Cletus, from the same fate.

Mattingly entered the flight deck as Frade climbed out of the pilot's seat.

"How did things go?" Mattingly said, as they shook hands.

"Well, we had Yak-9s for company most of the time," Frade said. "But I was not afraid, as we have half of the Vatican in the back."

Mattingly chuckled. "Don't be cynical, Colonel."

"What I was wondering is where they got all the — what do you call it? — *clerical garb.*"

"Never underestimate Holy Mother Church," Mattingly said.

Von Wachtstein climbed out of the co-pilot's seat and offered his hand to Mattingly.

"There is some interesting news to report," Mattingly said. "The ASA intercepted a message to Pavel Egorov, the NKVD's man in Mexico City . . ."

Frade formed a "T" with his hands, making a *time-out* gesture.

"Explanation needed, Bob," Frade said.

"You're dealing with a couple of simple airplane drivers."

"The NKVD is the People's Commissariat for Internal Affairs," Mattingly explained. "Pavel Egorov has been running things — dealing with both the Mexicans and us — in Mexico City."

"Okay."

"He was ordered to Buenos Aires to assume command of OPERATION G. OPERATION G is 'find out what's going on with the Americans and Gehlen.'"

"Assume command from whom?" Frade asked. "The Russians don't even have an embassy in Buenos Aires."

"They're working on that," Mattingly said. "In the meantime, they have a trade mission, one man working on buying things from Argentina, one man working on selling things to Argentina, and about forty people — including a dozen women — spying on Argentina. The man in charge has been Oleg Fedoseev."

"I never heard any of this from Bernardo Martín."

"I'm sure that even a simple airplane driver such as yourself," Mattingly said sarcastically, "has considered the remote possibility that General Martín doesn't tell you everything he knows."

"He didn't," Frade said, just as sarcastically. "Does that mean I'll have to turn in my cloak and dagger? Or will bowing my head and beating my breast in shame suffice?"

"Anyway," Mattingly said, smiling, "Egorov has been ordered to take over from Fedoseev. That may pose some problems for you, as we can't — can we? — have the Soviets learn what you're doing."

"I always thought that the Russians here already knew what we're doing," Frade said, now seriously. "The problem is going to be keeping them from finding out which of the Gehlens — Good Gehlens and Bad Gehlens — we have in Argentina and where we have them stashed."

"To do that you may have to take out not only Egorov and Fedoseev, but whoever else is getting too close."

"All forty of them?"

"If it comes down to that, all forty of them, meanwhile making sure that Egorov and Company don't take you out."

"Jesus!" Frade blurted. "You're just a fountain of good news, aren't you, Bob?"

"I do have a little of that, but let's finish this part first. Have you room on this Argentine estancia I hear so much about to place — more precisely place *and* hide — an antenna farm?"

"What kind of an antenna farm?"

"Whatever kind the ASA needs to listen to the Russians."

124

"And who would operate this antenna farm?"

"A nine-man team from Vint Hill."

"Black, I presume?"

"The antenna farm would be black. But the operators could be technicians from Collins and Aircraft Radio Corporation sent down there to maintain SAA's radios."

Frade considered the request a moment.

"Just as long as they understand they'll be working for me, not the ASA."

"Agreed."

"And now the good news?" Frade said.

Mattingly looked at von Wachtstein.

"The MPs picked up your sister-in-law, Peter."

"What?" von Wachtstein said, his tone incredulous.

"I spoke with her on the telephone," Mattingly went on. "She said she was the widow of Major Karl von Wachtstein. I think it's her, but we've had experiences with people taking other people's identification. Would you be willing to go have a look at her?"

"What a stupid fucking question!" Frade flared.

"Where is she?" von Wachtstein asked softly.

"In Marburg an der Lahn," Mattingly said. "It's here in Hesse."

"I went to university there," von Wachtstein said.

"And I was there with el Coronel," Rodríguez said. "We went there to hunt wild boar."

"Clete," von Wachtstein said, "I know it'll screw up our flight plan but —"

"Another stupid fucking question," Frade interrupted. "Of course we go! Screw the flight plan."

"And presuming it is her, then what?" Mattingly said. "What would you like me to do with her?"

"Three stupid fucking questions in a row," Frade said. "We take her with us, that's what we'll do with her."

"I thought that might be the case," Mattingly said. "That's what the buses are for. To take your passengers for a long, long breakfast while we go to Marburg an der Lahn."

[FOUR]

Kurhotel Marburg
Marburg an der Lahn, Germany
0925 8 October 1945

There were four men in the enormous Horch touring car but only a driver in the Opel Admiral that followed the Horch up to the entrance of the Kurhotel.

Enrico Rodríguez was driving the Horch. Von Wachtstein sat beside him. Frade and Mattingly were in the back.

The driver of the Opel Admiral, Harold N.

Wallace, was wearing an insignia-less uniform. Wallace was in fact a major of the Signal Corps, but functioning as a field officer of the Office of Strategic Services. He was present because Colonel Mattingly thought it possible that he or the car or both might prove useful in some unforeseeable circumstance.

The cars stopped before the entrance of the Kurhotel and everybody got out and marched inside.

"Harry, go in there," Colonel Mattingly ordered, gesturing toward the dining room, "and order up breakfast for everybody plus two. Frau von Wachtstein has a CIC lieutenant sitting on her, and they'll have to be fed, too. Tell the waiter to snap it up. We're pressed for time."

"Yes, sir," Major Wallace said.

Mattingly marched to the reception desk, picked up the telephone, and ordered in perfect German that he be connected with Frau von Wachtstein.

Elsa picked up the telephone on the third ring, and to do so she had to lean across Jimmy, which movement caused her breast to brush his face. Jimmy took advantage of the situation by taking her nipple in his mouth.

"Hello?" she said.

"Frau von Wachtstein?"

"Yes."

"This is Colonel Robert Mattingly, Frau von Wachtstein. I hope I didn't wake you."

Jimmy could hear the conversation, and let go of Elsa's nipple.

"No, I was awake," she said, meeting Jimmy's eyes.

"I'm downstairs in the lobby, Frau von Wachtstein," Mattingly said. "I realize this is rude, but we're really pressed for time. How soon do you think you could come down?"

"Ten minutes."

"Fine. I'll explain what's going to happen over breakfast."

"That would be nice of you."

"I don't suppose you know where Lieutenant Cronley is at this hour?"

"Probably in his room. Next door."

"Well, I'll call him there."

"I'll call him. I can just knock on the connecting door. He's a sound sleeper."

"That would be fine," Mattingly said. "I'll expect you in ten minutes."

Mattingly hung up and Elsa followed suit.

"Oh, shit!" Jimmy said.

"You knew this was going to happen," Elsa said.

"That doesn't make it any better."

"It's probably better. Quick."

"Like having a tooth pulled?"

"Yes," she said. "Get up and get dressed, sweet Jimmy."

Elsa kissed him in the elevator.

"Write me," he said. "Promise?"

"If I can."

She's not going to write me.

The elevator door slid open.

"Oh, my God!" Elsa suddenly said. "Hansel!"

"Am I glad to see you!" Hans-Peter von Wachtstein said, his voice breaking.

He put his arms around Elsa.

"You presumably are Lieutenant Cronley?" Colonel Mattingly asked.

"Yes, sir," Jimmy said, then his eyes went to the others.

After a long moment, Jimmy said, "Don't give me that funny look, Cletus. You're the one wearing that ridiculous Mexican bus driver's uniform! What the hell are you up to?"

"Jimmy!" Cletus Frade said. "You little sonofabitch!"

Mattingly looked between them.

"May I presume from that exchange, Colonel Frade, that you are acquainted with Lieutenant Cronley?"

Neither replied. They moved closer and hugged each other.

When they finally broke apart, Frade said,

"Jimmy, this is Colonel Bob Mattingly of the OSS. Colonel, not that I wanted it this way, he happened to live next door, this is Jimmy Cronley, the next thing I have to a little brother."

"He's been corrupting my morals since I was in short pants, Colonel," Cronley said.

Hans-Peter von Wachtstein then put in: "Elsa, this is my best friend, the best man at my wedding, Cletus Frade."

"*And* godfather to his child," Frade added, offering his hand. "Has my little brother been taking good care of you, Frau von Wachtstein?"

"Oh, yes," Elsa said. "He's been very kind and thoughtful. I couldn't ask for a better friend."

"Then thank you, Lieutenant," Hans-Peter von Wachtstein said. "Thank you very much."

"My pleasure," Cronley said, suddenly aware of his choice of words.

"Into the dining room," Mattingly ordered. "If you plan to take off before noon, Cletus, we're running a little late."

"Take off for where?" Cronley asked.

"Lieutenant, you don't have the need to know," Mattingly said, almost as a reflex action.

"Argentina," Frade said.

Mattingly gave him a dirty look.

Frade was not cowed.

"I told you, Bob. He's my little brother."

"With a Top Secret security clearance and everything," Cronley said.

"You're not cleared for this, Lieutenant," Mattingly snapped.

"What are you doing in Argentina, Clete?" Cronley pursued, ignoring Mattingly. "The last I heard you were flying Marine fighters on Guadalcanal. And what's this 'colonel' business?"

"Bob, for Christ's sake, he's on our side," Frade said.

"He also has a flip lip, and you're as aware as I am, Colonel Frade, we can't afford people with flip lips. Subject closed."

"Sorry, Bob. But there's a problem with that. I know Jimmy well enough to know that if I don't tell him enough to satisfy him — and shut him up — he's liable to open the whole can of worms. And *that* we can't afford."

"I'm telling you, Clete — all right, I'm *ordering* you — to tell him nothing."

"The problem with that, Bob, is that you can't give me orders. I work for Allen Dulles, not you. And Dulles gave me the authority to do just about whatever I want to do. And you know that."

Cronley thought: *What the hell is going on here?*

Then Cronley looked at Elsa. She was following the confrontation with frightened eyes.

Her brother-in-law seemed to think it was funny.

Mattingly threw up his hands in disgusted resignation and glared at Cronley.

"Okay, Jimmy," Frade said. "What I'm going to tell you is all that you're going to get. Not subject to discussion. And you are to tell no one — including your commanding officer or anyone else — what you see or hear here. Understand?"

"Understand."

"When I came back from Guadalcanal, I was recruited for the OSS and sent to Argentina. Did you know my father was an Argentine?"

"I heard something about it. Your grandfather certainly hated him."

"That's a long story, and there's no time to get into it now. So we'll leave it that I went to Argentina in 1942, and have been there ever since. Don't ask me what I was doing during the war, or what I'm doing now. Colonel Mattingly is right about that — you don't have the need to know."

"Okay," Jimmy said. "Whatever it was, you must have done it right. If you're a colonel."

"Lieutenant Colonel," Frade said.

"What's going to happen to . . . Frau von Wachtstein in Argentina?" Jimmy asked.

"Still the Boy Scout, are you, Jimmy?" Frade said, chuckling. " 'Let me help you across the street, Poor Little Old Lady'?"

132

"So what?"

"You're talking to a senior officer, Lieutenant!" Mattingly snapped. "Watch your mouth!"

"Frau von Wachtstein will be well taken care of," Frade said. "Hansel here" — he pointed to him — "and I became friends in Argentina. The circumstances are none of your business. He married an Argentine girl, who was sort of a daughter to my father. She's my wife's best friend."

"You're married?"

"With two children. Hansel and Alicia have one, a boy . . ."

"And yours?"

"Two boys," Frade said. "Jimmy, the point of this is that Frau von Wachtstein will be part of the family. Hansel, his bride, and mine will see that she's taken very good care of."

"Good," Jimmy said, looking at Elsa.

Jimmy thought he saw her tears forming.

"And that's all you get, Jimmy," Frade said. "Maybe sometime down the pike . . ."

"Yeah."

Mattingly interjected: "You fully understand, I presume, Lieutenant, what Colonel Frade said, that you are to tell no one, *no one,* what you saw or were told?"

"You didn't see any of us here, Jimmy," Frade added, his tone deeply serious, "except Colonel Mattingly. Keep your mouth shut, Jimmy. It's really important."

"I got it," Jimmy said.

"Well, let's go have our breakfast," Mattingly said.

"I don't want any breakfast," Jimmy blurted.

"Well, in that case, Lieutenant," Mattingly said, "why don't you go to Frau von Wachtstein's room, bring her luggage down, and put it in my car? Then, you're relieved of your duty here and can report to Major Connell for duty."

"No," Frade said, looking from Mattingly to Cronley. "Come have breakfast, Jimmy. We'll send someone for Frau von Wachtstein's luggage."

"Please," Elsa said softly.

Jimmy met her eyes, then nodded.

Fifteen minutes later, standing outside the Horch, Elsa kissed Jimmy on the cheek, and told him she would never forget how kind he had been to her.

Then she climbed in the Horch, and the others followed.

Jimmy, hands on hips, stood and watched as, tires spinning and throwing gravel, the Horch raced away with the Opel Admiral in pursuit.

[FIVE]

"You have a problem, Cronley?" Major Connell asked, waving him into his office.

"No, sir. Sir, Colonel Mattingly came to the Kurhotel this morning and took Frau von Wachtstein away."

Connell waited for Cronley to go on. When he didn't, Connell asked, not pleasantly, "Well, what happened?"

"Sir, I just told you. Colonel Mattingly took Frau von Wachtstein away and told me to report to you for duty."

"Where did he take her?"

"Sir, I can't tell you."

"What do you mean, you can't tell me?"

"Sir, Colonel Mattingly ordered me to tell no one anything I heard or saw at the hotel just now."

"Certainly he didn't mean to include me in the 'no one' category, Lieutenant."

"Sir, Colonel Mattingly made it clear I was to tell no one, including you."

"Did you have any problems with Frau von Wachtstein? Was she satisfied with the way you took care of her?"

"I believe she was, sir."

"And Colonel Mattingly gave you no message to deliver to me?"

"No, sir. Except that I was to report back to you for duty."

Connell studied Cronley for a long moment.

"If anything went wrong, Cronley, now is the time to tell me."

"Nothing went wrong, sir."

Connell nodded.

"Okay. You might as well go back on the roadblock."

"Yes, sir. Now?"

"Yes, now, Lieutenant."

"Yes, sir."

[Six]

The Ministry of Labor and Welfare
Avenida Leandro N. Alem 650
Buenos Aires, Argentina
1405 8 October 1945

The building housing the Ministerio de Trabajo y Seguridad Social of the Argentine Republic was at the western end of Avenida 9 Julio, which was said to be the widest avenue in the world.

It was a large building, but not as large, luxurious, or impressive as the Edificio Libertador.

El Coronel Juan Domingo Perón — vice president, secretary of War, and secretary of Labor and Welfare of the Argentine Republic — maintained an office in the Labor Building, as well as offices in the Edificio Libertador and in the Casa Rosada.

Two identical Ejército Argentino Mercedes-Benz sedans and an Army Ford ton-and-a-half stake-bodied truck came up Avenida 9 Julio to the building. The first Mercedes stopped in front of the Labor Building. General de Brigada Eduardo Ramos and Capitán Ricardo Montenegro got out and stood on the sidewalk as if waiting for someone.

The second Mercedes and the truck — which carried twenty helmeted soldiers, each holding a Mauser rifle between his knees — turned into the alley beside the building, and then turned around so they faced Avenida 9 Julio.

When they had done so, a third Mercedes, a black sedan with civilian license plates, which had been parked on Avenida 9 Julio, started its engine and drove up behind the Mercedes stopped in front of the building.

A tall, fair-haired, light-skinned thirty-seven-year-old in the uniform of a *general de brigada de caballería* got out of his car and walked up to Ramos and Montenegro. He was Alejandro Bernardo Martín, chief of the Ethical Standards Office of the Argentine Ministry of Defense.

Montenegro saluted, and Ramos and Martín shook hands, somewhat stiffly.

Then the three of them entered the building, walked directly to the elevator bank, and went to the fifth floor, where the secretary of Labor and Welfare had his office. They walked down the corridor until they came to a lieutenant and a sergeant — obviously guards — sitting outside the office, but neither challenged them.

Ramos entered the outer office first. A secretary rose from behind her desk.

"Be so kind, señora," Ramos ordered, "as to inform el Coronel Perón that Generals Ramos and Martín wish to see him."

"Does the secretary expect you?"

"I don't know," Ramos said simply.

The woman went to the door, through it, closed it behind her, and then reappeared a moment later. She held the door open.

"The secretary will see you, gentlemen," she said.

Ramos entered Perón's office first, with Martín on his heels.

"Well, another unexpected pleasure," Perón said, not rising from behind his desk. "We don't often see you in uniform, General Martín."

Martín ignored that, then announced: "Colonel Perón, by order of his Excellency, the President of the Argentine Republic, you are under arrest."

"Et tu, Brutus?" Perón said to Ramos.

"For the love of God, Juan Domingo, don't make this any more difficult than it already is."

"What are the charges?" Perón asked.

"Violations of the Code of Honor of the officer corps of the Ejército Argentino," Martín said. "You will be apprised of the specifics at a later time."

"You knew this was coming," Ramos said. "I warned you it was coming."

"Colonel, I will require your sidearm," Martín said.

"And, as soon as I draw it from my holster, will you — with the greatest reluctance, of course — shoot me for resisting arrest?"

"And I told you this was for your protection," Ramos said. "You may yet get shot, Juan Domingo, but not by General Martín or me."

Perón didn't reply.

With exaggerated delicate motions to show he had no intention of grabbing the weapon, Perón took a gleaming Luger 9mm Parabellum pistol from a shiny, form-fitting black leather holster and, using only his thumb and forefinger, held it in front of him.

"Take that, Montenegro," Martín ordered. "See to it that there is no round in the chamber and give it to me."

"That is a personal, rather than an issued, weapon," Perón said. "It was a gift from el Coronel Jorge Frade. When we were at the Kriegsschule, we were given a tour of the Deutsche Waffen und Munitionsfabriken in Berlin. You remember, Eduardo?"

"I remember, Juan Domingo."

"And they offered to sell us special Lugers, highly polished like that one, as presentation pieces."

"And Jorge, who had been at the schnapps over lunch, said he would take a dozen," Ramos said. "I remember. I have one just like that."

"I wonder what happened to the others," Perón said.

"They're probably at Estancia San Pedro y San Pablo," Ramos said.

"The weapon is now safe, *mi General,*" Montenegro reported.

"Give it to General Ramos, please," Martín said. "He can return it to el Coronel Perón when this issue is over."

"An unexpected courtesy, General," Perón said. "Thank you."

"Colonel, I take no pleasure in this," Martín said. "I am here at the direct personal order of the president."

"Of course you are," Perón said sarcastically.

"Colonel," Martín then began, "we now come to the question of transporting you to your place of confinement —"

"Indeed?" Perón interrupted. "And where is that going to be?"

Martín ignored the question.

"Parked outside, next to the building," Martín went on, "is a staff car in which are two officers, both senior to you. There is also a truck with a platoon of riflemen of the Patricios Infantry Regiment in it. One option is that I send for the officers and place you in their custody. They would then take you out of the building, visibly under arrest, and transport you to your place of confinement.

"The second option is that you give General Ramos and myself your parole. If you do that, you, General Ramos, and Capitán Montenegro can walk out the front door of this building and get into General Ramos's staff car, giving the impression, I would suggest, that you are all going to lunch."

"You would not, under your second option, be joining us for lunch?"

"Colonel, my orders from the president are to see you safely to your place of confinement."

"My mysterious place of confinement, you mean?"

"For Christ's sake, Juan Domingo," Ramos flared. "Martín is going far out of his way to spare you the humiliation of being taken from here under arrest. If I have to tell you this — that would be all over the front pages of *La Prensa* and *La Nacíon*!"

"Forgive me, General Martín," Perón said sarcastically.

Martín ignored him again.

"And to do that," Martín went on, "under Option Two, my car, the staff car containing the two officers senior to you, and the truck with the mountain troops will follow, at a discreet distance, General Ramos's staff car to our destination. It is my intention to put Montenegro in my car, and I will ride with General Ramos and you."

"Very well," Perón said, his tone suggesting he was granting, rather than receiving, a favor.

"As I said, Colonel," Martín said calmly, "I will require your parole, under the Code of Honor of the officer corps of the Ejército Argentino."

"Very well," Perón said. "You have it."

The cars and trucks trying to follow General Ramos's staff car in the heavy traffic lost it before they reached the Colón Opera House, which was about halfway down Avenida 9 Julio.

"Pull over and wait until they catch up with us," Martín ordered.

That maneuver was repeated when the trailing vehicles again lost Ramos's car near the end of Avenida 9 Julio, by the French embassy.

"Turn left on Libertador," Martín ordered this time. "And stop there to wait for them."

"I gather my mysterious place of confinement is not to be the Circulo Militar," el Coronel Perón said.

The central officers' club of the Ejército

Argentino, which overlooked the Plaza San Martín, was the former mansion of the Paz family, which owned *La Prensa* newspaper. It was one of the most beautiful buildings in Argentina.

If they had been going there, they had just missed the turn.

"I'm afraid not, *el Coronel*," Martín said.

When the trailing vehicles finally caught up, Ramos's staff car led the convoy all the way down Avenida Libertador, past the polo fields and racetrack, and out of the City of Buenos Aires proper, into the Province of Buenos Aires.

"Now I'm really curious where you're taking me," Perón said.

No one replied.

They eventually arrived in Tigre, often described as Venice without the buildings. It was a large area of small islands in the Parana River Delta. The center had been developed around the turn of the century, and ornate Victorian mansions — some of them housing the English, French, Italian, and Swiss rowing clubs — lined branches of the Parana River.

There was also a commercial area, where boats plying the Parana brought fruits, vegetables, and firewood from upriver.

The Ramos convoy headed for the wharfs of the fruit market and disappeared into one of the warehouses.

"Now I demand to know where I'm being taken!" Perón announced.

"You'll soon find out, *el Coronel*," Martín said.

When Perón got out of the Mercedes, he saw that the soldiers of the First Infantry Regiment — the Patricios — were lined up in two facing rows.

"That way, if you will, *el Coronel*," Martín said, gesturing that Perón should walk between the lines of soldiers.

When he had done so, he found himself outside the warehouse, standing on a wharf. A fifty-foot-long boat was tied up to the wharf. Highly varnished and brightly painted, it was one of perhaps thirty such boats used to take people on cruises — luncheon included — through the islands of Tigre and out onto the River Plate.

"What are you going to do, General?" Perón snapped. "Take me out onto the Plate and throw me overboard?"

Martín ignored the question. He motioned for Perón to cross the gangway onto the boat.

When he had done so, the soldiers followed him. Ramos and Montenegro and finally Martín boarded the boat, which immediately began to move away from the wharf.

They entered the cabin of the boat, which was furnished with tables and chairs and, at stern end, a bar.

"Stand if you like, *el Coronel*," Martín said.

144

"But it's about an hour's ride, and you'd probably be more comfortable sitting."

Perón glared between Ramos and Martín.

"You're taking me to Isla Martín García?" he asked, but it was more of a statement — an accusation — than it was a question.

Isla Martín García was a small island — little more than half a square mile — off the Río de la Plata coast of Uruguay. In the 1820s it had been fortified by the Ejército Argentino to deny the Brazilian navy access to the Uruguay River.

This time Martín replied. "The president, *el Coronel,* told me I was to remind you that you would be marching in the steps of President Hipólito Yrigoyen."

The smile on Martín's face showed that he had no trouble at all obeying that order.

General Ramos chuckled.

Juan Hipólito del Sagrado Corazón de Jesús Yrigoyen Alem had twice been president of the Argentine Republic. In 1930, a cabal of officers who had briefly seized power held him prisoner for a short time on Isla Martín García. A young major named Juan Domingo Perón had been appointed private secretary to the minister of War as a reward for his role in the coup.

Perón glared at both of them.

"You will pardon me for not being able to share in the joke," he snapped.

"He also said, *el Coronel,*" Martín went on,

145

"to tell you that it was the safest place he could think of to keep you in this situation."

"One day, Juan Domingo," Ramos said, "there will no doubt be another bronze plaque, one with your name on it, affixed to the wall of the schoolhouse beside the one that now states, 'President Yrigoyen was held captive in this building in 1930.' "

Perón, his face red, glared at him.

"Capitan Montenegro will stay with you, *el Coronel*," Martín said, "and see to your comfort. He and the troops from the Patricios will guarantee your safety."

"Sit down, Juan Domingo," General Ramos ordered, impatient, his tone making it clear he had tired of Perón's combativeness. "Try to get it through your head that the president, Martín, and I are doing our very best to keep you alive."

[SEVEN]

Base Naval Puerto Belgrano
Punta Alta, Bahía Blanca
Bahía Blanca Province, Argentina
1305 9 October 1945

Vicealmirante Guillermo Crater was immediately notified by telephone that a Storch aircraft carrying General de Brigada Bernardo Martín had just landed unannounced.

Where the hell did Bernardo get an airplane?

146

"What kind of an aircraft did you say?" the admiral inquired.

"A Fieseler Storch, *mi Almirante,* a Fi 156."

The Storch was what the Wehrmacht had called a Ground Cooperation Aircraft. The small, high-wing airplane, used for liaison and artillery direction, could carry a pilot and two passengers and was capable of landing and taking off within remarkably short distances.

Where the hell did he get a Storch?

Why am I still surprised at anything he does?

"My compliments to el General," Crater said. "Tell him I will be there directly."

"Sí, mi Almirante."

"And put the aircraft out of sight in a hangar. And do not record that it's been here. This is a matter of national security."

"Sí, mi Almirante."

Vicealmirante Crater did not see a Storch anywhere on the field when his gray 1942 Buick staff car took him and his aide-de-camp, Capitán de Fregata Roberto Otero, there.

"Which hangar?" he wondered aloud.

"I would suggest the far one, *mi Almirante,*" Otero said, having overheard the conversation announcing the arrival of the Storch and Crater's orders to get it out of sight.

"Drive there," Crater ordered.

General Martín was standing by the Storch.

147

He had just about finished changing into his uniform.

"I like your new horse, Bernardo," the vice-almirante said. "Where'd you get it?"

Martín smiled and chuckled, and the two officers patted one another's backs.

"I drove to Estancia San Pedro y San Pablo and commandeered it," Martín said. "You said this was important."

"That's Cletus Frade's airplane?"

"It is now," Martín said. "It used to belong to the German embassy. I thought you knew that story."

Crater shook his head.

"The day after the bomb didn't kill Hitler at his headquarters, Himmler ordered the arrest of those he suspected were involved. And their families. That included Major Hans-Peter von Wachtstein of the German embassy here. Von Wachtstein and Boltitz were way ahead of them. They got in the embassy's Storch, filed a flight plan to Montevideo, took off — and disappeared.

"Everyone thought they had gone out over the River Plate and dove into it, to escape the tender ministrations of the SS. What they really did was fly out to Estancia San Pedro y San Pablo, where they put this" — he patted the Storch fuselage — "into Frade's hangar. Frade then flew them to the American airbase at Porto Alegre, Brazil, in his Lodestar, from which they were flown to the United

148

States. Nobody was any wiser —"

"Including you?" Vicealmirante Crater interrupted.

"Including me. I knew, of course, that Boltitz was Admiral Canaris's man in the embassy, and that Frade had turned von Wachtstein. But I didn't know what had happened to either of them until several days after the German surrender, when Frade flew to the United States and brought them back."

"And this airplane?"

"Frade kept it. When Argentina declared war on Germany, Frade — or his man in the American embassy, Major Pelosi — claimed it as captured enemy property. Pelosi then immediately sold it to an Argentine national — Cletus Frade — for ten pesos, and then Frade asked me to help him get it registered here."

"And you did."

"And I did. I thought it might be useful someday. And so it has proven to be."

"I didn't know you were a pilot."

"I don't advertise it, but yes. Cletus taught me how to fly . . . and did so in this aircraft."

"You're very good at what you do, aren't you, Bernardo?" the vicealmirante said admiringly.

"I would say we both are — the proof being we're still alive."

They smiled at each other.

"What's so important, Guillermo?" Martín

then asked.

"Those German submarines you've been so interested in?" Crater said. "One of them appeared here at first light this morning to surrender. U-405. I hid it between the *Rivadavia* and *Moreno* and put her crew aboard the *Rivadavia*."

To counter Brazil's two Minas Geraes–class battleships, Argentina had built two American-designed battleships. They had seen little service and no combat during World Wars I and II. They were kept manned and ready for service. By 1945, though, they were absolutely obsolete.

"Her captain," Crater went on, "denies having put anything, or anyone, ashore. I'm sure he's lying."

"Interesting."

"Which is why I called you," Crater said. "If we can tie him to Perón, that'd solve a great many problems. And you'll know how to find out if he is or not."

"I never asked, Guillermo, because I didn't want to know until just now. Are you part of the group who wants Perón either out of the government or dead?"

Crater did not respond directly. Instead, he said, "Perón is not only a disgrace to the officer corps and the government but a danger to the Republic, and you know that as well as I do."

"That doesn't answer my question," Martín said.

"I know it doesn't, Bernardo," Crater said. "But let sleeping dogs lie. Would you like to talk to this man before I have to report the submarine to Buenos Aires? As I already should have done."

Martín was not willing to let go.

"The president knows about the threats to assassinate el Coronel Perón —"

"Who told him?"

"I did. It was my duty."

"Did you give him names?"

"No. But I'm sure he's figured them out himself."

"Would you say I'm one of the suspects?"

Martín considered that. "I don't think so."

Crater did not reply.

"Guillermo, yesterday, at the order of President Farrell, General Ramos and I arrested Perón."

"And charged him with what?"

"For his own protection, President Farrell believes that if Perón is assassinated, it will mean civil war, and I'm afraid he's right," Martín said. "He doesn't want, I don't want, and I don't think you want, Guillermo, what happened in Spain to happen here."

"Of course not. But neither do I want Argentina turned into a South American version of Fascist Italy, or Nazi Germany, under Juan Domingo Perón."

"Well, then we'll both have to try to see that doesn't happen, won't we?"

"Where did you take the sonofabitch? To the Circulo Militar?"

"You know better than to ask me to answer that question."

"You can't hide him for long."

"We can try. And if these people do find him, I'll have the satisfaction of knowing I didn't do anything to reveal where he's being held."

Crater met Martín's eyes for a long moment.

"Why don't you see what you can get out of Fregattenkapitän Wilhelm von Dattenberg?"

"That name rings a bell," Martín said, almost to himself. "You say you have him on the *Rivadavia*?"

Crater nodded. "In her wardroom."

"Not alone, I hope?"

"No, Bernardo, not alone. I didn't want him to make himself another Langsdorff."

Kapitän zur See Hans Wilhelm Langsdorff, captain of the *Panzerschiff* (pocket battleship) *Admiral Graf Spee,* had in 1939 refused Hitler's order to "die fighting" by taking his seriously damaged vessel into combat against three British cruisers waiting for him outside the harbor of Montevideo, Uruguay.

Instead, once he had seen to the burial of his dead and the hospitalization of his wounded in Montevideo, and arranged for the internment of the rest of his crew in Argentina, he scuttled his vessel just outside Montevideo harbor.

He was taken to Buenos Aires. To prove that saving his crew, and not his own life, was the reason he had scuttled the *Graf Spee,* he then put on his dress uniform, stood over the German navy battle flag on the floor of his hotel room, and blew his brains out.

When Vicealmirante Crater and General Martín walked into the wardroom of the *Rivadavia,* Fregattenkapitän Wilhelm von Dattenberg stood and came to attention before his naval escort, Capitán de Corbeta José Keller, could put down his coffee cup.

"Please keep your seat, Kapitän," Crater said, in German, adding, "This is General Martín."

Von Dattenberg clicked his heels and bobbed his head.

"I understand you've told the admiral, Kapitän," Martín said, also speaking German, "that you came here directly from Germany, that you did not, in other words, touch somewhere else on our shores to unload either people or cargo before you appeared here."

Von Dattenberg did not reply.

"The trouble one has as an honorable officer, Kapitän von Dattenberg, is that when you're lying, this is as evident to other honorable officers as a wart on your nose would be. Both Vicealmirante Crater and myself like to think of ourselves as honorable officers. We clearly see the wart on your nose."

Von Dattenberg's face showed his surprise.

"Didn't they teach you that in the Kriegsmarine?" Martín pursued. "Or at Philipps University?"

The second question visibly surprised von Dattenberg.

Vicealmirante Crater had two questions in his mind:

Where the hell is Martín going?

And how the hell did he know where von Dattenberg went to university?

"We are now going to take a ride in my airplane, Kapitän von Dattenberg," Martín said.

Now what the hell? Crater thought.

"You may make the trip to my airplane trussed up like a Christmas goose," Martín went on, "and be loaded aboard by several of the admiral's more muscular sailors. Or, if you wish, you can give me your parole as an honorable officer, and not be trussed. The truth is that I only recently learned how to fly, and I'm not good enough at it to simultaneously fly and try to dissuade you of any notions you might have to exit this world *à la* the late Kapitän zur See Langsdorff."

Well, if Bernardo's intention was to really

baffle von Dattenberg, he's succeeded.

What the hell is he up to?

"May I ask, Herr General, where I am being taken?" von Dattenberg asked.

"The way that works here, Herr Kapitän," Martín replied, "as I'm sure it did in the former Thousand-Year Reich, is that the intelligence officer, not the prisoner, gets to ask the questions."

"I protest being separated from my men," von Dattenberg said.

"Protest duly noted," Martín said. "And you may also file a protest to the representative of the International Red Cross as soon as that opportunity presents itself. Now, what is your choice? Trussed or not trussed?"

"I will not willingly go anywhere with you, sir."

"Capitán Keller," Martín said, switching to Spanish, "would you please round up two or three of your more muscular sailors and, say, three meters of stout twine and bring them in here?"

Martín saw on von Dattenberg's face that he understood the order and thus spoke Spanish; he was not surprised.

"Sí, mi General."

Before the sailors and the twine appeared, von Dattenberg said, "You have my parole, Herr General."

"As an honorable officer?"

"As an officer of the Kriegsmarine, Herr

155

General."

"Good," Martín said, and switching to Spanish added, "*Mi Almirante,* would you be kind enough to take Capitán von Dattenberg and myself to my airplane?"

Nothing that happened in the next three hours did anything to assuage von Dattenberg's confusion or bafflement.

First they drove from the *Rivadavia* to an airfield on which sat an assortment of naval aircraft that had been obsolete before the war had begun. As they approached one of the hangars, its doors opened and sailors pushed onto the tarmac an aircraft with which von Dattenberg was familiar, a Wehrmacht Fieseler Storch.

This one, however, was painted flaming red and bore Argentine markings.

He was then loaded into it, General Martín climbed in, the engine was started, and perhaps ninety seconds later it had taxied to a runway and begun its takeoff roll.

Von Dattenberg remembered what General Martín had said about his only recently having learned how to fly.

A minute or two after that, looking down from no more than five hundred meters, von Dattenberg could see no signs of civilization at all, not even a road. They were flying over grasslands stretching to the horizon in all directions and punctuated here and there by clumps of trees. Cattle — more cattle than von Dattenberg could remember ever having seen — were scattered over the grassland.

Von Dattenberg put this together and decided they were flying over Argentina's famed Pampas, which he now recalled stretched for hundreds of miles. That made sense. His pilot was an army general. He was being taken to an army base. Army bases were often built in the country.

For the next hour and a half, von Dattenberg looked for signs — even a road — that would indicate they were approaching such an army base. He saw none as far as he could see in any direction — nothing but the Pampas.

He had just about decided that he was having one of those incredibly realistic dreams one had from time to time, and would soon wake up to find he had dozed off in the wardroom of the *Rivadavia,* when General Martín dropped the nose of the Fieseler and quickly descended to perhaps two hundred meters above ground level.

Von Dattenberg was now looking more or less sideward at the clumps of trees and the cattle — not down at them.

They flew at this altitude for perhaps two minutes. Then General Martín took the airplane even closer to the ground, which caused von Dattenberg to remember again that the general had only recently learned how to fly.

And then they were flashing over something constructed by man. Specifically, over the roofs of perhaps two dozen single-story buildings, one of them enormous and sprawling.

Von Dattenberg was trying very hard to get a better look out the rear of the Storch when General Martín put it into a very steep turn, leveled off, and then dropped the nose even closer toward the ground. He saw what looked like a dirt airstrip.

I am going to die in the middle of nowhere!

And then I will wake up in the wardroom of the Rivadavia.

And then the Storch touched down, bounced back into the air, touched down again, bounced back into the air again, and touched down again, this time staying on the ground.

At the end of the runway, Martín turned the Storch around and taxied down the runway. Von Dattenberg now saw two large hangars, one of which held an American twin-engine Lodestar passenger transport, also painted flaming red.

There were also four American Piper Cub airplanes.

And a welcoming committee — six armed men on horseback.

What the hell do they call those people who work the herds of cattle?

Gauchos! They call them gauchos!

Where the hell am I?

General Martín stopped the Storch, shut down the engine, and immediately answered von Dattenberg's unspoken question.

"Welcome to Estancia San Pedro y San Pablo, Kapitän von Dattenberg."

Martín pushed open the door of the Storch. A gaucho walked up to the airplane. Von Dattenberg studied his clothing with interest. He wore knee-high black boots, into which were tucked billowing black trousers. His waist was encircled by a wide leather belt, liberally studded with silver ornaments. Tucked into his waistband was an enormous silver-handled knife. He had on a billowing white shirt, and wore around his neck a yellow-and-red scarf. Topping everything off was a wide-brimmed black leather hat with a silver-studded hatband.

The gaucho waited until General Martín had gotten out of the Storch and then saluted him crisply.

"How did it go, General?" he asked in English.

"Very well, I think, *Jefe*," Martín replied, and then pointed back toward von Dattenberg. "That is Fregattenkapitän Wilhelm von Dattenberg, late master of U-405."

"No shit?" the gaucho blurted.

"Which appeared off the Puerto Belgrano Naval Base flying a black flag at first light this morning."

159

"I'll be damned! What are we going to do with him?"

"I think I'd better see what Doña Dorotea has to say."

"She's not here. There was a telegram from Lisbon. They'll be back probably early tomorrow morning, so she and Doña Alicia took everybody into Buenos Aires to meet the plane."

"That's good news," Martín said. "What we're going to have to do, *Jefe,* is keep the *fregattenkapitän* out of sight until Cletus and Peter can get out here."

"Not a problem," the gaucho said.

"I don't think I have to tell you he's not permitted to ask any questions, about anything, but especially about Cletus and Peter, do I?"

"No, sir."

"I want someone with him around the clock. I don't want him to try to emulate Kapitän zur See Langsdorff."

"I understand, sir."

"Or anyone to learn he's here."

"Understood, sir."

The gaucho walked to the airplane. Von Dattenberg was just stepping to the ground.

"Do you speak English, Fregattenkapitän von Dattenberg?"

"Yes, I do."

"I am Lieutenant Oscar Schultz, United States Navy. You will now consider yourself to be a prisoner of the United States Navy and conduct yourself accordingly. Understand?"

Von Dattenberg nodded, then blurted, "You're a U.S. Navy officer?"

"Yes, I am. When we get you out on the Pampas, you and I can sit around and swap sea stories."

I have to be dreaming, von Dattenberg thought. *Why can't I wake up?*

Martín walked up to them.

"What are your plans now, General?" Schultz asked.

"What I'm thinking, Jefe, is that it's a long drive to Buenos Aires. . . ."

"But a much shorter flight?"

General Martín nodded.

"What the hell, why not?" Schultz said. "Cletus and Peter are going to be pissed anyway when they hear you've been flying their toy."

"Then that's what I'll do," Martín said. He turned to von Dattenberg. "Go with Lieutenant Schultz. You'll be in good hands. We'll see one another soon."

■ ■ ■ ■

III

■ ■ ■ ■

[ONE]

Headquarters, XXIInd CIC Detachment
Alte Post Hotel
Marburg an der Lahn, Germany
0700 9 October 1945

Major John Connell turned impatiently from his bathroom mirror when his telephone rang.

He thought about not answering it, but finally did.

"Major Connell," he said, annoyance showing in his voice.

"Mattingly, Connell," his caller announced. "You took your time in answering your phone."

"Sir, I was shaving."

"And Cronley didn't answer his phone, period."

"Sir, I believe Lieutenant Cronley was probably on his way to the roadblock. They start to process refugees at oh seven hundred."

"What I want you to do, Connell, is retrieve that young officer from whatever you have

165

him doing, put him in a vehicle, and have him brought here. Have him bring enough clothing for at least three days."

"Yes, sir. Sir, where is here?"

"The Schlosshotel Kronberg. It's in Taunus. You know where that is?"

"No, sir, I'm afraid I don't."

"Looking at a map might be helpful," Mattingly suggested sarcastically.

"Yes, sir. Sir, is there anything I should know?"

"About what?"

"Lieutenant Cronley's performance of duty."

"It seems to me, Connell — he's your lieutenant — that you should be answering that question, not asking it."

"Yes, sir. Sir, would you like me to bring Lieutenant Cronley to you?"

"Just put him and a sergeant — and maybe a map — in a jeep and have the sergeant drive him here. Got it? Or is that too complicated?"

"No, sir. I'll get right on it, sir."

"You took your sweet goddamn time getting here, Cronley," Major Connell greeted Lieutenant James D. Cronley Jr. when the latter entered the former's office thirty minutes later.

"Sir, I came as soon as I got word you wanted to see me."

"Yesterday, I asked if anything . . . *unto-*

ward . . . had happened when you were taking care of Frau von Wachtstein."

"Yes, sir?"

"If you did anything that in any way displeased her, or made her uncomfortable, Cronley, goddamn it, now is the time to tell me."

"Sir, I can think of nothing like that."

"Well, I can only hope you're telling me the truth."

"I am, sir."

"You better be. At zero seven hundred, I had a telephone call from Colonel Mattingly. He wants you at his headquarters immediately, with three days' change of uniforms."

"Yes, sir. Where is his headquarters?"

"Near Frankfurt. Sergeant O'Duff will drive you. He will have a map."

Staff Sergeant Francis O'Duff was the motor sergeant.

"So one last time, Cronley — did anything happen between you and Frau von Wachtstein that I should know about?"

Well, we fucked our brains out for two days. Is that what you mean?

"No, sir."

"If the subject comes up with Colonel Mattingly, Cronley, I want you to be sure to tell him that I ordered you to immediately bring to my attention any problems, any problems at all, that arose."

"Yes, sir."

"And that you did not bring any such problems to my attention."

"Yes, sir."

"Quickly pack a bag and get going, Cronley. O'Duff is waiting for you."

"Yes, sir."

[Two]

Schlosshotel Kronberg
Kronberg im Taunus, Hesse, Germany
1215 9 October 1945

The massive structure looked like a castle. It was constructed of gray fieldstone and rose, in parts, five stories high. There was no sign of war damage whatever.

There was an assortment of vehicles in the parking lot, some jeeps and three-quarter-ton ambulances — with the Red Cross common to them painted over — but most of the vehicles were German. Most of these were Mercedeses, but there was a scattering of Opel Admirals and Kapitäns, and Cronley saw the Horch in which Elsa had driven away from the Kurhotel.

The place was well protected, casually. There were four jeeps at strategic points, each with a pedestal-mounted .50 caliber Browning machine gun, with a belt of glistening ammunition dangling from each. There were two soldiers at each jeep. They were all

168

enormous black men. They were eating their lunch, but not from mess kits, or even stainless steel trays, but from what looked like fine china, crystal, and silver laid out on the hoods of the jeeps.

O'Duff stopped the jeep before a wide, shallow flight of stairs leading to the building.

Almost immediately, a black soldier came down the stairs. He was even more enormous than the others. He had first sergeant chevrons and the patch of the Second Armored "Hell on Wheels" Division on the sleeves of his "tanker" zipper jacket. He held a Thompson submachine gun effortlessly in his massive left hand.

He saluted. Cronley returned it.

"I'm First Sergeant Dunwiddie," he announced. "You're late."

"Excuse me?"

"You're Second Lieutenant James D. Cronley Junior, right?"

"Right," Jimmy said.

"Then you're late," First Sergeant Dunwiddie said. "The colonel expected you in time for lunch." Then he effortlessly jerked Cronley's canvas bag from the back of the jeep and turned his attention to Sergeant O'Duff. "Okay, Sergeant, you can go. I'll take care of this officer from here on."

It was only as First Sergeant Dunwiddie led him through the lobby of the building that

Cronley realized it was a hotel, and not a castle.

Not too swift, Jimmy. It's the Schlosshotel Kronberg.

Schloss means *castle*, *but* hotel *means hotel in both English and German.*

Dunwiddie led him through the lobby to a large dining room filled with people in uniform — most without insignia of rank — having their lunch, and then through a smaller dining room, and through that to a door.

Dunwiddie knocked using the butt of the Thompson.

"Who?" a voice called.

"Tiny," Dunwiddie called.

"Come."

Dunwiddie pushed the door open and nodded for Cronley to enter.

There were three people sitting at a round table, which had places set for five.

One was Colonel Mattingly, as strikingly uniformed as he had been the day before. A second was the man who had also been at the Kurhotel when they had taken Elsa away. Cronley intuited that he was an officer, almost certainly a major or higher, although he was wearing an insignia-less uniform. Cronley could not recall hearing his name, beyond Colonel Mattingly calling him "Harry."

The third man was a slight, pale fiftyish man in an ill-fitting civilian suit that was almost certainly German. Confirmation of that suspicion came immediately when Colonel Mattingly announced in German: "We're all speaking German, Cronley."

"Yes, sir."

"Say it in German!" Mattingly snapped, in German.

"Jawohl, Herr Oberst."

"Better," Mattingly said. "Sit down, Tiny. You're involved."

"Jawohl, Herr Oberst," Dunwiddie said, and sat down.

"And you, too, Cronley," Mattingly said. "Sit there, eat your lunch, confine your conversation to brief responses to my questions, and volunteer nothing. Understood?"

"Jawohl, Herr Oberst."

"What I have to say to you, Cronley, or anything any of these gentlemen says to you, is classified Top Secret–Presidential. Do you know what that means?"

"No, sir."

"Simply phrased, it means that information thus classified is so important to the security of the United States that extreme measures — killing people — is authorized to protect it. Understand?"

Does he really mean that?

What the hell is this?

Does it have anything to do with Elsa?

Cronley nodded. *"Ich verstehen, Herr Oberst."*

171

Plates of pork chops, applesauce, mashed potatoes, and bread were laid before Cronley and Dunwiddie. And then two liter-sized mugs of beer.

"Where to begin?" Mattingly asked, rhetorically.

The others waited.

"How much do you know about the OSS, Cronley?"

"Not very much, sir."

"During the late unpleasantness, the Office of Strategic Services was charged with providing a number of clandestine services to the Armed Forces of the United States. Its director, Major General William Joseph Donovan, reported directly to President Roosevelt. You didn't know that?"

"There was a lecture when I was at Camp Holabird about other intelligence agencies. I guess I didn't pay much attention."

Harry shook his head.

"You didn't make the connection between General Donovan of the OSS and your father's old Army buddy Donovan from World War One?"

"Not until this moment, Colonel."

"And now that you have?"

"The Colonel Donovan I know — not a General Donovan — is my father's New York lawyer. He used to come to the ranch when I was a kid."

"So he told me last night," Mattingly said

drily. "He has fond memories of you. . . . He said you were expelled from Saint Mark's School in Dallas at age fourteen for bootlegging and operating a poker game. True?"

Jimmy grinned. "Yes, sir. Guilty."

"Actually, I got that story from Colonel Frade yesterday, on the way to Rhine-Main," Mattingly said. "And then Colonel Frade suggested the high probability that your father and General Donovan were close, as a result of their service together in World War One. The circumstances being what they are, I telephoned General Donovan immediately after dropping Frade and company at Rhine-Main.

"Colonel Frade was correct. As I said, General Donovan remembers you fondly. He said to give you his best regards. The circumstances being what they are, that is tantamount to your being approved for service with the OSS."

"Yes, sir."

"Aren't you going to ask me about the circumstances to which I refer?"

"Sir, I don't have a clue what you're talking about," Cronley confessed.

"On October first — eight days ago — President Truman issued an Executive Order disbanding the Office of Strategic Services," Mattingly said. "You are witnessing the death throes of that organization."

"Sir, I'm confused."

"The order calls for the dispersion of our assets, human and otherwise, to the Army, the Department of State, the Federal Bureau of Investigation, and, so help me God, the Treasury Department," Mattingly went on. "For example, I have been sent back to the Army, which in its wisdom has assigned me to the CIC, specifically as deputy commander, CIC, USFET."

And Major Connell has heard that.

That is why he's so afraid of Mattingly.

"There was a flicker of interest in your eyes just now, Cronley. Why?"

What do I do now?

"Don't give that question serious consideration, Lieutenant. Answer with what popped into your mind."

When in doubt, tell the truth.

"Sir, I was thinking that Major Connell has probably heard about that."

Mattingly nodded, then made a *go on* gesture.

"That's why he's so afraid of you," Cronley said.

Harry chuckled, and Cronley saw that First Sergeant Dunwiddie was smiling.

At my stupidity?

"You picked up on that, did you?" Mattingly said, with a faint smile. "For your general fund of knowledge, Cronley, it is often useful to have people be a little — or a lot — afraid of you."

174

Cronley didn't reply.

"We may now move into that area classified as Top Secret–Presidential, Cronley. But I think I should ask for advice. Tiny?"

"My people have always held Aggies in high regard, Colonel," Dunwiddie said. "I'll vote yes. But one question for the lieutenant, sir?"

Mattingly nodded.

"How well do you get along with Negroes, Lieutenant?" Dunwiddie asked.

What the hell does he mean by that?

His mouth ran away with him.

"When they're as large as you, Sergeant, I try to be very obliging."

"That being the case, Colonel," Dunwiddie said, "I vote yes."

"Harry?"

Harry was now smiling broadly.

"Colonel," he said, "I would suggest that anyone who was expelled at fourteen for bootlegging and running a poker game is our kind of guy."

Mattingly nodded and turned to the man in the ill-fitting German suit.

"General?"

General?

"I would suggest that this young officer — and not only because of his command of the German language — would be quite suitable for our needs, Colonel."

"The motion carries," Mattingly said. "So, with something less than great enthusiasm, we turn to the Top Secret–Presidential area. Lieutenant, please understand that it was not hyperbole when I said before that information thus classified is so important to the security of the United States that extreme measures are authorized to prevent, or punish, its disclosure. Are you sure you understand that the definition of 'extreme measures' is the taking of life?"

"Yes, sir."

"Harry," Mattingly said, and gestured for Harry to speak.

"During the late unpleasantness, Lieutenant," Harry began, and then interrupted himself. "If you don't mind, I think I'll call you Jimmy. All right?"

"Yes, sir."

This guy speaks German as well as I do.

"During the late unpleasantness, Jimmy, there was a section of the German High Command Intelligence Service known as Abwehr Ost. It dealt with the East — the Soviets. It was commanded by Colonel, later General, Reinhard Gehlen."

Who is probably the guy sitting across from me.

"When it became apparent that German defeat was inevitable, just a matter of time, General Gehlen made contact with Allen Dulles, who headed the OSS in the European Theater of Operations, and proposed a deal. He would turn over to the United States all of his assets — including his human assets, which included agents in place in the Kremlin — if we promised to keep his people, and their families, out of the hands of the Russians.

"He gave us, as proof of the value of the intelligence he was offering, the names of Soviet spies who had infiltrated our Manhattan Project, the development of the atomic bomb. We had no idea who these people were, but on investigation, learned that they were indeed Russian spies.

"Mr. Dulles took the proposal to General Eisenhower, who authorized the deal. Neither General Donovan nor President Roosevelt were made aware of the arrangement —"

"Why not?" Cronley blurted.

"Because General Donovan would have felt duty bound to inform President Roosevelt, and if that had happened, the Russians would have immediately learned of it. There were people around the President — including his wife — who genuinely believed the Soviets were incapable of spying upon the United States. And there were others, including specifically the secretary of the Treasury, who were so outraged by the abominable behavior of the Nazis that they were more interested in retribution and punishment than anything else."

"Morgenthau," Mattingly interjected, "formally proposed that the senior one hundred

Nazis, and all SS officers, be shot out of hand — it's understandable, he's Jewish — on the spot wherever and whenever located."

"And there were Nazis, and SS, in Abwehr Ost?" Cronley asked.

"Yes, there were," Mattingly said, and again motioned for Harry to continue.

Harry nodded. "When President Roosevelt died, Mr. Dulles went to President Truman and told him of the deal he'd made. Truman gave him permission to continue with the deal until he'd had time to think it — as well as the the entire question of the OSS — over."

"I don't understand. . . ."

"The OSS was not popular with either the Army establishment or with the FBI — Mr. Hoover believed the FBI should have been in charge of both intelligence and counterintelligence — or the State Department or the Navy or, as I said before, especially the Treasury Department. There had been calls for our disbandment even before the war was over. On becoming President, Truman was subjected to enormous pressure to immediately put us out of business."

"And I think he would have," Mattingly spoke up again, "had his feelings not been hurt by his not having been told about the atomic bomb. If it hadn't been for that, he would have gone along with the Army brass, Hoover, and Morgenthau."

"Excuse me," Cronley said. "If it hadn't

been for what?"

"The day after Truman became President," Harry said, "Lieutenant General Leslie Groves, who headed the Manhattan Project, went into the Oval Office and said, in effect, 'Mr. President, there's something you have to know. We have a secret weapon of enormous power, an atomic bomb.' "

"He was Vice President and didn't know about the atomic bomb?" Cronley asked, incredulously.

"He was Vice President and didn't know about the atomic bomb," Mattingly confirmed. "Roosevelt didn't think he had the need to know. Which I believe was good for us, the OSS. Truman began to question the motives of those calling for our destruction. He did not shut us down immediately, and he gave Mr. Dulles permission to continue our arrangement with General Gehlen."

"But you said he did order the end of the OSS," Cronley said.

"He did. We're officially shut down. But Mr. Dulles was able to convince the President that the arrangement with General Gehlen was too important not to continue. It could not be turned over to the Army or anyone else. If that had happened, it would have been exposed, and public outrage would have killed it once and for all."

"Public outrage about what?"

"General Gehlen proposed the arrangement for two major reasons," Mattingly said. "First, he genuinely believed the Soviets were evil and intended to take over all of Europe and then the world. And that the only thing that could stop them was us, the United States Army. And he knew how valuable his assets would be to us.

"Second, Gehlen knew there would be enormous pressure on Eisenhower to turn over to the Soviets anyone connected with Abwehr Ost. He knew that that meant his people and their families would be interrogated — tortured — and then either killed or shipped off to Siberia to be worked to death.

"So the price for his assets was the protection of his people. And we agreed to protect them."

"Including the Nazis?" Cronley asked softly.

"Yes, including the Nazis. There weren't many of them, but there were Nazis. And of course their families."

"How could you do that?" Cronley asked.

Mattingly glanced at Harry, then went on: "The Nazis posed the greatest problem, still pose it. The non-Nazis — I'll get into this in a minute — could be kept in Germany. But Nazis are — and should be — subject to arrest for investigation of what they might have done, and then be brought before a war crimes tribunal. Once they were arrested, the Russians would demand they be turned over

180

to them."

"So, what did you do?"

"We got them, are getting them, out of Germany."

"To Argentina," Cronley blurted.

Mattingly nodded. "We entered into an unholy alliance with the Vatican — how's that for a turn of phrase? — who for their own reasons were helping Nazis — and Nazi collaborators, French, Hungarian, Czech, et cetera — escape the wrath of the victors."

"Jesus Christ!" Cronley said softly.

"Right now, the Nazis don't concern us as much as what we've come to call the 'Good Germans' — the officers and non-coms who were just soldiers doing their duty — which is where you come into the equation."

He motioned for Harry to resume the narration.

Harry said, "General Gehlen — Abwehr Ost — buried all their intelligence files in steel barrels in the Bavarian Alps and then moved north. On May twenty-second, 1945, Gehlen and most of his senior officers surrendered to the CIC at Oberusel, which is not far from here. That arrest was reported to SHAEF, and SHAEF dispatched a CIC team to thoroughly interrogate them."

"Commanded by Major Harold N. Wallace, Signal Corps, of the OSS," Mattingly furnished, "newly equipped with the credentials of a CIC special agent, through the courtesy

181

of a senior SHAEF intelligence officer whose name you don't have the need to know but probably can guess."

Cronley looked between Mattingly and Harry.

In other words, you, Mattingly.

And that means Harry is Major Wallace.

Harry Wallace saw the look on Cronley's face, nodded his confirmation, and then went on: "Meanwhile, our people — the OSS — were retrieving the material buried in Bavaria, and taking it to a former monastery in Grünau, Bavaria. The monastery was made available to us by the Vatican in exchange for services rendered."

Mattingly, glancing at Tiny, added: "Enter First Sergeant Dunwiddie and Company C, 203rd Tank Destroyer Battalion, Second Armored Division, which, less officers, had been placed on temporary duty with the OSS sometime before to provide security for OSS Forward. No officers because we didn't want a captain and four lieutenants about to be returned to the United States for discharge or reassignment to regale the fellows in the Fort Knox officers' club, or their hometown VFW, with tales of the interesting things they saw here at Kronberg Castle or at a monastery in Bavaria.

"When Tiny said that 'his people' have always held Aggies in high regard, he was referring not only to his family but to other black soldiers, cavalrymen, who have a proud and extensive history of service to the U.S. Army. The Ninth and Tenth Cavalry — black soldiers led, as was the 203rd Tank Destroyer, by white officers — did most of the Indian fighting on the plains after the Civil War. As Tiny will tell you — probably frequently — the Tenth Cavalry beat Teddy Roosevelt to the top of San Juan Hill in Cuba during the Spanish-American War."

"The Buffalo Soldiers," Cronley said.

"You know about them, Lieutenant?" Dunwiddie asked, as he patted the tight black curls of hair on his head. The Indians had thought the hair of the black soldiers they were fighting was like the hair on buffalo.

Cronley nodded and smiled. Dunwiddie smiled back.

"Most of Tiny's men are already at the Grünau monastery, as are just about all of General Gehlen's officers and some of their families," Major Wallace then went on. "Good Germans and some Nazis that we haven't yet been able to get to Argentina. The rest of Charley Company will move there in the next couple of days, when OSS Forward goes out of business and this place becomes a senior officers' club.

"Ultimately, the South German Industrial Development Organization, which is our new name for Abwehr Ost, will set up in a little *dorf* called Pullach, south of Munich. The engineers are now erecting a double fence around a twenty-five-acre compound, and rehabilitating the houses inside. And the barracks, just inside the outer fence, to house Company 'C,' which has just been placed on indefinite temporary duty with the newly formed Twenty-seventh CIC Detachment, Major Harold Wallace commanding."

Wallace then looked at Mattingly, who said: "Tiny has pointed out that a company of black soldiers with no visible white officers is liable to make people curious, and that's the last thing we want. My problem in that regard is that I have no one to fill that role."

"Which is where I fit it?" Cronley said.

Mattingly nodded. "Almost all of my people are going home, and in any event, most of them are senior captains and better, and wouldn't want the job anyway. So, yes, Lieutenant Cronley, that's where you come in. Interested?"

"Yes, sir."

"Right now — Tiny will fill you in on the details — what we're doing at the monastery is trying to stay inconspicuous — keeping the Nazis inside in case they decide to leave before we can get them out of Germany, and keeping out everybody else in the world."

"Yes, sir."

"Unless you have a reason, a very good reason, to go back to Marburg, I'd like to send you to Grünau right away."

"I have no reason to go back to Marburg, sir."

"Okay. Major Connell will be informed that you have been transferred to the Twenty-seventh — which is in Munich — and instructed to send to you whatever property you left."

"Yes, sir."

"Tiny, take Lieutenant Cronley to Grünau and get him settled."

"Yes, sir."

"There's no reason that I can see for you to come back here. Is there?"

"No, sir."

"I'll call the strip at Eschborn and have them wind up the rubber bands of one of our puddle jumpers," Mattingly said. "You ever have a ride in an L-4, Cronley? It's a small, high-wing single-engine Piper Cub."

"Yes, sir. I even know how to fly one. We had Cubs on our ranches, and Clete's . . ." He paused.

"Don't stop," Mattingly said, gesturing for him to continue.

"*Colonel Frade's* Uncle Jim — who raised him — taught him to fly theirs, and then promised to teach me when I turned fifteen. Before I turned fifteen, Colonel Frade took me out on the prairie and taught me how to fly his. So the first time I got in our Cub for my first flying lesson, we told Uncle Jim and my father there was a phone call for one of them at the house. When they went to find out about that, Cletus spun the prop for me and I took off. My father came out and found Clete there and me and the Piper gone. He shit — He got pretty upset."

Mattingly shook his head in wonder. "I think I should tell you, Lieutenant, that I am beginning to question the wisdom of taking you into the fold."

"No, you're not, Bob," Major Wallace said. "The more you hear about him, the more you have to agree that he's our kind of guy."

"Anytime you're ready, Lieutenant," First Sergeant Tiny Dunwiddie said, getting to his feet.

Forty-five minutes later, sitting in an L-4 "puddle jumper" on the active runway of what had once been a German fighter aircraft base, Cronley watched as a stick of parachutists floated from a Douglas C-47.

Tiny Dunwiddie, who was in a second L-4, had told him that the field was being used to provide a crash course in parachute jumping to replacements headed for the 508th Parachute Infantry. The 508th was charged with protecting the I.G. Farben Building, which would now house Eisenhower's Headquarters, U.S. Forces European Theater.

But Cronley wasn't really interested. Nor was his mind full of the incredible story he

186

had just been told at the Schlosshotel Kronberg.

What Jimmy was thinking as the parachutists came to earth, and as the pilot of his L-4 shoved the throttle forward and the Piper started roaring down the runway, was that it seemed entirely possible that his new duties would offer him the chance, sooner or later, to see Elsa again.

[THREE]

Kloster Grünau
Schollbrunn, Bavaria, Germany
1705 10 October 1945

The olive drab Piper Cub — painted with the stars-and-bars insignia of a U.S. Army war plane, and bearing the Army nomenclature L-4, was otherwise identical to the one in which Jimmy Cronley had soloed some months before he had turned fifteen — touched down somewhat roughly on a narrow strip of road.

Immediately, two jeeps, each with two large black soldiers and a pedestal-mounted Browning .50 caliber machine gun, appeared. Cronley saw that they didn't train the weapons on the aircraft — or him — but seemed quite ready to do so if that should become necessary.

"Okay, Lieutenant," the pilot said. "Here

we are. You can get out now."

The pilot was a young staff sergeant wearing pilot's wings superimposed with an "L," for Liaison.

Cronley, taking his canvas suitcase with him, got out of the airplane and stood on the road. The puddle jumper turned, taxied back down the road, turned again, and immediately roared toward him and took off.

As soon as that aircraft was airborne, the L-4 with First Sergeant Tiny Dunwiddie aboard came in and landed. It came to a stop, its engine still turning, near Cronley.

Dunwiddie squeezed himself out of the airplane, and it immediately turned and taxied back down the road and turned again and took off.

"Did those clowns salute you, Lieutenant?" Tiny asked.

Cronley shook his head.

"Salute Lieutenant Cronley!" Dunwiddie ordered. "And say, 'Welcome to Grünau, sir,' to your new commanding officer."

The sergeants standing by the pedestal-mounted Brownings saluted, and all four soldiers repeated, "Welcome to Grünau, sir."

Cronley returned their salutes.

"You," First Sergeant Dunwiddie said, pointing to the sergeant at the Browning in the nearest jeep, "get our luggage and put it and you in the other jeep." He next pointed to the driver. "And you get in the back of this one."

The driver hurriedly complied with his orders.

Dunwiddie waved Cronley into the passenger seat of the jeep, got behind the wheel, and headed down the road.

On hearing that they were headed to "the Grünau Monastery," Cronley's mind filled with images of ancient heavy stone monasteries, most of which he'd acquired from motion pictures starring Errol Flynn in tights.

What he found, instead, was a large tent city surrounded by two lines of barbed wire enclosing what he guessed to be at least five, maybe more, acres. Hung on the wire, spaced at twenty-five-yard intervals, were signs reading EINGANG VERBOTEN!

In the center of the tent city was a masonry building. An American flag flew from a pole in front of it. After first one and then a second gate in the barbed wire was pulled aside by heavily armed and uniformly huge black soldiers wearing "tanker" jackets with the shoulder insignia of the Second Armored Division, Dunwiddie drove them to the building.

As they did so, Cronley saw that there were a large number of Germans in uniforms stripped of insignia. They were either marching purposely between the tents, or just milling around. There also was a scattering of obviously German women and children.

"This is the command post, Lieutenant," Dunwiddie announced. "We're home, so to speak, in what used to be the prior's house when this place was a Carthusian monastery."

He gestured for Cronley to get out of the jeep and go into the building.

"This is not what I expected," Cronley announced.

"This is what you get," Dunwiddie said, and then smiled and asked, "What did you expect, monks walking around in black robes with their heads bowed in prayer?"

He bowed his head and put the tips of his fingers together.

"Yeah. I guess," Cronley admitted, chuckling.

"That hasn't happened here for a long time," Dunwiddie said. "From what I've been able to find out, they shut down the monastery here in 1802 during the Secularization."

"During the what?"

"The secular state — in those days, the kings, dukes, et cetera — took the property of the church away from the bishops and abbots, et cetera."

"What are you, Sergeant, some kind of historian?"

"In a way. I was majoring in history at Norwich," Dunwiddie said.

"You went to Norwich?"

Dunwiddie nodded, and then asked: "So

190

why am I not a commissioned officer and gentleman, such as yourself?"

Tiny chuckled when he saw the uncomfortable look on Cronley's face, and then went on: "Why don't I answer that while we're having a little nip to cut the dust of the trail?"

One of the rooms in the old building had been converted to a mess hall, and at one end of it was a well-stocked bar.

"This is the ex-officers' mess," Dunwiddie explained, "membership limited to former majors and better of the Abwehr. No Nazis or SS — which is usually the same thing — allowed. I think we can sneak you in, despite that gold bar. The rules are also waived for me and a couple of my senior non-coms."

He turned to the row of bottles. "Bourbon or scotch?"

"Bourbon, please," Cronley said.

Dunwiddie made the drinks and handed one to Cronley.

"With your permission, Lieutenant, I will introduce you to the German officers at the evening meal, which is served at eighteen hundred. Most of them are good guys, typical officers. Of course, they can't figure me out. Not only am I black, but an enlisted man, and when Major Wallace isn't here — and he's not often here — I'm *der Führer.*"

"I can't figure you out either," Jimmy confessed. "Or the way things are run. Or, for that matter, what we're doing here."

"Colonel Mattingly said I was to bring you up to speed on that. So where to start?"

"Norwich?" Cronley suggested.

Norwich University, in Northfield, Vermont, was the oldest of the small group of private military colleges — The Citadel, Virginia Military Institute, and a very few others — producing officers for the armed forces. The graduates of one generally knew all about their brother schools.

"Why not?" Dunwiddie said. "There I was, in the spring of 1944, in beautiful Vermont, finishing my third year at the Norwich School for Boys, a major in the Corps of Cadets, when I had an epiphany. . . ."

"You were a junior at Norwich in 1944?" Cronley asked in surprise.

Dunwiddie nodded.

"Then you can't be much older than me. I'm class of '45 at A&M."

"I would have been in the class of '45. I became legally able to drink this stuff about nine months ago," Tiny said, holding up his glass.

"You look a hell of a lot older than twenty-one," Jimmy said.

"Maybe it's my complexion. May I continue?"

"Please."

"As I said, I had an epiphany. I realized that unless I got out of my snazzy Norwich

uniform and into an olive drab one, I was going to be one of those very pathetic members of the officer corps who got their commissions a week after they called the war off. So I enlisted."

"You dropped out of Norwich to enlist?" Cronley asked incredulously.

"As a corporal, because of my Norwich training. It wasn't quite as selfless as it sounds. I had heard there was a shortage of second lieutenants in ETO — the European Theater of Operations — and that they were meeting the shortage by running a six-week officer candidate school. The plan was that I would get myself sent to Europe right out of basic training, go to OCS, and be a second lieutenant commanding a tank platoon in combat while my classmates at Norwich were still waiting to graduate."

"Jesus!"

"But, as you may have heard at A&M, the best-laid plans of mice and men sometimes go agley. Sure enough, just as soon as I arrived at the Second Armored Replacement Company, an officer — a light colonel by the name of Mattingly — showed up to take me to the commanding general . . ."

"Why?"

". . . who was Major General Isaac Davis White, Norwich '23, a classmate of my father's. I suspect Pop wrote him I was coming. General White suggested — and when

I. D. White suggests something, by comparison it makes Moses's graven-on-stone Ten Commandments seem like a grocery list written on toilet paper — that the thing to do was send me to the 203rd Tank Destroyer Battalion.

"White officers, black troops. There, in a couple of months, I could pick up a little experience, maybe make sergeant, or even staff sergeant, and he would then feel justified in directly commissioning me. All OCS was, General White said, was the ETO version of Rook year at Norwich, and I'd already gone through that.

"Five weeks later, I was acting first sergeant of Charley Company of the 203rd."

"How did that happen?"

"When the 203rd started taking out German armor, the Germans shot back. They were very good at that. Charley lost a lot of good people, including most of our officers and non-coms. Mattingly showed up at my hospital bed —"

"You were wounded?"

Tiny nodded.

"Not badly. Anyway, Mattingly told me that General White 'suggested' that since Charley Company had to be reconstituted — filled with replacements and trained — what the company needed more than a second lieutenant was a good first sergeant. He'd worry about making me a second lieutenant later.

194

So I did that.

"And then, later, after Mattingly had made bird colonel, he decided he needed a company of good troops for OSS security and laid that requirement on General White, who sent him Charley Company — less officers, because he didn't want them seeing things they shouldn't and then running their mouths when they went home — on indefinite temporary duty. So here I am."

"That's a hell of a story," Cronley said.

"Yeah."

"So, what happens now? About you getting a commission?"

"Well, that was finally offered. But if I took it — the Army doesn't like to leave directly appointed second lieutenants where they've been enlisted men — I knew I'd wind up as a platoon leader in, say, the 102nd Quartermaster Mess Kit Repair Company, or in some other outfit unimportant enough to let black officers command black troops, and I didn't want that."

He met Cronley's eyes, and added, "What's going on here is important. I wonder if you understand just how important."

Cronley said aloud what he was thinking: "It doesn't seem fair."

"You are a naïve second lieutenant, aren't you, Lieutenant? With all possible respect, Lieutenant, sir."

"There was a tactical officer at A&M who

195

was always saying the first thing a second lieutenant should do is find a good non-com and listen to him. It looks like I've found him."

"I would say that's a fair assessment of our situation," Dunwiddie said. "May I refresh the lieutenant's libation, sir?"

"Thank you. And I don't mean that just for the Jack Daniel's."

[FOUR]

Aeropuerto Coronel Jorge G. Frade
Morón, Buenos Aires Province, Argentina
1005 10 October 1945

Despite several large signs in Spanish and English proclaiming ONLY AUTHORIZED VEHICLES BEYOND THIS POINT, a number of unauthorized vehicles were lined up on the tarmac in front of the passenger terminal.

There were two Mercedes-Benz and one Leyland buses, a spectacular flaming red with black fenders Horch soft-top touring sedan, a custom-bodied 1940 Packard Super 180 convertible, an only slightly smaller 1940 Packard 120 convertible, and a 1939 black Mercedes closed sedan.

The occupants of all the vehicles were awaiting the arrival of South American Airways Flight 207. It had originated in Berlin, and then — after stops at Rhine-Main

Airfield, Frankfurt am Main, Lisbon, Portugal, and Dakar, Senegal — had headed out over the Atlantic Ocean.

Just over an hour before, it had established radio contact with the SAA station in Montevideo, Uruguay — 120 miles east of Buenos Aires — and reported its estimated time of arrival at Aeropuerto Coronel Jorge G. Frade. SAA Montevideo had then telephoned to SAA Jorge Frade — and to some other interested persons — the imminent arrival of the *Ciudad de Rosario,* a Lockheed Constellation aircraft.

Even with its landing gear extended and its flaps fully down as it made its approach to Jorge Frade, the *Ciudad de Rosario* was, in the opinion of both her pilot in command, Cletus Frade, and her first officer, Hans-Peter von Wachtstein, one great big beautiful bird.

"Hansel," Frade ordered, "inasmuch as our women and little ones are probably down there watching, please try very hard to get us on the ground without splattering us all over the runway."

Von Wachtstein responded with a gesture, holding up his left hand balled into a fist, except for the center finger, which was extended. Then he moved that hand to the throttle quadrant and, with a gentle touch that most surgeons would envy, began to retard engine power.

■ ■ ■ ■

As the *Ciudad de Rosario* turned on final, the two men in the huge Packard got out and walked to the Horch.

"Dorotea," General de Brigada Bernardo Martín, who was in mufti, said to Señora Dorotea Mallín de Frade, "we need a quick word with Cletus, and we should have it in private."

Señora Frade — often referred to as Doña Dorotea, a term recognizing her position within the Argentine social hierarchy — was a tall, long-legged, twenty-two-year-old blue-eyed blonde with a marvelous milky complexion. She looked like what came to mind when one heard the phrase "classic English beauty."

"I gather you want this 'private word' before I see him?" she asked.

Martín nodded.

"Go to hell, Bernardo," she said. "Wives go to the head of the line."

She indicated the woman sitting behind her, twenty-two-year-old Señora Alicia Carzino-Cormano de von Wachtstein. Alicia was the Spanish-Italian version of Doña Dorotea. She had glowing olive skin, lustrous black hair, and dark eyes.

The two had been friends since infancy.

"Dorotea," the Reverend Kurt Welner, S.J., asked, smiling, "why can't you ever be as sweet as you look?"

Father Welner liked to refer to himself as a simple priest, but that was some distance from reality. He was recognized to be the *Éminence Grise* behind the thrones of both the Cardinal Archbishop of Buenos Aires and the Papal Nuncio to Argentina. He was confessor to President Farrell and many other very prominent Argentines.

"And you can go to hell with Bernardo," Doña Dorotea said.

"This is important, Dorotea," Martín said.

"I really don't understand why you keep doing this," Doña Dorotea said. "You know damned well that the moment I finally get to see my husband, he's going to tell me everything you said."

"But you won't have heard it from us," Martín said.

She threw up her hands in a mocking gesture of surrender.

"You can have three minutes with him," she said. "After which Alicia and I will appear at the foot of the steps with our weeping children in our arms."

The children to whom she referred were in the backseat of the Horch under the care of a nanny.

"Fair enough," Martín said, chuckling and smiling. "Thank you."

The *Ciudad de Rosario* touched down

199

smoothly. Immediately came the roar of its four eighteen-cylinder radial Wright R-3350 engines as the propellers were moved into reverse pitch.

The aircraft slowed, not quite quickly enough to make the first turn off the runway, but enough to easily make the second. It taxied toward the passenger terminal and the cars and trucks on the tarmac.

This triggered a series of actions. Two Ford pickup trucks — one with a flight of stairs and the second with a conveyor belt mounted in their beds — came onto the tarmac and waited for the Constellation to park. A second set of stairs, much narrower and mounted on wheels, was pushed onto the tarmac by ground handlers.

Four officers of the Immigration Service of the Argentine Republic got out of the Leyland bus, and a priest and two nuns got out of each Mercedes bus.

As soon as the *Ciudad de Rosario* stopped and the engines began the shutdown procedure, the truck-mounted wheels and conveyor belt were put against the rear passenger door and the smaller stairs against the door behind the cockpit.

General Martín and Father Welner started up the narrow stairs. They were about halfway up when the door behind the cockpit opened. Enrico Rodríguez stood in it, and turned to announce their presence, whereupon the door was slammed closed.

The cockpit door was not opened for some time, and not until after Martín had hammered on it with his fist.

In the Horch, Doña Alicia laughed, then said, "Good for you, my darling!"

Father Welner entered the airplane first.

Hans-Peter von Wachtstein was still in the co-pilot's seat. Cletus Frade was standing in the area behind the pilot's and co-pilot's seats doing some sort of administrative work with two other men in SAA pilot's uniforms — there were two complete crews on each flight; it was a long way between Berlin and Buenos Aires — and Father Welner waited until he had finished before speaking.

"Let us all thank the Lord for another safe flight," he said.

"Thank Hansel, Your Holy Eminence," Frade said, not very pleasantly. "The only thing God provided was a lot of turbulence and one hell of a headwind."

The priest did not seem offended.

"Bernardo," he said, "I suspect our Cletus woke up on the wrong side of his airplane."

"If I didn't need you two," Frade said, "you'd still be outside on the ladder."

He pointed at Martín, and went on: "The only way you could have known when we were coming is because you've slipped someone into SAA Montevideo who called you and told you. Now I'm going to have to fire everyone there and replace them with people who work for me, and not the Bureau of Internal Security."

Von Wachtstein climbed out of the co-pilot's seat.

General Martín did not deny the accusation, instead asking, "You say you need us? Curiosity overwhelms me."

"Hansel and I have gone into the smuggle-deserving-Germans-into-Argentina business ourselves," Frade said. "We need to smuggle someone out of the airport, and we need a *libreta de enrolamiento* for our friend right away, this afternoon. Whatever your other faults, you two are very good at arranging things like that."

Von Wachtstein was now smiling broadly. The other two SAA pilots, who knew who the priest and Martín were, looked uncomfortable.

"Well, you've got my attention," Martín confessed. "Are you going to tell me where you found this deserving German?"

"Some friends of ours who were looking for her found her," Frade said.

"You mean some of your OSS friends?" Martín said.

"I've told you and told you, Bernardo, we don't even know what those initials stand for. And besides, don't you read the newspapers? The OSS no longer exists."

"I read that, but I'm having a hard time believing it," Martín said. "Where is this deserving German?"

"Enrico, would you ask Frau von Wachtstein to come up here, please?"

"Frau von Wachtstein?" Father Welner blurted.

"Don't add bigamy to your list of Hansel's other sins, just yet, Your Eminence," Frade said. "Try to give him the benefit of the doubt."

Martín chuckled.

Elsa appeared in her Officer Equivalent Pinks and Greens skirt and tunic uniform.

"Gentlemen, may I present my sister-in-law, Frau Elsa von Wachtstein?" von Wachtstein said.

Father Welner quickly recovered.

"My dear child, I'm Father Welner. Welcome to Argentina."

"Thank you," Elsa said.

"Does that mean we get the *libreta de enrolamiento*?" Frade asked.

"That's no problem," Martín said. He put out his hand to Elsa. "Frau von Wachtstein, I'm General Martín."

"How do you do?"

"What I suggest we do," Martín said, "is that I put Frau von Wachtstein in my car and drive her to the house on Libertador. That'll solve the problem of getting her through Immigration and off the airfield . . ."

There was not an Argentine police officer — or any other official — who would dare stop a car driven by the chief of the Bureau of Internal Security for any reason, much less to demand the identity documents of anyone in it.

Peter von Wachtstein saw the look on Elsa's face.

"I'll go with you, Elsa," he said.

". . . leaving Father Welner to explain to your wives what you two are doing with this beautiful young woman," Martín concluded.

"Thanks, Bernardo," Frade said. His tone of voice reflected his sincerity.

"*De nada,*" Martín said. "Enrico, open the door and see if they're finished out there."

"*Sí, mi General,*" the old soldier said, and pushed the door open and looked out. He pulled his head back in and reported, "Not quite, *mi General.*"

Martín nodded.

A line of people, mostly adults, many of the latter in the religious garb of nuns, priests, and brothers, were moving slowly but steadily down the stairway at the rear door of the Constellation. At the foot of the stairs, their documents were examined by immigration officers. Some of the arriving passengers were directed to the Leyland bus, but some of the people in clerical garb and all the children were escorted to one of the Mercedes buses by priests and nuns.

It was clear that everybody knew what had to be done and how to do it efficiently.

Which also made it clear that this was not the first time passengers like these had been off-loaded from an SAA flight originating in Berlin.

"They are finished, *mi General,*" Enrico reported.

"Let me go first," Father Welner said.

He went down the stairway and walked to the Horch.

"Your three minutes were up long ago," Doña Dorotea said. "What's going on?"

"Alicia," the priest said, "your husband and General Martín are about to come down with a beautiful young woman. As they walk to General Martín's car, I suggest you smile and wave at them."

"Why the hell should she do that?" Doña Dorotea demanded.

"Because she's Alicia's sister-in-law," the priest said.

"Oh, my God!" both young women said, almost in unison.

[FIVE]

The five-story turn-of-the-century mansion sat behind a twelve-foot-tall cast-iron fence across Avenida Libertador from the Hipódromo de Palermo.

A 1940 Ford station wagon was parked at the curb. A legend painted on its doors read FRIGORIFICO MORÓN. The Frigorifico Morón — Morón Slaughterhouse and Feeding Pens — no longer existed to process cattle from Estancia San Pedro y San Pablo. The 1,500-hectare property in Morón was now the site of Aeropuerto Coronel Jorge G. Frade.

When Martín's Mercedes turned off Avenida Libertador and stopped before the double gates in the fence, two burly men got quickly out of the Ford and walked to the Mercedes. One held a Remington Model 11 twelve-gauge riot gun parallel to his trouser seam. The other had his hand under his suit jacket on the butt of a Ballester-Molina .45 ACP pistol, the Argentina-manufactured version of the Colt Model 1911-A1.

The two men were part of what had come to be known — if not in public — as Frade's Private Army. Like the others in it, they had been born, as had their fathers and grand-

206

fathers and great-grandfathers, on Estancia
San Pedro y San Pablo. They had left it to do
their military service and returned to it either
after their conscription period, or after retir-
ing from twenty-five years of service with the
Húsares de Pueyrredón.

There was nothing mocking or pejorative in
references to Frade's Private Army. For one
thing, there was nothing amateurish about it.
And for another, everyone recognized he
needed one.

El Coronel Jorge G. Frade had been assassinated on his Estancia San Pedro y San
Pablo, and there had subsequently been five
attempts to assassinate his son, Cletus. While
the threat of future attempts to assassinate
him, or members of his family, had dimin-
ished with the surrender of Germany, it had
by no means disappeared.

The threat of assassination also applied to
Hans-Peter von Wachtstein and his family.
The SS in Argentina — Peter only half-
jokingly said that there were more SS in
Argentina now than there ever had been at
the SS-Junkerschule in Bad Tölz — had been
furious when Major von Wachtstein, then the
assistant military attaché for air of the German embassy, had disappeared following the
monstrously cruel execution of his father for
his father's role in the July 1944 bomb plot
against Hitler.

The rage intensified when they learned that

Major von Wachtstein — the recipient of the Knight's Cross of the Iron Cross from the hands of the Führer himself — had been spirited out of the country by Cletus Frade because von Wachtstein had been a traitor to the Third Reich, working all along for Frade and the OSS.

When one of the ex-Húsares saw who the Mercedes held, he saluted. The other signaled impatiently toward the house. The huge gates began to creak open. When they were fully open, the Mercedes drove through them to a ramp leading to the mansion's basement garage, whereupon the gates immediately began to close.

They were almost closed when the rest of the convoy appeared. First, the Horch, with Enrico at the wheel, Doña Dorotea beside him, and Cletus Frade in the back with the nanny holding his sons. Then came Father Welner's enormous Packard, with Alicia, her son, and the nanny in it, and finally her Packard, now carrying former *sargentos* of the Húsares de Pueyrredón Rodolfo Gómez and Manuel Lopez, bodyguards to Doña Dorotea and Alicia respectively.

The gates creaked back open and the cars went through them and disappeared down the ramp to the basement.

There they found Hans-Peter von Wachtstein and Elsa von Wachtstein standing beside

Martín's Mercedes.

Alicia got out of Welner's Packard and trotted to her husband and Elsa.

"Frau von Wachtstein, say hello to Frau von Wachtstein," Hansel tried to wisecrack, but his voice was broken.

Tears were now running down the cheeks of both women. They embraced.

"You'll have to excuse Alicia, Elsa," Hansel said. "She's an Argentine, and they tend to get quite emotional."

Doña Dorotea was by then out of the Horch and had walked up to them.

"Shut up, Hansel," she snapped. "You're as bad as Cletus not knowing when to keep quiet!" Then she turned to Elsa. "I'm the other big mouth's wife. Do I get to give you a welcoming hug?"

Elsa and Alicia parted wide enough to admit Dorotea to their embrace.

That embrace lasted a full sixty seconds, and then the three women, Elsa in the center, walked first to the Horch, where they collected the children, and then toward the stairs leading from the basement.

Hans-Peter von Wachtstein met Martín's eyes.

"Thank you," von Wachtstein said.

Martín shrugged.

"And now shall we go find a telephone so we can get started on the *libreta de enrolamiento*?" Frade asked.

Martín nodded.

"And after that," he said, "Father Kurt and I have to talk to you. Both of you."

The men went to the library off the foyer. Enrico Rodríguez and the other bodyguards arranged themselves, without being told, in armchairs from which they could cover the front door, the stairs leading to the upper floors, and of course the library.

Once the men were inside the library, a distinguished-looking elderly man wearing a gray butler's jacket appeared almost immediately. Antonio Lavalle had been el Coronel Jorge Frade's butler. Now he was head of all of Dorotea's crews of servants at all of the Frades' homes, running everything for her everywhere.

"Welcome home, Don Cletus," he said.

"Thank you, Antonio. What happened to the ladies?"

"They went upstairs, Don Cletus."

Antonio looked at Martín, the priest, and von Wachtstein. "Gentlemen," he said with a nod.

"Upstairs for what?" Frade asked.

"I would hazard the guess, Cletus, that they are going to get Frau von Wachtstein out of that uniform," Father Welner said.

"You're going to tell me about that uniform, right?" Martín asked. "It's what your women soldiers wear, yes?"

"Our women officers," Frade said.

"Women should not wear uniforms," Martín proclaimed.

"You better get used to it, it's the wave of the future," Frade said. "Antonio, while General Martín uses the phone, those of us not on duty would like a little something to drink. Are you on duty, Your Eminence?"

"Haig & Haig, please, Antonio," the priest said. "Not too much ice." Then he smiled and added, turning to Cletus, "By now you should understand, my heathen son, I am not going to let you provoke me."

"My little brother told me Elsa walked all the way across Germany from Pomerania," Frade began.

"Your little brother?" the priest said. "That's the first I've heard —"

"He's the closest I have to one. He lived next door to me in Midland. He didn't have a big brother, and I didn't have a little one, so we adopted one another."

"And where did he encounter Frau von Wachtstein?" Martín asked, from where he was speaking on the telephone. "The *new* Frau von Wachtstein. That's going to cause confusion. Would she be offended if I called her 'Frau Elsa'?"

"If you get her that *libreta de enrolamiento*," Peter said, "I'm sure she'll be happy to let you call her anything you want."

"If you come over here, Peter, and give me

her personal data, I'll get her a *libreta de enrolamiento,*" Martín said, then added, "You were saying, Cletus, where your little brother — what's his name, by the way? — encountered *Frau Elsa?*"

"If I didn't know better, Bernardo, I'd suspect you were gathering data for a dossier on the lady," Frade said.

"That's because you have a suspicious nature," Martín said. "Probably something you acquired in the OSS." He handed the telephone to von Wachtstein. "I don't see any reason you can't tell Major Careres what he needs to know about Frau Elsa."

Antonio Lavalle had by then opened the library bar and, with the skill of a master bartender, had just about finished preparing the drinks.

Martín walked to the bar, raised his hand to decline a large, squat glass dark with scotch whisky and instead picked up a glass of soda water. He raised it in toast.

"I give you Don Cletus's previously unknown little brother," he said. "What did you say his name was, Cletus?"

Frade laughed.

"His name is James D. Cronley Junior," he said. "Want me to spell it for you?"

"Cronley with a 'C' or a 'K'?" Martín asked, unabashed.

" 'C,' " Frade said. "And now that I think about it, you'd probably like him. You're both in the counterintelligence business. We call ours the CIC."

"And your CIC was looking for Frau Elsa? What were they going to charge her with?"

"For being the daughter of Generalmajor Ludwig Holz," Frade said, "who was hung with piano wire from a butcher's hook for being involved in the July 1944 bomb plot."

"Jesus Christ!" Martín said. "I'm sorry. Peter, I deeply apologize."

"It's okay," von Wachtstein said.

"No, it's not," Martín said. "That was stupid and cruel of me."

"Forget it," von Wachtstein said.

"We were looking for her," Frade said. "As we're still looking for Karl's father."

" 'We' being the OSS, you mean?" Martín asked.

This time Frade did not pretend not to know even what OSS stood for.

"What they did," he said, "was add the names of people we wanted to help, if possible, Karl's father, for example . . ."

Kapitän zur See Karl Boltitz had been the naval attaché of the German embassy. His father, Vizeadmiral Kurt Boltitz, and Admiral Wilhelm Canaris had been deeply involved in the bomb plot to kill Adolf Hitler. Canaris had been immediately arrested and placed in the Flossenberg Concentration Camp in Bavaria. When the 97th Infantry Division of

213

the Third U.S. Army liberated Flossenberg, they found Admiral Canaris's naked, torture-scarred, decomposing body hanging from a gallows.

Admiral Boltitz, like his son a submariner, had been in Norway, at the German submarine pens in Narvik, when his arrest order had gone out. He disappeared before the SS could find him. It was not known whether he had tried — was still trying — to hide in Norway or had decided that jumping into the frigid Norwegian waters was preferable to arrest, torture, and certain execution.

Frade had gotten both von Wachtstein and Boltitz out of Argentina and to the secret POW camp for senior enemy officers at Fort Hunt in Virginia as much for their services to the United States as for their friendship.

". . . and people like Elsa to the list of Nazi officials and SS officers we — our Military Police — were looking for," Frade continued. "Elsa turned up at an MP checkpoint in Hesse. Lieutenant Cronley — did I mention my little brother is a second lieutenant, Bernardo? You wouldn't want to leave that out of your dossier — was sitting there in his jeep.

"He notified the OSS. The OSS was waiting when we landed in Frankfurt on our way back from Berlin."

"And they knew the connection between Peter and Frau Elsa?" Martín asked.

Frade nodded. "So we went to Marburg — it's about sixty miles north of Frankfurt — and got her. I didn't know Jimmy was involved — or even in the Army, or in Germany — until we got there."

"Jimmy wanted to know why Clete was wearing that Mexican bus driver's uniform," von Wachtstein furnished as he pointed. "Clete had no answer."

"Then we loaded Elsa onto the *Ciudad de Rosario* and brought her here," Frade said. "End of story."

"*Frau* von Wachtstein," Martín said. "What about her husband? Where's he?"

"My brother was killed in Russia," Hansel said.

"My condolences, Peter," Martín said.

Von Wachtstein shrugged. "He was a good man and a fine officer."

"Does that complete your dossier, Bernardo?" Frade asked.

"Just about, thank you," Martín said. "Which permits the conversation to turn to why Father Kurt and I went to the airfield to meet you."

"Which is?"

"President Farrell sent us," Martín said.

"Now *you* have *my* attention, Bernardo," Frade said.

"El Coronel Juan Domingo Perón has been arrested at President Farrell's order," Martín said.

215

"And how did my Tío Juan offend el Presidente? I'm almost afraid to ask."

"Perhaps Bernardo should have said, 'has been taken into custody,'" Father Welner said.

"Well, which was it? And what's the difference?"

"For his own protection," the priest said. "He's done nothing wrong."

"You know better than that, Your Eminence," Frade said.

"I went to the president with credible intelligence that a group of officers is planning to assassinate Juan Domingo," Martín said.

"Maybe you should have kept your mouth shut," Frade said.

"Cletus, Juan Domingo is your godfather!" the priest said.

"And you know better than that," Martín said. "My duty required that I inform the president of something like that. El Coronel Perón is the vice president —"

"And the minister for War and the secretary of Labor and Welfare," the priest added.

"What happened when you told Farrell that some people want to blow Juan Domingo away?" Frade asked.

"It took him some time to accept it," Martín said. "And the first thing he thought was that it had something to do with Señorita Duarte."

"No!" Frade said, in sarcastic surprise. "I

216

can't imagine the officer corps being at all offended that the minister for War is running around with a semi-pro hooker half his age. Every senior colonel should have a blond tootsie like Evita to help him pass his idle hours."

"You don't know that for a fact," the priest said, "that she's a semi —"

"If it waddles like a duck, quacks like a duck, et cetera," Frade interrupted.

"You're repeating gossip," the priest said disparagingly.

"You remember when our Hansel was ordered back to the fatherland?" Frade asked. "Well, let me tell you what happened that night at the Alvear Palace."

The Alvear Palace Hotel was Argentina's best hotel, and one of the best hotels anywhere in the world.

"Clete, let that lie," von Wachtstein said.

Frade considered the request.

"Okay, Hansel," he said.

"What happened that night at the Alvear?" Martín asked.

"Hansel wants it forgotten — it's forgotten," Frade said seriously, and then smiled. "Suffice it to say, *mi General,* on that memorable night I saw Señorita Evita waddling and going 'quack, quack.' It went over Hansel's head. But not mine."

Martín raised his eyebrows, then went on: "General Ramos and I went to see el Coronel Perón, and —"

"You went to see him or the president *sent* you to see him?" Frade interrupted.

"President Farrell suggested to General Ramos and me that it might be helpful if we had a talk with el Coronel Perón," Martín said.

"About his blond tootsie?" Frade asked.

"To tell him that there was credible information about talk in certain factions within the officer corps about assassinating him —"

"Is there?" Frade again interrupted. "You believe it?"

Martín nodded. "For conduct unbecoming an officer and a gentleman, bringing disgrace upon the officer corps."

"The unbecoming conduct meaning his cohabitation with Señorita Evita?" Frade said. "Parading all around town with her on his arm? Or did that include his younger — much younger — other lady friends?"

"That came up," Martín said. "But there's more."

"What more?"

"The officers in question know about the passports Rodolfo Nulder took to Germany."

"I can't say that breaks my heart," Frade said. "But I didn't tell them. I've been scrupulously neutral in the trouble the officer corps has been having with my beloved Tío Juan."

Martín ignored the response.

"The officers we're talking about are the ones who had to keep their mouths shut before we declared war on Germany," Martín said. "Now they feel free to criticize not only the Nazis, but also — maybe especially — those officers who leaned toward Germany. And Perón certainly heads that list."

"So you and Ramos said, 'Get rid of the blonde, Juan Domingo, *and* the girls of doll-carrying age, *and* your Nazi sympathizer pals like Nulder — or you're likely going to get shot'?"

Martín nodded. "And General Ramos phrased it just about that crudely."

"Did he believe you? Did he think these officers are angry enough to be serious about assassinating him?"

"I don't know," Martín said.

"Let me guess what he said when you told him this, Bernardo: 'Go fuck yourselves, and tell the boys at the Circulo Militar to do the same.' "

"Actually, he said, 'Don't hold your breath.' "

"And when you reported this to General Farrell, his Irish temper flared, and he said, 'Arrest the sonofabitch!' "

"What President Farrell said, very calmly, was that we could not afford to have the officer corps split in two as it would be if there were an attempt — successful or not — on Juan Domingo's life. Therefore, the obvious thing to do was protect him until the problem of the unhappy officers could be resolved —"

"And did he say how he was going to do that?" Frade interrupted.

Martín ignored the question.

"And since el Coronel Perón would almost certainly not accept any such protection willingly, that left no choice but to arrest him."

"And you did? I mean, Farrell gave you that dirty job?"

"El Coronel was arrested by General Ramos and myself," Martín said.

"Where? At the Edificio Libertador? Or did you — I hope — go to his apartment and pull him out of the loving arms of his tootsie?"

"To spare him the embarrassment of being taken from the Edificio Libertador in arrest, we waited until we knew he was in his office in the Labor Ministry."

"And took him where?"

"I'm not at liberty to tell you that," Martín said.

"Why are you telling me any of it?"

"At the orders of President Farrell. General Farrell also directed me to tell you that this is none of your affair."

"What's that all about?"

"I think he is concerned that you might try to free el Coronel."

"There's not a chance in hell of that, and you know it. And he should."

Father Welner said, "President Farrell is aware that Juan Domingo is not only your godfather —"

"Ah, so that's your role in this," Frade said. "I was wondering where you came in."

"— but was your father's lifelong best friend," the priest concluded.

"General Farrell didn't say this," Martín said, "but I think he's concerned that if you tried to free el Coronel Perón, it might trigger an eruption between those who think his personal life is no one's business."

"That would be those who want to shoot him?"

Martín nodded.

"You can tell General Farrell that I don't care if he keeps my Tío Juan locked up from now on. Incidentally, where did you lock him up?"

"I told you I don't think that's any of your concern, Cletus," Martín said.

"Well, I guess I'll just have to turn to my ER," Frade said. "Curiosity overwhelms me."

"To your what?" Father Welner asked.

"Bernardo has his BIS, Your Holy Eminence, and I have my ER. It stands for Enrico Rodríguez."

"I don't understand," the priest said.

"I'll bet my Horch against your Packard that right now Enrico is patiently waiting for me to come out of here so that he can tell me Juan Domingo has been arrested and say where he's being held. The Ejército Argentino — like the U.S. Marine Corps — has no secrets safe from its sergeants major."

Martín laughed. "He's right, Father. Cletus, el Coronel is on Martín García Island."

"Where the hell is that?"

"It's a small island off the coast of Uruguay," Martín said. "Have I your word you will go nowhere near it?"

"Right now, I have absolutely no intention of going anywhere near it, much less of springing my Tío Juan from his cell. But this is Argentina, and we never know what's going to happen next, do we?"

"Is that really what you want me to tell General Farrell?" Martín asked.

"I don't care what you tell him," Frade said, and then reconsidered. "No. Tell him I understand that whatever he has chosen to do with el Coronel is none of my business."

"I will," Martín said.

"What I don't understand is why Farrell is so interested in keeping Juan Domingo alive," Frade said. "Farrell's no fool. He has to know Juan Perón has his eye on the Casa Rosada."

"You don't know what happened in Spain, Cletus," Father Welner said. "A half million people died —"

"At the risk of sounding callous," Frade interrupted, "the Germans killed ten times that many Jews, Gypsies, and other so-called undesirables."

"— and he is determined there will be no civil war here," Welner finished.

"And so am I," Martín said. "Which brings us to something else. At dawn yesterday, the U-405 appeared off our naval —"

"The U-405?" von Wachtstein interrupted.

Martín nodded.

"— our naval base at Puerto Belgrano flying a black flag and surrendered."

"You're sure it was the U-405?" von Wachtstein asked.

Martín nodded again.

"The U-boat skipper told Vicealmirante Crater that he came directly to Puerto Belgrano from Denmark — that is, without making a stop somewhere else to off-load a cargo in secret — but the admiral and I think he's lying."

"You don't have the U-boat captain's name by any chance?" von Wachtstein asked.

"I heard his name," Martín said. "Let me see if I can remember it."

"Hansel, he's pulling your chain," Frade said. "Where did you take Hansel's pal, Bernardo?"

"As we speak, he and el Jefe are swapping sea stories on Estancia San Pedro y San Pablo," Martín said.

"I gave up on Willi von Dattenberg," von Wachtstein said. "After all this time, I was sure he was gone."

"Why are he and Schultz swapping sea

stories, Bernardo?" Frade asked.

"What I would like to happen is to hear from Fregattenkapitän von Dattenberg who and what he put ashore and where, and then get him back to Puerto Belgrano before he is interrogated by anyone else. I think we'd be better off if the people he put ashore, and the people who were waiting for him, don't know we know."

"Well, let's go talk to him," von Wachtstein said. "Fly down there right now. He'll tell me anything we want to know."

"There's a small problem with that, Hansel," Frade said, and held up his glass.

"I haven't been drinking," Martín said. "I can fly."

"The problem with that, *mi General,*" Frade said, "is the only airplane you know how to fly — using that term very loosely — is at the estancia."

"I took the liberty of borrowing the Storch to fly to Puerto Belgrano," Martín said, "and then from there to Estancia San Pedro y San Pablo with von Dattenberg."

Frade shook his head. "And then, flushed with success, and with the complete confidence of pilots with maybe thirty hours' total time usually have, you flew it here?"

Martín nodded.

"You are a devious and dangerous man, *mi General,*" Frade said. "I say that with the greatest admiration."

Frade set his glass down.

"Let's go before the wives come back. It's always easier to beg forgiveness after doing something than it is to ask for permission that'll probably be denied to do it."

■ ■ ■ ■

IV

■ ■ ■ ■

[ONE]

Estancia San Pedro y San Pablo
Near Pila
Buenos Aires Province, Argentina
1315 10 October 1945

Lieutenant Oscar Schultz, USNR, at the wheel of a wood-paneled 1937 Ford station wagon, pulled up in front of the Big House of Estancia San Pedro y San Pablo. Fregattenkapitän Wilhelm von Dattenberg, in the front passenger seat, noted that the eight-year-old vehicle, with its steering wheel on the right, was unbelievably well maintained — it looked as if it had left the showroom last week.

Schultz then motioned for his passenger to get out.

Von Dattenberg no longer believed he was having a dream, but that did not mean he had any idea what was going on, or even where he was. Everything seemed surreal.

Schultz had driven him from the airstrip

out onto the Pampas to a small cluster of buildings.

There he had introduced him to a man who rode up to them on a really beautiful horse. He was wearing boots, riding breeches, and a polo shirt. A polo mallet rested on his right shoulder.

"Kapitän, this is Technical Sergeant Jerry O'Sullivan, U.S. Army," Schultz said. "And this, Sergeant, is Fregattenkapitän von Dattenberg. He is our prisoner. I have told him there's little point in trying to escape as he can't possibly know where to try to escape to. But he may not believe me. Get the Winchester .22, and if he tries to run, shoot him in the leg. We want him alive."

"Yes, sir."

"And when you're in the house, tell my Dorotea to start lunch and to bring us a bottle of the '41 Estancia Don Guillermo Cabernet Sauvignon. We'll be on the veranda."

"Yes, sir."

Fully aware that he should not allow himself to become besotted in the situation in which he found himself, von Dattenberg nevertheless accepted a glass of wine. It had been a long time since he had had anything alcoholic to drink; he had finished his "emergency bottle" of cognac more than a month before.

And then luncheon was served. It consisted of the largest filet mignon he had ever seen, a

230

baked potato, a tomato and onion salad, and some freshly baked hard-crusted bread. There was a bowl holding at least a half kilo of butter and another holding that much thick cream. It had been a long time since he'd seen either.

When the polo-playing sergeant extended to him the bottle of the great Cabernet Sauvignon to refill his glass, he accepted.

He was eating dessert — a pear soaked in wine — when a flaming red Fieseler Storch flashed over the house at no more than fifty meters off the ground.

"That has to be the colonel," Schultz announced. "I don't think the general would try to fly that low — he just learned how to fly. As soon as we kill the rest of the Cabernet, we'd better get up to the Big House."

The red-tile-roofed building had looked large when von Dattenberg had gotten a quick look at it when they first flew over it. Now it looked huge.

Six gauchos on horseback appeared, and von Dattenberg now noticed the gauchos were heavily armed. Two of them held what looked like Mauser rifles, their butts resting on their legs. The other four held American-manufactured Thompson submachine guns.

There was an assortment of cars parked in front of the house, two late-model Ford station wagons, and two Buicks, a four-door sedan and a convertible coupe.

Three men clearly waiting for them were standing on the veranda of the house. One of them was General Martín. The other two were wearing blue uniforms heavy with gold braid. Von Dattenberg could not at first remember ever having seen them, but after a moment he recognized one of them.

The last time that Fregattenkapitän Wilhelm von Dattenberg had seen Hans-Peter von Wachtstein had been in Berlin, and the latter had then been wearing his Luftwaffe major's uniform, to which that morning the Führer himself had pinned the Knight's Cross of the Iron Cross.

"Wie geht's, Willi?" von Wachtstein called cheerfully from the veranda. "Welcome to Estancia San Pedro y San Pablo."

Von Dattenberg walked onto the veranda.

"It's been a long time," von Wachtstein said emotionally, as he grasped von Dattenberg's shoulders. And then he blurted: *"Mein Gott,* you're skinny!"

"Peter, what is that uniform you're wearing?" von Dattenberg asked.

"South American Airways. We just came back from Germany, and there hasn't been time to change."

"You just came back from Germany?" von Dattenberg asked incredulously.

"This morning," von Wachtstein said. "And guess who we had aboard?"

"Let's go into the house," Frade said impatiently.

Von Wachtstein gave him a look of annoyance.

"We're really pressed for time, Peter," Martín said.

"My name is Frade, Kapitän —"

"Cletus is my best friend, Willi," von Wachtstein interrupted. "He's the godfather of my son, and Karl Boltitz and I are godfathers to both of his."

"— I'm a lieutenant colonel, U.S. Marine Corps, and have been in charge of the OSS in Argentina. What we have to do is get some answers from you, and then get you back to Puerto Belgrano before the wrong people know you've been gone."

Von Dattenberg clicked his heels and shook the offered hand, but his face showed that he had no idea what was going on and that he didn't like it.

"Come on in the house, Willi," von Wachtstein said. "We'll get you something to eat and we can talk while you're eating."

"I just ate," von Dattenberg said.

"Then this way, if you please, Kapitän," Frade said.

Von Dattenberg allowed himself to be led into the house and through a large foyer to a large room, the walls of which were lined with books.

"Right over there, please," Frade said,

indicating a chair at a table.

A middle-aged woman wearing a starched white maid's apron and cap entered. She pushed a wheeled cart to them and placed coffee cups on the table as the others arranged themselves at it.

Frade and Martín put briefcases on the table and took from them several folders, legal pads, and writing instruments.

My God, von Dattenberg thought, *I expected to be interrogated by my captors again, but I never dreamed that Peter would clearly be one of them.*

"We are really pressed for time, Kapitän von Dattenberg," Martín said. "And there may not be time for all the details right now. So let's start with the names of the people who you put ashore and what cargo."

I am an officer of the Kriegsmarine and I have given my word.

"As I told Vicealmirante Crater, Herr Oberstleutnant, I came to Argentina, to Puerto Belgrano, directly from Germany."

"You sailed from Narvik, Norway," Frade said unpleasantly.

"We know that, Willi," von Wachtstein said.

Von Dattenberg began: "Under the Geneva Convention —"

"Oh, for Christ's sake!" Frade said disgustedly, and then went on: "Cutting to the chase, let me tell you what's going to happen, Kapitän, if in the next thirty minutes you do not answer fully and honestly any questions we put to you —"

"Give me a minute, Clete," von Wachtstein said.

Frade looked at him for ten seconds.

"I'll give you three minutes, Hansel," Frade said. He raised his left wrist and punched a button on his Marine Corps–issued pilot's chronometer. "Have at it. The clock is running."

"Willi —" von Wachtstein began.

"Under these circumstances, Major von Wachtstein, please do me the courtesy of addressing me by my rank," von Dattenberg said.

"As you wish, Herr Fregattenkapitän," von Wachtstein said softly, after a moment. "We must never forget for a moment that we are officers and gentlemen in the service of our beloved Germany, correct?"

"Who both swore a holy oath of loyalty to the Führer," von Dattenberg said.

"I'm sure Claus von Stauffenberg, who we both know was always a better Christian than either of us, Herr Fregattenkapitän, had that holy oath in mind when he placed that bomb under the map table at Wolfsschanze. And had it in his mind the next day when he was standing against the wall on Bendlerstrasse waiting for the SS to shoot him for high treason."

"Claus was — may God forgive him — a

traitor," von Dattenberg said.

"And so apparently was my father, and I'm sure he had that holy oath in mind when he was hanging naked in the execution hut in the Bendlerblock, being very slowly choked to unconsciousness, and then revived, and then choked again — over and over again, until God, in his mercy, took his life."

"Treason is treason," von Dattenberg said, his voice on the edge of breaking.

"Get him talking, Hansel, or I'll kill the sonofabitch right here and now," Frade said. "To hell with flying him to your beloved fucking Germany for trial —"

Von Wachtstein held up his hand to silence him.

"We've learned, Willi," von Wachtstein went on calmly, "that Claus's last words were 'May God save our beloved Germany.' We don't know what Admiral Canaris was thinking when he was hung, naked, from a gallows at the Flossenbürg Konzentrationslager, of course. . . ."

"Admiral Canaris was hung?" von Dattenberg asked softly.

"He was as much a traitor as was Claus and my father — and Karl Boltitz's father."

"Karl? Is Karl alive?"

Von Wachtstein nodded.

"He is in Narvik, looking for his father. Unfortunately, it looks as if Admiral Boltitz chose jumping into a Norwegian fjord over facing a People's Court for treason and being strangled to death."

"And Karl was a . . ."

"Was Karl a traitor? Yes, he was. And, I tell you proudly, my old friend Willi, so am I. Not a traitor to the Code of Honor under which the von Wachtsteins and the von Dattenbergs have lived for hundreds of years. But, yes, a traitor to the Austrian corporal and all the evil men around him who brought to our beloved Germany shame and —"

"Time's up, Hansel," Frade said, tapping his wristwatch crystal.

Von Wachtstein, ignoring him, went on: "What my honor as an officer demands now, Willi, is that I do whatever is necessary to keep Nazis from finding refuge here in Argentina. I demand that you not only tell us who, where, and what you put ashore from U-405, but that you give me your word as a German officer that you will do whatever General Martín asks you to do."

"My cup runneth over," Frade said. "I have had more of this honor-of-the-officer-corps bullshit — German and Argentine — than I can swallow. See if you can make your pal understand that he's about sixty seconds from getting shot and being buried in an unmarked grave on the Pampas."

"Cletus!" General Martín said warningly.

"Cletus what?" Frade snapped. "The fucking Nazis murdered my father, and Hansel's father, and this smug sonofabitch sits here and says, 'Sorry, my officer's honor doesn't —,' "

"Herr Oberstleutnant," von Dattenberg interrupted.

Frade looked at him. He saw tears running down von Dattenberg's cheeks.

"What?" Frade snapped.

"I will tell you, and may God forgive me, whatever it is you wish to know."

"I really hope you mean that, von Dattenberg," Frade said, after a long moment.

"I will tell you whatever you wish to know, Herr Oberstleutnant," von Dattenberg repeated.

"Okay. Your immediate problem with me is that by asking you some of these questions I will be telling you things you have no right to know, and I can't run the risk of you telling anyone what I have asked. I really don't like killing people, but I will kill you without hesitation if I decide that is what has to be done to keep this information out of the wrong hands. You understand what I'm saying?"

Von Dattenberg nodded slowly. "I understand, Herr Oberstleutnant."

"Clete, Willi's given his word," von Wachtstein said.

"Are we back to that German officer's honor bullshit, Hansel?" Frade snapped.

"It was my German officer's honor that

238

forced me to warn you that there would be an attempt on your life," von Wachtstein said softly.

Frade looked at him for a long moment.

"Touché, Hansel," he said finally. "You really know how to go for the gut, don't you?"

Von Wachtstein didn't reply.

"What our mutual friend, Hansel, is talking about, Willi," Frade explained, "is that shortly after he came to Argentina, he learned from Oberst Karl-Heinz Grüner — the SS guy at the German embassy — that, to send a message to my father and the Argentine army officer corps, assassins had been hired to whack me —"

" 'Whack'?" von Dattenberg parroted.

"Kill, assassinate, eliminate," Frade clarified. "And, cutting to the chase, he warned me."

"And you were able to stop them?" von Dattenberg asked.

"What he did, Fregattenkapitän," General Martín said, "was kill both of the men sent to kill him."

"But not before the bastards had cut the throat of Enrico's sister, who was my housekeeper. Later, Oberst Grüner arranged the successful assassination of my father. Nice guy, Oberst Grüner. Enrico later put a seven-millimeter slug in his brain when Grüner was unloading stuff from a Spanish merchant ship onto the beach at Samborombón Bay.

"The reason I'm telling you all this, Willi
— and the reason I'm calling you Willi — is
that you just got a pass. Hansel has vouched
for you — that makes you one of the good
guys. In other words, after you finish answering my questions, I will not shoot you."

"And you had planned to do that?"

"Let's say I considered it one of my likely
options."

"One of the difficulties I have encountered
in dealing with Colonel Frade, Fregattenkapitän," Martín said, "is that I never really
know if he means what he says."

"Well, Willi, now that you're suitably terrified, there's a number of questions I have for
you. Let's start with the most important
subject in which my government is interested.
U-234."

"Before I ask what's your interest in
U-234," von Dattenberg said, and looked at
von Wachtstein, "I will clarify that prior to
surrendering my *U-boot,* I carried out orders
to put ashore SS-Brigadeführer Ludwig Hoffmann and fifteen other SS officers with five
wooden crates, contents unknown, in the San
Matias Gulf."

Frade noticed that his tone showed that he
didn't seem at all terrified. Not as he went
on answering von Wachtstein's and Frade's
and Martín's detailed questions about the
secret landing. And not as he almost conversationally finally said, "Now, what's your

240

interest in U-234?"

"I think the stories about large numbers of U-boats leaving Germany for Argentina in the last days of the war are bullshit," Frade said. "But U-234 is different. Credible intelligence has been developed by the OSS that U-234 left the submarine pens in Norway bound for Japan carrying not only the to-be-expected cargo of Nazi officers and cash and diamonds, but also several German nuclear physicists and five hundred sixty kilograms of uranium oxide. Do you know what uranium oxide is, Willi?"

"It has something to do with your atomic bombs," von Dattenberg said.

"It is the essential ingredient in nuclear weapons," Frade said. "Did you know that the Germans had a program to make nuclear weapons?"

"No. But I'm not surprised."

"Our intelligence has it that when imminent defeat became apparent to the Nazi hierarchy, they decided to send their stocks of uranium oxide and their best nuclear scientists to Japan, in the hope the Japanese could finish the work. Do you know, or have you heard anything, about that?"

"No. But it also doesn't surprise me. I know we sent at least one, and possibly more than one, of our jet fighter aircraft, the ME-262, to Japan by submarine. Same idea, I would suggest, that the Japanese could possibly use them against the English and Americans."

"One unpleasant, if wholly credible, scenario is that the senior Nazi officers aboard U-234 — once they heard the Japs had surrendered, and that would have happened before they could have reached Japan — would contact the Russians by radio and see what the Russians would offer, including sanctuary from war-crimes trials, for both the uranium oxide and the nuclear scientists.

"My own variation of that scenario is that the Russians would promise the Nazis the moon, and then when U-234 tied up in a Russian port, the Russians would seize the uranium oxide, put the German scientists to work on their nuclear weapons program, and either execute the Nazis on the spot or after they had been thoroughly interrogated.

"It's obviously of great importance to the United States that the Russians get neither the scientists nor the uranium oxide," Frade went on. "Or that the Soviets even learn that both had left Germany on a submarine bound for Argentina. So, what I need from you right now, Willi, is everything you know, or have heard, or intuit, about U-234."

Von Dattenberg nodded, collected his thoughts, and then began: "Colonel —"

"Now that we're pals, Willi, you can call me Cletus."

Von Dattenberg nodded again. *"Cletus,"* he said. "This would be good news, except that

I don't think you're ready to accept good news from me."

"Meaning what?"

"I knew that U-234 — more accurately I *suspected* that U-234 was coming here. She's the same kind of boat — a VIIC, built as a minelayer, converted to a transport — as my U-405. Both vessels were sort of reserved for important missions like Argentina transport because of their greater range.

"We can assume she didn't make it to Japan. If she did, as you suggest, try to go to Russia — I think this is unlikely, as she was probably close to Argentina when she heard the Japanese were out of the war, and establishing radio contact with any Russian base would be very difficult. Even if that unlikely circumstance happened, she would not have had enough fuel to make it to any Russian port.

"One possibility is that she went to South Africa, put the money, the crew, and passengers ashore, and then was scuttled. But that's a remote possibility, at best. So, if I were you, I'd stop worrying about U-234."

"If that's good news —"

"I hope you accept it as such. It's the best I have to offer."

"Well, Willi, since Hansel got you a pass, I don't have any other options, do I?"

"El Jefe," General Martín said, "please take Fregattenkapitän von Dattenberg onto the veranda and give us a moment alone."

"Open another bottle of the Cabernet," Frade said. "Quickly. This won't take long."

Martín waited until von Dattenberg had followed Schultz out of the library before asking, "Well? Is he telling the truth, Peter?"

"Yes," von Wachtstein said. "I think — what is that line from court trial movies? — I think we got 'the truth, the whole truth, and nothing but the truth.' "

"Cletus?"

"Either that, or he's a better actor than John Barrymore," Frade said. "Those were real tears."

"You were a pretty good actor yourself," Martín said, "with that line about him being sixty seconds from getting shot."

"What the hell makes you think I didn't mean it?" Frade asked.

"I think what broke him," von Wachtstein said, "was what Clete said about the 'honor-of-the-officer-corps bullshit.' Willi — he's really a good man — had to know that oath of loyalty we 'swore' to Hitler was . . . well, bullshit."

"Since we're all playing psychiatrist," Frade said, "I think what made him open up was hearing what happened to Hansel's father and Admiral Canaris."

"The question now is whether he will keep his mouth shut about talking to us," Martín said. "But let me back up. The people he put

244

ashore on the San Matias Gulf — anybody important, Clete?"

"According to the list of people we are looking for —"

" 'We' again meaning the OSS?" Martín interrupted.

"Don't start that crap again, Bernardo. The OSS no longer exists."

"I may not be very bright, Cletus, my friend, but I'm smart enough to know when not to — what is it you say? — pull your chain. I just want to know what list."

Frade looked at him for perhaps five seconds, and then tapped the thick stack of paper held together with a metal clip with his fingertips.

"I got this in Germany," he said. "This is the list of people the U.S. government — and all the Allies, which theoretically includes Argentina — are looking for." He paused, and then went on: "For a lot of reasons. That same list allowed us to find Elsa von Wachtstein."

"Are you going to give me a look at it?"

"How come you don't have a copy, Bernardo? I'm sure the Argentine embassy — or whatever it's now called — in Berlin was given a copy."

"Would you be shocked to learn there are people in my government who would rather I didn't have access to the information in your list?"

"Nulder, you mean?"

"Nulder and others," Martín said.

"I'll do better than giving you a look," Frade said. "I'll have el Jefe shoot it with his trusty Leica."

"I would be grateful," Martín said.

"According to the list, SS-Brigadeführer Ludwig Hoffmann is a three-star sonofabitch. We really want him. And of the other fifteen SS officers, nine are of 'special interest,' which means if they weren't here, and we caught them, they'd be on death row waiting to be hung. Unless the Brits found them first — seven of von Dattenberg's Nazis are on the Special Air Service's 'execute on locating' list. I've got a copy of that, too, which, if you'd like, el Jefe can also photograph."

"Thank you."

"I'll probably learn more when I send the list to . . . to somebody I know in Germany."

"Your little brother, you mean?" Martín asked.

"Yeah, my little brother," Frade said, smiling. "Like most second lieutenants, he knows everything about everything. So, what happens to von Dattenberg now?"

"Well, presuming we can get him back to Puerto Belgrano without attracting too much attention —"

"Define 'too much attention,' " Frade interrupted.

"No eyebrows will be raised if the chief of

246

BIS is reported to have been at Puerto Belgrano to see what he can find out about U-405. That's my job. The same eyebrows would go way up if it got out that I took him away for all this time."

"And if they don't go up?"

"I will report to General Farrell that I interviewed von Dattenberg, and that he told me he had not put anything or anyone ashore anywhere. I will recommend that he and his crew join the internees of the *Graf Spee* in Villa General Belgrano in Cordoba, until it can be decided what to do with them. I think Farrell will go along with that. Once they're there, certain people will go there to try to find out what, if anything, he told Admiral Crater and me about his passengers and cargo.

"I think 'certain people' will either be el Coronel Perón's good friend former Teniente Coronel Nulder, or one of Rudy's charming associates. With a little bit of luck, von Dattenberg's crew will tell them he ordered them to say nothing about their putting anything ashore in the San Matias Gulf."

"His crew will do what he asked them to," von Wachtstein said flatly.

"I really hope so, Peter," Martín said.

"So, what happens to him now? To them? After they're in Villa General Belgrano?"

"We'll just have to wait and see what happens, Peter," Martín said. "What we have to

247

do now is get him back to Puerto Belgrano as discreetly as possible. And as quickly."

"Quickly would be in the Lodestar," Frade said. "But that airplane seems to attract attention, doesn't it?"

"Just a little," Martín agreed. "Maybe because it's fire-engine red?"

"I could fly Bernardo and Willi to Puerto Belgrano in the Storch," von Wachtstein said. "And then take Bernardo to Buenos Aires. Your driver is here, right?"

Martín nodded.

"By the time you and I could get to Jorge Frade, he could be there with your car," von Wachtstein finished.

"That would work," Martín said.

"And I could shoot the lists and send the film with your driver," Schultz said.

"That would really be helpful," Martín said.

"A beautiful plan which will probably destroy Hansel's happy marriage, when Alicia gets home and he's not there," Frade said.

"Absence makes the heart grow fonder," von Wachtstein said. "I thought you knew that."

[Two]

Half of a section of one of the book-lined walls of the library that von Dattenberg had noticed when he was brought into the house was swung open. It revealed a small desk on which sat several devices. But of course von Dattenberg was not privvy to the secret compartment; as far as he knew, the library bookshelves were simply that.

One device on the desk was a Collins Radio Corporation Model 7.2 transceiver, usually — but not today — capable of establishing communication around the world.

"It's the fucking sun," Lieutenant Oscar Schultz, USNR, diagnosed.

It was an expert opinion. Schultz had once been chief radioman, USN, aboard the destroyer USS *Alfred Thomas,* DD-107.

"Can we get through to Vint Hill?" Frade asked.

Vint Hill — officially Vint Hill Farms Station — was a small, highly secret base in Virginia, not far from Washington and the Pentagon. It was the home of the Army Security Agency, which provided, among other services, "secure" — in other words, encrypted — communications between the Pentagon and Army headquarters around the world. It had provided such services to the Office of Strategic Services and — by VOPO-TUS, Verbal Order President of the United States — had been directed after the OSS disestablishment to continue to provide such services between Allen Dulles, Colonel Robert Mattingly, and Lieutenant Colonel Cletus Frade in connection with the unnamed operation everyone had come to think of as

249

OPERATION EAST.

El Jefe adjusted several controls on the Collins and then typed for perhaps ten seconds on the keyboard of another device, this one itself classified Top Secret, and called the SIGABA. He then pushed a switch marked TRANSMIT.

Thirty seconds later, a strip of paper, a quarter inch in width, began to come out of the SIGABA.

He looked at it and announced, "We're up, boss."

Frade handed him a typewritten message. Schultz took it and turned to the SIGABA keyboard, and with a speed most secretaries would envy, retyped it. This caused two things to happen. The message itself appeared as it would on a typewriter, and the SIGABA started to emit more of the quarter-inch paper.

When he had finished, he handed the "typewriter" copy to Frade, who read it carefully.

```
TOP SECRET–PRESIDENTIAL

URGENT

VIA VINT HILL SPECIAL

FROM TEX 0013 10OCT45

EYES ONLY ADDRESSEES

TO BERN AT WHITE HOUSE

TANKER AT HQ USFET

FLAGS AT XXVII CIC MUNICH
```

"Tex" was Frade; he was from Texas. "Bern" was Allen Dulles, who had run OSS operations in Europe from Bern, Switzerland, and had been given access to the White House communications network. "Tanker" was Colonel Robert Mattingly, now deputy commander of the CIC at Headquarters, U.S. Forces, European Theater in the I.G. Farben Building in Frankfurt. "Flags" was Major Harold N. Wallace, whose lapels bore the crossed semaphore flags of the Signal Corps, and who was now commanding the XXVII CIC Detachment in Munich.

HOOVER BROUGHT TO FARM FRE-
GATTENKAPITÄN WILHELM VON
DATTENBERG HEREAFTER SUB-
MARINE WHO SURRENDERED U-405
TO ARMADA ARGENTINA AT PUERTO
BELGRANO 0520 9OCT45.

SUBMARINE TOLD FRIENDLY AR-
MADA ADMIRAL HE CAME DIRECTLY
TO PUERTO BELGRANO FROM GER-
MANY BUT AFTER MEETING WITH
GALAHAD REVEALED HE HAD SE-
CRETLY PUT ASHORE SIXTEEN SS
OFFICERS INCLUDING SS-
BRIGADEFÜHRER LUDWIG HOFF-
MANN AND FIVE CRATES UNIDENTI-
FIED CONTENTS. LIST OF SS
OFFICERS WILL BE SENT AS MES-
SAGE TEX-0014.

"Hoover" was General de Brigada Bernardo Martín, whose Bureau of Internal Security was something like the FBI, which was under J. Edgar Hoover. "The Farm" was Estancia San Pedro y San Pablo.

Frade did not see any point in identifying "Friendly Armada Admiral" as Vicealmirante Crater. "Galahad" was von Wachtstein. "Irish" was President Edelmiro Julián Farrell. "Tío Juan" was Colonel Juan D. Perón.

UNDERSIGNED BELIEVES WE ARE GETTING ABSOLUTE TRUTH FROM SUBMARINE AFTER HIS MEETING WITH GALAHAD, AND THAT HE WILL PROVIDE FURTHER ANSWERS TO ALL QUESTIONS WHEN THERE IS OPPORTUNITY TO ASK.

HOOVER INFORMED IRISH OF CREDIBLE PLOT TO ASSASSINATE TIO JUAN. IRISH, BELIEVING EVEN UNSUCCESSFUL ATTEMPT WOULD TRIGGER CIVIL WAR, ORDERED ARREST OF TIO JUAN FOR HIS OWN PROTECTION. HE IS BEING HELD IN SECRET LOCATION KNOWN TO UNDERSIGNED, WHO IS TAKING NO REPEAT NO ACTION.

URGENTLY REQUEST FULLEST DOSSIERS ON SS OFFICERS LISTED IN TEX-0014.

TEX

TOP SECRET–PRESIDENTIAL

"Send it," Frade ordered.

Schultz tore the tape hanging from the SIGABA and then inserted it into another slot of the machine. He then pushed the TRANSMIT button again. The SIGABA began to slowly suck the tape into its innards. No more than sixty seconds later, there was a *ping* sound and the tape began to eject.

"It's there, boss," Schultz announced. "Now what?"

"I'm going to get out of my Mexican bus driver's uniform, have a shave and a shower, and then — God knows I've earned it — a strong drink."

" 'Mexican bus driver's uniform'?" Schultz parroted.

"That's a long story that'll have to wait until I get out of it."

"I'll wait until I get acknowledgment of receipt, and then close up," Schultz said.

Frade came back into the library ten minutes later, now wearing khaki trousers, a polo shirt, and Western boots. Schultz was still sitting at the SIGABA.

"Acknowledgments from both places in Germany," he announced. "But not from the White House."

"That's good enough," Frade said. "What I want is the dossiers. Shut it down. God only knows where Dulles might be, but the White House switchboard will find him."

"How are they going to get the dossiers to us?" Schultz asked. "Sixteen dossiers is a lot to feed through the SIGABA."

"Mattingly will think of something," Frade said.

"Tell me about your Mexican bus driver's uniform."

Frade began to do so, and by the time he had finished, Schultz had shut down the Collins and the SIGABA and closed the section of bookcase. There now was not even a suggestion that something was hidden behind it.

Frade, meanwhile, had pulled another section of the bookshelves open, this time revealing a well-stocked wet bar.

He was making drinks, pouring from a bottle of Johnnie Walker Black, when a buzzer sounded.

"Now what the hell?" Frade muttered.

"It's probably Doña Dorotea," Schultz said, and went to a telephone — an Argentine copy of the U.S. Army EE-8 Field Telephone — hidden behind a row of books.

There was no gate to the enormous Estancia San Pedro y San Pablo, just a sign reading BIENVENIDO!

This was not to say the estancia went unguarded. At least two of the more than two hundred gauchos working the estancia around the clock always had the entrance in sight. If a vehicle entering the property was not known to them, it would be stopped by gauchos on horseback suddenly appearing somewhere on the eight-kilometer road between the BIENVENIDO! sign and the Big

255

House complex.

If the vehicle was known to be welcome, the gaucho who made this decision would ride to the nearest field telephone — all of the phones were mounted six feet up in eucalyptus trees; the gauchos disliked having to dismount — and call the Big House.

"It's an embassy car," el Jefe announced as he returned the telephone to its hiding place.

"I wonder what Tony wants?" Frade asked rhetorically.

Frade couldn't think of anyone else from the U.S. embassy who would come to Estancia San Pedro y San Pablo either unexpectedly or uninvited.

Major Anthony J. Pelosi, CE, USAR, now an assistant military attaché of the embassy, had come to Argentina in 1942 as a second lieutenant, accompanying then–First Lieutenant Cletus Frade, USMCR.

They had been charged by the OSS with a dual mission: blowing up a "neutral" merchant ship or ships known to be replenishing German submarines in Samborombón Bay, and with attempting to make contact with the man the OSS believed would become the next president of the Argentine Republic, and then to attempt to make this man tilt as far toward the United States as he was then tilting toward the Third Reich.

Lieutenant Pelosi had been well qualified for his task. His family in Chicago had been

demolishing buildings in the Windy City for more than a century. Tony at the age of twelve had "taken down" his first structure — a 120-foot-tall grain elevator — with trinitrotoluene charges.

Lieutenant Frade, who had been flying fighter aircraft off Fighter One on Guadalcanal, had only one qualification to accomplish his mission: The man the OSS believed was about to become president of Argentina was his father.

Frade could never remember having seen el Coronel Jorge G. Frade. All he knew about him was that his grandfather never referred to him except as "that sonofabitch," or more commonly, "that miserable three-star Argentine sonofabitch."

Frade later learned that the OSS never had any real hope that either mission would be accomplished, but had decided that giving it a try was well worth putting the lives of an Army second lieutenant and a Marine Corps first lieutenant at risk.

Against odds, they succeeded. And within a year, Frade was a captain and Pelosi a first lieutenant. Frade had been awarded the Navy Cross — the nation's second-highest award for valor — and Pelosi the Silver Star — the third-ranking medal for valor. The citations accompanying the medal were more than a bit vague and obfuscatory. Sinking neutral merchant vessels in neutral waters posed a

number of diplomatic problems.

And el Coronel Jorge G. Frade was murdered by the SS as he drove across his Estancia San Pedro y San Pablo. Reichsführer-SS Heinrich Himmler had ordered his assassination to make the point to the Ejército Argentino officer corps that growing too close to the Americans would not be tolerated.

It didn't work.

Cletus Frade, who had made his peace with his father only six weeks before, fell heir not only to Estancia San Pedro y San Pablo — which was slightly larger than New York City, all of it, Manhattan, Queens, the Bronx, and Brooklyn, too — but also to everything else that made up what Frade thought of as "El Coronel, Inc."

This probably would have been enough for the OSS to decide to keep him in Argentina, but what settled the question once and for all was Allen Welsh Dulles's pronouncement, echoed by Colonel Alejandro Graham — the OSS deputy directors for Europe and the Western Hemisphere, respectively — that they had never encountered anyone who seemed more born to be an intelligence officer than Cletus Frade.

Frade was named OSS commander for Argentina, Uruguay, and Paraguay.

Then Frade had arranged for Pelosi to be assigned to the American embassy. For one thing, it made his presence in Argentina

legitimate. For another, Pelosi kept him abreast of what was going on in the embassy.

Fifteen minutes after the field telephone call, one of the maids came into the library carrying a small silver tray. He looked at her curiously, but picked up what the tray held, an engraved calling card.

> Bosworth Stanton Alexander
>
> Ambassador Extraordinary
> and Plenipotentiary
>
> of the
>
> President of the
> United States of America
>
> to
>
> The Republic of Argentina

"Heads up, *Jefe*," Frade called, and when Schultz looked at him, went on, in Spanish, "Please show the ambassador in."

He had heard there was a new ambassador, but knew nothing beyond that.

The first impression Frade had of Ambassador Alexander was that he looked like Allen W. Dulles. He was younger and had no mustache, as did Dulles, but was built about the same and wearing the same kind of single-breasted suit and button-down-collar shirt and bow tie that Dulles habitually wore.

"Thank you, Colonel, for receiving me without notice," the ambassador said.

He sounds like Dulles, too. Pure Boston.

"Welcome to Estancia San Pedro y San Pablo, Mr. Ambassador," Frade said as he walked toward Alexander.

He realized the hand he wanted to extend held his whisky glass, then moved the glass.

Alexander's handshake was firm.

"May I offer you . . . ?" Frade asked, holding up his whisky glass.

"Very kind of you," the ambassador said.

"Jefe," Frade ordered in Spanish. "See what the ambassador will have."

"A little of that Jack Daniel's, if you please, Lieutenant Schultz," the ambassador said in perfect Spanish. "Over ice."

The ambassador smiled shyly. "I've seen el Jefe's photograph," he said. "So let's get that out of the way. I know a good deal — not everything, of course, but a good deal — more about you than an ambassador usually does about the American citizens whose well-being and property he is charged with protecting."

Schultz made the drink and handed it to the ambassador.

He raised it. "The United States of America, gentlemen, and our President."

260

Schultz and Frade raised their glasses, and they all sipped.

"I'm sure you're curious about the sources of my information," the ambassador said.

"I can't imagine why you'd think that," Frade said.

Alexander smiled shyly again.

"I hardly know where to begin," Alexander said. "Well, at his request, I paid a courtesy call on Treasury Secretary Morgenthau shortly after I was confirmed by the Senate. He seems to feel that you are facilitating the movement of Nazis from Germany to Argentina, which understandably distresses him."

"Mr. Ambassador . . ." Frade began.

Alexander cut him off with a raised palm. "I'm not asking you for confirmation or denial."

"Where did you see my photograph?" Schultz asked.

"Your photo, Lieutenant, and yours, Colonel, were in the dossiers given to me by the Navy. Since word hasn't yet reached you — I asked my naval attaché to hold off on contacting you — you have both been relieved of your assignment to the now defunct Office of Strategic Services and are now assigned . . . as unassigned officers to the Navy Department — the Navy uses very strange terminology, as you may have noticed — with temporary duty station, the U.S. embassy, Buenos Aires.

"The Navy has directed my naval attaché to issue the appropriate orders to you to return you to the United States for reassignment or relief from active duty.

"The War Department has done very much the same thing for the Army personnel formerly assigned to OSS Western Hemisphere Team 17, code name Team Turtle. Specifically, Majors Maxwell Ashton the Third and Anthony J. Pelosi, Master Sergeants William Ferris and Sigfried Stein, and Technical Sergeant Jerry O'Sullivan. They are now assigned to Fort Meyer, Virginia, with temporary duty station at the embassy here."

Frade thought: *He recited all that from memory. And without a pause.*

"That's the bad news," Alexander went on. "I've learned that it's often best to get to that right away. The good news is — this seemed to surprise both my military and naval attachés — that as the ambassador, I am the senior officer of the United States in Argentina, which means that they can comply with their orders from the War and Navy departments only with my permission. I have not given either of them permission to contact you, or to order any of you anywhere.

"Next, and this is, I would say, a mixture of good and bad news, I had dinner just before I left with President Truman, Rear Admiral Sidney W. Souers, and my old friend Allen

262

Dulles. Just the four of us.

"An unnamed intelligence operation called, for convenience, Operation East was discussed. To save time, let me say I became privy to the President's opinion of the enormous value of the intelligence we've received and, it is to be hoped, will continue to receive from General Gehlen.

"I am also aware of the price of General Gehlen's cooperation. More important, I was made aware of the enormous damage to the President — indeed, the nation — disclosure of any details of Operation East would cause.

"Allen Dulles told me, Colonel Frade, that you are the best natural intelligence officer that he has ever known, so I don't have to waste our time by going into details, but let me touch briefly on just a few problems.

"Secretary Morgenthau's suspicions that we are facilitating the movement of Germans known to be Nazis to sanctuary in Argentina are well founded. Nothing is going to cause him to stop looking for proof.

"FBI Director J. Edgar Hoover would love to be able to hold something like Operation East over the President's head.

"As would the Argentines, if only to justify their frankly disgusting relations with the Nazis in the past and now.

"As would the Soviet Union. I think you take my point.

"The priority obviously is the protection of

263

the President. The President, therefore, obviously could not have ordered you to proceed with this unauthorized and highly illegal project that you call Operation East.

"As the President's ambassador extraordinary and plenipotentiary, the same is true of me. We have never met. I was never here, and you have not been, nor will you ever go, to the embassy.

"I may, however, on my own, or when a little bird whispers in my ear that I should, travel to visit my fellow ambassadors in Chile, Uruguay, and Brazil. My staff tells me that South American Airways provides the best service. I also understand that South American Airways, as a courtesy and mark of respect, often offers traveling ambassadors a tour of the aircraft cockpit while in flight."

Frade met his eyes and thought, *Where we could have a little chat . . .*

Ambassador Alexander stopped, smiled shyly again, and asked, "Would you say that covers everything?"

"Yes, sir, I would say it does."

"I have not presumed to suggest how you should deal with your men, Colonel, but I think I should point out that they are all entitled to go home. They have been here since 1942, and the war — at least, World War Two — is over."

Frade said, "What I have been thinking —"

264

Alexander again shut him off with a raised palm.

"If I don't know what you're thinking, Colonel, then I could not relate that, either inadvertently or in answer to a question, could I?"

"Point taken."

"One last thing," Ambassador Alexander said. "I told my secretary I was going to Mar del Plata to see about renting a house for two weeks at the beach. My driver is sure to report to General Martín of the BIS that I stopped off here en route. Is that going to pose any problems, do you think?"

"You have an Argentine chauffeur?" Frade asked, surprised.

"Why not? I have nothing to hide. If I use one of the Marine guards to drive me, General Martín has to have someone follow me."

"I don't think there will be any problems, Mr. Ambassador, no matter what your driver might tell General Martín," Frade said.

"That's good to know," Alexander said.

He finished his drink in two healthy swallows, went to Frade and Schultz, wordlessly shook their hands, and walked out of the library.

[THREE]

Hotel Cóndor
San Carlos de Bariloche
Río Negro Province, Argentina
1545 10 October 1945

Large, double-pane windows in the suite on the top — sixth — floor of the hotel provided a splendid view of Lake Nahuel Huapi and, beyond that, the foothills of the Andes Mountains.

There were three middle-aged men in the "sitting" area. They were gathered around a low table that was just about covered with hors d'oeuvres, bottles of wine, champagne, and spirits.

El Coronel Hans Klausberger of the Tenth Mountain Division was in full uniform, but did not exactly cut a military figure. He was portly and rather short.

One of the others — Señor Franz Mueller, who owned the Hotel Cóndor — was elegantly dressed in a double-breasted suit. Compared to him, the third man, SS-Brigadeführer Ludwig Hoffmann, wearing the best suit he had had in Germany, and which he had put on shortly before getting off U-405, looked positively dowdy.

Hoffmann had just reached for another — his fifth — piece of prosciutto wrapped around a melon chunk when there was a

266

knock at the door. Señor Mueller went to the door, unlocked it, and admitted another elegantly dressed middle-aged man.

"We were about to give up on you, José," Mueller said.

Señor José Moreno was the assistant managing director of the Banco Suisse Creditanstalt S.A.

"I had some difficulty getting the *libreta de enrolamiento* for Herr Hoffmann," Moreno said.

"But you have it?" el Coronel Klausberger asked.

Moreno's face showed he didn't like the colonel talking to him as if he was a subordinate.

Before answering, Moreno went to the table, politely asked, "May I?" and then helped himself to a glass of wine. He ate a prosciutto-wrapped chunk of melon. And then another.

Finally, Moreno nodded at Klausberger.

"Of course I have it," Moreno said. "And then Aeroposta Argentina canceled my flight. They apparently have no aircraft capable of reaching another airfield if they can't land here because of the weather."

"But you are here," Hoffmann said.

"Brigadeführer Hoffmann?" Moreno asked. "Pardon my bad manners, sir. Welcome to Argentina."

He walked to Hoffmann and they shook hands.

"Oberst Klausberger has been telling me that under the circumstances, it would be best not to refer to me by my rank," Hoffmann said.

"That was stupid of me," Moreno said. "It won't happen again."

Hoffmann's acknowledgment of the apology — a brief nod — was that of a general officer acknowledging an apology for a blunder by his aide-de-camp. Moreno didn't like that very much either.

Moreno decided that while courtesy is often important, tolerating discourtesy is often taken as an admission of subordination, and he had no intention of letting Hoffmann think he was in a position to order him around.

I'll fix that right now.

"I see you're wearing the insignia of your old regiment, Hans," he said with a smile. "May I infer from that that your little difficulty has been put to rest once and for all?"

El Coronel Klausberger glared at him.

"You may," he said icily.

"What little difficulty was that?" Hoffmann asked.

"Well, for a while there, it looked as if Hans was going to stand before a wall with a blindfold over his eyes," Moreno said.

With a broad smile on his face, Moreno

mimed a firing squad rifleman taking aim.

And, as he thought he would, Klausberger lost his temper.

"Goddamn it! You know it never came close to that. I was never even formally charged."

"Oh, really? I thought you had been charged, and then when General Rawson turned over the presidency to General Farrell, Farrell decided that charging you with treason for being a little too friendly with the late el Coronel Schmidt was going a bit too far and instead assigned you to the Edificio Libertador staff."

Innkeeper Mueller decided the subject should be changed, and quickly.

"How did you get here, José?" he said. "If the Aeroposta flight was canceled?"

You know very well how I got here, Franz. What you are doing is changing the subject.

So what?

Hoffmann is going to ask about Klausberger's "difficulties" until he knows all about them. And that's even better for my purposes than hearing them from me.

"Well, South American Airways' Lodestars, Humberto Duarte told me with a rather infuriating smugness —"

"Who?" Hoffmann interrupted.

Good. He wants to know everything.

"Humberto Valdez Duarte, Señor Hoffmann," Moreno explained. "He's managing director of the Anglo-Argentinian Bank. He's also a director of SAA." He paused, and then went on, "As I was saying, Humberto told me SAA's Lodestars have sufficient range to go back to Buenos Aires if they can't land here."

"I don't understand why you called Duarte," Klausberger said.

"Because the SAA flight here was full. I already knew that. That's why I made a reservation on Aeroposta. And when they canceled that flight, I had to have someone with influence get me on the SAA flight. I tried to call Juan Domingo — that's el Coronel Perón, Herr Hoffmann, who's also an SAA director — but no one seems to know where he is right now. So I had no choice but to call my dear friend Humberto. And here I am."

"I can't imagine you not being able to get through to el Coronel Perón," Mueller said.

"I wouldn't read anything into that," Moreno said. "He's probably off to Mar del Plata — or may even be here — with the fair Evita."

He refilled his wineglass and helped himself to several crackers on which he spread Brie and then topped that with black olive.

"Well, I don't have much time," he announced. "So if I may make a suggestion?"

"Please do," Hoffmann said, and then parroted, " 'Don't have much time'?"

"My flight to Buenos Aires leaves at five oh

five," Moreno said. "And I don't want to miss it."

"Excuse me, Señor Moreno," Hoffmann said. "I was under the impression that we were going to discuss, in detail, the . . . financial situation."

"That's going to be impossible in the time I have, I'm afraid," Moreno said.

"And I'm afraid I'm going to have to insist," Hoffmann said.

"Señor Hoffmann, at the risk of sounding disrespectful, you are not in a position right now to insist on anything," Moreno said.

"You're talking to SS-Brigadeführer Hoffmann, Señor Moreno," Klausberger said indignantly.

Well, here goes . . .

"I'm talking to *former* Brigadeführer Hoffmann," Moreno said matter-of-factly. "Herr Hoffmann, you have a choice. You may either listen to me tell you how things are —"

"Or what, José?" Klausberger challenged.

"Or I walk out of here right now and find a taxi to take me to the airport."

"You wouldn't dare!" Klausberger said.

After a moment, Hoffmann said: "I think we should hear what Señor Moreno has to say, Oberst Klausberger. Please go on, Señor Moreno."

That "courteous" response was intended to be menacing.

He'll have to learn right now that he's no

271

longer in a position to menace anyone.

"Thank you," Moreno said. "I have received from Banco Suisse Creditanstalt a list of people the Americans are looking for. It was provided to the Swiss border authorities. I'm sure you won't be surprised to learn, Herr Hoffmann, that you are on that list. I would be surprised if the names of the other SS officers who came here with you aren't also on that list.

"For the moment, you are relatively safe here. *For the moment.*

"I don't know if you're aware of this, Herr Hoffmann, but U-405 surrendered to the Armada Argentina early on the morning of nine October."

"Surrendered?" Hoffmann asked. "I ordered von Dattenberg to scuttle his vessel."

"Her captain?" Moreno asked, and when Hoffmann nodded curtly, went on, "Well, the vessel was surrendered intact. The BIS — the Bureau of Internal Security, Herr Hoffmann, corresponding to the former Sicherheitsdienst —"

"I know what the BIS is," Hoffmann interrupted.

"As I was saying, the BIS was apparently notified. The same day U-405 surrendered, Brigadier General Martín, the head of BIS, flew to the Puerto Belgrano Naval Base and interrogated her captain. I understand the captain said that he had come directly from

272

Germany — that, in other words, he denied any knowledge of putting anyone or anything ashore.

"I'm sure General Martín and Vicealmirante Crater did not believe him. And that it's simply a matter of time before it comes out that U-405 did in fact put you, the other officers, and your cargo ashore —"

Klausberger interrupted: "Brigadeführer Hoffmann ordered this man to —"

Hoffmann silenced him with a raised palm.

Moreno went on: "— At which time, if not before, General Martín will turn his attention to you, el Coronel Klausberger. He is aware of your previous roles in assisting el Coronel Schmidt in bringing people and cargo from German submarines ashore, and, if I have to say this, General Martín does not like you.

"General Martín, Herr Hoffmann, is not only a very good intelligence officer, but a very powerful man. He has the ear of President Farrell. He does not need to ask for permission to carry out what he sees as his duty, and only President Farrell can tell him not to do so.

"You can therefore expect, el Coronel Klausberger, that the barracks of the Tenth Mountain Regiment in San Martín de los Andes — and any other place where he thinks fleeing German officers and what they brought with them might be concealed — will shortly be searched by BIS personnel.

"So far as the other German officers are concerned, I think they will be safe in the homes of the loyal Argo-Germans to which Señor Mueller arranged for them to be taken.

"The cargo — in other words, the currency, gold, other precious metals and diamonds, et cetera — is something else. Its discovery would mean not only its loss, but an intensification of the search for you and your officers.

"The obvious thing to do is twofold: You and your officers will have to remain in deep hiding for at least a month, possibly longer, until the search for you is, if not called off, then less intense. The cargo will have to be taken somewhere where it cannot be found. In my judgment, the most safe place for it is in the vaults of the Banco Suisse Creditanstalt in Buenos Aires, and its branches in Rosario, Mendoza, and elsewhere.

"To that end, when I heard you were here, I dispatched an armored car, with a crew that has worked for me for years and can be trusted, to San Martín de los Andes. I told the driver to drop off sufficient bank bags — you know the type, heavy leather and lockable — at el Coronel Klausberger's office.

"What I want you to do now, Klausberger, is go back to San Martín and load those bags with the contents of the crates. My driver will take the bags off your hands at noon tomorrow."

Klausberger looked alarmed.

"I've cared for the . . . the special cargo . . . often before," he protested. "I can see no reason . . ."

Moreno glanced at him, then turned to Hoffmann.

"I don't wish to debate this, Herr Hoffmann," Moreno said. "If you prefer to leave the 'special cargo' in Colonel Klausberger's care, that's fine with me. My armored car will return to Buenos Aires, you and el Coronel can deal with General Martín, and I will conclude that our relationship is over."

"Over?" Hoffmann said softly.

"Over," Moreno confirmed. "Bluntly, if our business relationship is going to continue, it will have to be on my terms. I have no intention of putting Banco Suisse Creditanstalt — or myself — at risk."

"Now see here, Moreno!" Klausberger began, and was again silenced by Hoffmann's raised palm.

"We will, of course, listen to your wise advice," Hoffmann said. "But there is one question I hope you will have time to answer before you leave."

"Which is?"

"What about the assets in Uruguay?"

"You're referring to the Confidential Special Fund?"

Hoffmann nodded.

"I can understand your interest," Moreno

said. "I still don't have all the details, but this is what I know: SS-Brigadeführer Ritter Manfred von Deitzberg came here — aboard U-405, now that I think of it — in October 1943.

"I don't *know* this — I'm a banker, not a member of the Sicherheitsdienst — but I have concluded his orders were to take charge of the assets of the Confidential Special Fund."

Hoffmann said nothing.

"Herr Hoffmann, if I'm going to tell you what I know, or believe, you're going to have to do the same," Moreno said.

"Your information is correct," Hoffmann said.

"The Confidential Special Fund was then controlled by Sturmbannführer Werner von Tresmarck, the security officer of the German embassy in Montevideo, Uruguay."

He paused and waited for Hoffmann to say something.

"It was," Hoffmann said, after a pause.

"Anton von Gradny-Sawz, of the German embassy here, procured an Argentine identity document — a *libreta de enrolamiento,* same as I just got for you — for von Deitzberg in the name of Jorge Schenck. Von Deitzberg/Schenck then took the overnight steamer to Montevideo.

"His purpose was to see von Tresmarck, presumably to relieve him of the assets of the Confidential Special Fund. Frau Ingeborg von Tresmarck told him that her husband and his good friend Ramón Something were in Paraguay."

"Von Tresmarck is a homosexual, Señor Moreno," Hoffmann offered. "That is the reason he was sent to Uruguay to manage the Confidential Special Fund. Since his alternative was being sent to a *konzentrations-lager* with a pink star pinned to his breast, I thought he would appreciate the benefits of doing nothing that would annoy me, or even arouse any suspicions on my part about his performance of his duties."

That, Moreno thought, *was intended to remind me how important Brigadeführer Hoff-mann was in the Third Reich.*

I don't think he really understands that the Third Reich is finished and so is whatever authority he had.

"Yes, I knew that," Moreno said. "Well, von Deitzberg waited until von Tresmarck and his friend returned from Uruguay, and then had him transfer title of all the assets of the Confidential Special Fund to him. Then he gave him a large sum of money — nearly the equivalent of a million U.S. dollars — and then strongly suggested that he and his friend Ramón disappear.

"Von Deitzberg returned to Buenos Aires. I later learned from our branch manager in Montevideo that the embassy had reported to the police that both — husband and wife — had disappeared. The police had no idea where von Tresmarck was, but they had learned that Frau von Tresmarck had taken the steamer to Buenos Aires the next night.

"The Buenos Aires authorities learned that Señora von Tresmarck had taken a room at the Alvear Palace Hotel. She had then gone shopping, leaving a message to that effect with the hotel switchboard. She never returned to the Alvear Palace, and has not been seen — at least as Frau von Tresmarck — since.

"However, a woman matching her description, and calling herself Señora Schenck, was seen two weeks later in San Martín de los Andes, in the company of Señor Jorge Schenck, el Coronel Juan D. Perón, and Señorita Evita Duarte. El Coronel Perón went there to purchase a small estancia in the name of Señorita Duarte.

"While they were there, Brigadeführer von Deitzberg was shot to death in the men's room of the Rio Hermoso Hotel.

"Neither el Coronel Perón nor Señorita Duarte nor Señora Schenck was interrogated by the police about Señor Schenck's murder. This was probably at the order of President Rawson, who was then in the area dealing with the problem of el Coronel Schmidt."

"What problem was that?"

"Would you like to tell Herr Hoffmann, *el*

Coronel?" Moreno asked. "Or should I?"

"You'd better be damned careful what you say!" Klausberger said.

That bluster wasn't very convincing, Klausberger.

"Well, if I get anything wrong, please feel free to correct me," Moreno said. "As I understand the situation, el Coronel Schmidt was leading his regiment to an estancia outside Mendoza owned by Cletus Frade. He believed that there was an illegal cache of arms on the estancia and two diplomats who had disappeared from the German embassy in Buenos Aires —"

"Traitors, Herr Brigadeführer," Klausberger put in.

Hoffmann met his eyes and said, "You were the one, Herr Oberst, who suggested we no longer use my rank."

Hoffmann turned back and said, "Please go on, Señor Moreno."

"Once Schmidt had confiscated the arms cache, he apparently intended to stage a coup against President Rawson. Am I right so far, el Coronel Klausberger?"

Klausberger nodded curtly.

"Rawson, however, had learned of the plot. He and Señor Frade and some troops of the Húsares de Pueyrredón met the regiment on the highway. Schmidt attempted to place President Rawson under arrest, whereupon Frade shot Schmidt and at least one of the officers with him. The regiment was then placed under the command of its sergeant major and ordered to return to its barracks. Which it did. Did I get anything wrong, Klausberger, or leave anything out?"

Klausberger didn't respond.

"What I believe happened," Moreno went on, "was that President Rawson, on learning that el Coronel Perón was in San Martín, feared that Perón might be connected with Schmidt's coup. I don't think he was, but Rawson had no way to know. Permitting Perón to return immediately and quietly to Buenos Aires, and then pretending not to know he had been there, solved that problem.

"I have subsequently learned that Señora Schenck was awarded all of her late husband's property — the Confidential Special Fund assets — by judges known to be friendly to el Coronel Perón and that, presumably as an expression of her gratitude, she subsequently transferred half of what she received to Señorita Duarte."

"Who shot von Deitzberg?" Hoffmann asked.

"I really have no knowledge of that, but it probably has something to do with the German officers — members, I have heard, of the former Abwehr Ost — Frade is rumored to have brought here from Germany."

"And what is that all about?" Hoffmann asked.

"I have no idea," Moreno said. He looked at his wristwatch. "Well, I really have to go. And so do you, Klausberger. Can I offer you a ride?"

"No, thank you," Klausberger said.

Moreno walked to each of them in turn, wordlessly shook hands, and then left the room, stopping only to help himself to the hors d'oeuvres on the table.

When he had been gone at least sixty seconds, Klausberger said, "I'd like to kill that Swiss bastard."

"So would I," Hoffmann said. "Even more, Herr Frade. He's given us trouble ever since he came to Argentina. But we won't take them out just yet. We still need Moreno, and I want to find out what Herr Frade is doing with General Gehlen's Abwehr Ost people before we kill him."

■ ■ ■ ■

V

■ ■ ■ ■

[ONE]

Hotel Vier Jahreszeiten
Maximilianstrasse 178
Munich, American Zone, Germany
1820 10 October 1945

There were two signs over the door to the off-the-lobby restaurant of the hotel. One read RESTAURANT MAXIMILIAN and the other OFFICERS' OPEN MESS.

"Let's get something to eat," First Sergeant Tiny Dunwiddie said to Second Lieutenant James D. Cronley Jr. as he pointed to it.

First sergeants are enlisted men and don't get to eat in an officers' mess. Cronley didn't say anything, but his surprise registered on his face and Dunwiddie saw it.

"Not to worry, Lieutenant, sir. This place is loaded with CIC, and I can probably pass myself off as one of those special agents, like you, sir."

A headwaiter led them to a table without questioning Dinwiddie's right to be messing with his social betters.

A waiter appeared.

"Two glasses of your finest beer, if you please, Herr Ober," Dunwiddie ordered in flawless German. "And then a menu."

Then he made a pointing gesture to Cronley with the hand he had resting almost regally on the linen tablecloth.

Cronley followed the pointing to the next table, at which sat a spectacular — tall, very blond, and magnificently assembled — female and her escort, a plump young man, no older than twenty-one, who looked Jewish and was wearing pinks and greens with "civilian triangles" sewn to the lapels.

"Spectacular," Cronley said.

"My sentiments exactly," Dunwiddie said. "He's probably regaling her with tales of his exciting life in the CIC, which I would say is going to see him in her bed — or vice versa — in the near future."

Cronley could hear enough of the couple's conversation in German to conclude that Tiny was right on the money.

The couple finished their meal and left just as Tiny's and Jimmy's entrees were being served. The blonde, who they now saw towered at least a head over her escort, was even more spectacular when viewed from the rear.

Dunwiddie again read Jimmy's mind: "I have always been an ass man myself," he said, and when Cronley smiled, went on: "I never asked. Did you leave a fur-line behind in

Marburg?"

"No," Cronley replied immediately. When he saw the look on Tiny's face, he explained, "My father met my mother in Strasbourg after the First World War."

"And you're uncomfortable 'taking advantage'?"

"I guess."

"Oddly enough, so am I," Dunwiddie said, and then asked, "You haven't gotten laid since you came to Germany?"

"I didn't say that."

"Who is she?"

"Didn't Norwich teach you that gentlemen don't tell?"

"What Norwich taught me was to seek inspiration from great leaders."

"Meaning what?"

"General George S. Patton, who I suggest qualifies as a great leader, said, 'A soldier who won't fuck won't fight.' I have taken that advice to heart."

"So, you have a fräulein?"

"I didn't say that. What I did was agree with the opinion of Oscar Wilde, who said, 'Celibacy is the most unusual of all the perversions.' "

Cronley chuckled. "I never heard that."

"We of Norwich tend to have greater erudition than you Aggies."

"So then what do you do?"

"Well, since I certainly don't want to be accused of practicing the most unusual of all perversions, I decided that I would have to enter into business relationships with practitioners of the world's oldest profession."

"You find yourself a whore," Jimmy said.

"When my libido gets out of control, I find a *prostitute,* not a whore."

"What's the difference?"

"You pay a prostitute for services rendered, and that's the end of it."

My God, he's got it right. That's what I should do.

I can't spend the next two years — or however long I'm going to be in Germany — with a perpetual raging hard-on.

Dunwiddie again read his mind.

"Why, Lieutenant, do I think I have just solved one of your more pressing problems?"

"Where would I find one of these professional ladies?"

"In Munich. I shall have to make discreet inquiries. What you should not do is go to one of the ladies walking up and down on the sidewalk. You saw the movies — your male appendage turns black and falls off. You must have seen those movies."

"I saw them. And then you go crazy and die."

"Exactly. I'd love to know where that fat little man met the blonde."

"Maybe we can find him and ask."

"He's funny-looking, but he also looked

smart. He wouldn't tell us, and in any event, we don't know what Major Harold N. Wallace has in mind for us to do."

Cronley had a very clear mental image of Elsa in her see-through underwear and then of her without it.

A business relationship it is going to have to be.

I can't go on this way.

Cronley followed Dunwiddie down the carpeted fifth floor of the hotel looking for Room 507.

"Here it is," Dunwiddie announced.

There was a small, neatly lettered sign nailed to the door: XXVII CIC DET.

Dunwiddie pushed it open, went in, and Jimmy followed.

This isn't a room, Cronley immediately decided when he saw how the room was furnished.

More like the Presidential Suite. Or the Reichsführer Suite.

The plump young man from the dining room was sitting behind an ornate gilded desk.

"What do you want?" the young man challenged in a thick German accent.

"Who are you?" Tiny Dunwiddie challenged.

"I am asking the questions," the young man said.

It came out *"duh k-vestions"* — the accent so thick that Cronley smiled.

"Well, you don't get any answers until I hear who you are," Dunwiddie replied.

An interior door opened and Major Harold N. Wallace, wearing insignia-less pinks and greens, came into the room.

"Well, I see you've found us in all this squalor," Wallace said.

"Yes, sir," Tiny and Jimmy said in chorus.

"Say hello to Sergeant Friedrich — Freddy — Hessinger," Wallace said. "Freddy, this is First Sergeant Dunwiddie, and I think I should warn you that his bite is just about as bad — maybe a little worse — than his bark. And this is Second Lieutenant Cronley, who unlike most second lieutenants seems to know what he's doing."

Hessinger smiled uncomfortably and said, formally, "How do you do?"

Cronley had to smile again at both the formality and the accent.

"Well, come on in," Wallace said, and waved them through the door. "You better come, too, Freddy."

Through the door was a luxuriously furnished sitting room, equipped with a desk even more ornate than Hessinger's, and off of which three doors opened. One of them was ajar and Cronley could see an enormous bed.

"Sit," Wallace ordered, indicating two chairs

and a couch, all ornately carved and upholstered, facing his desk.

"We have heard from our master, now
ensconced in the I.G. Farben Building, right
behind the throne of Eisenhower," Wallace
said. "So where to begin?" he asked rhetorically, and then began.

"Welcome to the CIC, Tiny," he said.

"Sir?"

Wallace opened a drawer in his desk, took
out something — Cronley thought it looked
like a leather CIC credentials wallet — and
tossed it to Dunwiddie. He examined it, then
tossed it to Cronley.

It was indeed a set of CIC special agent
credentials, badge and plastic-sealed identity
card providing the photo, physical description, and name of the agent: CHAUNCEY L.
DUNWIDDIE.

"Chauncey?" Cronley asked, smiling.

"Fuck you, with all possible respect, Lieutenant, sir."

"Colonel Mattingly said to tell you that
while he thinks these credentials will probably prove useful, he doesn't think you should
tell anybody about them, or rush off to the
Officers' Sales Store to buy pinks and greens.
Got it?"

"Yes, sir."

"Just get another Ike jacket and sew the
triangles on it, for use as needed," Wallace
said, pointing to one of the small blue tri-

angles with the letters "US" inside them on his lapels.

"Yes, sir."

"Those ordinarily come with a .38 S&W snub-nosed," Wallace said, indicating the credentials. "You want one?"

"Absolutely," Tiny said.

"Colonel Mattingly thought you would think the .38 was beneath the dignity of a cavalryman," Wallace said. "That you would prefer the 1911-A1 .45."

"I'm curious. I've never shot one of those little snub-nose .38s."

"Freddy here shot Expert on the range at Camp Holabird with one," Wallace said. "Which brings us to him. Or, more precisely, to that subject.

"Freddy, like you, Jim, is a graduate of one of those abbreviated classes at Holabird. The CIC needs German-speaking people to run down Nazis. Many of them, like Freddy, are German Jews who have a personal interest in seeing that Nazis are rounded up. While this is of course a noble endeavor, it is somewhat at odds with our mission. How many of you were there on the plane, Freddy?"

"There were twenty-two of us, sir."

"Colonel Mattingly had a chat with each of the twenty-two," Wallace said. "And he liked Freddy for two reasons. One, Freddy wants to be an historian when he gets out of the Army, and the colonel, as you know, was a professor of history."

Second Lieutenant Cronley thought: *Mattingly was a what?*

"The second thing that caused the colonel to look fondly upon Freddy," Wallace went on, "is that he said Freddy was the only one who had ever heard of the Communists — frankly, I think this was a bit of hyperbole — much less regarded them as a major threat to anything.

"After giving Freddy what has now become a standard cautionary note vis-à-vis Operation Ost — 'Reveal any of this to anyone and we'll kill you' — the colonel told him what we're doing here.

"This included telling him that while, thank God, Secretary of the Treasury Morgenthau has left government service, he left in place a large number of people as devoted as he was to running down Nazis wherever found. For example, in Kloster Grünau or even in Argentina.

"He also told Freddy of his concern that — with the most noble of motive — the CIC Nazi hunters, especially those of the Hebrew persuasion, would happily share with these people whatever they had heard — fact and rumor — about Nazis being in Kloster Grünau or even in Argentina, and this would be unfortunate for Operation Ost.

"The colonel told me he realized that there should be — had to be — two branches of the CIC in USFET — one dedicated to finding Nazis and the other to frustrating the Soviets. And he realized that the structure to do this was fortuitously already in place, the Twenty-seventh CIC Detachment. At the time, there were only two personnel assigned to the Twenty-seventh, Second Lieutenant Cronley and myself. Now there are four, counting you two.

"The colonel also told me he realized the Twenty-seventh would itself have to have two divisions, one of them nameless and secret and charged with the support and security of General Gehlen and his people — Operation Ost. The other would perform more or less routine counterintelligence operations involving the Soviets. The colonel feels their activities will provide a credible cover for the activities of the unnamed section. They will know nothing of the unnamed section."

He paused, looking between them.

"Getting the picture?" Wallace said.

"Where does Hessinger fit in?" Dunwiddie asked.

"General Gehlen told the colonel he thinks we have to expect the Soviets will try to kidnap anyone they think knows anything about Operation Ost. While Freddy will know no more than he absolutely has to about the details of Operation Ost — in case the Soviets grab him, the less he knows the better — but he will serve as the contact between Kloster

Grünau and me."

"Got it," Dunwiddie said.

"And turning to the subject of contact," Wallace said. "There is no way I could operate a semi-clandestine radio station in the Vier Jahreszeiten, so you get the Collins and the SIGABA."

Collins? SIGABA? Cronley thought.

Semi-clandestine radio station?

What the hell is he talking about?

"Yes, sir," Dunwiddie said.

"Bring Lieutenant Cronley up to speed on that."

"Yes, sir."

"What are you driving?"

"A Kapitän, sir."

"I'm not sure the Collins and the SIGABA will fit in a Kapitän," Wallace said. "But that's not going to be a problem. I got you another three ambulances . . ."

Three ambulances?

Oh, the ones with the Red Crosses painted over.

". . . so you can put the SIGABA and the Collins in one of them and drive home. They're in the basement garage."

"Yes, sir."

"*You* drive the ambulance, Mr. Dunwiddie, as second lieutenants are not supposed to drive ambulances. It's beneath their dignity, and we don't want to draw attention to us with an undignified lieutenant, do we?"

295

"No, sir."

"And when you get home, send someone to pick up the other ambulances. I want to get them out of here before anyone asks where I got them."

"Yes, sir."

"Spend the night here — I don't want to risk damage to the SIGABA if you hit a pothole. Leave first thing in the morning."

"Yes, sir."

"Can you think of anything else, Hessinger?" Major Wallace asked.

"No, sir."

"What do we do, sir? Check into the hotel?" Dunwiddie asked.

"Not necessary. I requisitioned this entire floor. I don't know what I'm going to do with all the space, but I didn't want anybody else in it."

Wallace looked at his watch.

"Well, that's it. I'm off to see the Wizard . . ."

Now what the hell does that mean?

". . . call Freddy when you're set up with Vint Hill."

"Yes, sir."

"Code phrase 'I talked to Virginia.' The Wizard really doesn't want anyone to know about the SIGABA and the Collins, and I don't think we should trust the ground lines between here and the Kloster."

"Should I try to call Argentina, sir?"

"Yes, and set up a schedule. The Wizard can't put an antenna on the Farben building either."

Aha! The Wizard is Colonel Mattingly.

"Yes, sir."

"Oh, what a tangled web, right, Tiny?" Wallace asked.

"Yes, sir."

"I told Freddy to get you anything you need," Wallace said, as he offered his hand to everybody in turn. Then he walked out of the room.

Anyplace else, we'd have been called to attention, been dismissed, and then exchanged salutes.

Welcome to Oz, Lieutenant Cronley!

"I have the keys to your rooms outside," Hessinger said. "Is there anything you need tonight before I go?"

You're back to that spectacular blonde, you mean?

They followed him to the outer room. He handed them enormous keys attached to even larger brass room number tags.

"Is there anything?" Hessinger repeated.

"We understand why you're so anxious to leave, Hessinger. We saw the blonde," Tiny said.

"She seeks employment as a translator," Hessinger said simply. "I am trying to help her."

"Of course you are," Tiny said.

297

"If you are asking if she is available, of course she is. But not for a box of Hershey bars."

"Never buy cheap shoes or rent cheap courtesans, Hessinger. You agree?"

Hessinger bent over his desk and scrawled an address on a slip of paper.

"It's not far. I recommend that you walk."

"Presumably she has friends?"

"Many friends."

"May we say that you sent us?"

"Of course."

"There is something you can do for me, Sergeant," Cronley then said.

"Yes, sir?"

"You have access to the files on the people we're looking for?"

Hessinger nodded. "Of course, sir."

Tiny's curiosity was visible on his face, but he said nothing.

"We recently picked up a woman, a Category Four. You know what that means?"

"Yes, sir."

"I'd like a look at her dossier. Can you get it for me?"

"Right now, sir?"

"Before we go back to the Kloster."

"If you and First Sergeant Dunwiddie are going out, sir, I could have it waiting for you in your room by the time you come back."

"That'll do fine. Her name is Frau Elsa von Wachtstein. Should I spell that for you?"

"That's enough, sir."

"Good man, Hessinger," Jimmy said.

In the elevator, Tiny said, "Because I am now a CIC agent and a simulated gentleman, I won't ask you what that was all about."

"Good, because it's none of your fucking business."

Two hours later, their mission to find companionship having been successful, Tiny pointed to a sign in the lobby of the hotel reading OFFICERS' CLASS VI SALES.

Class VI was the Army euphemism for distilled spirits.

"One way for you to show me your gratitude for finding that energetic redhead for you would be for you to go in there and buy us a bottle of Rémy Martin."

"To drink while I now wait for my dick to turn black and fall off?"

"To drink while we consider our philosophical discussion of the differences between whores and courtesans."

"What the hell — why not?"

There was a well-stuffed manila envelope on the desk in Cronley's room. It bore a red mark across it, on which the word SECRET was printed.

There was a handwritten note on it: *I hope this is the right one. Sgt Hessinger.*

"Let me wash a couple of glasses," Tiny said. "There's some on that table."

Cronley sat down at the desk and ripped open the envelope flap.

The envelope contained several folders. In the second were four photographs of Elsa. Three showed her with a man who was obviously the late Oberstleutnant Graf von Wachtstein. The fourth showed her in a skimpy bathing suit on the bank of a narrow river.

God, she's beautiful!

Tiny set a brandy snifter on the desk.

"Is that the lady causing you to wallow in remorse because of your recent infidelity?"

"How the fuck could I be unfaithful to her? She thinks I'm a boy. And she's in fucking Argentina."

"Hans-Peter von Wachtstein's widowed sister-in-law? That's who you . . . found sexual relief with?"

"Fuck you, Tiny."

"You promised her something — or implied something — to get in her pants and didn't deliver? Is that what's bothering you?"

"I didn't know about the brother-in-law. Before Mattingly showed up in Marburg, before I knew what was going on, I told her she didn't have to worry, I was . . . I was in a . . . a position to help her."

"You told her you were rich?"

Dunwiddie then saw the look on Cronley's face, and explained: "Mattingly showed me

300

your dossier before you came down from Marburg."

"Yeah. And her reaction was to make me promise I would never tell another German woman. She was afraid they'd take advantage of me."

"And they would. She was right."

"I'm in love with her."

"She is thirty-something. You're twenty-one. And you better hope Mattingly never finds out you screwed her."

"I don't really give a damn if he does."

"Come on! Operation Ost needs you."

"Needs *me*? I'm a twenty-one-year-old second lieutenant."

"Charged with protecting what is probably the number one secret project going. Maybe somebody could do that better, but you have the job. You and me, *Lieutenant.* This is for real."

"So, what should I do?"

"Close that dossier and give it back to Hessinger and forget it and her."

"And then what?"

"Pull your necktie back up and we'll go back to the whorehouse and tie one on. We don't have to leave first thing in the morning. Wallace won't be back until late tomorrow, if then."

When Cronley didn't reply, Dunwiddie said, "Drink your cognac."

Cronley stood. He picked up the cognac

snifter and drained it.

Then he bent over the dossier, opened the metal fastener over the photos, and removed the picture of Elsa in her bathing suit.

"That's not smart, Jimmy," Dunwiddie said as Cronley closed the metal clasp.

"She's gone. Nobody's going to open this and count pictures."

"I meant for you. Are you going to get all wet-eyed every time you look at it?"

"I don't know. I hope not. We'll just have to see."

He pulled his necktie in place.

"I have another confession to make."

"Oh, Christ, now what?"

"That was the first time I was ever in a whorehouse."

"I would not have suspected that, judging by your behavior. You seem to have a natural talent for that sort of recreation."

[Two]

Kloster Grünau
Schollbrunn, Bavaria, Germany
0950 11 October 1945

"Well, let's see if it works," Dunwiddie said.

"How do we do that?" Cronley asked.

"Pray, and then try this."

He typed rapidly on the SIGABA keyboard. A strip of paper came out of the machine.

Dunwiddie ripped it off and showed it to Cronley.

FROM TANKER TWO TO VINT HILL SPECIAL SIGNING ON NET ACKNOWLEDGE

Dunwiddie then fed the strip into the SIGABA, which swallowed it.

"Now what?"

"This is where we pray again."

Thirty seconds later, a paper strip began to come out of the SIGABA. After thirty seconds, it stopped. Dunwiddie tore it off, read it, and handed it to Cronley.

"Thank you, God," Dunwiddie said.

That didn't sound sarcastic, Cronley thought.

As he began to read the strip — *FROM VINT HILL TO TANKER TWO WELCOME TO THE NET MESSAGES FOLLOWING HAVE NOT REPEAT NOT BEEN ACKNOWLEDGED BY TANKER OR FLAGS PLEASE RELAY IF POSSIBLE AND ACKNOWLEDGE RECEIPT OR FAILURE* — tape began to stream from the machine again.

This took about five minutes, and this time Dunwiddie didn't even try to read it, instead feeding it back in the SIGABA machine. The teletypewriter-like keyboard began to clatter, as if invisible hands were pushing the keys.

What this produced on the teletypewriter were the two messages — TEX-0013 and TEX-0014 — Frade had sent from Estancia San Pedro y San Pablo just after noon the day before.

After Dunwiddie had explained the code

names and the general meaning of the message, which took more than enough time for Cronley to decide he was in way over his head with whatever this was, Dunwiddie made it worse.

"Well," Tiny announced, "here's where you start earning your keep, even if you are a twenty-one-year-old wet-behind-the-ears second john who can find only — and with difficulty — one cheek of his ass with both hands."

"When you are finished with kissing said ass, First Sergeant Dunwiddie, you are going to explain that, right?"

"Well, the reason the colonel didn't get these is because he can't hang a Collins antenna out his office window in the Farben building — people might ask questions — any more than Major Wallace can hang one out his bedroom window in the Vier Jahreszeiten. Which means, since this is obviously important, I have to get it to them.

"The problem there is that the landlines are not secure, which means I can't get on the telephone. The ASA —"

"The what?"

"The Army Security Agency, which not only listens to Russian radio traffic but is also charged with providing secure communications to people like us."

"Okay."

"The ASA is right now installing such

secure communications for the South German Industrial Development Organization in Pullach."

"That's what we're going to call Operation Ost, right?"

"You get a gold star to take home to Mommy for remembering that. But since that's not yet up, and anyway we're here, not at Pullach, that's not a solution to our problem.

"Which means I'm going to have to go back to Munich. Maybe Wallace will be able to solve our problem. But maybe Wallace won't be there.

"Which means I probably will have to go to Frankfurt.

"Which means you will be here dealing with the dossiers. When I'm at the Vier Jahreszeiten, I will tell Sergeant Hessinger to send his blonde back to the village and get these dossiers from wherever he got the one about your girlfriend. But as I suspect Gehlen's people have better dossiers than G-2 does, you will get the dossiers from them while I'm gone. Got all that?"

"How am I supposed to get Gehlen's dossiers?"

"Well, off the top of my head, asking General Gehlen might work."

"General Gehlen personally?"

"If you ask anyone else, Herr — former Oberst — Mannberg, for example, I think ol'

Ludwig would go ask the general if he should give that Wet Behind the Ears *Ami* Leutnant the time of day, much less any dossiers from their files. If you ask General Gehlen first, it'll save time."

"And if General Gehlen says, in effect, go fuck yourself, Herr Leutnant Cronley, then what do I do?"

"Be firm."

"Tiny, you can't leave me alone to handle this."

"Say 'Post,' " Dunwiddie said.

"What?"

"Say 'Post.' "

"Post."

"Yes, sir!" Dunwiddie bellowed, then popped to attention, saluted crisply, performed a perfect about-face movement, and marched out of the room.

"I'll be a sonofabitch!" Cronley said aloud, although he was now alone.

After sitting deep in thought for at least a minute, he got out of his chair and went to the building entrance.

Technical Sergeant Abraham L. (for Lincoln) Tedworth, who was nearly as large and almost as black as First Sergeant Dunwiddie, sat in an armchair with a Thompson submachine gun in his lap.

He stood as Cronley approached.

"Sir?"

"I need to see General Gehlen."

"Yes, sir. I'll give the general your compliments, sir."

Five minutes later, Herr (formerly Oberst) Ludwig Mannberg walked into the office.

Mannberg, who had ranked high in the Abwehr Ost hierarchy, was wearing a finely tailored uniform from which the insignia had been removed. His breeches still bore the red stripe identifying members of the General Staff Corps.

He didn't salute but he came to attention and clicked his heels.

"Herr Gehlen is not available," he said, in perfect, British-accented English. "May I be of some assistance?"

I'm not going to let you get away with that, Herr Oberst.

"I need to know what information, perhaps the dossiers, Abwehr Ost has on these people," Cronley said in German. He handed him TEX-0014.

"You speak German like a Strasbourger," Mannberg said.

"My mother is a Strasbourger."

"So is mine," Mannberg said.

He examined the list of names.

"At least half of the people on this list learned from us," he said.

"Excuse me?"

"They managed to have themselves reported as having been killed," Mannberg said. "This fellow, SS-Brigadeführer Ludwig Hoffmann, is a particularly nasty bastard. May I ask where you got this list?"

Among the many things Good Ol' Tiny didn't tell me was what, if anything, I could tell Gehlen's officers.

Fuck it! If this has been dumped on me, I'll deal with it my way.

"They are reported to have been landed in Argentina from a submarine. U-405."

"That U-boat used to be commanded by a friend of mine — actually a family friend, our fathers were friends and my younger brother was with him at university, Philipps, in Marburg. That's presuming we're talking about Fregattenkapitän Wilhelm von Dattenberg."

"That's the guy," Cronley said.

Should I have admitted that?

He's a very bright, very senior intelligence officer. One easily capable of taking advantage of a wet-behind-the-ears second lieutenant who has no idea what the fuck he's doing.

Once again, fuck it. Go for broke.

"That makes sense," Mannberg said. "Von Dattenberg was one of the better U-boat skippers. Himmler would order the best to get them out of Germany. I will undertake this task with pleasure, Herr Leutnant. These are the people who brought Germany to what and where it is today. They should not be allowed to escape the wrath of decent Germans. I presume you want this information quickly?"

"The sooner the better."

"I'll get right on it. Is there anything else?"

"Not right now."

"Then with your permission, Herr Leutnant," Mannberg said, popped to attention, clicked his heels, and walked out of the office.

[THREE]

Office of the President
Casa Rosada
Plaza de Mayo, Buenos Aires, Argentina
1215 12 October 1945

General de Brigada Bernardo Martín marched into the president's office, stopped in front of the presidential desk, and saluted.

General Edelmiro Julián Farrell, the twenty-eighth president of Argentina, who was slightly built and whose pale skin reflected his Irish ancestry, returned the salute. He then rose and came around the desk, offered his hand, and patted Martín's back.

"We don't often see you in uniform, Bernardo," Farrell said. "What's the occasion?"

"Sir, I was in Puerto Belgrano, at the naval base arranging the movement of the U-405 crew to General Villa Belgrano. Dealing with the navy, I thought being in uniform . . ."

Farrell nodded his understanding.

"Did you manage to get that submarine captain to say anything?"

"He finally admitted to have put sixteen SS officers and five heavy wooden crates ashore on the San Matias Gulf. He said he didn't know what was in the crates, sir, but almost certainly it was currency and other valuables."

"And where are they, and these crates, now?"

"I don't know, sir. My fault. A week before this happened, I pulled my coast watchers off the job. I thought we'd seen the last of the German submarines, and I needed my people to deal with our other problem."

"But you have suspicions?"

"Only suspicions, sir. Nothing I can prove."

"If you had to guess?"

"In Patagonia, sir."

"You think el Coronel Klausberger was involved with smuggling these people into Argentina?"

"Sir, you asked me to guess."

"When I became president, el Coronel Perón made the point to me that el General Rawson had gone much too far when he charged Klausberger with treason."

Martín did not reply.

"You didn't," Farrell said. It was both a question and a statement, and again Martín did not reply.

"Bernardo, the last thing I want — and the

last thing you want — is a Spanish Civil War here. Court-martialing Klausberger — or even bringing him before a court of honor — might well have triggered such a war. So I accepted Juan Domingo's suggestion that I assign Klausberger to duty in the Edificio Libertador. And then, more than a year later, I accepted Perón's suggestion that he be given command of the Tenth Mountain Regiment. And there was no civil war during that year."

Martín remained mute.

"And you think I made a mistake," Farrell said, and again it was both a question and a statement.

"*Mi Presidente,* I serve you. I never have and never will question your decisions."

"I know. And I hope you know how much I appreciate that." He paused and then went on: "Is my returning Klausberger to the Tenth Mountain Regiment one of the reasons half of my officer corps talks of assassinating Perón? They think he has too much influence on me?"

"Sir, I believe that to be the case. And then there is Señorita Duarte."

"Who, as we speak, is mobilizing the — what does she call them? 'The Shirtless Ones'? — to protest Perón's arrest?"

Again it was both a question and a statement, and again Martín did not reply.

"How difficult a situation is that going to

be?" Farrell asked.

"I don't know, sir. I do know that Señor Rodolfo Nulder is assisting Señorita Duarte's efforts with the shirtless ones. And I believe, sir, that el Coronel Perón's association with Nulder is another reason some in the officer corps are annoyed with him."

"They're not just annoyed with him, Bernardo. They want to kill him."

"I'm afraid that's true, sir."

"How safe is he for the moment?"

"As far as I know, sir, no one in that group of officers knows we have him on Isla Martín García. But it's only a matter of time until they find out."

"We have to keep Juan Domingo alive. If he is hurt in any way, much less assassinated, we will have civil war. What about Cletus Frade? Is he going to . . . do anything?"

"Señor Frade told me, and I believe him, that he is going to do nothing with regard to el Coronel Perón unless you ask him to."

"God, I wish his father were alive and in this office!" President Farrell said. "He'd know how to deal with this."

"I've often thought the same thing, sir."

"Well, he's not. So I have to deal with what's going on. And the only thing I'm sure of is that we cannot allow Perón to be assassinated. And the only person I know who can do that, General Martín, is you."

"I will do my best, *mi Presidente*."

"I know," Farrell said. "But now, if you have nothing else for me?"

"With your permission, *mi Presidente*, I would like to parole the officers of the U-405, and then see where they go and who they contact."

"Do what you think has to be done."

Martín came to attention, saluted, did an about-face movement, and walked out of the room.

[FOUR]

Estancia San Pedro y San Pablo
Near Pila
Buenos Aires Province, Argentina
1620 12 October 1945

There was no airfield in the small mountain village of General Villa Belgrano, just a stretch of road on which a skilled pilot could land a small aircraft such as a Piper Cub or a Fieseler Storch.

Aware of these — and his own — limitations, General Bernardo Martín had driven directly from President Farrell's office in the Casa Rosada to Estancia San Pedro y San Pablo intending to first find Cletus Frade and then, if he was lucky, Hans-Peter von Wachtstein.

He was lucky, really lucky. Both were in one of the hangars at the airstrip, watching as

313

a mechanic did something to the engine of the Storch.

Wordlessly, they shook hands and patted each other's back. Martín waited for the inevitable needling he was to get over his uniform.

It came immediately.

"Let me guess, *mi General,*" Frade said. "You've just come from posing for a recruiting poster."

Martín ignored him, instead asking, "Is something wrong with the Storch?"

"Nothing that can't be fixed in a month," Frade said. "Why? Do you want another flying lesson?"

"I need a ride to Villa General Belgrano. I was hoping Peter could fly me there."

Nothing had ever been said, much less written, when Martín had arranged for the Argentine registration of the German embassy Storch that Tony Pelosi had somewhat grandiosely "seized in the name of the United States of America as booty of war" and then sold to Frade for ten pesos. But it was understood that Martín had certain rights in the now-civilian aircraft.

But both Frade and von Wachtstein were really uncomfortable when Martín elected to fly the aircraft himself, although both had taught him the basic — very basic — techniques of flying.

As Frade repeatedly warned him: "Thirty-odd hours in the air does not a Charles Lindbergh make, so to speak."

So neither had any problem with Hansel flying Bernardo anywhere. Not only was he a good guy, but they were deeply in his debt for many favors.

"You are going to tell us why, right?" Frade said.

"Because I don't think I can land the airplane on that dirt road," Martín said.

"Frankly, neither do I," Frade said, "but my question was: Why do you want Hansel to fly you to Villa General Belgrano?"

"Two reasons," Martín said. "The obvious, I don't want to crash trying to land on that road."

Von Wachtstein had a good deal of experience landing a Storch on the dirt road at Villa General Belgrano.

When the crew of the pocket battleship *Graf Spee* had been interned after the Battle of the River Plate, it had been decided to put them in Villa General Belgrano. Some said this was simply a decent thing to do. Settled by Germans starting in 1930, the village looked like it belonged in the Bavarian Alps; the internees would be comfortable there.

Others said the internees had been placed there because its location and the sympathies of the German population would facilitate the escape of the internees. Credence to the latter theory came when most of the officers and skilled technicians escaped within a year of their internment.

When Hansel had been Major von Wachtstein, the assistant military attaché for air of the embassy of the German Reich, he had flown to Villa General Belgrano at least twice a month, and sometimes more often, to deliver mail, pay the internees, and handle other administrative matters. He had flown in what was now Frade's flaming red Storch, then painted in the camouflage pattern of the Wehrmacht, and with a large swastika painted on its vertical stabilizer. The heroic recipient of the Knight's Cross of the Iron Cross had then been a welcome visitor.

"And the second reason?" Frade asked.

"I want Peter to have a word with von Dattenberg for me."

"He's there?" von Wachtstein asked, in surprise.

"He — and the rest of his crew — will be there by the time we get there."

Von Wachtstein looked at his wristwatch.

"Another two problems, Bernardo," von Wachtstein said. "If we left right now — and we can't — it would be dark by the time we got there."

"I'd hoped you could pick me up at Jorge Frade very early tomorrow morning," Martín said.

"You didn't have to drive all the way out here to ask me that," von Wachtstein said.

"And you know it. But I said 'two problems.' By now, Bernardo, they know. Somebody is sure to have told them."

What von Wachtstein did not say — did not have to say, because Martín had known almost from the first — was that for most of the time he had been a decorated hero of the Luftwaffe he had also been a traitor to der Führer and the Thousand-Year Reich by being Frade's — the OSS's — mole in the German embassy.

"I'm counting on that," Martín said.

"What the hell does that mean?" Frade challenged.

"You're the one who told me that the most amazing thing you found in Berlin was that there were absolutely no Nazis and everybody hated Hitler."

"Touché, *mi General,*" Frade said, with a chuckle.

"Why should the internees be any different, Peter?" Martín asked. "What nine out of ten of them are doing now is trying — desperately — to figure out how they can avoid getting shipped back to Germany and can stay, settle down, permanently in Villa General Belgrano. If you were popular delivering the payroll and their mail, wait until you see how they love you when they learn you're a close friend of the head of the BIS."

"Beware, Hansel," Frade said. "El General has some Machiavellian plan in mind."

"I'm just a simple airplane pilot . . ." von Wachtstein began.

That caused Frade to snort.

". . . so you'll have to explain that to me," von Wachtstein finished.

"There are several things I'd like to learn in Villa General Belgrano," Martín said. "One: Who has been aiding the escape of the *Graf Spee* officers?"

"Would you be surprised to learn that it was my beloved Tío Juan?" Frade asked sarcastically.

"Not at all," Martín said, ignoring the sarcasm. "But I just left President Farrell, and if I had photographs of Perón rowing SS-Brigadeführer Ludwig Hoffmann ashore in the San Matias Gulf, he wouldn't take any action against him if it looked to him — and it would — that it might set off a civil war. But if I can learn who actually had done the work for Perón, that's something else."

"How so?" von Wachtstein asked.

"If somehow that proof — and it would have to be incontrovertible — somehow came into the hands of the American ambassador and he presented it to the Foreign Ministry . . ."

"That won't work, Bernardo," Frade said.

"Why not?"

"Because you couldn't give it to Ambassador Alexander. I would have to."

"All right. You developed the intelligence.

You give it to your ambassador. What's wrong with that?"

"Ambassador Alexander came to see me. After he told me that our meeting never took place, he told me that I was never to go anywhere near the embassy."

"Because of your Operation Ost?"

Frade nodded.

"It would be bad enough if we were caught bringing Gehlen's people — some of whom are really nasty Nazis — here. Imagine the damage if it came out after we were self-righteously demanding the Argentine government stop doing the same thing."

Martín exhaled audibly.

"You're right," he said finally.

"Maybe we'll get lucky and the people who want to take out Juan Domingo will," Frade said.

"You don't mean that," Martín said.

"I don't know if I do or not," Frade said.

"And you weren't listening to what I said about starting a civil war," Martín said.

"I don't want a civil war," Frade said.

"I was in Spain for theirs," von Wachtstein said. "No, you don't."

"So, what do we do?" Frade asked.

"I don't know, but I still think going to Villa General Belgrano — having Peter fly me there — and seeing what we can find out is a good idea."

Frade nodded.

"Hansel," he said, "do not, repeat not, let Bernardo fly."

[FIVE]

General Villa Belgrano
Córdoba Province, Argentina
1520 13 October 1945

Oberleutnant zur See Rudolf Wechsler and Oberfähnrich zur See Erwin Vogel, who were interned members of the *Panzerschiff Graf Spee,* sat drinking beer at an outside table of the Café Wietz. They watched as the flaming red Storch taxied to the far end of the ad hoc runway — the road — turned, accelerated toward them, then took off.

In the U.S. Navy, Wechsler would have been a lieutenant (junior grade) and Vogel a chief petty officer. But they had other, secret, ranks as well. When they had been interned Wechsler had held the rank of *obersturmführer* of the Sicherheitsdienst and Vogel had held that of an SS-*sturmscharführer.*

On the *Graf Spee,* they had looked for any signs of disloyalty to the Führer or talk of defeatism. They had continued to do so in internment. Wechsler had been promoted to SS-*obersturmführer* and Vogel had been commissioned as an *untersturmführer* for their services in helping *Graf Spee* officers escape and return to Germany. And they had, of course, continued to look for disloyalty and defeatism among their former shipmates.

They had passed this information to the resident Sicherheitsdienst officer, SS-Oberst Karl-Heinz Grüner, the military attaché of the German embassy, whenever Major von Wachtstein had come to General Villa Belgrano.

Or they thought they had.

Now they knew better. Von Wachtstein had probably — laughing while he did — tossed their reports out of the Storch and Grüner had never seen them.

"Gottverdammter Verräter," Vogel said, sliding his beer mug on the table.

"Von Wachtstein certainly is a traitor," Wechsler agreed. "But we don't *know* that von Dattenberg is, do we?"

"With respect, he was ordered to scuttle his *U-boot* and instead surrendered it," Vogel said. "And he was not loaded onto that Storch in handcuffs, was he?"

"True," Wechsler agreed. "In any event, we have to bring this to Brigadeführer Hoffmann's attention. And we can't use the telephone to do that. So you'll have to drive to San Carlos de Bariloche."

[SIX]

Estancia San Pedro y San Pablo
Near Pila
Buenos Aires Province, Argentina
1910 13 October 1945

"Well, we won't have to go all the way to Estancia Santa Catalina," Peter von Wachtstein's voice announced in Fregattenkapitän von Dattenberg's headset over the Storch's intercom. "There they are."

Von Wachtstein pointed out the left window.

Von Dattenberg looked where he pointed.

A very large convertible sedan, roof down, was speeding along a macadam road that cut through the grassland of the Pampas. At first they couldn't see it very well, but that quickly changed as the Storch sort of dived at it.

"What is that, a Rolls-Royce?" von Dattenberg asked.

"My mother-in-law's," von Wachtstein confirmed. "Apparently, they're already on their way to Estancia San Pedro y San Pablo."

"How can you tell they're going there?"

"That's the only place the road goes, Willi."

They were now much closer to the ground — dangerously close, in the non-professional opinion of von Dattenberg — and moving very slowly. It was possible to see the occupants of the vehicle. There was a woman in the front seat beside the driver, and two younger women in the backseat.

One of the younger women in the back waved as the plane passed.

"That's my wife, Willi. The woman beside her is my sister-in-law, Elsa. You knew her, right? Karl's widow? She just got here."

Von Wachtstein stood the Storch on its wing, made a 180-degree turn, and flew over the Rolls again, this time approaching it from the rear.

The woman in the front seat stood and, holding on to the windshield that was between the front and rear seats, shook her fist at the Storch.

"And the formidable one is Claudia, my mother-in-law," von Wachtstein said, laughing. "She doesn't like to be buzzed. When we get to Estancia San Pedro y San Pablo, I'll tell her you were flying."

He retracted the flaps, added several hundred feet of altitude, and flew down the road.

Doña Claudia Carzino-Cormano, a svelte woman in her late fifties who wore her luxuriant gray-flecked black hair pulled tight on her skull, had just about regained control of her temper in the fifteen minutes it took the Rolls to drive to Estancia San Pedro y San Pablo from where it had been intercepted on the road.

She descended graciously — even regally — from the front seat of the Rolls and advanced on the party waiting for her, embracing first Doña Dorotea Mallín de Frade and then Doña Dorotea's husband.

"Just like your father, Cletus, always showing off," Doña Claudia said. "Even when you're endangering your life and those of others."

"With God and Dorotea as my witness, Claudia," Frade, smiling broadly, replied, "that was not me in the Storch. It was our Hansel."

"And you know he hates being called Hansel," Doña Claudia said.

She turned to Peter, giving him first her hand and then her cheek to kiss.

"I don't believe for a moment that was you, darling," she said.

"Momma, I don't even know what you're talking about," Peter said.

"The hell you don't! You're as bad as Cletus," she snapped.

"And that's bad," Frade said. "Shame on you, Hansel!"

"Momma, may I present my old friend Fregattenkapitän Wilhelm von Dattenberg?" Peter said.

"Welcome to Argentina," Doña Claudia said.

Von Dattenberg took the extended hand, bowed, and clicked his heels. "An honor, madam."

"You're going to have to break that habit,"

Clete said, and when von Dattenberg looked at him in confusion, mockingly bowed far deeper than von Dattenberg and clicked his heels.

Von Dattenberg nodded.

Von Wachtstein frowned, but decided to let it ride.

"Willi, this is Alicia," Peter said.

"Peter's told me so much about you," Alicia said. "Welcome to Argentina."

"The baroness is as gracious as she is beautiful," Willi said.

"Beautiful yes, baroness no," Peter said.

Von Dattenberg looked at him in confusion.

"Unfortunately, with Karl and Kurt dead in Russia," Peter said evenly, "when those swine murdered my father in the execution hut in Berlin-Ploetzensee, I became the Graf von Wachtstein. This flower of Argentina is the Gräfin von Wachtstein."

"And I am His Magnificence Grand Duke Cletus the First of San Pedro y San Pablo," Frade said. "The blonde is the Grand Duchess Dorotea, and the fat little boy — by the way, his diaper needs changing — she's holding is His Royal Highness, Prince Cletus Junior."

Everyone looked at him in shock.

"Cletus," Doña Dorotea said, "that's not funny. It's cruel."

Frade was unrepentant.

"And the last time the Graf von Wachtstein here visited the family castle it looked to me — five to one — as if he was going to be nailed to the castle door to make it easier for the Red Army to skin him alive . . ."

"My God, Cletus!" Doña Claudia said, horrified.

". . . to send the message to his loyal subjects that the old days were gone, and the Soviets were now in charge. And if my little brother hadn't pulled Elsa there" — he pointed to her — "from a mile-long parade of refugees, she'd still be in Germany, wondering where she could find a crust of bread." He paused, then concluded, "This is Argentina, and this is now. And I've heard all I want about who ranks where in the *Almanach de Gotha*."

"Cletus!" Doña Claudia said furiously. "You owe Peter and Fregattenkapitän von Dattenberg an apology and —"

"And that's my point," Frade interrupted her. "He's no longer a *fregattenkapitän,* Claudia."

"— and one to the Baroness von Wachtstein," Claudia finished.

"Do you think of yourself as the Baroness von Wachtstein, Elsa?" Frade asked evenly.

Elsa met his eyes and shook her head.

"No," she said. "I don't. I thought about that last night at dinner, and at breakfast this morning. Looking at all that food, I realized that I had stopped thinking of myself as anything like that from the moment Jimmy took me to dinner in the American officers' club in Marburg an der Lahn."

She stopped and looked at von Dattenberg.

"Yes, Willi, where you and Kurt and Peter went to university. Jimmy took me to dinner in the Kurhotel. Remember that?"

"Jimmy?" Claudia asked. "Who's Jimmy?"

"He's sort of my little brother, Claudia," Frade said.

"Of course," von Dattenberg said. "I remember it well."

"Jimmy first got me some clean clothing — that uniform I was wearing when I arrived here — and then took me to dinner. It was more food than I'd seen in years. A huge steak and a baked potato and corn on the cob. The only reason I didn't gorge myself was that I knew what would happen if I did."

"I don't understand," Claudia said.

"If you've been starving for a while," Frade expained, "and then eat a good meal, and quickly, the body reacts."

He mimed throwing up.

"Good God, Cletus!" Claudia snapped.

"He's right," Elsa said. "So Jimmy waited patiently until I'd eaten maybe half of what I was served. And then we went to the basement of the hotel and Jimmy burned the clothing I had been wearing. When there was nothing left of it but ash, I told Jimmy, 'So ends my old life, and begins my new one.' "

She raised her eyes to von Dattenberg.

"Willi, I can't tell you how glad I am that you came through, and to see you here. But please don't call me baroness. That was in another life, a long time ago."

Doña Claudia wrapped her arms around her.

"I still don't understand any of this," Claudia said. "I didn't know until just now, Cletus, that you have a little brother."

"If I explained it to you, Claudia, I'd have to kill you," Frade said.

"Goddamn it, Clete!" Doña Dorotea said furiously.

"What I think we should do now," Frade said, "is open some wine. But before we do that, I'm going to take Willi with me and get him out of his sailor suit."

"Excuse me?"

"I didn't tell you, Willi," Peter said, "but you've just escaped from Villa General Belgrano."

"But I gave my parole to General Martín," von Dattenberg protested.

"He's released you from it," von Wachtstein said. "He's the one who told me to tell you you've escaped."

■ ■ ■ ■

VI

■ ■ ■ ■

[ONE]

Kloster Grünau
Schollbrunn, Bavaria, Germany
1400 15 October 1945

Second Lieutenant James D. Cronley Jr.,
First Sergeant Tiny Dunwiddie, and former
Oberst Ludwig Mannberg were sitting
around the large table that normally served
as the commanding officer's desk. It was literally covered with stacks of files.

Mannberg had suggested that "care be
exercised" to make sure that as few people as
possible knew what they were doing with the
files. Tiny had instructed Technical Sergeant
Abraham L. Tedworth that no one — not
even "Honest Abe" himself — was to open
the office until permission had been granted
over the telephone.

All three of them looked up with mingled
surprise, concern, and annoyance when they
heard the door open without so much as a
knock.

A moment later, all three sprang to attention.

Colonel Robert Mattingly was the intruder.

"At ease, gentlemen," he ordered, slapping his gloves against his leg. "But the next time I arrive — even unannounced — please have the band waiting to play 'Hail to the Chief.' "

Mattingly had added an Air Corps pilot's leather jacket to his usual somewhat spectacular uniform. That had not been a surprise; very little of his uniform was authorized in the first place.

Jesus Christ, Cronley thought, *he looks like Clark Gable — or at least some other movie star.*

Mattingly walked to each of them and offered his hand.

"I suspected that you would be sitting here twiddling your thumbs hoping for something to do to pass the time, so I brought you an L-4 full of more documents concerning the passengers of U-405. Plus an enormous stack of same that I held, not without discomfort, in my lap in my puddle jumper."

"We have a plethora of information, Colonel," Mannberg said in precise, British-accented English. "What we have been doing, so to speak, is separating the wheat from the chaff."

"That was the original intention, but there has been a change of strategy," Mattingly announced. "I will explain. I have always held the thought of how nice it would be if we could enlist General Martín in our cause."

"The man who heads the . . . ?" Mannberg began to ask.

"The Argentine Bureau of Internal Security, the BIS," Mattingly furnished. "He has been cooperating for a long time. If he was going to betray us, he would already have done so. I think he believes, either professionally or philosophically, that allowing these people to establish themselves in Argentina is not in Argentina's best interests. And Colonel Frade trusts him completely.

"How nice it would be, I thought, if we could show the general our appreciation for his past services by giving him access to our intelligence — including of course that of the South German Industrial Development Organization regarding the Nazis who have made it safely to Argentina. Doing so would, I thought, encourage him to continue, perhaps even with enthusiasm, his cooperation in the future.

"I realized this would be difficult — virtually impossible — for several reasons, including that I hadn't yet found a solution to get the dossiers of these scoundrels Colonel Frade asked for to Argentina.

"The problem, as I'm sure you all have realized, was twofold. First of all, the dossiers should really never leave our control, even to accommodate Colonel Frade. All we can do

333

in this situation is make new files from the material you pluck from General Gehlen's originals.

"The only way around this problem would be if we had the capability to copy all of US-FET G-2's, and General Gehlen's, files. And there is no such capability. Right?"

"No, there is not," Dunwiddie said with finality. "Maybe we could use the Corps of Engineers' blueprint machines. That's sort of a photocopy. But that would take forever."

"It would take forever," Mattingly agreed. "And if we made copies using the Army's 'Certified True Copy' procedure — typing everything, or hand-drawing maps, et cetera, and then having each page signed by a commissioned officer swearing on his honor as an officer and a gentleman that the page is a true copy — that would not only take forever, but I doubt if General Martín would be very impressed with that, even if signed by our very own Second Lieutenant Cronley."

He paused long enough to let that sink in, and then said, "Two days ago, I somewhat reluctantly attended a briefing in the Farben building. It was presented by the Signal Corps Intelligence Service. That is the official euphemism for the unit charged with seeing what of a technical nature can be stolen from one's defeated enemy.

"They demonstrated a number of devices, including a gadget that permits recording on wire. It is fascinating. I requisitioned three of these devices, and when Major Wallace and I are finished playing with them — Wallace is, you will recall, Signal Corps and presumably knows how to deal with such things — we will send one here for your edification and amusement.

"The last device they showed us was at the very end of their presentation — so late that it was only by the grace of God that I was still awake, proving once again that the Lord looks fondly upon the pure in heart. You may wish to write that down, Cronley. It may keep you out of brothels."

What? Cronley thought.

The only way he could have known about that is Sergeant Freddy Hessinger told him.

And that fat little sonofabitch probably also told him I asked for, and he gave me, Elsa's dossier!

"This device," the Mattingly lecture continued, "was developed by the Ernst Leitz people — they make those wonderful Leica 35-millimeter cameras — in conjunction with the Zeiss people, who used to make the lenses for Leica cameras in what is now the Russian Zone of Germany. It is a copy machine. I have absolutely no idea how it works — how *they* work. The Signal Intelligence people had four of them, two of which are as we speak en route here in the care of Major Wallace — but what they do is copy documents, make photos of them, so to speak, on special paper with astonishing speed.

"The only problems with it are: One, the factory making the paper was blown up in the closing days of the late unpleasantness. I requisitioned all of the paper they liberated and would let me have, and several trucks loaded with it — it comes in huge rolls, like newspaper printing paper — are also en route here.

"Two, documents fed to it have to be flat, without creases. That means anything that is not flat or has creases will have to be ironed. I have acquired the necessary irons and ironing boards. They are in the trucks."

"Ironing?" Dunwiddie said. "Who's going to do the ironing?"

Mattingly did not immediately answer the question.

He instead said, "The machines will be accompanied by technicians I have pressed into service. You, Ludwig, will have to impress upon them that there will be dire consequences if they run at the mouth after we let them go several months from now."

"They will be so impressed," Mannberg said. "I have several people very skilled in that sort of thing."

"Nevertheless, these technicians should not be permitted to read what is being copied, either when it is being fed into the machine, or should it require pressing before insertion.

That means, to answer your question, Tiny, that we are going to have to do the pressing."

"We"? Cronley thought. *In a pig's ass!*

The last person I expect to see standing at an ironing board is Mattingly, dressed up like Clark Gable, ironing documents.

Well, face it, Jimmy. All those movies where Clark Gable and Alan Ladd, et cetera, are intelligence officers, spending their time in romantic saloons exchanging soulful looks with Ingrid Bergman or some other erotic tootsie — they're all bullshit.

In the real world, intelligence officers such as myself stand at an ironing board flattening bent sheets of paper and getting their romance in a whorehouse.

"What we will do is make two copies of everything Herr Mannberg and Sergeant Hessinger have found," Mattingly said. "One set of copies will go to Colonel Frade in Argentina and the other be held for incorporation into the files of whatever the reborn OSS is called, whenever that occurs."

"If that occurs," Tiny said.

"Oh, ye of little faith," Mattingly said. "I believe it will, perhaps not soon, but inevitably. But as I was saying before I was interrupted: We can guarantee the safety of these files by transferring them only amongst us. For example, from Lieutenant Cronley, who will take them under heavy, but inconspicuous, guard in one of our ambulances to

Rhine-Main, where he will personally place them in the hands of Colonel Frade, and Colonel Frade only, just before Frade takes on fuel to fly to Lisbon on his way back to Argentina.

"After all the files Colonel Frade has requested, and those others I think he ought to have, are copied, we will begin to copy the files of Abwehr Ost so they can be incorporated into the files of the reborn OSS. We will continue to do that until the available copying paper is exhausted. By then I hope to have an additional supply of the special paper. Samples have been sent to the United States for analysis, and to determine how we can make it ourselves."

The translation of that is that I will be here ironing paper for the next three to four years.

"I think that about covers everything," Colonel Mattingly said. "Are there any questions?"

Silence ensued.

"In that case, I have to get back to the Farben building. Keep your seats, please, gentlemen."

Then Mattingly marched out of the room.

[Two]

Estación Retiro
Plaza San Martín, Buenos Aires, Argentina
2030 15 October 1945

SS-Brigadeführer Ludwig Hoffmann — whose new *libreta de enrolamiento* identified him as Ludwig Mannhoffer, born November 5, 1899, in Dresden, Germany, and as a citizen of the Argentine Republic since 1917 — walked down the platform of what was officially the Ferrocarril General Bartolomé Mitre railway station. He was thinking that the way he was dressed, compared to the other passengers in the first-class car, made him look like a failed door-to-door toilet-brush salesman.

His annoyance turned to concern as he got closer to the terminal building and began to worry that something had gone wrong and that no one was here to meet him. The concern grew when he considered his options if no one had.

He would have to get into a taxi and go to a hotel. He was reasonably sure his new *libreta* would stand scrutiny.

But then what?

If something happened to keep Raschner from coming to the station — and he knew how important meeting me was — does that mean that gottverdammt *Martín is going to be wait-*

339

ing for me here? That's a credible scenario. . . .

Thank God, there he is!

A short, squat, bald-headed man in his late forties was coming down the platform, smiling.

Look how he's dressed! No one's going to mistake him for a toilet-brush salesman!

"Let me take your bags, Señor . . . ?" the man said in Spanish.

"Mannhoffer," he provided. "Ludwig Mannhoffer. And you are?"

"Richter, Señor Mannhoffer, Erich Richter. And Señor Konrad Fassbinder is outside at the curb with a car."

The last time Mannhoffer had seen Richter had been in the SS Headquarters on Prinz Albrechtstrasse in Berlin. He had then been SS-Sturmführer Erich Raschner.

A light gray 1941 Plymouth was standing at the curb outside the railroad station. When the driver saw them coming he quickly got from behind the wheel and opened the rear door. The last time Mannhoffer had seen the driver was also at the SS headquarters. SS-Hauptsturmführer Konrad Forster, now known as Konrad Fassbinder, had been wearing his black uniform.

"This is Señor Mannhoffer, Fassbinder," Richter said in Spanish.

"It's good to see you again, sir," Fassbinder said.

Their Spanish is fluent; they sound like they've been here all their lives.

I do not sound as if I've been here since 1917.

Richter put Mannhoffer's suitcase in the trunk of the Plymouth and then got in beside him. The car pulled away from the railroad station.

"This is Avenida Libertador," Richter said, gesturing. "Which we are now going to cross, pass through Plaza San Martín, and then turn right until we come to Avenida 9 Julio, where we will turn left. About halfway down 9 Julio we will come to the Colón Opera and the Obelisk. The Obelisk was built in 1936 by us — Siemens, working with Grün & Bilfinger — in thirty-one days."

"Fascinating," Mannhoffer said sarcastically. "And the apartment?"

"The apartment we're going to is behind the opera on Calle Talcahuano."

"Is it safe?" Mannhoffer asked.

"The embassy rented it for years. Its last occupants, before he deserted his post, was commercial attaché Wilhelm Frogger and his wife —"

"What do we know about them?" Mannhoffer interrupted.

"As far as I know, Herr Brigadeführer —"

Mannhoffer interrupted him again, this time angrily.

"That was the last time you will ever refer to me by my rank! You understand?"

341

"I beg your pardon, sir."

After a significant, and icy, pause, Mann-hoffer asked, "The Froggers?"

"As far as I know, señor, they are still at Frade's estancia in Mendoza."

"Isn't Mendoza near the Andes?"

"Yes, sir. It is."

"I was under the impression Frade's estancia was somewhere near Buenos Aires."

"He has more than one estancia, sir. This one, the one in Mendoza, Estancia Don Guillermo, is where he is holding the Froggers."

"Estancias? How many estancias does Frade have?"

"I don't know, sir. At least five. Probably more than that. Oberst Frade, the father, was a very wealthy man."

"And this *gottverdammt* American son of his inherited them all?"

"Yes, sir. And all the veterans of the Húsares de Pueyrredón."

"Explain that to me."

"Oberst Frade, and his father before him, commanded the Húsares de Pueyrredón cavalry regiment. Most of the men in the regiment were from one of his estancias. When they completed their conscript service, or retired, they went back to their estancias. They have transferred their allegiance to the son. The result is what people are calling Frade's Private Army. They protect him, his

342

family, and all of his properties, including Estancia Don Guillermo."

"These ex-soldiers are armed?" Mannhoffer asked incredulously.

"Very well armed."

"And the government permits this?"

"It's not illegal, sir."

"You just said these people were armed. The government permits this?"

"The people here have the right to be armed, to go about armed."

"That's insane."

"That's how it is, sir."

"Weapons in the hands of people cannot be tolerated. The Führer forbade private citizens to have arms."

"They have them here, sir."

"Tell me more about the Froggers."

"Yes, sir. Frade has them — Herr Frogger and his wife, and their son, Oberstleutnant Frogger — at his estancia in Mendoza."

"Their son? He was captured in North Africa."

"Yes, sir. Frade brought him here from the United States."

"You're saying the son is also a traitor?"

"It seems obvious, sir."

"Well, that's one more that has to go," Mannhoffer said. "Tell me about this apartment."

"Sir, when Herr Frogger deserted his post, I realized that it would be useful if the Final

Victory . . . didn't come as quickly as we hoped . . . and I stayed behind. So I suggested to Ambassador von Lutzenberger that the apartment lease be allowed to expire. It was then rented by a man named Gustav Loche, an Argentine of German ancestry, whose son, Günther, was an employee of the embassy."

"Can this man be trusted, in the changed situation?"

"He is a great admirer of the Führer and National Socialism. More important, he is a devout Catholic who believes that National Socialism is the last defense against the Antichrist, the Communists. And finally, I have kept him and his son on the payroll."

"Tell me about von Lutzenberger. Where is he now?"

"He and his wife — and just about all the diplomats — have been interned in the Club Hotel de la Ventana, in the south of Buenos Aires Province."

"Graf von Lutzenberger is one of two things, Richter," Mannhoffer said. "He is either an incredibly stupid diplomat who never understood that his naval attaché and his military attaché for air were traitors, or he is a traitor himself."

"I never thought von Lutzenberger was stupid, Señor Mannhoffer," Richter said.

He looked out the Plymouth's side window.

"That's the opera, Herr Mannhoffer. One

of the largest in the world. Larger than Vienna and Paris."

"And Berlin?"

"And Berlin. The apartment is almost right behind it. There is an underground garage, so no one will see us go in."

"Except perhaps agents of General Martín," Mannhoffer said. "One should never underestimate one's enemies, Richter."

"I try very hard not to, Señor Mannhoffer."

[THREE]

Apartment 4-C
1044 Calle Talcahuano
Buenos Aires, Argentina
2105 15 October 1945

"Do we have a tailor we can trust?" Mannhoffer asked.

He was sitting in an armchair by a window through which the Colón Opera House could be seen across a park.

"Excuse me?" Fassbinder asked.

"That was a simple question, Fassbinder. Do we have a tailor we can trust? Answer yes or no."

"A *tailor!* I thought you said a *tailor.* Yes, sir. We do."

"Get in your car and bring him here."

"I don't understand, Herr Mannhoffer."

"Look at me, Fassbinder. I look like a Bible

salesman. I need new clothing, and I need it now."

"Sir, I can get on the telephone and ask —"

"We don't know, do we, Fassbinder, whether or not General Martín's agents are listening to calls made on that telephone? Go get him! And bear in mind I don't like having to explain my orders."

"Yes, sir. Immediately, Herr Mannhoffer."

As soon as the door closed behind Fassbinder, Mannhoffer turned to Richter.

"He's not one of Wernher von Braun's rocket scientists, is he?"

"He's a good man, Herr Mannhoffer. Reliable."

"I sent him away because I need new clothing, and I need it now . . ."

"That will not be a problem, sir."

". . . and I didn't want him here when we have our little chat."

"Yes, sir."

"Let's start with money," Mannhoffer said. "I am presuming we have sufficient cash for all Operation Phoenix requirements?"

"Yes, sir."

"And what, if anything, is left of the Confidential Special Fund assets?"

"You do know what happened to them?"

Mannhoffer nodded. "Señor Moreno of the Banco Suisse Creditanstalt told me that Brigadeführer von Deitzberg went to Montevideo, where he had Sturmbannführer von Tresmarck transfer all of the assets of the Confidential Special Fund to him. Is that your understanding?"

"Yes, sir. I heard he permitted von Tresmarck to retain approximately one million U.S. dollars, which was to finance von Tresmarck's disappearance."

"That was to get him out of Uruguay without his making a fuss. The second part of that scenario was to later run him down in Paraguay, eliminate him and his boyfriend, and reclaim that money. Obviously, that did not happen."

"I never heard of the plans for him in Paraguay, sir."

"No reason that you should have. The fewer people who know something, the less chance the wrong people will learn of it."

"I've heard that, sir."

"Frau von Tresmarck also disappeared at the same time. She appeared in San Martín de los Andes, as Señora Schenck. Inasmuch as von Deitzberg was now using that name, I'm afraid we have to presume — he was notorious for this — that the late *brigade-führer* once again was careless with his zipper.

"Moreno also told me that after von Deitzberg was murdered by parties unknown — any thoughts, Richter, on them?"

"I believe he was murdered by someone in

Abwehr Ost, one of those Frade brought to Argentina."

"Why would they want to murder him?"

"Either at Frade's order, or simply because he could recognize one of them and get word back to Germany that some of Gehlen's people were in Argentina. The war was still on."

Mannhoffer grunted.

"In any event," he went on, "von Deitzberg died. Moreno told me that a court — or at least judges — favorable to Oberst Perón quickly granted the former Frau von Tresmarck all of her husband's — Señor Schenck's — assets. In other words, the Confidential Special Fund. And that she almost immediately transferred half of them to Señorita Evita Duarte, Oberst Perón's good friend, as an expression of her gratitude for their friendship and support in her time of grief. Is that your understanding, Richter?"

"Yes, sir. That sums it up very well."

"How many men do we have here?" Mannhoffer asked.

"You're speaking of SS?"

Mannhoffer nodded.

"Directly subordinate to me, sir, there are fifty-two. Eleven junior officers, the rest other ranks. And there are perhaps a hundred others who can be pressed into our service — SS personnel sent here for other reasons. I'm compiling a roster."

"I thought there were a few more than that. Immediately subordinate to me, I mean."

"We lost sixteen of them, sir."

"What do you mean 'lost'?"

"Shortly after the Froggers deserted their post at the embassy, we learned that they were being held at a small estancia — one of Frade's — in Tandil. A raid was staged with the mission of eliminating them. Four SS officers and twelve other ranks were assigned to the mission, to augment troops of the Argentine Tenth Mountain Regiment. After the initial assault, the Argentines left and our people stayed behind to make sure the Froggers had in fact been eliminated. None of the SS men were seen or heard from again. They are probably buried in unmarked graves on the Pampas."

"Sixteen SS troopers just vanished?"

"Yes, sir."

"Leaving me just fifty-two. Well, we'll have to use what we have. They are, after all, SS."

"To do what, sir?"

"As incredible as this might sound at first, the future of National Socialism is now in the hands of two men, neither of whom can any longer use their names, much less their ranks."

Richter did not reply.

"Think about it, Richter. The Führer is dead. Joseph Goebbels is dead. Heinrich Himmler is dead. Hermann Goering is a prisoner and will probably be hung. Everyone who served in the SS is being arrested. We're all that is left."

He paused to let this sink in, then said fervently, "But National Socialism is not dead! It will rise, phoenix-like, from the ashes. Because of us, Señor Richter."

Richter, who looked uncomfortable, again did not reply.

"If you have something to say, Richter, say it!" Mannhoffer snapped.

Richter nodded, then carefully began, "I've had a lot of time to think our situation over, Herr Brig— Señor Mannhoffer."

"And you have concluded?"

"That for the immediate future, until time passes, it would be best if we just lay low, do nothing that would call attention to us. Then, as I said, when time passes we can begin our work."

Mannhoffer didn't reply for a long moment.

"I, too, had a good deal of time to consider our situation," he began finally. "On that *gottverdammt U-boot.* There's not much else to do on a U-boat. Well, I initially came to the same conclusion. But then I thought a little deeper."

"Yes, sir?"

"I realized that disappearing into the woodwork was not the thing to do. We have to have continuity, Richter. *Continuity.*"

"I'm afraid I don't understand, sir."

"We have to be a *continuation* of the Third Reich, of National Socialism, not a small group of former National Socialists who, after escaping to Argentina, decided to see what they could do about bringing National Socialism back. People have to believe we are members of the Third Reich *continuing* to fight its battles."

"Yes, sir. Sir, how are we going to do this?"

"By doing what soldiers always do in a war, Richter. By killing our enemies and our traitors."

Richter did not reply.

"The image of ourselves in the public's imagination that I intend to build is of a secret organization — a large secret organization — dedicated to the maintenance of National Socialist principles. Now, try to follow my reasoning. We will eliminate someone, say von Wachtstein. No one will know who did it. But they will wonder, 'Who did this and why?'

"And they will first remember that he was a traitor to the Reich when he was an attaché at the embassy. 'Is it possible he was killed for being a traitor?' they will ask, and then they will answer their own question."

"Yes, I see."

"But caution is the handmaid of victory, Richter. Whatever we do cannot fail. Therefore I think we should start with the von Tresmarcks. Give us a little practice, so to speak. How many SS are in Paraguay?"

"Twenty-two, sir. I should have included them in the number of those who are immediately subordinate to us. Two junior officers and twenty other ranks. I just don't know how many SS there are in Paraguay not officially subordinate to us."

"Find out. What I intend to do is make sure that the SS who mistakenly believe they are 'not officially subordinate' to me are reminded, forcibly if need be, that I am the senior SS officer in Argentina and Paraguay — actually in all of South America."

"Yes, sir."

"Is Fassbinder capable of going there and taking charge of the SS we now control in a mission to locate von Tresmarck, eliminate him, and recover the cash von Deitzberg gave him? Or would you prefer to do that yourself?"

"I'm sure Fassbinder can handle it."

"Tell him not to kill the boyfriend. Rough him up. Badly rough him up, but leave him alive so the word will get out the SS punished von Tresmarck."

"Yes, sir."

"And locate Frau von Tresmarck — or whatever she is calling herself these days. In this regard, while she will have to be eliminated eventually, I would like to recover the Confidential Special Fund assets before we do that. So, for the moment, just locate her."

"Yes, sir."

"Is this tailor Fassbinder went to fetch any good?"

"Very good, sir."

"I simply can't go around looking like this," Mannhoffer said. "It would attract the wrong kind of attention."

[FOUR]

4730 Avenida Libertador General San Martín
Buenos Aires, Argentina
1015 16 October 1945

Don Cletus and Doña Dorotea Frade were taking breakfast with their children on the balcony of the top-floor master suite of the mansion when the elevator door opened with a squeal.

They didn't pay any attention. The children's dog, a large black Labrador retriever named Poocho, was dragging Master Jorge Howell Frade, aged eighteen months, across the floor by his diaper. The toddler was howling. Doña Dorotea was yelling. Don Cletus was laughing.

"You sonofabitch!" Doña Dorotea screamed.

"Are you referring, my dear, to your husband or the dog?"

Doña Dorotea and Don Cletus looked

toward the elevator.

Cletus Marcus Howell, wearing a seer-sucker suit and holding a cigar in one hand and a stiff-brimmed straw hat in the other, stood there.

"Both," Doña Dorotea said.

"Well, I'll be goddamned," Don Cletus said.

The old man whistled shrilly. Poocho let go of Jorge's diaper, trotted to the old man, sat on his haunches, and offered his paw. The old man solemnly shook it.

Jorge stopped howling.

Doña Dorotea snatched him off the floor and went to the old man and kissed him.

"I just happened to be in the neighborhood," Cletus Marcus Howell said. "And I thought I might as well just drop in and see my grandson, my great-grandsons, and the beautiful and charming mother of the latter."

"How did you get here?" Clete asked.

Frade knew that, it being Monday, the next Pan American–Grace flying boat from Miami wasn't due until Tuesday. He was keenly aware of the details because a shipment of radio parts for SAA had been "misrouted" by Panagra, and only recently "found" and promised on the Tuesday flight. Clete had strongly suspected Juan Trippe's hand caused that delay.

"In some comfort," his grandfather said. "I will tell you all about it, but that will have to wait until the ladies — now powdering their noses — are finished gushing over you and your children."

"Ladies? Plural? You brought everybody with you?"

Before Howell could answer, the door to the suite opened and three women entered.

"Thank you ever so much for sending the elevator back down for us, Dad," said one of them sarcastically. She was a stocky, short-haired blonde in her late forties. "All you had to do was close the damned door!"

"Sorry," the old man said, not very sincerely. "In the States, they close automatically."

The woman was Martha Williamson Howell. She was Howell's daughter-in-law and the only mother Clete had ever known. With her were two young women, her daughters, Elizabeth, known as Beth, a tanned and athletic twenty-two-year-old, and her sister, Marjorie, twenty, sort of a smaller version of her sister. They were Clete's cousins, but he had grown up with them and thought of them as his sisters.

Martha Howell went to Clete and wrapped him in a bear hug.

"Well," she said, "I can see that Dorotea has been feeding you."

"Almost every day," Clete said.

He looked at Beth.

"No, he's not," Clete said, answering her unasked question. "And I really don't know when he will be."

"You bastard!" she said.

"Isn't that what you were going to ask me?" Clete asked.

"She's right," Martha Howell said. "You can be a bastard. You have your grandfather's genes."

"And his father's," the old man said. "We can't leave Ol' Horr-gay out of that equation, can we?"

"Enough!" Dorotea said furiously. "I don't know what the hell is wrong with all of you, but I've had enough of it."

"What I think we should do, Cletus," the old man said, "to escape the wrath of the females of the clan, is go somewhere — your splendidly equipped library comes to mind — and have a Sazerac."

"My God, it's half past ten in the morning!" Martha said.

"It is never too early for a Sazerac. As long as you have been married into this family, Martha, you should know that."

He headed for the elevator. By the time he reached it, so had Cletus.

[FIVE]

"Dare I hope that you have Peychaud's?" the old man asked as Clete stepped behind the bar in the library.

Peychaud's bitters were an absolutely

356

necessary ingredient to make a genuine Sazerac.

Clete held up a small bottle.

"I stole this from the house on Saint Charles Avenue."

"Jean-Jacques told me that you taught Dorotea to drink Sazeracs."

"A mistake — they make her mean," Clete said as he looked for, found, and triumphantly held up a bottle of Templeton Straight Rye Whiskey.

"I never heard what you were doing there."

"And you never told me what you're doing *here.* Or how you got here."

"The grandson said, mistakenly believing the grandfather to be so far into his dotage that he will not realize the subject has been changed."

Clete smiled, then said, "So how did you get here?"

"In a Lockheed Constellation. They're really the only way to fly."

Clete finished making the cocktails and handed his grandfather one of them.

"Whatever the circumstances, I'm glad you're here," Clete said.

They touched glasses.

"No matter how you got here," Clete added.

"I just told you. In a Lockheed Constellation."

"You're kidding, right?" Clete said, after a moment.

The old man shook his head, smiling.

"Whose Constellation?"

"Mine."

"Now, that I don't believe."

"Have I ever lied to you?"

"Yes, you have. And sometimes they've been whoppers."

"But always, you must admit, with good intentions. This, however, is not one of those occasions."

"This time you have evil intentions?"

"Well, if you're really curious, Clete . . ."

"I am beside myself with curiosity."

"The Air Corps canceled a contract with Lockheed for a VIP-outfitted Constellation — the one in which, I understand, you were flown to Berlin to meet the President —

Jesus Christ, how did he hear about that?

"— and Howard let me have it cheap but with caveats."

"Cheap?"

"As you may have heard, the war is over. There is now what is known as 'war surplus.' "

"How cheap is war surplus?"

"I'm embarrassed to tell you."

"And the caveats?"

"I could not resell it for a year, and even then not to a foreign corporation, such as South American Airways. Apparently, Juan Trippe thinks you already have enough

Constellations and had a word with his senator."

"I never even thought of getting some 1049s from war surplus," Clete said, as much to himself as to his grandfather.

"You should have," the old man said. "Perhaps you could have gotten to our senators before Trippe got to his. Anyway, there's a lot of bargains out there. I just put in a bid for six Navy tankers."

"What are you going to do with six tankers?"

"If you paid just a little attention to the family's petroleum business, you might have an idea. And I bought the Flying Brothel."

"Whatever for? Do you have any idea how much it costs to operate one?"

"To the last dime."

"So why?"

"A number of reasons. For one, I wanted to come down here to see you, and I didn't want to have to call Juan Trippe and say, 'Please find me a seat on one of your flying boats.' I can't stand that sonofabitch."

"I thought you were pals."

"So tell me how goes your war against the godless Communists?"

Where the hell did he hear about that?

As if reading Clete's mind, the old man went on, "I ran into a mutual acquaintance of ours, purely by coincidence, in the restaurant of the Hay-Adams, and he told me, as he waved a small American flag back and forth, that the reason you can't come home is that you're the nation's last defense against Joe Stalin and all his wicked works."

Is he talking about Colonel Graham? Allen Dulles?

"You talked to Colonel Graham?"

"I think that's his name. Fat Mexican. He used to be a friend of mine."

Used to be? They have been close friends, personally and professionally, for years.

When Howard Hughes caught his uncle with his hand too deep in the Hughes Tool cash box, he turned to them. They provided the lawyers — the expensive lawyers — Howard needed to get himself legally declared to be an adult so he could take over Hughes Tool in his own right.

" 'Used to be a friend'? Now you're warring with Graham?"

Howell didn't have time to answer the question before Antonio Lavalle opened the door and announced, "Don Cletus, your guests have arrived. May I show them in?"

Clete didn't have time to answer that question, either, before Doña Claudia Carzino-Cormano pushed past the butler and entered the library.

"Antonio told me you were having a cocktail in the library," she announced indignantly. "At half past ten in the morning . . ."

She stopped when she saw Cletus Marcus Howell.

"Well, look who's here," the old man said. "Will you join us, Claudia? The more the merrier, I always say."

"Señor Howell," she said. "What an unexpected pleasure."

She didn't sound very sincere.

"I thought we were on a first-name basis," the old man said. "Have I done something to offend?"

Hans-Peter von Wachtstein and Wilhelm von Dattenberg came into the room. Through the open door, Clete saw Alicia von Wachtstein and Elsa von Wachtstein in the foyer.

"Did I hear the word 'cocktail'?" Peter asked.

"You'll have to ask your mother-in-law if you can have one," Clete said.

Claudia snorted and walked out of the library.

"Hansel, you've never met my grandfather, have you?" Clete said. "Grandfather, this is Peter von Wachtstein."

"I've heard a good deal about you, sir," Peter said.

"And I've heard a good deal about you, too," the old man said. "From my chauffeur."

"Uh-oh," Clete said.

"Do you realize, Cletus, that it took Alex Graham —"

"Your fat Mexican former friend?" Clete

interrupted. "That Alex Graham?"

"— and both of my senators to get Tom out of that mess you put him in?"

"What mess was that?" Clete asked innocently.

"You spirited your friends here out of that Top Secret POW camp in Virginia and then left poor old Tom to face the music. The FBI wanted to charge him with aiding and abetting a prison break, and the Army wanted to add high treason," the old man said, then realizing Clete was pulling his leg, and concluded, "As you goddamn well know."

"I told Tom to tell the FBI that I held a gun on him," Clete said. "He said he hadn't had so much fun since driving you around dodging revenuers during Prohibition."

The old man ignored that and turned on von Dattenberg.

"You're the other one, right?"

"Excuse me?"

"The other German my grandson helped to escape from Fort Hunt. The one trying to take advantage of my granddaughter."

Clete laughed out loud. Von Wachtstein chuckled and smiled.

"It's not funny, goddamn it, Cletus!" von Dattenberg said.

"Grandfather, this is Willi von Dattenberg, late *fregattenkapitän* of the submarine service of the Kriegsmarine," Clete said. "An officer and a gentleman who has never even met

362

Beth. The one trying to take advantage of Beth — actually, when I think about it, it's the other way around — is Karl Boltitz."

"Huh," the old man snorted.

Doña Dorotea and Doña Alicia came into the library.

"Claudia," Dorotea announced, "says to tell you she's not going to the Jockey Club if you're drunk."

"Can you get that in writing?" Clete asked.

"Cletus, it was your idea to show Willi and Elsa a good time," Dorotea argued.

"And so it was," he said, after a moment. "Grandfather, sorry, but that's your last Sazerac."

"The hell it is," the old man said. "But you, my dear, may assure Señora Carzino-Cormano that whenever we get wherever we're going, Cletus will comport himself as a gentleman."

"That'll be a first," Dorotea said. "But I'll tell her."

She and Alicia left the library.

"Where did she say we're going?" the old man asked.

"To the Jockey Club."

"Isn't that way the hell out in San Izzie-something?"

"There's another one in San *Isidro*," Clete said. "The one we're going to is right across the street."

[Six]

The Hipódromo de Palermo was in fact right across Avenida Libertador and they could have walked there in three or four minutes.

But that would be too damn simple, Clete thought, equally annoyed and amused.

What had happened, instead, was that, forty-five minutes later, everyone more or less followed instructions to assemble in the basement. There, under Señora Carzino-Cormano's strict direction, they were loaded into automobiles according to her sense of protocol.

She put Cletus Marcus Howell and Martha Williamson Howell in the backseat of her Rolls-Royce. Cletus Frade, following her signals, got in the front beside her chauffeur. She installed Peter von Wachtstein and Wilhelm von Dattenberg in the front seat of Clete's Horch, and Doña Dorotea, Doña Alicia, and Elsa von Wachtstein in the backseat. Beth and Marjorie Howell were seated last, in front of them, on jump seats unfolded from the floor.

Clete's 1941 Ford station wagon held the bodyguards.

When she was satisfied, she got in the backseat of her Rolls-Royce with the old man. There she stood — looking not unlike General George S. Patton urging his armored columns onward to the Rhine — and signaled to the driver of the station wagon to get the show on the road.

The convoy went up the ramp of the garage, through the enormous gates, and onto Avenida Libertador. Then it went around the block, which was not as simple as that sounded, as the block held both of the Ejército Argentino's National Polo Fields, the stables to house the horses therefore, and other buildings.

Finally they returned to Avenida Libertador and rolled up to the cast-iron gates of the Jockey Club. The gates opened as they arrived. Once inside the grounds, they drove to the members' door of the Jockey Club.

The bodyguards got quickly out of the station wagon, half of them eyeing the people on the wide steps warily, and the other half opening the doors of the Horch and the Rolls-Royce.

Everybody went into the Jockey Club and then up a wide flight of stairs to the second-floor foyer, where they were greeted by the maître d'hotel of the dining room.

"Señora Carzino-Cormano, welcome!" he announced. "Your table is of course ready. But perhaps a glass of champagne before you go in?" "Splendid idea," Cletus Marcus Howell answered for her. "Never turn down a glass of champagne is my motto."

She glowered at him.

"I don't believe I know this gentleman,"

the maître d'hotel said.

"Cletus Marcus Howell," the old man announced. "Of New Orleans, Louisiana, USA." He pointed at Clete. "I'm his grandfather."

"An honor, sir," the maître d'hotel said.

"Raul, I believe we'll have the champagne at the table," Doña Claudia ordered.

The maître d'hotel led Claudia — who had taken the old man's arm and was leading him — through double doors into a large, glasswalled room overlooking the racetrack. A long table had been set up formally, complete with cards indicating who should sit where.

Doña Claudia led the old man to one end of the table, pointed to the card at the head of the table, and said, "Well, here I am. I wouldn't be surprised if you were down there, near the other end."

"Not a problem, dear lady," the old man said. "Just so it's not far from the bubbly."

When he got to the far end of the table, he saw that Clete was seated at the head, with the submarine captain on one side of him and the other Frau von Wachtstein on the other. He was seated next to the submarine captain — he wasn't sure if he believed that or not, but he couldn't think of his name beyond von-Something — which meant that neither of them would be able to watch what was going on on the track without having to look over their shoulders.

Clete had said that the submarine captain was not the one Martha had told him Beth fancied herself in love with. Maybe that was so. Beth was paying absolutely no intention to Captain von-Something, and he seemed to be fascinated with the other Frau von Wachtstein.

Why can I remember that von, but not the other?

He found that seated next to him was the von Wachtstein woman, an Argentine beauty, who was married to the German pilot Clete had broken out of Fort Hunt. Alex Graham had told him the pilot's father had been executed — brutally — for his role in trying to blow up Hitler, so it was doubtful the son was a Nazi. At least not anymore.

From where he was sitting, he could see a row of oil portraits of ornately uniformed Argentine men hanging on the wall.

The uniforms those guys are wearing make them look like characters in an operetta.

And they all look like Nazis.

"What is that, Cletus?" the old man asked. "The local version of the post office wall with pictures of J. Edgar Hoover's ten-most-wanted men?"

Clete smiled.

"Those are the founders of the Jockey Club," Clete said. "The handsome one, third from this end, is my grandfather."

"He's dead, right?"

Clete nodded. "Before I was born."

"Then he *was* your grandfather. Past tense. So why don't you do something nice for your *living* grandfather and scare up a waiter with the champagne the Queen promised me?"

Elsa von Wachtstein giggled.

Clete looked at her.

"Sorry," she said.

"What for? The whole idea of this was to make you and Willi smile."

"I'm not sure if I want to smile or cry," she said. "Your grandfather is just like my father. My father in happier times."

"Smile, please," Clete said.

"I'm a little numb with all this," Elsa said. "Here, it's as if there never was a war. Look at this table. The hors d'oeuvres alone would feed a family for a week in Germany. There must be a half kilo of cream in that bowl."

"There never was a war here, Elsa," Frade said. He met von Dattenberg's eyes. "Except for the one people like Willi and me brought here. And now people like Willi and me are trying to wind that one down."

Von Dattenberg nodded, just perceptibly.

"Let me get my grandfather his champagne," Clete said, and looked around for a waiter.

Clete didn't take any of the champagne when it was served, and he turned over the three empty wineglasses placed before him to indicate he also wished not to be served any of the grape.

He didn't know why, but somehow he knew that he should get and stay completely sober.

The first thing he thought was that his total sobriety would pour a little oil on the troubled waters between him and Claudia.

And between me and Martha.

Or maybe it's because I know I'm taking off for Berlin at nine tonight.

I don't believe that pilots have to go off the sauce twenty-four hours before takeoff, but they should turn off the alcohol valve eight hours before starting the engines.

He had looked down the table when he had that thought. He saw Hansel's glasses were also turned over.

Well, either ol' Hansel believes that twenty-four-hour business, or Alicia got to him.

Or he saw that I'm not drinking.

Or it may be that I don't want to make Elsa uncomfortable.

Or maybe because, if I'm really sober, I may pick up something from what von Dattenberg says, or how he acts. I'm still not sure if I trust him with that honor of the officer corps bullshit.

Or maybe I'm just trusting my intuition.

Whatever the reason, get thee behind me, Demon Rum!

Clete had, almost two hours later, just about finished his *postre* — a small mountain of strawberries just about concealed by whipped cream — and was on the cusp of deciding that a little cognac — one only — to top off the meal would not see him qualify as a flying drunk when the maître d'hotel bent over him and whispered in his ear.

"Don Cletus, Father Welner asks if you can have a word with him."

"Send him in."

"He asks that you join him in the foyer, Don Cletus."

What the hell does he want?

Why didn't he come in?

"Okay."

He turned to Elsa.

"Excuse me, please. I'll be back in a moment."

The priest was standing to one side of the foyer. On either side of him were men in civilian clothing. Both of them Clete recognized as agents of Martín's Bureau of Internal Security. One of them held, as Enrico so often did, a Model 11 Remington twelve-bore riot gun against the seam of his trousers; it was, Clete realized, a surprisingly effective way of hiding a shotgun. The other BIS agent, making no effort to conceal it, held a Thompson submachine gun cradled in his arms.

What the hell is going on?

Where the hell is Enrico?

"You can let Father Welner go," Clete

greeted them. "I'll vouch for him."

No one was amused.

"This way, please, Don Cletus," one of them said, and indicated a door opening off the foyer.

Martín was inside a small room apparently used as someone's — *maybe the maître d'?* — office. Martín was in uniform, which was unusual, and far more unusual than that, he was armed. A Ballester-Molina .45 ACP semiautomatic pistol was in a shoulder holster.

"Sorry to interrupt your lunch," Martín said.

"Bernardo, what's with all the guns?" Clete asked.

"Clete, where's the Storch?"

"At Jorge Frade. Why?"

"God, I hope you didn't drink your lunch," Martín said. "Have you?"

Jesus Christ! I knew I should be sober, but what the hell is this all about?

"What's all this sudden interest in my sobriety and airplane?"

"They've put the plan to assassinate el Coronel Juan Perón into play," Martín announced.

"Who's 'they,' and how do you know?"

"I told him, Cletus," Father Welner said.

"Who told you?"

"I can't tell you that," the priest said.

"I have to take it on faith, right?"

371

"Yes, you do, remembering that I'm a priest."

"How do you know? I mean, how do you know it's not just the boys sitting around the Circulo Militar, or the Officers' Casino at Campo de Mayo, drinking too many martinis?"

"Because Phase A of the outline calls for the assassination of General Martín," the priest said.

"That's what all the guns are for? You don't really think they're going to come into the Jockey Club and try to whack Bernardo, do you?"

"Whack?" the priest asked.

"Shoot, kill, assassinate," Clete said, somewhat impatiently.

"Phase A called for the assassination of Bernardo as he left his home to try to stop this," Father Welner said. "They regard him as their greatest obstacle to carrying this out."

"Well, don't go home, Bernardo," Frade said.

"I warned him," the priest said.

"And now what?"

"It was necessary to take the lives of three of the plotters," Martín said. "Two other men have been taken to Cosme Argerich. They are not expected to live."

And then he clarified, "The Central Military Hospital Dr. Cosme Argerich."

"I know what it is, Bernardo," Frade said

softly. "You put me in there the night they tried to whack me and killed Enrico's sister."

"That's right. I'd forgotten."

What I think it is, General, is that for the first time in your life you've been on the receiving end of someone shooting at you. Before this, it was other people getting shot at.

Don't be self-righteous, Cletus, Old Veteran: Remember your first time. When you got back to Fighter One and saw all those holes in your Wildcat, you threw up.

"You got five of them?"

Martín nodded.

Which means this is the real thing.

"Major Habanzo and Captain Garcia," Martín said, pointing in the general direction of his men in the foyer, "managed to get there before . . . the other people did."

They call them assassins, Bernardo.

Not "plotters" or "other people."

Then he said it out loud: "The term is 'assassins,' General."

Martín nodded.

"Well, what are you going to do now?" Clete asked.

"We have to get el Coronel Perón off Isla Martín García," Martín said. "And to a place of safety. We need your help to do that."

"Phase B of the outline is already under way," Father Welner said.

"What's Phase B?" Clete asked.

"A company of the Horse Rifles —"

"The what?" Clete asked incredulously.

"Officially," Martín said, "the Eighth Cavalry. It's known as General Necochea's Own Horse Rifles."

"— is en route by boat from La Plata to the island," the priest finished.

Clete said what he was thinking.

"That's a long trip. Are they bringing their horses?"

The sarcasm went over Martín's head.

"They knew my men were keeping an eye on the logical places to mount an operation like that," Martín said. "So they left from La Plata, which I was not watching."

"They intend to try to convince the men of the First Infantry Regiment, who are guarding el Coronel, that they are far outnumbered and resistance would be futile," the priest said. "If they don't give up — and the Patricios have a proud tradition and may resist however untenable their position . . ."

Heroism, and the glory that comes with it, sounds easy to people who've never been shot at.

"And the first shots of the civil war will have been fired," Bernardo said. "We have to prevent that."

He's probably right.

Hell, he is right.

"How do you plan to do that?"

"You fly us to the island," Martín said. "We pick up el Coronel and fly him to Jorge

374

Frade, where a platoon of the Patricios will be waiting for us. We then take el Coronel Perón to the Central Military Hospital, where he will be safe until this mess can be sorted out."

Frade exhaled audibly.

"Bernardo, I hate . . . I *really* hate . . . to rain on your parade. But there are so many holes in that plan that I hardly know where to begin."

"Begin," Martín said.

Frade shook his head in resignation.

"Okay. Let's start with President Farrell telling me to keep my nose out of this."

"That no longer applies, Cletus," Father Welner said.

"It doesn't? Does General Farrell know that?"

"We came here from the Casa Rosada," Welner said. "His message is now: 'Sorry that you have to get involved, but I can see no other alternative.' "

I'm not sure I'd believe Martín telling me that; he's really shaken up.

But I don't think even the devious Jesuit would come up with that as an outright lie.

Clete looked at his watch.

"Problem two," he said. "The reason I have not been drinking is that I take off for Europe at nine. That means I have to be at Jorge Frade at seven. That's not enough time —"

"For God's sake, Cletus!" Martín said. "Try

375

to understand that we're preventing a civil war —"

"And the loss of life that that means," the priest interjected.

"— and that's far more important than you flying anywhere," Martín picked up. "You're not SAA's only pilot."

"I'm the only one skilled at bringing back all those passengers traveling on Vatican passports," Frade replied. "Let's not forget that, Father."

"You're going to have to do this, my son," the priest said. "Among other things, it's your Christian duty to your godfather."

Oh, Jesus H. Christ!

"How do you figure that?"

"For one thing, Juan Domingo loves you," Welner replied. "If you don't do this, he will be killed. And others will die, not only on Isla Martín García today, but all over this country in the civil war that will follow. Hundreds, perhaps thousands, of innocent people."

Maybe he's right.

"Bernardo said before," Clete replied, "something about me flying 'us' to this god-damned island. Who's 'us'?"

"Father Welner and me," Martín said.

"What's Welner going to do on the island?"

"Several things," Martín said. "For one, if he's there — unless the both of you are there — el Coronel probably can't be disabused of his suspicions that I'm party to the assassination. If he still believes that, he'll refuse to get in the Storch with you."

"He can't anyway — you can get only three people in the Storch. Or are you planning to stay on the island?"

"I will stay there," Welner said. "The idea is that after you have taken Juan Domingo off the island — before the Horse Rifles arrive — I can talk the Patricios out of resisting the Horse Rifles, and permit them to land. And once they have landed, with God's help, I can talk whoever's commanding the Horse Rifles into going back to La Plata."

That'd work. Neither the Patricios nor the Horse Rifles is going to shoot a priest.

Or are they?

Hansel told me that in the Spanish Civil War priests were what the Marine Corps calls Targets of Opportunity.

A lot of them were shot on sight. By both sides.

But maybe he can talk them into going back to La Plata.

Blessed are the peacemakers, as it says in the Good Book.

And Operation Ost cannot work in the middle of a civil war, and that's your priority, Colonel Frade.

So, unless you have a better idea, Master Spy . . . ?

"Two things," Clete said. "One, I'm going

377

to have to tell Peter von Wachtstein what's going on. He'll want to know why I'm not going to Germany, and he'll have to be told how to handle the Vatican passport people in Berlin and Frankfurt.

"Second, how am I going to explain my sudden disappearance from here?"

"I'll have Captain Garcia get von Wachtstein out here," Martín said.

"And how do we satisfy Claudia's curiosity?" Clete asked. "And my wife's? And Peter's?"

Martín and Welner were still thinking about that when the answer came to Clete.

"You go in there, Your Eminence," he said, "and tell the ladies that both Peter and I are, under your wise guidance, doing their Christian duty, and that you will explain things later, but not now."

The priest considered that for a moment. "That'll work."

Then he walked out of the small office.

■ ■ ■ ■

VII

■ ■ ■ ■

[ONE]

Aeropuerto Coronel Jorge G. Frade
Morón, Buenos Aires Province, Argentina
1645 16 October 1945

The platoon of infantrymen from the Patricios Regiment that General Martín said he had ordered the regimental commander to send for the protection of el Coronel Perón were not at the airport when Clete Frade, General Martín, and Father Welner arrived.

This made Frade uneasy.

It was his professional opinion that the Patricios were not needed. The SAA security guards at the airfield were all former members of the Húsares de Pueyrredón. Thus, they were capable of guarding Perón — probably more so than the Patricios, because, most important, Frade's Private Army was as loyal to Clete as they had been to his father.

Which brought up what really made him uneasy.

Frade wondered if Martín had considered the possibility that the Patricios' commander would not really have his heart in protecting Perón. Frade thought it was just as likely the commander was one of the malcontents, one of those officers deeply offended by Perón's relationships with Señorita Evita Duarte, the disgraced former Teniente Coronel Rodolfo Nulder, and the Nazis.

And — adding to Frade's unease — since Martín obviously had ordered the troops to be sent before he had gone looking for Frade and finally finding him at the Jockey Club, there had been plenty of time for the Patricios to get to the airfield before the three of them had arrived there from the Hipódromo.

So why the hell aren't they here?

Frade reminded himself that Martín usually knew what he was doing, and kept his mouth shut.

He did, however, take Enrico Rodríguez aside and told him to order whoever was in charge of the SAA security guards to avoid confronting the Patricios if and when they showed up. He also told the old soldier to get into a security guard uniform and to go to the control tower and wait there to see how the rescue operation played out.

It was also Frade's professional opinion that the scenario to rescue el Coronel Perón had several problems. He chose not to share this with his fellow rescuers. He didn't think they would understand what the hell he was talking about.

The biggest problem was that there were no maps of the island showing a suitable place where he could land — even in a Storch that could land damn near anywhere — or where he could take off.

The maps Frade did have showed where the island was — a few miles off the coast of Uruguay — which only gave him two options. He could either fly along the shore of the River Plate estuary and try finding it that way, or fly there directly.

The first option would require a flight at least twice as far as the second, adding problems of time and fuel consumption. The second option would require dead reckoning navigation over water, which carried with it the strong possibility of getting lost and not being able to find the goddamn island at all.

It would also be useful if he knew where General Necochea's Own Horse Rifles — "the invasion force," so to speak — was floating around on the River Plate Estuary. Martín knew only that they had left from La Plata. Martín did not know when they'd left and of course had no idea what kind of speed the invasion fleet was capable of making.

As Frade lifted off in the Storch from the Jorge Frade airfield — with Martín and Welner aboard — he had a poetic thought, one based on the work of Alfred, Lord Tennyson:

Patricios to the left,
Horse Rifles to the right,
Forward the light airplane,
Onto the island of death
Flew the Three Stooges!

Clete picked up enough altitude so that the Storch wouldn't attract attention and then flew over and just beyond Buenos Aires, far enough out over the River Plate so that he would be out of sight of anyone on the shore.

This thinking, he reasoned, would also be in the mind of whoever was commanding the Horse Rifles invasion force — stay close enough to the shore so as not to get lost sailing up the estuary, and yet far enough offshore to avoid detection.

[Two]

En route to Isla Martín García
River Plate Estuary, Argentina
1655 16 October 1945

"I think we have found the invasion fleet," Cletus Frade announced over the intercom. He pointed downward to the right.

There was no response from his passengers.

Six "river" boats, each maybe fifty feet long, were moving up north in a rough double "V" formation. That seemed unnatural for anything but an invasion fleet.

He pushed the nose of the Storch sharply

384

down to get a closer look.

"Why else would those boats be moving in a formation like that?" he wondered aloud over the intercom.

And again there was no response from his passengers.

He looked over his shoulder at Father Welner and General Martín. They were crammed in the backseat. Neither of them wore the rear headset.

Well, that explains their silence, especially after that dive.

He had two thoughts as he mimed for them to put on the headset.

Both look terrified — as if they are going to piss their pants.

I wonder if Otto Skorzeny and Benito Mussolini looked like that when another heroic Storch pilot such as myself on a rescue mission such as this flew them off that mountaintop in Italy?

Then he had another thought: *Will Tío Juan's fate follow Il Duce's violent end?*

Father Welner got the headset on first.

"What are we doing?" he asked, with great concern — or maybe terror — in his voice. "Is something wrong with the airplane?"

Why does it surprise me that he got the headset on before Martín?

By now I should have learned to never underestimate the wily Jesuit.

With great effort Clete resisted the temptation to solemnly advise the priest to prepare

385

to meet Saint Peter at the Pearly Gates.

"I think we have found the invasion fleet," he repeated.

Thinking, *The last time I did this was in an L-4 Piper Cub off Tulagi in the Solomons looking for Japanese barges,* he dropped to two hundred feet above the water and then flew over the boats twice, once approaching them from the front, and a second time from the rear.

These boats are really getting tossed around. Why is that?

Because, Stupid, when the water in the River Plate estuary, always shallow, is affected by the tide and the winds, it can get really choppy.

And these boats are not intended for rough water.

He saw that the soldiers were sitting on the flat deck behind the wheelhouses, rifles held between their knees, getting drenched by water coming in over both the bow and the sides.

At first he thought the Horse Rifles had not brought their horses. Then he saw that every boat carried at least one horse and several had two.

Of course. Officers ride into battle. Waving the troops on with their sabers.

How are they going to get the horses off the boats? Make them jump?

Then he saw that each of the boats had a World War I Maxim heavy machine gun mounted on a wheeled carriage.

He picked up altitude and took up a course — he hoped — that would take him on a direct vector to Isla Martín García.

"Ask Bernardo," he said into the intercom microphone, "if the Patricios have Browning automatic rifles."

"Two BARs . . ." Martín replied.

Well, guess who finally remembered he's the general in charge of this operation and took the headset away from the priest?

". . . and two air-cooled Browning .30 caliber machine guns. Why do you ask?"

Does he really have to ask?

"Bad news, Bernardo. Two BARs and two .30-cal Brownings firing from shore can chew those boats up pretty easily. And, bobbing around the way those boats are, the Horse Soldiers won't be able to effectively return the fire. Unless we can keep both sides from shooting, there's going to a lot of dead Horse Soldiers."

"Well, maybe Father Welner can do that."

"The power of prayer, right?"

"Have you any better ideas?"

"If I think of something, I'll tell you when I land on your goddamn island. Presuming I can find it."

The island appeared, dead ahead, twenty minutes later. He did the math in his head. He was making, give or take, a hundred knots. Divided by three, that meant the invasion fleet was thirty-three miles behind him. Getting tossed around by the choppy water the way it was, the fleet was making no more than, say, fifteen knots. That meant they would reach the island in a little more than two hours.

Two hours to land, load Tío Juan aboard, and take off seems like plenty of time.

Presuming the Patricios don't use their BARs and light Brownings to shoot us out of the sky.

Or, more likely, shoot us dead the moment we land.

If we can land.

It took him five minutes to reach the island, and another ten minutes to fly back and forth looking for some adequate place to set down the Storch.

He saw that he again had two options: to land on the beach or in the tiny square in the center of the island. There were problems with the beach. The Patricios had set up their Brownings to cover the beach, the only place the invaders could land.

If I try to land on the beach, I'll be presenting the Patricios with a nice, easy moving target.

Like those metal ducks in a carnival shooting gallery.

Even if they didn't shoot, I don't know if the beach sand will support the weight of the Storch — either when landing or when I stop.

If the gear sinks into the sand, I'll never be

able to take off.
That leaves the town square.

When he flew over the town square — right at stalling speed — he saw that there would be several problems if he tried to land there.

For one, it looked like a postage stamp.

For another, about twenty soldiers of the Patricios were taking aim at the airplane with their 7mm Mauser rifles.

Frade had a sudden inspiration.

"Bernardo," he ordered. "Pass me your cover."

"My what?"

The Ejército Argentino does not refer to their uniform caps as covers, Stupid!

"Pass me your goddamned hat!"

"Why?"

"I'm going to throw up in it and I don't want to dirty the airplane."

General Martín, with great reluctance, passed his uniform cap, an ornate, tall, crowned leather-brimmed item of uniform decorated with all the gold braid appropriate for a *general de brigada.*

Frade raised the Storch's side window and then made another pass over the town square. When he was almost directly over it, he threw the hat out.

He made another 180-degree turn, came in low over the square, and landed.

The airplane was immediately surrounded

389

by troops of the Patricios. Most of them had their Mausers aimed at the airplane. But three of them — all officers, Clete saw — *Thank you, God!* — were examining the general officer's headgear that had just floated down to them.

And one of those officers, Clete saw, as he quickly turned around the Storch, thinking he might have to try to take off in a hurry, was el Coronel Juan Domingo Perón.

"Bernardo," Clete said to his microphone, "why don't you get out and see if el Coronel Perón will give you back your hat?"

When Martín, immediately followed by Father Welner, climbed out of the Storch, Clete saw that the officers with Perón immediately recognized Martín and saluted. That caused the soldiers with the Mausers to lower their weapons.

He saw, too, that a moment later surprise came to Perón's face when he saw the Jesuit. Perón's eyes then widened even farther when he recognized the Storch pilot.

When Martín walked up to Perón — who should have saluted Martín but didn't — Perón almost absentmindedly handed Martín his uniform hat. The crown had been crushed when the hat met terra firma, and Martín immediately started trying to carefully mold it back in place.

Why not? With all that gold braid on it, it probably cost him a month's pay.

Frade climbed out of the airplane in time to hear Perón demand, "What's going on here?"

"What we feared would happen, el Coronel, has happened," Martín announced.

"What are you talking about?" Perón demanded.

"What he means, Tío Juan," Clete said, not very pleasantly, "is that General Necochea's own Horse Rifles are on their way here to shoot you."

Perón considered that for a moment. "Cletus, that's nonsense. El Coronel Lopez commands the Horse Rifles. He's an old friend of mine."

"Cletus speaks the truth, Juan Domingo," Father Welner said.

Perón looked at Martín.

"You're telling me Fernando Lopez is one of the malcontents?"

"It would appear so, el Coronel," Martín said.

Perón considered that a moment, then said, "I refuse to believe el Presidente would permit any serious attempt by anyone in that handful of malcontents, including Lopez, to try to do something like trying to assassinate me. I am vice president of the Argentine Republic. It would be treason."

"Then why do you suppose," Frade said, "that Farrell sent us to get you off this island before your old friend Lopez gets here?"

That the question surprised Perón was visible on his face.

"General Farrell sent you?"

"There I was, minding my own business, having a pleasant lunch at the Jockey Club," Clete said, "when these two showed up and said, 'The president asks that you get your Tío Juan off that island before he gets shot.' Or words to that effect. Father Welner told me it was my Christian duty to do so. So here we are."

"I find that hard — impossible — to believe!" Perón said.

"What Cletus just said is the truth, Juan Domingo," the priest said.

"You don't really expect to fly me off the island in that?" Perón asked, pointing at the Storch. "I'm not going anywhere in that little airplane."

"Well, you could swim to Uruguay, I suppose. That's the only other option I can see you have," Clete said.

"You seem to think this is funny, Cletus," Perón snapped.

"I do see elements of humor in it. Mussolini was damned glad to see the Storch that flew onto that mountaintop to rescue him from a firing squad. The last thing I expected to hear was that you would be afraid to get in my Storch."

Perón didn't reply to that, but Clete saw on his face that he knew about how Otto Skorzeny, of the Waffen-SS, had rescued the Italian dictator from Italian troops who — waiting for orders to shoot him — held Il Duce prisoner at the Campo Imperatore Hotel high in the Apennine Mountains.

"*Afraid?* You dare to accuse me of cowardice?"

"That's what it sounds like, Tío Juan."

"Cletus!" Father Welner said warningly.

"What did you expect to hear?" Perón snapped.

"Something along the lines of 'Thank you, godson, for interrupting your lunch and risking your life to come here not only so I wouldn't get shot, but to keep Argentina from having a civil war.' You can say that in your own way, of course."

"Civil war? What are you talking about?"

Frade met Perón's eyes for a long moment, then shook his head disgustedly.

"You pompous fool! Stopping a civil war from getting started is what Farrell is concerned about! Not you. He doesn't give a rat's ass about keeping you alive any more than I do!"

"Cletus, you know you don't mean that!" the priest said.

Frade ignored him.

"Tío Juan," Frade challenged, "are you going to stand there with a straight face and try to tell me you don't know what your girlfriend and your old pal, former Teniente Coronel

Rodolfo Nulder, are up to?"

"I have no idea what you're talking about," Perón said arrogantly.

"Then pay goddamn attention! It's probably the reason your old friend el Coronel Lopez and the other malcontents have finally decided to stop their wishful thinking and get on with shooting you."

"I advise you, Cletus," Perón said evenly, wagging his right index finger in Frade's face, "to be very careful what you say. There is a limit to my patience."

"And I have passed my limit," Frade snapped. "The lady — and I use the term loosely — and Nulder have been in the slums organizing the workers — she calls them 'the shirtless ones.' They are going to march — have begun to march — on Buenos Aires, up Avenida 9 Julio to the Ministry of Labor Building, and then over to the Casa Rosada, to protest your arrest."

"How in the world did you hear about that?" Father Welner blurted.

"I didn't tell him," Martín said, directing the comment to Perón.

Frade glared at Martín. "But you are the one who's always making those unsupported allegations that I'm an intelligence officer, right, Bernardo?" He turned to Perón. "Are you really going to deny any knowledge of this?"

"I've heard some rumors," Perón said.

"Jesus! You're unbelievable, Tío Juan."

Perón glared at him.

"Even if the rumors are true," he pronounced, "a peaceable demonstration of the shirtless ones to protest the wholly unjustified arrest of the Labor minister — whom they know to be a friend — is not the sort of thing that would start a civil war."

"It's enough to get your old friend el Coronel Lopez and the other malcontents off their asses and on the road to kill you. And when everybody hears what's probably going to happen here, a civil war seems to me to be a sure thing."

"And what do you think is going to happen here?"

"What I would like to see happen here is what Father Welner and General Martín — and now that I think about it, what General Farrell — want to happen here, which is that nothing happens. Not a shot is fired by anybody.

"Just as soon as you and I and General Martín take off, the Patricios get back on their boats and go back where they came from . . ."

"Tigre," Father Welner furnished.

". . . taking the Good Father with them, as he won't fit in the airplane," Clete continued, ignoring him.

The priest was not going to be ignored.

"I thought the plan was that I would meet

the Horse Rifles when they arrived and reason with them."

"That was your plan, Padre. Mine's better. Think about it. When the Horse Rifles get here and find nobody here but the officer — what is he, a captain? — normally in charge . . ."

"He's a major," Martín finished, nodding toward one of the officers standing beside Perón.

". . . of this bucolic outpost to greet them — in other words, no Patricios and most important, no el Coronel Perón, to stand against a wall — they are going to feel — especially if they conduct a thorough search of the island and don't find him — more than just a little foolish. They will then do one of two things."

"What?" Martín asked.

"They will get back on their boats and go back where they came from, or they will stay here thinking that el Coronel Perón may come back. In either event, no shooting, no dead people, no starting a civil war."

"Cletus is right, Father," General Martín said. "It would be best if the Horse Rifles saw for themselves that there's nothing on this island that shouldn't be."

"And what, if I may be so bold as to inquire," Perón asked, thickly sarcastic, "do my captors plan to do with me?"

"We fly you to Jorge Frade," Martín said.

"I have arranged for a platoon of the Patricios to be there. They will provide all the protection you'll need as we take you to the Military Hospital."

Now he sounds like a general.

But where has that confident tone of command been up to now?

"No matter how anxious they are to shoot you," Frade said, "none of the malcontents is going to try to get at you in the Military Hospital. The barracks of the Patricios is right next door."

"I can see no reason that I have to fly off the island," Perón said. "I can return to the mainland the way I came. By boat."

"Jesus Christ!" Clete exploded. "Are you really that stupid? How did you get to be a colonel?"

"Cletus," Father Welner said, "you cannot talk to your godfather that way. He deserves your respect!"

Clete turned angrily to him.

"What the hell has he ever done to earn my respect, Padre? I'm trying to keep him alive, and you're not only of no goddamn help, but getting in the way. So shut the hell up!"

He turned to Perón.

"Tell me, Tío Juan," he said sarcastically, "in your long military career didn't someone, somewhere, sometime try to teach you that knowing what the enemy is likely to do is at least as important as knowing what you want to do?"

"Your father, Cletus, would have slapped your face for talking to a man of God that way," Perón said. "Or, for that matter, to me."

"Answer the goddamn question!"

"Then you tell me 'what the enemy is likely to do,' " Perón said icily.

"I think they're likely to have a platoon," Clete said, "maybe a company of the Horse Rifles in Tigre waiting to see if you show up there. Can you admit that remote possibility?"

Perón's face showed that the remote possibility had not occurred to him.

"Now, unless you want to get shot on the dock in Tigre, or against a wall here, get in the goddamned airplane!"

"El Coronel," Martín said, "you have no other option."

"You'll be with me in the airplane?" Perón asked.

Martín nodded.

"Very well then," Perón said.

Jesus Christ! He acts like he's doing us a favor!

[THREE]

There were a number of problems with flying off from the Isla Martín García town square, problems Clete elected not to share with either of his passengers.

For one thing, with three people aboard, the Storch was overloaded. That of course had been true at Jorge Frade Airfield when they had taken off from there, but there he had had the luxury of several thousand meters of runway.

Here he had no more than 150 meters of what would have to more or less pass as a runway. The Storch was capable of taking off within forty-five meters, but that meant a Storch not exceeding maximum takeoff weight. And he'd never actually tried to take off after a forty-five-meter takeoff roll.

Another problem was that it had grown dark. The landing light only barely illuminated the "runway." He knew that the town square was ringed with trees, which meant that he would not only have to get off the ground but gain enough elevation to miss the trees.

And, presuming he did get into the air, he again faced the problems of navigation he had when flying to the island — except now they were exacerbated by the darkness.

And the fuel gauges indicated he had less than half-full tanks.

In other words, in the darkness over the River Plate, he not only would have to navigate by the seat of his pants but would not know if he had enough fuel to get where he was going, wherever that was.

"Attention, passengers," he said over the intercom. "Extinguish all smoking materials, put your seats in the full upright position, and fasten your seat belts. Thank you for flying with us today."

Then stepping as hard as he could on the brakes, he moved the throttle forward to full takeoff power. The 237-horsepower Argus As 10C-3 engine then attempted to move the aircraft forward. With the brakes firmly locked, this resulted in the aircraft bouncing and shuddering in place.

When the needle on the tachometer seemed to have moved upward as high as it was ever going to go, he turned on the landing light and released the brakes.

The Reverend Kurt Welner, S.J., was now in view at the end of the runway, his hand raised as he invoked the blessing of the Deity on the flight.

The Storch sort of jerked into motion.

In the instant Clete got his feet off the brakes and put them on the rudder pedals, he felt life come into the controls. He pushed the nose forward to get the tail-dragger wheel off the ground, then eased back on the stick. He felt the Storch grow light on the landing gear, and then the rumble of the wheels stopped.

I'll be a sonofabitch! We're flying!
Thank you, God!

Navigation, if not fuel remaining, ceased to be a problem thirty seconds into the flight as he reached two hundred meters.

There was a yellowish glow on the horizon to his right.

That has to be coming from the Paris of South America. Or at least the outskirts thereof. Maybe Tigre on the right?

And if that's Tigre, I'm not lost and I'm not going to run out of gas. Tigre's only twenty miles, give or take, from that island.

He moved the nose of the Storch so that it was pointing at the right of the glow on the horizon.

Five minutes later, he could see the floodlights on the wharves of Tigre.

"Bernardo," he ordered, "look ahead to your right. That's the wharves in Tigre. Did you leave some of the Patricios there?"

"No. But there's Army trucks down there."

"I noticed. Give Tío Juan the headset."

"Hello, hello, can you hear me?" Perón's voice demanded.

"Not if you're talking, Tío Juan. Shut your mouth and look down and to the right. Those are the trucks of the Horse Rifles I told you would probably be waiting for you."

Perón did not reply. Clete hadn't expected him to.

He made a low pass over the wharf, then picked up the nose and went to an altitude of 250 meters. Ninety seconds later, he saw below him a steady line of headlights moving in both directions.

He turned to the left and flew south, parallel to what he thought had to be National Route 8.

"Give General Martín the headset," Clete ordered.

Perón didn't reply, but a moment later Martín's voice came over the headset: "I have the earphones on."

"On our left is Route 8," he said. "Don't tell him, but we're going to have a look at Avenida 9 Julio and see how many shirtless ones his girlfriend and his pal Nulder were able to muster."

Ten minutes later, now at two hundred meters, they were flying up what someone had once told Frade — and he had no reason not to believe — was the widest avenue in the world.

Avenida 9 Julio, named for Argentina's Independence Day, was usually crowded, but not like now.

Lines of automobiles, trucks, and buses were running up and down the various lanes, but they were now sharing the avenue with hordes of people.

Clete came to the Obelisk near the Colón Opera House. He thought of it as a miniature version of the Washington Monument in Washington.

The area around it and the streets leading from Avenida 9 Julio to the Casa Rosada were jammed with people, as was the avenue from the Obelisk to the Labor Ministry Building.

"It looks like my Tío Juan's girlfriend has really roused the rabble," Clete said. "There must be a hundred thousand people down there."

"I've never seen anything like it," Martín said, and then, as they approached the Ministry of Labor building, asked, "What do we do now?"

"Get the rest of the bad news," Clete said, as he switched to the radio function.

"Jorge Frade, SAA One."

He had to call three times before he got a reply.

"SAA One, Jorge Frade."

"SAA One is ten kilometers to the south."

Clete switched back to intercom mode.

"Bernardo, please tell me you recognize that voice, and that he works for you."

"Is that Muñoz?" Martín asked.

"Ask again, after I switch to radio," Clete said, moved the switch, then made a *thumbs-up* gesture.

403

"Is that Muñoz?" Martín repeated.

"A sus órdenes, mi General."

Clete switched back to intercom.

"Okay. He knows it's you. Ask him if he's alone, and if he says yes, ask him if Rodríguez is with him."

He switched back to radio and made another thumbs-up.

"Muñoz," Martín asked. "Are you alone?"

"Suboficial Rodríguez is with me, *mi General.*"

"No one else?"

"There was a lieutenant from the Horse Rifles, *mi General,* but at the moment he's taking a . . . he's in the toilet."

"There are no Patricios there? The ones I sent out there?"

"Shortly after you left, *mi General,* a platoon of the Patricios arrived. Ten minutes after that, a company of the Horse Rifles arrived. The Horse Rifles put the men from the Patricios into Hangar Two, *mi General.*"

"The Patricios went willingly?"

"No, *mi General.*"

"Were shots fired?"

"No, sir. But there was a company of the Horse Rifles, and the Patricios had no choice."

"Have the Patricios been disarmed?"

"The lieutenant in charge of the Patricios gave his parole to the captain in charge of the Horse Rifles."

"I'll have him shot!" Martín declared furiously.

That's right, General. Remain calm.

Never lose your temper.

"Enrico?" Clete called.

"*Sí*, Don Cletus?"

"Listen carefully. I want you to go out on the tarmac right now — without anyone seeing you. Go to the line of Lodestars. Go to the Lodestar nearest the runway. Untie the airplane and remove the wheel chocks. Then open the door."

"*Sí*, Don Cletus."

"What I'm going to do is land. Have Muñoz turn on the runway lights in five minutes — that should give you enough time to get out to the Lodestar. As soon as I'm on the ground, I'm going to taxi to the Lodestar and get out. I'll have el Coronel Perón with me. General Martín will then slowly taxi the Storch to the terminal. El Coronel and I will get in the Lodestar and take off. Got it?"

"Where are we going, Don Cletus?"

"Mendoza."

"*Sí*, Don Cletus."

Clete switched to intercom.

"You heard all that, Bernardo? Including the part about taxiing slowly to the terminal? I'm going to need all the time I can get."

"I understand."

"Give the headset to el Coronel."

"What's going on, Cletus?" Perón demanded thirty seconds later.

"There's a company of Horse Soldiers at the airfield looking for you."

"What about the Patricios? Martín said the Patricios would be here to protect me."

"When the Horse Soldiers came, they put the Patricios in Hangar Two."

"So where are you going to take me now? Campo de Mayo? Or Estancia San Pedro y San Pablo? Your men there — they're all ex–Húsares de Pueyrredón troopers — can protect me."

Tío Juan, why do I think it's finally sunk in that people are trying to kill you?

"I don't have enough fuel to fly to Estancia San Pedro y San Pablo."

"My God, what are you going to do?"

"I may be able to keep all three of us alive if you do exactly what I tell you and do it when I tell you to do it — not after you think it over. Agreed?"

That started out as bullshit, but now that I think about it, it's right on the money.

Martín and I are no longer spectators. El Coronel Whatsisname — Lopez, Fernando Lopez — of the Horse Rifles is a good deal more competent than I would have thought.

Not only did he get the whole Shoot Perón

406

Show actually under way, but he seems to know just what he's doing.

Like covering his flanks.

He had to know that General Farrell was sending Martín and Father Welner to get me to fly Tío Juan off that island. Which means somebody told him. And since that wasn't General Farrell, it had to be someone in Farrell's inner circle.

The proof of that is the company of Horse Rifles showed up at the airfield twenty minutes or so after we took off for the island.

Even if Lopez had somebody here who called him the minute we had taken off, there's no way he could have gotten a company of the Horse Rifles here in twenty minutes unless they were already formed somewhere close awaiting the order to get on the trucks and head for the airfield.

And where is Lopez?

You should have thought of this before, Stupid!

He's probably on one of the boats about to land on the island.

Because he's commanding the operation.

And because if he expects to shoot my Tío Juan, he's going to try to do it by the book, not just murder him. By the book means the convening of a summary court-martial, having the court find him guilty of treason, and then, and only then, standing him against a wall facing a firing squad.

And what is Lopez going to do when he learns that Tío Juan is not on the island?

There has to be a Plan B — maybe even Plans B, C, D, and E. So far Lopez has had a plan for everything.

And once he got on those boats and headed for the island, he knew he was committed. There was no going back.

So what's Plan B?

Jesus Christ! You should have thought of this a long time ago, Super Spy!

"If el Coronel Perón is not on Isla Martín García, or for some other reason manages to escape arrest and thus avoid court-martial, then he will be shot to death whenever or wherever he is located."

The one thing Lopez can't allow to happen, now that he's actually started this operation, is have Tío Juan get away.

Lopez knows that failure means Lopez gets the firing squad. He's going to do whatever he can to stay alive. If that means killing Perón — and whoever's with him — out of hand, then so be it. . . .

Frade's chain of thought was interrupted when he heard Perón's voice in his headset.

"What are you thinking of doing, Cletus?"

"As soon as I land, while we're still on the runway, you and I are going to get out of the Storch as quickly as possible. You and I will lie in the grass by the side of the runway. Martín will then taxi toward the terminal.

When he's out of our sight, we'll run to the nearest Lodestar and get in it and fly to Mendoza. Got it?"

"Don't you need a second pilot to fly a Lodestar?" Perón protested.

"I don't. Now give the headset to General Martín."

"Yes?" Martín then said.

"Change of plans, Bernardo. We're all going to get in the Lodestar."

"Why?"

"Because I think that the Horse Rifles are going to shoot first and ask questions later."

Martín didn't reply.

"What I'm going to do is leave the runway and taxi to the first Lodestar. I'll get out and get Perón out and drag him to the Lodestar —"

"What I will do is taxi halfway to the terminal," Martín interrupted him. "Then I will stop, get out, and raise my hands . . ."

"And that's when they'll shoot you," Clete said.

". . . and do whatever I can to stall the Horse Soldiers. The priority is to keep el Coronel Perón alive. The more time you have to get in the Lodestar, start the engines, taxi to the runway —"

"So long, Bernardo. It's been nice to know you."

"God be with you, Cletus," Martín said.

"You sonofabitch," Clete said.

409

■ ■ ■ ■

The runway lights came on. There was no time to argue with General Martín.

Clete moved the stick hard over, stood the Storch on its left wingtip, straightened out, dropped the nose, and put the flaps down.

With a little bit of luck, I can get this onto the ground before those bastards figure out what's going on.

Enrico was standing by the open door of the Lodestar when Clete taxied the Storch up to it.

Clete jumped out, ran to Rodríguez, and grabbed his arm.

"Get el Coronel into the airplane and close the door."

"*Sí,* Don Cletus."

Clete got into the Lodestar, made his way to the cockpit, and threw the MASTER BUSS switch. The instrument panel lit up.

Clete was vaguely aware that the Storch was moving past him, onto the taxiway.

He looked back and saw Enrico boarding with Tío Juan.

The port engine hesitated, belched flame, shook, and started to run very roughly. Clete moved the throttle forward and the Lodestar began to move. By the time he reached the runway, he had the starboard engine running.

Clete got the Lodestar to the end of the runway and turned around. He saw that not one of the engine gauges was in the green. He didn't know what would happen when he moved the throttles to TAKEOFF POWER, but there were a number of possibilities, most of them unpleasant.

He put his hand on the throttles and shoved them to TAKEOFF POWER.

The Lodestar began to roll.

When he passed the taxiway, he had a moment's glance at General Martín, who was standing by the Storch with his arms raised in the universal sign of surrender.

And he saw something else he hadn't seen in a very long time: the muzzle flashes of machine guns, at least three of them, maybe more.

And then he was past the taxiway.

"So long, Bernardo," he said softly. "It's been nice to know you. *Vaya con Dios*."

He inched the yoke forward and sensed the tail-dragger wheel leaving the runway.

He felt life come into the controls, eased the yoke back, and a moment later the rumble of the landing gear stopped.

He reached for the landing gear retract lever, pulled it, and when he got a green light, pulled a little farther back on the yoke and made a shallow climbing turn away from the airfield.

The last thing he saw as he took off — and

he was flying low enough and slow enough to see it clearly — was a silver Lockheed Constellation parked out of the way near the end of the runway. There was an American flag painted on each of the three vertical stabilizers, and the legend HOWELL PETROLEUM CORPORATION painted across the fuselage.

The old man's right. If I had any sense at all, I would be in the States.

Tending to the family business instead of being here, getting shot at.

Enrico came into the cockpit five minutes later, just as Clete thought he might have solved a problem he hadn't thought of at all until he'd begun his climb to cruising altitude: How do I navigate to Mendoza without charts?

Every SAA pilot of course had his own set of charts, consisting of maps of wherever he might be expected to fly, the radio frequencies of the control towers at airports to which he might fly, plus the frequencies of the rare Radio Direction Finding transmitters he might encounter en route to wherever he was going, as well as all sorts of other interesting and necessary information.

Clete's charts were in his office at Aeropuerto Coronel Jorge Frade, where he had expected to pick them up before flying to Berlin at nine.

There of course had been no opportunity

to pick up his charts during this brief visit to Aeropuerto Coronel Jorge G. Frade.

All he had was his memory of many flights to Mendoza.

He knew, for example, that Mendoza was to the west of Buenos Aires.

He knew the only Radio Direction Finder transmitter en route to Mendoza was in San Luis, which was, give or take, five hundred miles from Buenos Aires, and that it had a range of no more than fifty miles — when it worked.

But there were roads, masquerading as highways, leading to Mendoza. National Route 8 and National Route 7, which ran more or less parallel across Argentina from Buenos Aires. After passing through Rio Cuarto, Route 8 jogged to the south and joined Route 7 about a hundred miles east of San Luis.

Clete was reasonably — not absolutely — sure he could simply follow the highways.

He had just found what probably was Route 8, and had turned the Lodestar so that he would be flying to the left of it, when Enrico came into the cockpit.

Frade motioned him into the co-pilot's seat. When Enrico had put on the headset, he said, "I wondered where you were."

"Putting a bandage on el Coronel."

"A bandage? What happened to him?"

"He's got a cut on his face."

Enrico drew his index finger across his cheek to show where. Clete saw dried blood on Enrico's fingers.

"Is it serious? What happened?"

"It's not as serious as he thinks it is. He was squealing like a stuck pig."

"What happened?"

"We took at least nine hits from those machine guns," Rodríguez said matter-of-factly. "Five of them went straight through the plane, in the right side and out the other. One of them took out the window where el Coronel was sitting. A piece of that artificial glass . . ."

"Plexiglas," Clete furnished.

". . . got him here." He drew his index finger across his face from his right ear to the chin. "Sliced him open pretty good, but I don't think it got any muscles. There's always a lot of blood with head wounds."

"But you've bandaged him?"

"Sort of, Don Cletus."

"What does that mean?"

"When I went to the first aid kit by the door, it was gone. Somebody must have stolen it."

"So?"

"So I went to the toilet. You know those pads women use, Don Cletus?"

Frade nodded.

"I used one of those."

If I laughed, or even smiled broadly, at the

414

mental image of the vice president of the Argentine Republic sitting there feeling sorry for himself while holding against his face whatever they call a Kotex down here, I would really be a sonofabitch, wouldn't I?

That thought was immediately replaced by a far more sober one: *Would you be laughing, Red Skelton, if one of those bullets had hit him in the head?*

[FOUR]

Aeropuerto Coronel Jorge G. Frade
Morón, Buenos Aires Province, Argentina
1915 16 October 1945

"I regret that you have been wounded, *mi General*," the major of the Horse Rifles said, looking down at General de Brigada Bernardo Martín. "I have sent for a surgeon."

Martín, who was lying on the taxiway ten meters from the Storch, raised himself on his elbow and looked down at his left leg. There was a lot of blood, but he saw that he had been lucky. The machine gun bullet had gone into the fleshy part of his thigh and he didn't think it had hit either artery or bone.

"Not as much as you will later," Martín snapped, and immediately thought, *That was not smart, Bernardo. He has a gun.*

And is apparently so shaken by this that he hasn't taken mine.

415

Another major appeared, this one a *cirujano mayor,* a doctor.

"I'll put a quick tourniquet on your leg, *mi General,* and then give you something for the pain."

Good. It's starting to throb. That will soon be followed by pain.

But I can't take any morphine; I need to think.

"No morphine," Martín ordered.

"Let's get your trousers off," the cirujano mayor said.

The Horse Rifles major suddenly raised his hands in the universal sign of surrender.

Martín looked toward the terminal building.

Major Habanzo and Captain Garcia of the BIS, pistols drawn, were running toward them, followed by what looked like an entire company of Patricios.

The Horse Rifles major dropped his pistol onto the taxiway.

Martín immediately thought how that could have been reported: *"General Bernardo Martín died of a second wound suffered when his captor, who never should have been allowed to get near anything more lethal than a water pistol, dropped his pistol onto the taxiway, whereupon it went off."*

"You'll be shot," Habanzo said to the Horse Rifles major.

"Not by you," Martín said.

"How bad is el General?" Habanzo demanded of the cirujano mayor.

"He is in no immediate danger, and we can have him at the hospital in twenty minutes," the doctor said.

"I'm not going to the hospital," Martín announced.

"*Mi General,* you're wounded!" Captain Garcia said.

"I noticed," Martín said. "Garcia, get a stretcher and bearers and take me to Señor Frade's office in the terminal building."

"And the cirujano mayor?" Habanzo asked. "What do we do with him?"

"You don't do anything with him. But what you do now is seal off the airport. Nobody in or out."

"Including the passengers who were going to fly to Berlin?"

"Including everybody," Martín said.

"*Mi General,* you really should go to the hospital," the cirujano mayor said.

"Do what you're told, Major," Martín said. "Get me on a stretcher and get me to Don Cletus's office!"

"Aside from what you did to my trousers, which were nearly new, what's the damage?" Martín, after finding Frade's bottle of Rémy Martin and taking a long swig, inquired of the cirujano mayor.

"You were lucky, *mi General.* There is

417

simply a good deal of muscle damage. You will be on crutches for six weeks or so. But there is no bone damage, no arterial damage. I repeat, you belong in the hospital. You should be x-rayed and you should have a couple of liters of blood. And you should not be drinking that."

"It has reduced the pain from excruciating to barely tolerable," Martín said. "And with that in mind, I think I will have another little taste of the Rémy Martin before you admit the people waiting to see me. I would not want them to see me, as the senior officer present, drinking on duty."

Martín picked up the bottle of cognac again and took another healthy swallow.

"Please let my people in, Cirujano Mayor," he then said.

Major Habanzo and Captain Garcia came into the office followed by a *teniente coronel* of the Patricios — whose face Martín knew but whose name would not come — and Hans-Peter von Wachtstein, who now was wearing the uniform of an SAA first officer.

"You first, please, el Coronel," Martín said. "What's the situation?"

"The airfield is secure, *mi General*. The press is at the gates demanding entrance and to know what's going on. I have told them nothing except that they will be arrested if they try to force their way in."

"And the Horse Rifles?"

"They have been disarmed and placed in Hangar Two, *mi General.*"

"Habanzo, what about the passengers for the Berlin flight? Where are they?"

"In the passenger terminal, *mi General.* And they demand to know what's going on."

Flight 2230 was scheduled to depart at nine P.M. It would fly across the Atlantic Ocean to Dakar, and then to Lisbon, Portugal, Frankfurt am Main, Germany, and ultimately Berlin. Its passengers would include a half-dozen senior Argentine diplomats and other government officials; three priests, one of them a Jesuit; and seven prominent Argentine businessmen. The pilot-in-command was supposed to be SAA Captain Cletus Frade.

"What happens now, Peter, without Cletus?" Martín asked. "Can you go without him?"

"No," von Wachtstein said simply.

"Why not? He's not the only SAA pilot."

"The four pilots here now are qualified to fly the airplane, but none is certified for Berlin. During the flight we were going to teach them how to fly across the Russian Zone into Berlin."

"You and Frade were to teach them, you mean."

"Right."

"Why can't you do that yourself?"

"Because it has to be done by the pilot-in-command, and the pilot-in-command has to

419

be a captain. I am only a first officer."

"SAA has other captains certified to fly into Berlin, right?"

"Five other captains."

"Why can't we use one of them?"

"We need two. We'd have to find them and get them out here to the field. That would take at least two hours. Is that what you want me to do?"

Martín bit off the reply that came to his lips.

You're more than a little drunk, Bernardo. Your mind is not as badly muddled by all that Rémy Martin as it would have been by morphine. But there's no question that while the four ounces — at least — of the cognac you gulped down took some edge off my pain, it was at the price of at least partial intoxication.

Which is probably why I think I am facing a Kasidah situation.

And almost certainly why I suddenly clearly remember discussing the Kasidah with Frade, when both of us sat in his library suffering the effects of having consumed most of a bottle of Rémy Martin . . .

"Cletus," Martín had said, "have you ever heard of the Kasidah?"

"The what?"

"I think of it as a splendid one-sentence philosophy for people in our profession."

"We say, 'Don't look in the mirror,' " Frade said.

"Meaning, 'Never forget your enemy doesn't think like you do'?"

"Precisely."

"*The Kasidah of Haji Abdu El-Yezdi* says, 'The truth is a shattered mirror strewn in myriad bits and each believes his little bit the whole to own.' "

Frade had considered that for a moment, and then replied, just a little thickly: "I like that. I adopt it herewith. 'The truth is a shattered mirror,' et cetera — whatever you said — 'so don't look in the mirror.' "

"Better yet," Martín had replied, " 'don't look in the mirror, because the truth,' et cetera, et cetera."

"Okay. Who was the genius who thought this up? Some Arab?"

"Actually, Haji Abdu El-Yezdi was the pen name of an Englishman, Sir Richard Francis Burton."

"The dirty book guy?"

"I gather you're familiar with the *Kama Sutra*?"

"I was thinking of the translation of *One Thousand and One Nights* with all the dirty parts left in it. What's the *Kama Sutra*?"

"An ancient Hindu book offering illustrated practical instructions on how to perform sexual intercourse."

"How did I miss that?"

"I can't imagine."

"Wait. I know," Cletus had said. "I'm a Texan. We don't need practical instructions on sexual intercourse. It comes to us naturally. But I'm not surprised you Argentines need an illustrated 'How to Screw' manual."

Before Martín could reply to that, Doña Dorotea Mallín de Frade had come into the library, causing a change of subject.

. . . The situation here at Aeropuerto Coronel Jorge G. Frade, Martín now thought, *is like a broken mirror. And not only do all the players believe they have the truth, but they are determined that no one else learn anything about their truth.*

The official purpose of the Argentine diplomats and other government officials going to Germany was to facilitate the return of Argentine nationals who had been trapped in Germany to their homeland.

Martín was deeply suspicious of this on-the-surface noble purpose, wondering why so many of his countrymen had been trapped there in the first place. Until Argentina had declared war on Germany on March 27, 1945, not quite six weeks before the Germans surrendered unconditionally on May 7, Argentines, as neutrals, had been perfectly free to leave Germany simply by taking a train to Sweden or Switzerland.

The stated purpose of the Argentine businessmen in going to Germany was to protect their business interests in what had been the Thousand-Year Reich.

Commerce between Germany and Argentina had been one-way since 1940. The Germans had bought all the Argentine foodstuffs, leather, and wool that they could. But nothing had gone the other way because the Germans had nothing to sell. And what the Germans had bought they paid for with U.S. dollars, British pounds, and Swiss francs. The reichsmark, for all practical purposes, was worthless. And now all that remained of foreign currency in what had been the Reichsbank was controlled by the Allies, who were holding it for reparations. Germany could not buy anything from anyone, and had nothing to sell to anyone.

So why did just about every SAA flight to Germany carry Argentine businessmen?

The answer to this question, in Martín's mind, also applied to the question of why the government was so interested in repatriating its citizens from Germany.

It was one word: corruption.

He didn't know for sure — although he had come up with a number of pretty good scenarios — how the businessmen or the government officials were enriching themselves illegally by traveling to Germany, or repatriating Argentines, but there was no question in his mind that they were.

He didn't care.

Protection of the Argentine Republic was his business, not corruption. There had been corruption in Argentina from its beginnings. The army and the navy — usually — stood aloof from it, and generally military officers lived by a Code of Honor. Martín tried to.

The three priests on Flight 2230 were something else. He knew that the Jesuit answered to Father Welner, and at least one — probably both — of the others also did. What they were doing — arranging for Nazis and their families to find refuge in Argentina — was illegal, but the priests were serving Holy Mother Church, not enriching themselves personally.

Why the Vatican was spiriting Nazis — and Hungarian, French, Belgian, Norwegian, Danish, Austrian, and other collaborators with the Thousand-Year Reich — out of Europe so they could escape the justified wrath of the Allies wasn't clear. Except that it had to do with the Vatican's war against the Communists, who they believed were the Antichrist.

Just about everyone in Argentina was Roman Catholic and, if asked, would agree with Holy Mother Church that the Communists were the Antichrist. After all, that's what the Pope had said.

But virtually none of his countrymen

thought of the Antichrist as a real threat to Argentina. Russia was a long way away, and the Soviet Union didn't even maintain diplomatic relations with the Argentine Republic. And besides, the Germans had really bloodied the Russian Bear's nose. They would be too busy rebuilding their own country to even be thinking about turning Argentina into one more Soviet Socialist Republic.

Frade — and the reports he had received from a BIS officer he had had in the Argentine embassy in Berlin, and from the SAA pilots who worked for the BIS and had been to Germany — had convinced him that the Soviet Union posed a real and immediate threat to Argentina.

Martín knew enough about the Soviets to know how skillful they were in taking advantage of chaos. He didn't think they had anything at all to do with the plot to assassinate Juan Domingo Perón, but if it succeeded or the stopping of it resulted in a civil war — that would really play into their hands.

And of course Martín knew all about OPERATION OST, Frade's smuggling into Argentina — often assisted by the Vatican — former officers, some of them Nazis, of General Gehlen's Abwehr Ost.

Frade had promised, and Martín believed him, to share his intelligence vis-à-vis the Soviets with him. Martín knew there was no other way he could get such intelligence. In this connection, Frade had told him that when he returned from his next flight to Berlin, he was going to have a good deal of intelligence to share with him.

"Conclusions to be logically drawn" — in the terminology of an intelligence analysis — from all he knew and believed were that his first priority was to keep Juan Domingo Perón alive. Failing to do so would result in chaos and possibly civil war.

For the moment, Cletus Frade had Perón safe in Mendoza.

If Flight 2230 did not depart for Germany, all the government officials, diplomats, businessmen, and priests would have to be permitted to leave Aeropuerto Coronel Jorge G. Frade. And once they got back to wherever, they would report what they had seen at the airport.

The news that an attempt to assassinate Perón had been made would be all over Argentina within an hour. Martín realized he could not permit that to happen.

And he understood that he could not present the problem to General Farrell, asking for permission to do what he knew should be done. He knew what Farrell's reaction to that would be: "Let's not act in haste. Let's see how this looks tomorrow."

Martín thus saw it as his duty to do what he thought should be done, and to worry about President Farrell's reaction to it later.

■ ■ ■ ■

"Who are the four captains scheduled to make this flight, Peter?" Martín now asked.

Von Wachtstein recited their names.

God is with me, Martín decided, and ordered, "Get Captain Lopez in here, please."

SAA Captain Paolo Lopez, like a half-dozen other SAA captains, was an officer of the Bureau of Internal Security.

Lopez appeared within minutes.

"How are you, *mi General?*" he asked.

Martín did not reply, but he addressed Lopez by his military rank.

"Major Lopez, you are aware that Captain Frade cannot take Flight 2230 to Berlin. My solution to that problem is to designate First Officer von Wachtstein as pilot-in-command. Do you have any problem with that?"

After a long moment, Lopez said, "No, *mi General.*"

"Advise the other pilots of my decision. It is not open for discussion. The only option they have is to go, or not go. In the latter case — don't tell them this until they indicate what they are going to do — they will be confined in Hangar Two with the Horse Rifles until I decide what to do with them."

"Sí, mi General."

"Peter, how soon can you take off?"

"As soon as we load the passengers and dinner."

"Have a nice flight," Martín said.

[FIVE]

Above Provincial Route 60
Mendoza Province, Argentina
2305 16 October 1945

It wasn't hard to find Casa Montagna on Estancia Don Guillermo. Clete Frade had come to think of it as Fort Leavenworth South; he had converted what had been a romantic retreat looking down at an enormous vineyard until it was, like Leavenworth, both a fort and a prison. The floodlights shining down from it made it stand out like a beacon on the hilltop — elsewhere it would be called a mountaintop — in the foothills of the Andes mountain range.

"What do you say we wake everybody up, Enrico?" Frade said, pushing the yoke forward and pointing the nose of the Lodestar at Casa Montagna. "Put a little excitement into their lives?"

"El Coronel?" Rodríguez asked.

"My Tío Juan needs a little excitement, too, to take his mind off" — in the last moment, he stopped himself from saying "the Kotex on his face" and instead said — "his many other problems."

428

Frade buzzed Casa Montagna twice, flashing over the hilltop enclave at no more than two hundred feet, first from the north and then from the south, and then he turned the Lodestar toward the Mendoza Airfield.

He had to buzz that three times after he learned that he had no air-to-ground communications over which he could order the runway lights be turned on. Obviously, some of those machine-gun bullets, if they hadn't hit the radio compartment itself, had taken out the antenna, or at least one of the antenna supports.

The runway lights finally came on, and he lined up with the runway with plenty of time to consider yet another unpleasant set of possibilities.

Had machine-gun bullets taken out the hydraulics necessary to lower the landing gear?

And/or punctured the tires?

He had no choice but to land. He wasn't sure he had enough fuel to make it through the Andes to Chile. Even if he was able to pull that off, he didn't want to land in Santiago in a bullet-riddled airplane carrying the vice president of the Argentine Republic. There would be questions.

The green GEAR DOWN AND LOCKED light came on five seconds before he got to the threshold of the runway. Ten seconds after that, as the Lodestar had not swerved out of control off the runway, he was able to draw the reasonable conclusion that there was air in the landing gear tires.

He taxied to an SAA hangar and shut down the engines.

He went into the passenger compartment.

El Coronel Juan D. Perón was nothing to smile over, much less laugh at. His uniform was black with blood and so was the leather of his seat. His face was pale from loss of blood.

Jesus Christ!

Next step is shock. I've got to get him to a doctor!

"We'll have you out of here in just a minute, Tío Juan. Hang on. Try to stay awake."

Perón grasped Clete's arm.

"God bless you, Cletus," he said emotionally.

Enrico had the door open by the time Clete got there. When he went through it and jumped to the ground, Clete found himself facing the headlights of three Ford pickup trucks. On the roof of one was an air-cooled .30 caliber machine gun.

Have we gone through all this only to get blown away the minute we land?

"My God, Don Cletus!" a voice called. "What happened?"

Clete couldn't see who it was.

"It's a long story," Clete said. "I need one of the pickups to go to the Little Sisters' Hospital, and one of the others to go with us.

430

Then get this airplane into a hangar, close the door, and don't let anybody get near it."

"How many injured, *mi Coronel?*" the same voice asked.

Clete still couldn't see who it was.

"Just one," he said, and after a moment added: "El Coronel Perón. And no one is to know."

While flying to Mendoza, Frade had thought that the Horse Rifles commander and others involved in the plot would probably think he had flown Perón to Uruguay, which was sort of the traditional destination for Argentine leaders who had to get out of the country in a hurry. He knew he had to keep them thinking that as long as possible.

"Understood, *mi Coronel.*"

"I buzzed Casa Montagna before I came here. Major Ashton will probably be here shortly. When he — or whoever — shows up, send them to the Little Sisters' Hospital."

"*Sí, mi Coronel.*"

"Enrico, let's get el Coronel out of the plane and into the front seat of that pickup."

Clete then pointed to the men standing by the pickup.

"You get in the back," he ordered. "I'll drive."

431

[Six]

Halfway to the hospital, Clete realized that the worst way to keep the presence of the blood-soaked vice president of the Argentine Republic in Mendoza from becoming public knowledge would be to take him to a hospital. So he drove instead to the convent, jumped out of the pickup, and pounded on the door.

The Mother Superior of the Mendoza Chapter of the Order of the Little Sisters of Santa María del Pilar finally came to the door. She was leathery-skinned, tiny, and of indeterminate age.

"What's going on, Cletus?" she demanded. "God help you if you've been drinking!"

"I really need your help. I've got an injured man in the pickup."

"This is the convent, not the hospital," she snapped.

"Please take a look."

She walked to the pickup.

"Get out of there, Enrico," she ordered.

Rodríguez propped up Perón as well as he could and got out. The nun climbed into the cab, and immediately recognized Perón.

"Who did this to you, Juan Domingo?" she

432

demanded.

"They're trying to kill me, Mother Superior," Perón said weakly.

"You don't mean Cletus and Enrico, I hope."

"No. They're the only reason I'm alive."

"What's your blood type?" she demanded.

He called it forth from memory: "AB."

"Well, that's one problem solved," she said.

"For obvious reasons, I didn't want to take him to the hospital," Clete said. "No one must know he's here. And in that condition."

"Really?" she said sarcastically, then looked at Perón. "Put your head between your knees, Juan Domingo. We don't want you passing out."

She backed out of the cab.

"Don't just stand there, Enrico," she ordered. "Get back in there!"

She turned to Clete. "Take Juan Domingo to Casa Montagna. Put him in a bed in the infirmary. Cover him with blankets. See if you can get some liquid in him. I'll get my bag and be there as soon as I can."

"You can't come with us?"

"I'm too old, Cletus, to ride in the bed of a truck. Now get going!"

[Seven]

About ten kilometers down Provincial Route 60, which was deserted at this time of morning, Clete saw unusually bright headlights. A vehicle was coming down the road in the direction of Mendoza at a high rate of speed.

That's probably Ashton.

Confirmation of the guess came a moment later when an unusual automobile flashed past the pickup. It was a 1940 Lincoln Continental, unusual in its own right, but in this case more unusual because it was custom bodied.

The Lincoln had been shipped from the States as a birthday present from Clete's uncle, Humberto Duarte, to his wife, Beatrice, who was Clete's father's sister. At the time of course Clete had never laid eyes on el Coronel Jorge G. Frade and had no idea he had an aunt and an uncle and a cousin his own age named Jorge.

He learned of this only when he first went to Argentina and coincidentally arrived just before his cousin Jorge returned to his home-

434

land in a lead-lined casket from Stalingrad. Jorge had been an Ejército Argentino captain serving as an observer when the Russians shot down the Storch he was in.

For this act of heroism — Clete thought that voluntarily exposing oneself to enemy fire was absolute stupidity — it was decided at the highest levels of the Thousand-Year Reich to award the fallen Argentine the Knight's Cross of the Iron Cross, a decoration on a par with the American Distinguished Service Cross. Doing so, Joseph Goebbels, the Nazi Propaganda Minister, had successfully argued, would remind the Argentines that Germany was fighting the godless Communists who had killed Captain Jorge Duarte.

By the time the body of Jorge arrived — accompanied by a bona fide German hero, Captain Hans-Peter Ritter von Wachtstein, who had received his Knight's Cross of the Iron Cross from the hands of Adolf Hitler himself for his service as a fighter pilot — Clete's Aunt Beatrice had been literally driven out of her mind by the death of her son.

She clearly belonged in a mental institution. But she was a Frade, married to a Duarte, and Clete learned that Argentines of that class simply are not carted off to a funny farm just because they were as bonkers as a March hare.

To solve the problem, el Coronel Frade had turned over his Estancia Don Guillermo to his brother-in-law. He had not returned to the place since the last time he had been there with his wife, Clete's mother, shortly before she had died in childbirth.

Following a generous donation to the Little Sisters of Santa María del Pilar, which permitted them to add a wing to their Mendoza hospital, the nursing order took over the care of Beatrice Frade de Duarte with the understanding they would do so for the rest of her life. A sort of one-room psychiatric hospital was constructed for her in a wing of Casa Montagna. She was driven there in her Lincoln.

Aunt Beatrice surprised everyone by regaining enough of her mental health to the point where, suitably drugged, she could resume her role in society and return to Buenos Aires. The Lincoln stayed in Mendoza. It triggered unpleasant memories for Aunt Beatrice.

Clete had known nothing of Estancia Don Guillermo, even after his father had been murdered and it — and everything else his father had owned — became his. It was brought to his attention when he needed a place to hide the Froggers, after Herr Frogger deserted his post in the German embassy. Enrico had matter-of-factly suggested that since "the Nazi woman was crazy," housing her at Casa Montagna would solve that problem. Clete then learned that his father had charged the old soldier with keeping an eye on the place after he had left it for the last time.

When Clete and Dorotea visited Casa Montagna, they became the first to be in the master suite since the day Clete's mother and father had left there. No one, in fact, had been in the house at all, save for the period during which his Aunt Beatrice was being nursed in what was euphemistically called "the Infirmary" by the nuns of the Little Sisters of Santa María del Pilar.

In a room off the master bedroom, Dorotea found a bassinet, baby powder, a stack of diapers, and a stuffed toy tiger waiting for a baby. She wept when she realized a moment later that that baby was now her husband.

Dorotea had immediately fallen in love with Casa Montagna and shortly thereafter was using Clete's bassinet and other items for their firstborn, Jorge Howell Frade, who was delivered in the Infirmary under the care of the Mother Superior of the Order of the Little Sisters of Santa María del Pilar.

After the Lincoln flashed past the pickup, its taillights quickly disappeared from Clete's rearview mirror. He was afraid that, after being directed to the Little Sisters' Hospital from the airfield and then not finding Clete there, Ashton would draw unwelcome attention to his presence simply by asking questions.

But shortly afterward, the bright headlights appeared in Clete's rearview mirror. They grew, and moments later the Lincoln pulled alongside the pickup and Clete found himself looking at Major Maxwell Ashton III.

Clete gestured toward the estancia. Ashton nodded and pulled ahead of the pickup.

Clete followed him to the vineyards of the estancia, through them, and then up the steep road to the house enclave.

The gates were open when he got there, but there were machine guns trained on them, just in case.

They helped el Coronel Perón from the pickup truck and into the infirmary and into a bed.

Clete and Enrico, not without difficulty, had just finished getting Perón out of his blood-soaked uniform when Mother Superior, trailed by two nursing sisters, came into the room.

"Lie down, Juan Domingo," the tiny nun ordered, "and let me have a look at that."

He docilely obeyed.

She pulled the pad from his face.

"There are a lot of blood vessels in the face, and whatever did that to you cut many of them," she announced. "You'll live, and there won't be much of a scar; jagged wounds leave

438

less scar than neat ones. But before I sew you up, we're going to get some of Cletus's blood in you. You lost a lot."

Frade thought, *Cletus's blood?*

Mother Superior turned to one of the nuns. "We need another pressure pack on that. Get one. A proper one." She considered what she had said. "But that one did a pretty good job, I must admit."

Then she turned to Enrico.

"Drag that bed next to this one," she ordered. "And you, Cletus, take your jacket and shirt off and get in it."

"How do you know I have the right kind of blood?" Cletus asked.

"Because when you were an adorable baby I typed it. And then when your son was born, and I thought your poor wife might need a little blood, I went to your records and there it was. Any other questions, or have I your kind permission to get on with this?"

Clete got in the bed. Ninety seconds later, blood began to flow from his vein into his godfather's.

Frade saw Ashton standing in the doorway, and motioned for him to come to the bed.

"Yes, sir?" Ashton said.

Mother Superior snorted.

"Get on the Collins to Estancia San Pedro y San Pablo," Clete ordered. "Tell el Jefe —"

"Colonel, it's quarter to two in the morning. No one will be standing by the radio."

"Then get on the telephone and call them and tell them — without mentioning my name — to get on it. When that happens — make sure this is encrypted — tell el Jefe to get out to the Jorge Frade airport and find out what happened there after we left. Specifically, what happened to General Martín. And also what happened to the nine-o'clock flight to Europe. Did it get off on time? Get off at all? If not, what happened? Don't tell him Enrico and I are here, or that Colonel Perón is with us."

"Colonel," Ashton said hesitatingly, "if I call them on the Collins, el Jefe will know where you are."

Frade considered that for a moment.

"You're right," he said. "I guess I'm not thinking very clearly."

"I wonder why not?" Mother Superior said, as she took his pulse. "When was the last time you had something to eat?"

"Lunch," he said.

Mother Superior looked at Ashton.

"When el Coronel Frade is finished giving his orders, wake up a cook and have him ready to prepare a couple steaks for these two when they wake up."

"Yes, ma'am," Ashton said.

"Wake up?" Clete challenged. "What makes you think I'm going to sleep? I can't afford to go to sleep."

She snorted.

"And have el Jefe find Dorotea," Frade went on, "and tell her we're all right. Personally. Not over the telephone."

"Yes, sir."

"Is that all?" Mother Superior asked. "If so, just lie there quietly and let the transfusion work."

"I'll take care of everything, Colonel," Ashton said.

Clete lowered his head to the pillow, and then had one more thought and raised his head.

"Make sure no one gets off the hill and starts talking," he said. " 'You'll never believe who's in the infirmary.' "

"No one will," Ashton said.

Then Clete had one more thought.

"Do something about Colonel Perón's uniform. Get it cleaned somehow."

"Yes, sir."

"I said lie there quietly!" Mother Superior ordered, then waved everyone out of the room.

Clete lowered his head again and looked at the ceiling.

The ceiling lights went out, leaving only a small table light to illuminate the room.

He looked at Perón and found Perón's eyes on him.

"Now that they've gone, I've got something to say," Perón said.

Now what?

"We both know there has been bad blood between us, Cletus. But the blood flowing from your veins into mine has wiped that slate clean. God has changed all that. I have realized the godfather-godson relationship works both ways: God sent you to help me, to help Argentina just when we needed help most!"

Jesus Christ, does he believe that?

Even more incredibly, does he expect me to believe it?

"Greater love hath no man than to lay down his life for another," Perón went on. "You did that for me. General Martín did that for me. Even Suboficial Mayor Rodríguez did that for me. For Argentina!"

He's delirious! Out of his gourd!

Clete closed his eyes.

If I'm not looking at him, maybe he will shut the hell up.

VIII

VIII

[ONE]

The Infirmary
Casa Montagna
Estancia Don Guillermo
Kilometer 40.4, Provincial Route 60
Mendoza Province, Argentina
0815 18 October 1945

When Clete opened his eyes, he saw that sunlight filled the room. He also saw Major Maxwell Ashton III standing at the foot of his bed.

I guess I passed out listening to Tío Juan's babbling.

He looked at the adjacent bed. It was empty.

"Where's Perón?"

"Mother Superior is sewing him up. She said she waited until he had a little rest. She just started. She said I should wake you up."

Clete grunted.

"So good morning," Ashton said. "How do you feel?"

445

"Peachy keen. What do we hear from el Jefe?"

"I couldn't get him on the Collins until the regular schedule at oh-six-hundred. By now, he should be getting close to the airport."

"Which means we won't hear from him for another two hours and something. Not before eleven hundred, probably."

"Later even, depending on what he finds at Jorge Frade. You hungry?"

"Starved."

"Mother Superior put Enrico to work on breakfast. You're to get steak and eggs, orange juice, bread and butter, and not more than two glasses of wine."

"She's letting me have wine?"

"She's insisting on it. Says you need it after the transfusion."

"And where is this feast to take place?"

"In the dining room of your apartment. You need some help?"

"Do I look that bad?"

"Since you ask, Colonel, right now you look like death warmed over. And that's a hell of an improvement over how you looked at oh-one-thirty. You must have had a hell of a day yesterday."

"And the fun may just be beginning," Clete said, as he sat up and swung his legs out of bed.

He felt a little dizzy, but managed to get on his feet and stay there.

446

■ ■ ■ ■

The dining room of Clete's apartment was the master suite of the big house. He didn't make it that far. The aroma of searing meat caught his attention as he walked down the corridor and he followed his nose into the kitchen.

Enrico, wrapped in a white apron, was standing at a *parrilla* and holding a large knife against a large, three-inch-thick *bife de chorizo.*

"When you finish making that inedible," Frade said as he slipped into a chair at a large kitchen table, "I'll eat it here."

"I cooked at this *parrilla* for your father before you were born, Don Cletus. I know what I'm doing."

"You want the wine?" Ashton asked.

"I never challenge Mother Superior's medical opinions."

Ashton opened a bottle of Don Guillermo Cabernet Sauvignon 1940 and poured all of it into three glasses, handing one to Enrico and one to Frade and raising the third.

"What do we drink to?"

"Perón is still alive," Frade said seriously. "And maybe we can avoid a civil war."

"That really worries you, doesn't it?" Ashton asked. "A civil war?"

"Not only would that really fuck up Opera-

447

tion Ost for us, but I've heard a lot more than I wanted to about the one they had in Spain."

"From who?"

"From Hansel as we were flying back and forth across the drink. Spain's was apparently really bad, and I don't want that to happen here. And not only because of what it would mean for this operation."

"Well, we should be hearing from el Jefe pretty soon about what happened at the airport." Ashton raised his glass. "Long life to your Tío Juan!"

As if the toast had been his cue, el Coronel Juan Domingo Perón came into the kitchen.

He was in a sort of ratty cotton bathrobe, thin, washed out, and not quite large enough for him. He had a bandage covering most of his cheek. He looked pale but somewhat better.

"Very kind of you, señor," Perón said. "But I don't believe I have the privilege of your acquaintance."

Clete took a healthy sip of his Cabernet Sauvignon and was surprised at how quickly — immediately — he felt the effect of the alcohol.

I guess that's because I've been bled.

"Colonel Perón," Clete said, "may I present my deputy, Major Maxwell Ashton the Third? Max, this is my Tío Juan."

The two shook hands.

"Aside from my godson, Major, you're the

first member of the OSS I've ever actually met."

"Of the what, Colonel?" Ashton asked.

Clete thought: *Why do I think this is going to be a disaster?*

"Enrico," Frade ordered, "get el Coronel a glass of wine, and then go in the wardrobe and get him a decent bathrobe. I think there's a couple still in boxes. And where's my breakfast?"

"Right away, Don Cletus," Enrico said, gesturing for the plump, pleasant-looking middle-aged woman who was "el patrón's cook" to take over the *parrilla.*

She dropped what looked like a half pound of butter into a fire-blackened frying pan on the *parrilla* and then — seemingly without looking — began to break eggs into a bowl with one hand.

My God, my mouth is actually watering!

Enrico returned carrying a gray box printed with the legend *Sulka et Cie, Rue de Castiglione, Paris.*

"Oh, my God!" Perón said. "If that's what I think it is!"

"What would that be?" Frade asked.

He took another swallow of the wine.

I'm about to get fed, why not?

"You were with us, Suboficial Mayor," Perón said. "Remember?"

"I remember, *mi Coronel*," the old soldier said.

"We had time off — I forget why — from the Kriegsschule and your father took me and Eduardo Ramos to Paris," Perón recalled emotionally. "We stayed at the Hotel Continental. We had lunch, with a good deal of wine. No. Now that I think of it, your father was drinking cognac and water — the French call it *'fin de l'eau,'* which means 'the end of water.' And after lunch we went across the street to Sulka, where your father bought shirts . . ."

"There's still boxes of them in the wardrobe," Enrico furnished.

". . . and then he saw the robe," Perón finished.

Enrico opened the box. He held up what Clete realized was a "dressing robe" rather than a bathrobe. It was of padded blue silk with a white collar and lapels.

"That's it," Perón said. "And your father said, 'I'll take all you have. Send them over to the hotel.' Your father was like that, Cletus. Generous to a fault. I always thought he was going to give one to Eduardo and me, but that didn't happen. . . .

"But now he has! He's given me not only the robe, but his son, as well!"

Oh, shit! Frade thought, looking over the rim of his wineglass as he sipped.

Enrico held out the robe for Perón to put it on.

"There's a mirror in there," Perón said, pointing, and then marched out of the kitchen toward the apartment.

Enrico asked permission with his eyes, and when Clete nodded, Enrico followed Perón.

The cook put a plate before Clete. It held the large *bife de chorizo,* now covered with four sunny-side-up eggs, and a pile of what he thought of as "home-fried" potatoes.

Clete looked up from his breakfast as Tío Juan came back in the kitchen wearing the robe.

Even with that bandage on his face, he is a good-looking sonofabitch.

He looks like someone in charge, someone who can be trusted.

Unless you know him well, in which case you know not to trust him half as far as you can throw him.

"Sit down and have some breakfast," Clete said, as he dipped a piece of potato in an egg yolk.

"That was my intention, Cletus," Perón said, his tone making it clear he didn't like being told what to do. "And I believe I will have a taste of the wine."

As the wine had had a near-immediate effect on Clete, so did the steak and eggs.

He really thought he could feel strength

451

come back into his body.

Christ, how much of my blood did Mother Superior pump out of me and into my Tío Juan?

Or is it just the wine making me feel better?

That seems logical.

"Well, where do we stand in dealing with our problem?" Perón asked as he sipped his wine and awaited his plate.

"Our problem"?

It's you they're trying to kill, not me!

"We're waiting to hear from Buenos Aires, to learn what happened at the airport," Clete said. "For example, is General Martín still alive?"

"And if someone calls here to provide that information, Cletus, they will know that you're here and that I am almost certainly with you."

"We have a way around that."

"When do you expect to hear from Buenos Aires?" Perón demanded.

"Before noon."

"Then we have time for you to tell me exactly what's going on around here," Perón said.

Oh, shit. This is what I've been afraid of.

And I can't say it's none of his goddamn business, either.

I guess I could, now that I think about it, but that would (a) sure piss him off and (b) make him determined to find out.

Unless of course he does get himself killed.

"Okay. I'll tell you what I can."

"You'll tell me everything. And I think we had better have this conversation in private. Major Ashton, will you excuse us?"

"Stay right where you are, Max," Clete snapped. He turned to Perón. "Let's clear the air. You don't issue any orders here. Your status is that of an officer under arrest by order of President Farrell. My status is that I am acting at the orders of the president. Until the president releases you from arrest — or General Martín, the only other person who can issue an order to me right now, does, and we don't know what happened to him — that makes you my prisoner."

"I can't believe what I just heard!" Perón said. "How dare you talk to me that way!"

"You better believe it, and tell me you do or I'll have Major Ashton lock you in a room and keep you there until this mess is resolved."

"You wouldn't dare!"

"Major Ashton, get a couple of the Húsares," Frade ordered, "and take Colonel Perón to the detention facility."

Ashton popped to his feet.

"Yes, sir."

"The Húsares? There are Húsares here?" Perón asked, visibly shocked.

I meant to say "ex-Húsares."

But if he wants to think that . . .

453

"And they call me 'Coronel,' " Clete said. "Now, shall I have Major Ashton get a couple of them? Or are you going to behave?"

Perón considered that option for a full thirty seconds.

"The worst thing that could happen under these circumstances is that there be more bad blood between us," he said finally. "Will you accept my parole?"

"Accepted. Sit down, Major Ashton."

"Yes, sir," Ashton said, and did so.

Okay, now what?

I guess I'd better tell him everything. I don't see any other option.

"As to what we are doing here," Clete began, "shortly before the German surrender, when General Reinhard Gehlen, who ran Abwehr Ost, realized that defeat was inevitable . . ."

Telling that story took just over half an hour, during which Perón asked a number of pertinent questions. They reminded Clete that while Juan Domingo Perón was a three-star asshole, he didn't get to be a colonel, much less simultaneously vice president, secretary of War, and secretary of Labor and Welfare of the Argentine Republic, by being stupid.

"I have always regarded the Bolsheviks as a monstrous danger to Christian society," Perón announced. "It was for that reason that

I supported National Socialism, even after I learned of the horrible things the Nazis were doing."

Well, here comes the bullshit.

What did I expect?

"And I'm proud, deeply proud, that my godson, the son of the best friend I have ever had, is fighting this menace. What I can't understand — what hurts me deeply — is why I have been kept in the dark about this."

"You think you can handle the answer, Tío Juan, if I tell you why?"

"I would be grateful if you would."

"No one trusts you. Not only is there good reason for people — your brother officers — to believe that you are getting rich getting Nazis out of Germany to escape getting hung, but your personal life — specifically your sex life — including your refusal to get rid of that pervert Nulder — does not tend to make people think well of you."

Clete expected an explosion — *What the hell, get it over with* — but it didn't come.

"As far as profiting," Perón replied calmly, "if you wish to call it that, from the current problems senior members of the former German Reich are experiencing is concerned — guilty as charged. But there are two reasons, one of which I'm more than a little ashamed of. That is, my personal finances. I have been a poor man all of my life."

He patted the quilted robe.

"I've never been able to say, 'I'll take all you have.' I've never been able to take a two-minute look at an automobile on the Kurfürstendamm and then tell them to ship it to Argentina, the way your father did with his beloved Horch.

"But getting personally rich from the Nazis, as you put it, was not my motive when I decided to part them from their money. That came later. When this started, and it started in 1942, not six months ago, my intention was to accumulate the funds to enter politics. You cannot seek public office without access to vast sums of money. Which I did not have. When I realized it was my fate to lead Argentina, indeed, South America, in the postwar years . . ."

Does he expect me to believe this horseshit?
Does he believe it himself?
I'll be goddamned if I know.

". . . I knew I would need a fortune and I went after getting one in the only way I knew how. And is it so terrible to turn dirty money toward a good purpose?

"I confess — and it is shaming — that I have diverted some of these funds, a very small percentage of the total, to my own use. I am not a perfect man.

"And as far as Rudy Nulder is concerned: Politics is a dirty business, Cletus, perhaps especially in Argentina. Sometimes — for good reasons — unpleasant things have to be

456

done. I needed — I need — someone to do them for me. Nulder fills that role. I'm not proud of that, either, but that's the way things are.

"Now, as far as my personal life is concerned, my sex life, as you put it, I've never been married. I knew if I was to rise in the army, I could not afford a wife and a family. It's been a lonely life, Cletus."

Which you dealt with by taking thirteen-year-old girls into your bed.

"I'm not proud of some of the things I did to satisfy the natural lusts of a healthy man. But that's all in the past. I now have Evita."

"A hooker half your age!" Clete exploded. "Jesus Christ, how do you justify that?"

"They said the same thing about Wallis Warfield Simpson. They said that she was a woman of questionable morals, and very possibly she was. Nevertheless —"

"What — or who — the hell are you babbling about now?"

"The Duchess of Windsor. King Edward the Eighth gave up the throne of England because of his love for her."

"Oh, yeah," Clete said, vaguely remembering.

" 'But you must believe me,' " Perón began to quote, " 'when I tell you that I have found it impossible to carry the heavy burden of responsibility and to discharge my duties as King as I would wish to do without the help

457

and support of the woman I love.' "

Jesus, I remember that. I heard it on the radio.

"And I cannot lead Argentina into the problems of the rest of this century without the help and support of the woman I love. Eva Duarte."

"You're going to marry her?" Clete asked incredulously.

"As soon as it is politically practical."

"After you become president, you mean?"

The sarcasm went right over Perón's head.

"Either after I become president, or when I'm sure I will be."

Jesus H. Christ!

There came a knock at the kitchen door.

Enrico grabbed his shotgun and went to see who it was.

He turned from the door and announced, "It's Major Habanzo and Captain Garcia."

"Who?" Clete said, then remembered. They were the BIS officers who had come to the Jockey Club.

"They want to see you, Don Cletus," Enrico added.

"Tío Juan, you get behind the *parrilla,*" Clete ordered. "Now. Don't show yourself."

Clete went to Enrico and said, "Give me your pistol."

Ashton had already taken his .45 from his holster and was racking a round into it.

"I knew they'd find me here!" Perón said.

"Shut the hell up!" Clete said in a furious

458

whisper.

When he was satisfied Perón was out of sight, he held Enrico's .45 behind him and opened the door.

Both officers saluted him.

They don't look menacing.

"What happened at the airport yesterday?" Clete said.

"Where is el Coronel Perón?" Major Habanzo asked.

"What the hell happened at the airport yesterday?" Clete demanded angrily.

"I am here," Juan Domingo Perón announced suddenly. "I am not going to hide behind a *parrilla.*"

Major Habanzo saluted again.

"*Mi Coronel,* I present the compliments of the president of the Argentine Republic. He asks that you attend him immediately. And you, too, Don Cletus."

"Where's General Martín?" Clete demanded.

"With the president, Don Cletus."

"Is he all right?"

"He suffered a wound to his left leg."

"What happened at the airport?"

"Ten minutes after you left, Don Cletus, a battalion of the Patricios arrived and placed the Horse Soldiers in the same hangar where earlier the Horse Soldiers had placed the platoon of Patricios."

"Did the flight to Berlin get off all right?"

459

"Yes, sir."

"How did you get here?" Clete asked.

"On the regular eight-twenty SAA flight, Don Cletus. It is now being serviced for the return flight to Buenos Aires."

[Two]

Headquarters, U.S. European Command
The I.G. Farben Building
Frankfurt am Main, Germany
1115 18 October 1945

Brigadier General H. Paul Greene, chief, Counterintelligence, European Command, waved Mattingly into a chair in his fourth-floor office and got right to the point.

"I've always believed, Colonel Mattingly, that the air between myself and my subordinates should be perfectly clear. I'm sure you can understand that."

"Yes, sir."

"The air between us, as I'm sure you will agree, is anything but clear. The phrase 'dense fog' comes to mind."

Mattingly didn't reply.

"And you'll understand why I can't permit that situation to continue."

"General, I have no idea what you're talking about."

"Indulge me, Colonel, I'm getting to it."

"Yes, sir."

460

"I know a good deal about you, Colonel. Not as much as I would like to know, but a good deal. I know, for example, that you are — perhaps more accurately, *were,* now that he has left the European Command — a protégé of Major General I. D. White. Would you say that's a fair statement?"

The way he said that implied that he believes General White left EUCOM under some sort of cloud. That he was booted out.

That's the impression Eisenhower wanted the Russians — and the State Department and the handwringers in EUCOM — to have.

But it's not the real story.

And it's damn surprising that Greene doesn't know it.

General White had told Mattingly that Eisenhower had called him into his office. Ike told White that not only the Russians were seriously miffed that White had taken "Hell on Wheels" into Berlin and thrown the Red Army out of the American Sector. There also was a large cabal of Americans in the Farben building, the Pentagon, and, maybe especially, in the Department of State.

They believed — or at the very least were seriously worried — that White, like General George S. Patton, was trying to start World War III, this time fighting the Russians.

That was nonsense, of course, but it had to be dealt with. And what Eisenhower had come up with proved again his diplomatic skills. He had arranged to remove White — temporarily — from the European Command. White would be given command of the Cavalry School at Fort Riley, Kansas.

White had told Mattingly: "Since neither the handwringers nor the Russians can credibly argue that I'll start World War Three while sitting on a horse in the middle of Kansas, that will silence both."

White went on: "What I'll really be doing at Fort Riley will be the final planning for the Constabulary. Which is what we're going to call the Occupation Police Force. Essentially, what we're going to do is take most of the tanks from three armored regiments, replace them with fleets of M-8 armored cars and jeeps, then train the troopers to become sort of policemen.

"I'll be back in Germany in about two months, and the Constabulary will be activated the day I get back. I'd offer you one of the Constabulary regiments, Bob, if I didn't think what you're doing with General Gehlen's intelligence operation was more important."

"General," Mattingly said to Greene, "I was privileged to serve under General White in 'Hell on Wheels,' if that's what you mean."

"Before you went to the OSS, you mean, right?"

"Before I went to the OSS. Yes, sir."

"And then when the OSS was dis-established — and not a day too soon, in my judgment — you found yourself as sort of a stay-behind to finish a project the OSS did not trust G-2 to take over. Is that about right, Colonel Mattingly?"

What is this bastard up to?

"Excuse me, sir?"

"From what I've been able to put together, General White went to Eisenhower's chief of staff, General Walter Bedell Smith, and explained the problem to him . . ."

Who the hell has Greene been talking to?

". . . and between the two of them, they decided that the best place to hide you and this secret OSS project you're running was in my Counterintelligence Corps. So Beetle Smith went to the EUCOM G-2, Lieutenant General Seidel, and told him to arrange it. I don't know how much General Seidel was told, but I do know him well enough to know he didn't like it at all . . ."

He was probably told nothing. And certainly as little as possible.

For two reasons.

The fewer people who know a secret, the better.

And if Operation Ost blows up, and Seidel knows nothing about it, he probably won't get burned.

". . . But being the good soldier General

463

Seidel is, he said, 'Yes, sir,' and came to me. And told me I was about to get a new deputy — you — and maybe a dozen people you'd bring from the former Office of Strategic Services.

"I told General Seidel I already had a very competent deputy. He told me that was fine, I should change his title and keep him, as you and your people would be fully occupied with your own project, which he was not at liberty to discuss with me. So being the good soldier I am, I said, 'Yes, sir.' "

Greene paused, looked at Mattingly, and said, "And that was the way things were going — until yesterday."

"Sir?"

"Yesterday, Colonel Mattingly, my inspector general, Lieutenant Colonel Tony Schumann, and a team of his men were driving either to or from Munich — I'm not sure which because when I talked to him this morning he was still pretty upset — near a little dorf called Schollbrunn . . ."

Oh, shit!

". . . when they came across a monastery surrounded by concertina barbed wire. What caught Colonel Schumann's attention was a number of signs attached to the concertina. They said the area was under the control of the Twenty-seventh CIC Detachment and entrance was strictly forbidden.

"Colonel Schumann found this interesting,

as he had no previous knowledge of a Twenty-seventh CIC Detachment. So he thought he'd better have a look. He had of course not only the authority to do so but also the duty, as anything involving the Counterintelligence Corps is of interest to its inspector general.

"They — there were three Opel Kapitän sedans in his little convoy — were intercepted by two jeeps. The jeeps had pedestal-mounted .50 caliber machine guns, and the personnel in them were all Negro non-commissioned officers whose uniforms bore the insignia of the Second Armored Division.

"Colonel Schumann identified himself and asked to be taken to the commanding officer. He was told the area was off-limits and he would not be given access to it.

"After some fruitless discussion with the sergeant, Colonel Schumann then ordered his driver to drive past the jeeps. When he attempted to do so, the machine gun on one of the jeeps fired into the front right tire of Colonel Schumann's Opel Kapitän. The projectile went through the tire and into the engine, shattering the block.

"Comment, Colonel Mattingly?"

Mattingly did not hesitate.

"The sergeant did what he had been ordered to do, General. That compound is classified Top Secret–Presidential, and unauthorized personnel are not allowed past the outer ring of concertina wire."

"Ordered by whom, Colonel Mattingly?"

"By me, sir. The sergeant was authorized to take any action, including the taking of life, to prevent a breach of the area."

General Greene took his time considering that.

"We'll return to that extraordinary statement in a moment," he then said. "What happened next was an officer appeared — I presume he was an officer, Schumann reported that he was a young white man whose uniform bore no insignia of rank, but the Negroes in the jeeps saluted him — and spoke with Schumann.

"After Schumann identified himself as the inspector general of the CIC in the European Command and again demanded access to the compound, this officer, after demanding and receiving proof of that, said that because Colonel Schumann was the CIC IG, he and his men would not be arrested. Then he said that any questions should be directed to you, Colonel Mattingly."

General Greene let that sink in for a long moment.

"So here we are," he then said. "Just what the hell are you up to, Mattingly?"

Mattingly at first thought it was more a rhetorical than a serious question, but Greene immediately made it specific.

"What *are* you up to at Kloster Grünau, Colonel? What *exactly* are you up to?"

"Sir, I must respectfully decline to answer that question."

"Mattingly, you're not in a position to decline, respectfully or not, to answer my questions."

"Sir, with respect, I'm afraid I must."

"I'm the chief of Counterintelligence for the European Command. Before that, I was chief of Intelligence for Supreme Headquarters, Allied Expeditionary Force. I have security clearances you never even heard of. I even knew about the Manhattan Project. And you're telling me I don't have the proper clearance to learn what you're doing?"

"Yes, sir. That unfortunately seems to be the case."

"Colonel, you are ordered to answer my questions. If you refuse to do so, you will consider yourself under arrest."

"General, I respectfully request sixty seconds to address this issue."

"So long as you understand you're under arrest, you can have sixty minutes to address this issue."

"Thank you, sir."

"You understand you're under arrest?"

"Yes, sir."

"Okay. Go ahead."

"What happened yesterday at Kloster Grünau was the one thing I didn't foresee when I set it up. That the one person — one of two persons, the other being you, sir — in the European Command with the authority to go past a barrier erected by the CIC would show up at a mountaintop monastery and try to go past that barrier.

"I'm sorry it happened, and I accept full responsibility. What you're going to have to do now, sir, as I doubt if Colonel Schumann would accept this from me, is tell him to forget he and his men were ever at Kloster Grünau."

"You're out of your mind, you know that? Your sixty seconds are up. Report under arrest to your quarters, Colonel Mattingly."

"Request to make one telephone call, sir, to report that I'm under arrest and the circumstances."

"Denied."

"If I don't make this call, sir, members of my staff will make it for me. It would really be best if I made the call."

"Who are you going to call, Colonel, General Eisenhower?" Greene asked sarcastically. "Okay. Make your goddamn call, then get out of my sight."

Mattingly leaned over Greene's desk and dialed a two-digit number.

"Colonel Mattingly for General Eisenhower," he said to whoever answered.

General Greene slammed his hand on the base of the telephone, breaking the connection.

"Now, just a moment!" he said, staring

down Mattingly.

"I respectfully suggest, General, that there is no reason for me to involve General Eisenhower in this, providing you release me from arrest and deal with Colonel Schumann as I outlined."

After a long moment, Greene, tight-lipped, nodded.

"Permission to withdraw, sir?" Mattingly asked.

Greene nodded again.

Mattingly came to attention, saluted, did an about-face movement, and marched toward the door.

He had almost reached it when General Greene called out to him.

"You ever hear, Mattingly, that he who laughs last lasts best?"

Mattingly turned, said, "I'm sorry you feel that way, sir," then marched out of the office.

The problem, he thought, *is that I understand why he's furious.*

In his shoes, I would be.

He didn't get to be chief of Counterintelligence by being slow.

This is not over.

[THREE]

Instead of the gray skies and drizzle — or worse — that South American Airways First Officer Hans-Peter von Wachtstein expected to find in Berlin, there was bright sunshine and not a cloud in the sky.

He could see Flughafen Berlin-Tempelhof from a long way off.

So could SAA Captain Paolo Lopez, who was in the co-pilot's seat of the Lockheed Constellation.

"My God, that's enormous!" Lopez said.

"Until the Americans built their Pentagon, it was the largest building in the world," von Wachtstein said.

There was a downside to the unexpected good weather. The ruins of the German capital — stretching for miles — could be seen just as clearly as could the graceful curved terminal of what was now U.S. Army Air Force Field Berlin (Tempelhof).

"Get on the radio, please, Captain," von Wachtstein ordered. "In English."

"Tempelhof, South American Zero One Zero."

"Go ahead, Zero One Zero. I read you five by five."

470

■ ■ ■ ■

As von Wachtstein taxied *La Ciudad de Mar del Plata* under the soaring arch of the airport, he saw a Horch like the one Colonel Robert Mattingly had in Frankfurt. He wondered who owned this one, then saw Mattingly himself leaning on it.

Former Kapitän zur See Karl Boltitz, now wearing what Peter thought of as the OSS uniform, an insignia-less U.S. Army officer's uniform, stood beside Mattingly. On the other side of the Horch were two huge black sergeants, one cradling a Thompson submachine gun in his arms.

He had expected to see Mattingly in Frankfurt. Frade had told him Mattingly would have General Gehlen's and the Americans' dossiers on the Nazis who had come off U-405 as well as some other intelligence they would bring back to Argentina. And he had not expected to see Boltitz, who he last heard was in Denmark trying to learn both what had happened to his father in the last days of the war and something about the fleet of U-boats that had supposedly left Germany and Norway just before the surrender.

Peter believed that Boltitz's mission had to be a wild-goose chase. He thought Admiral Boltitz, who knew what the Nazis had done to officers involved in the bomb plot, had chosen a quick end by drowning in the frigid waters of a Norwegian fjord — a sailor's death — over the humiliation and death by torture he knew he would receive if the Schutzstaffel could get their hands on him.

Von Wachtstein knew that his father would have welcomed that option.

And von Wachtstein thought the stories about as many as thirty submarines leaving Germany for South America were, as Frade had succinctly put it, bullshit. And he thought Karl should know better than to waste his time looking for something that never was.

He and Karl had been in the Fort Hunt Senior Enemy Officer POW Interrogation Facility outside Washington, D.C., during the last six weeks of the war. They followed the progress of the war on radio station WJSV, the owner of which, they were told, was presently serving as Eisenhower's naval aide-de-camp. There were almost daily reports of the concern at Eisenhower's headquarters over the *Werwolf.*

These were supposed to be fanatic SS troopers who would stay behind as the Allies advanced through Germany and then attack from the rear. They were going to do this in the Black Forest and elsewhere and ultimately at Berchtesgaden, Hitler's mountaintop retreat in Bavaria, where they would fight until the last of them was dead, killing as many Allied soldiers as possible.

Eisenhower's Supreme Headquarters seemed to know a great deal about *UNTERNEHMEN WERWOLF* — OPERATION WEREWOLF — including the name of its commanding officer, SS-Obergruppenführer Hans-Adolf Prützmann. It was said that after Berlin fell, General George S. Patton was prepared to use three armored divisions to deal with *WERWOLF.*

It turned out to be bullshit. *WERWOLF* didn't show up in the Black Forest — or anywhere else — and a platoon of paratroopers from the 101st Airborne Division captured Berchtesgaden without firing a shot.

It had been one last — and highly successful — act of psychological warfare concocted by Propaganda Minister Joseph Goebbels, and von Wachtstein thought the fleet of submarines supposed to be headed for South America was much the same thing. And had been about as successful for the Nazis as had the *WERWOLF* deception.

The Allies had launched a massive search for the submarines, primarily involving aircraft in Europe and B-24 bombers modified to be submarine hunters flying out of USAF bases in Brazil and North Africa, but also including naval vessels all over the North and South Atlantic oceans.

Aside from several U-boats sunk in or near the English Channel, none of the twenty —

or thirty, or sixty, depending on which scenario one used — submarines supposed to
be en route to South America was ever found.

The arrival of U-405 seemed to finally
settle the question. Willi von Dattenberg, her
master, was arguably the best and most
experienced of all U-boat skippers when it
came to sailing to Argentina to secretly put
ashore whatever cargo and people senior Nazi
officers wanted to smuggle into Argentina.

When Willi told Clete he thought Clete
could stop worrying about U-234 — which
implied stop worrying about any other submarines as well — that seemed to be the final
word.

So poor Karl had been on one wild-goose
chase.

When von Wachtstein now saw Mattingly
looking at him, he waved and then turned to
Captain Lopez.

"The people I have to see are on the tarmac," von Wachtstein said. "I'm going to have
to get out of here as soon as I can. The SAA
people and representatives from the Argentine
embassy are waiting for our flight. With them,
you can handle the shut-down, off-loading,
and paperwork. It shouldn't be a problem.
There's a restaurant in the airport hotel. The
U.S. Army runs it, but we can eat there. After
you've eaten and seen to the refueling, tell
the SAA station manager to give the crew a
tour of Berlin — better yet, tell them Señor

Frade told you to tell the station manager to get you a tour."

"You'll be where?" Lopez asked.

"When I know what's going on, I'll be in touch."

"How will I get in touch with you if I need you?"

"This is Berlin, Captain Lopez, not Buenos Aires. If you take the tour what you'll see is hundreds of hectares of rubble. I can't give you a phone number that I don't know. I'll be in touch."

Von Wachtstein unfastened his shoulder belt and got out of the pilot's seat.

[FOUR]

357 Roonstrasse, Zehlendorf
Berlin, Germany
1035 18 October 1945

When Colonel Robert Mattingly had seen von Wachtstein waving cheerfully at him from the cockpit window of *La Ciudad de Mar del Plata* he had been mildly surprised that Cletus Frade had not been flying the Constellation.

He walked to the foot of the stairway that the ground handlers had moved to the cockpit door. He stood there, wearing a smile, his hand extended, when von Wachtstein came nimbly down the stairs.

475

"Colonel Frade wasn't flying?" he asked.

"Colonel Frade's not on the airplane," von Wachtstein told him.

"Where the hell is he?" Mattingly snapped.

He heard the tone in his voice and realized his temper had been triggered.

And he knew why. The one thing he didn't need now was trouble with Lieutenant Colonel Cletus Frade, USMCR. He absolutely had had enough unexpected trouble in the last forty-eight hours and didn't need any more.

"I really don't know where Colonel Frade is, Colonel," von Wachtstein said. "Probably at Estancia Don Guillermo."

Mattingly saw on von Wachtstein's face that he had picked up on the tone of his voice and was both curious and displeased.

"What the hell is that?" Mattingly then said. "What's he doing there?"

And I just made it worse. What the hell is the matter with me?

"It's a vineyard he owns in Mendoza," von Wachtstein said, somewhat coldly. "And what he's doing is trying to keep Juan Domingo Perón alive."

And what the hell is that all about?

Get your temper under control, you damned fool!

He forced a smile.

"Well, that sounds interesting. You can tell me all about that at the house. I suspect you

476

could use some breakfast and a shower."

"Yes, I could," von Wachtstein said, and turned to Karl Boltitz. *"Wie geht's, Karl?"*

Boltitz gave him a fond hug.

"How's Willi, Hansel?" he asked.

Without thinking, von Wachtstein said, "The last time I saw him he was in the Jockey Club looking soulfully over a stem of champagne into the eyes of my sister-in-law."

He heard what he had just said.

Mein Gott, *where did that come from?*

"Your wife's sister?" Boltitz asked.

"No. Elsa. Karl's widow," von Wachtstein corrected him.

"Karl's widow?" Boltitz parroted, surprised.

Von Wachtstein nodded and repeated, "Elsa. Karl's widow."

"Well, isn't that interesting!" Boltitz said.

"I thought so," von Wachtstein said.

I thought so when I first noticed it, just before Father Welner came into the Jockey Club and took me away from the table.

Whereupon I apparently promptly forgot it.

I can't imagine it slipped my mind just because Welner and Martín told me that unless Cletus could fly the Storch — right then — to that island and get Perón off it to keep him from getting shot, Argentina was going to find itself in a civil war.

I can't imagine why a little thing like that would take my mind off Willi's sex life with my sister-in-law, except maybe watching Clete taking off

477

— without a co-pilot — from Jorge Frade in that Lodestar while three machine guns were firing at him.

I'm just going to have to learn to concentrate on the important things.

And what, if anything, am I expected to tell Colonel Mattingly about any of this?

They walked to the Horch and got in the backseat. The sergeants got in the front. They drove through the rubble surrounding Tempelhof and finally came to Zehlendorf, the suburb that somehow had escaped massive damage, and finally to what had been Admiral Canaris's home.

An American flag now flew where Canaris's admiral's flag once had flown, and a U.S. Army M-8 armored car and three jeeps carrying the markings of the Second Armored Division sat in front. The soldiers in the M-8 saluted, and von Wachtstein, in a Pavlovian reflex, returned it when Mattingly did.

Try to remember, Señor von Wachtstein, that you are now a civilian.

In the ten minutes it took von Wachtstein to shower, Mattingly went over again and again in his mind the problems he had faced before he learned that Frade was still in Argentina, and the additional problems both Frade being there and what was happening there posed for OPERATION OST.

His biggest problem, Mattingly recognized,

478

was himself.

Colonel Robert Mattingly seemed to have proved beyond any reasonable doubt he was not the calm, competent, and unshakable senior intelligence officer that he previously fancied himself to be.

It was absolutely inexcusable that he had not foreseen that someone from the European Command CIC Inspector General's office — or someone from the staff of the EUCOM Inspector General — would stumble across Kloster Grünau and insist on having a look at what was inside the concertina wire. He should have planned for something like that to happen, and he hadn't.

And he should have foreseen that General Greene had been looking for something to hang on him from the moment General Seidel had told Greene (a) that he was getting a new deputy named Mattingly and (b) that Mattingly was going to have duties that were none of Greene's business.

Instead of being prepared for someone stumbling on Kloster Grünau, he had been angry. So angry that when Greene had sarcastically asked if he was going to call General Eisenhower, he had dialed Eisenhower's number like a petulant child.

If Greene hadn't slammed his hand on the phone base, Eisenhower would have taken the call and more than likely told Greene he didn't have the need to know about Kloster

Grünau and/or OPERATION OST and to release Mattingly from arrest.

But there would have been an awful price
to pay for that.

For one thing, Eiscnhower would have
justifiably concluded that Colonel Robert
Mattingly was incompetent and shouldn't be
in charge of a project that, should it be
compromised and become public, would
greatly embarrass not only Eisenhower but
President Truman as well.

Even worse, Eisenhower, who had a well-
deserved reputation for his ability to both
quickly analyze the depth and nuances of a
problem and as quickly decide what to do
about it, could have quietly ordered, "Shut it
down, Colonel Mattingly, before it can hurt
the President."

That had been planned for.

If OPERATION OST was compromised, the
members of what had been OSS Team Turtle
would disappear. To a man, they had agreed
to do so. Hiding them in Argentina would be
no more difficult than integrating the "Good
Germans" had proved to be.

But there was a price they would have to
pay for that: They would be charged with being absent without leave and refusing the lawful order to return to the United States. After
ninety days, the AWOL charge would automatically convert to one of desertion.

So that meant that they could not return to

the United States in the foreseeable future, even, conceivably, ever. It was a price they were willing to pay. They would not turn the "Good Germans" and their families over to the Russians, after the deal had been made. And somehow they would see that intelligence produced by Gehlen's people would reach the appropriate intelligence agencies in Washington.

Whereupon, Mattingly thought, more than a little bitterly, the FBI, the G-2, the ONI, and the State Department would probably dismiss it out of hand as propaganda trying to be foisted on them by ex-Nazis hiding out in Argentina.

Frade obviously couldn't disappear in Argentina. But that hadn't seemed to be a problem until Mattingly heard about the attempted assassination of Colonel Juan Domingo Perón and the very real threat of a civil war that posed.

If that had not happened, Frade would not have to try disappearing within Argentina. He was an Argentine citizen and could have thumbed his nose at a summons to return to the United States to tell a Congressional Committee, under oath, everything he knew about smuggling Nazis out of Germany and into Argentina. His status would have changed from being a highly decorated — Frade had been awarded the Navy Cross — Marine Corps lieutenant colonel to deserter.

But he could have, would have, kept the secrets of OPERATION OST.

For that reason, ever since his confrontation with General Greene, against the near certainty that Greene would overtly or covertly try to find out what he was doing, Mattingly had been removing from his office safe the most damaging material regarding OPERATION OST. This included the names both of all the "Gehlen people" who had been sent to Argentina and the Russians whom Gehlen's agents in the Kremlin had learned the Soviets were sending to Argentina.

If there was a raid — by whatever name — on either his files or Kloster Grünau, there was nothing in either place that would expose Gehlen's people in Argentina. He was going to turn the files over to Frade for safekeeping.

More precisely, he intended to personally hand them to Frade, when Frade was next in Berlin, and at the same time deliver a little speech about how sensitive the material was. In the meantime, until Frade arrived, Mattingly had put the files into the safest place he could think of to put them: two canvas suitcases that he hid in the trunk of the Horch.

He polished this scenario, first by telephoning First Sergeant Dunwiddie and telling him to send Technical Sergeant Abraham L. "Honest Abe" Tedworth and one other responsible senior non-com to the I.G. Farben Building for about a week's special, unspecified, duty. One or the other, and usually both, kept an eye on the Horch around the clock.

Next, he augmented that protection — frankly feeling rather smug about it — by rigging both suitcases with thermite grenades that could be detonated by pulling on a nylon cord.

As he drove to Berlin, he managed to just about convince himself that he now had things pretty much under control. All he had to do now was put the two canvas suitcases into the hands of Cletus Frade.

"Well, that didn't take long," Mattingly said when von Wachtstein came into the kitchen. And then he noticed what he was wearing. Von Wachtstein had changed from his SAA uniform into an insignia-less U.S. Army officer's uniform.

"Why are you wearing that?" Mattingly heard himself demanding.

Von Wachtstein met his eyes for a long moment and then said icily, "Forgive me, Colonel, I was unaware that I needed your permission."

What the hell is wrong with me?

"Peter, I don't know why that came out the way it did. Of course you don't need permission. I was just curious."

Von Wachtstein considered that for a moment, and then, almost visibly, decided to let it pass.

"I'm going to go over to the Kurfürsten-damm," he said, as he slipped into a chair and helped himself to a cup of coffee, "and I thought I would attract less attention in this than I would in what that lieutenant . . . Cronley . . . ?"

Mattingly smiled and confirmed, "Second Lieutenant James D. Cronley Junior."

". . . so aptly described as a Mexican bus driver's uniform."

Boltitz laughed.

"Once again," he said, "unexpected wisdom from the mouth of a *leutnant.* I probably would have said Hungarian bus driver, but that's exactly what you look like in that SAA uniform."

"You can go to hell, Karl," Peter said.

"Who is this astonishingly wise young officer?"

"That's right, you didn't meet him, did you?" Peter said. "Or even hear the story."

Boltitz shook his head.

"We've got him to thank for Elsa. He's a CIC officer, and pulled her from a line of refugees trying to get to Marburg. Colonel Mattingly had a 'locate and report' order out on her, and when *Cronley* reported he had her, Colonel Mattingly —"

"I wish you would call me Bob," Mattingly interrupted.

Von Wachtstein looked at him, nodded, and went on. "When *Cronley* reported to *Bob* that he had her, Bob arranged for him to take care of her until we could get to Marburg. So we did, and when we walked into the Kurhotel, Cletus looked at him in utter surprise, whereupon Cronley said, 'Don't give me a funny look, Cletus, you're the one wearing that Mexican bus driver's uniform.' "

"He knows Cletus?"

"They grew up in Texas together. Cletus says he's the little brother he never had."

"What a marvelous story!" Boltitz said.

"He now works for me," Mattingly said.

"I didn't know that," von Wachtstein said.

"I put him in charge of the guards around Gehlen's people at Kloster Grünau. He's really a bright kid. And he is not burdened with the terrified awe most second lieutenants have for senior officers, which came in handy a couple of days ago."

Damn it. I don't need that story getting around. Change the subject.

"So, what are you going to do on the Kurfürstendamm, Peter?" Mattingly asked, quickly changing the subject.

"I'm looking for a couple friends of mine. Have you been over there? Seen the notes pinned to the wooden fence around the ruins of the Kaiser-Wilhelm-Gedächtniskirche?"

Boltitz nodded.

Mattingly shook his head.

"People looking for people — family, friends — leave notes there," von Wachtstein explained for Mattingly's benefit. "You put the name of the person you're looking for, and your name and address, on a card and pin it to the fence and hope that the other guy sees it. I've been doing that since the first time we flew in here. And every time since, I go look, and if necessary put up a new card."

"Who are you looking for?" Mattingly asked.

"Two Luftwaffe buddies. Actually one buddy and my — our — old commanding officer. Former Oberstleutnant Dieter von und zu Aschenburg and former Hauptmann Wilhelm Johannes Grüner, also known as Wild Willi."

"There's an Argentine connection, Bob," Boltitz said thoughtfully. "Grüner's father was Oberst Karl-Heinz Grüner, the military attaché — and Sicherheitsdienst man — in the embassy."

"The father arranged the assassination of Clete's father and the several failed attempts to kill Cletus," Peter added.

"And he's a *friend* of yours?" Mattingly asked softly.

Peter shook his head. "Not the father. But Dieter and I went to flight school together and flew as corporals in the Condor Legion in Spain. Hauptmann von und zu Aschenburg was our squadron commander. We were pretty close."

"You have some reason to think they survived the war?"

"I have a lot of reasons to think they probably didn't," Peter said.

"What happened to the father?" Mattingly asked. "Is he now interned in Argentina?"

"Enrico Rodríguez shot him on the beach of Samborombón Bay," Peter said. "While he was trying to unload crates of money from a Spanish freighter."

"And if you find either one of them, then what?"

"Then I take them to Argentina," Peter said.

Which brings us back to that, Mattingly thought, just before the kitchen door opened and one of the Second Armored Division sergeants entered.

"What is it, Sergeant?" Mattingly asked impatiently.

"Colonel, I thought I should tell you about this before I just ran him off."

"Ran who off?"

"There's a Kraut out there asking if we have a Kraut named Wachheim or something like that working here. . . ."

"Wachtstein?" Peter asked.

"Right. Working here. This guy was hanging around yesterday and the day before."

"Please show the Kraut in, Sergeant," von Wachtstein said.

"Yes, sir," the sergeant replied.

487

The sergeant turned and ordered, "In here, Fritz!"

A moment later, he motioned into the kitchen a tall, gaunt, balding, blond, fair-skinned man in his forties who was dressed in the ragged remains of an insignia-less Luftwaffe uniform.

Von Wachtstein and then Boltitz stood.

"I think this is where I get to say, 'Speak of the devil,' " von Wachtstein said in English.

"So it is you, Peter," the gaunt man said, and added, looking at Boltitz, "The both of you."

"Colonel Mattingly," von Wachtstein said, "may I introduce former Oberstleutnant von und zu Aschenburg? Dieter, this is Colonel Robert Mattingly."

Von und zu Aschenburg came to attention, clicked his heels, and bobbed his head in a bow. "Herr Oberst."

"You can forget all that, Dieter," von Wachtstein said. "The war's over."

"And we survived," von und zu Aschenburg said.

"And Willi?" von Wachtstein asked softly.

"He's out there," von und zu Aschenburg said, gesturing toward the street, "waiting to see what was going to happen to me when I asked for you."

"I'll go get him," Peter said. He looked at Mattingly, then asked, "With your permission, of course, Colonel?"

"Of course," Mattingly said.

Was that sarcastic?

Keep in mind that von Wachtstein does not work for you.

With you, but not for you. You can't give him orders.

Von Wachtstein walked quickly out of the kitchen.

Von und zu Aschenburg looked at Mattingly. "May I ask how well you speak German, Herr Oberst? My English —"

"Your English is fine, Colonel. But I speak German."

Von und zu Aschenburg then said, "When we found the notes on the Gedächtniskirche fence" — he waited to see if Mattingly understood, and when Mattingly nodded, went on — "I recognized the address, the home of Admiral Canaris. . . ."

"How did you know it?"

"I've been here many times," von und zu Aschenburg said.

"Bob," Boltitz began, "when Dieter was flying Condors to Buenos Aires —"

"Doing what?" Mattingly interrupted.

"Are you familiar with the Focke-Wulf Condor?"

"No," Mattingly said simply.

"It was a Lufthansa transport airplane," von und zu Aschenburg explained. "It looked something like your DC-3 except it was slightly larger, had four engines, and on short

489

hauls could carry twenty-six passengers. Considerably fewer than that of course when flying across the Atlantic."

"And you flew one of these airplanes to Buenos Aires?" Mattingly asked.

I never heard about that.

One more massive cavity revealed in the intelligence database of Colonel Robert Mattingly.

"I flew a lot of those airplanes to Buenos Aires," von und zu Aschenburg said.

"He flew diplomatic pouches back and forth between Foreign Minister von Ribbentrop and Ambassador Lutzenberger," Boltitz said, "and brought Admiral Canaris's orders to me. Fortunately, he was never caught."

Okay. So that makes this guy one of the good guys.

Why does that make me unhappy?

Because when I take von Wachtstein into a corner and tell him I'm sorry but I just can't allow you to try to smuggle your pals into Argentina, that such an act will add another risk we can't afford, von Wachtstein will say, "Fuck you. I don't work for you. I work for Cletus Frade. And since he's not here, that makes the Constellation my airplane. And besides, my pals have earned themselves a seat."

"How long did Lufthansa fly to Buenos Aires?" Mattingly asked.

"Until Hitler decided the Condors would be more valuable serving the Eastern Front," von und zu Aschenburg said drily.

"So you flew in Russia, too?"

"Until there were no more Condors. And then I flew Auntie Ju's — Junkers JU 52s, a tri-motor like your Ford. Until there were no more of them. And then I was allowed to fly Fw-190 fighters until we ran out of fuel for them. I was then impressed into the Volkssturm, from which I deserted."

I like this guy.

But that doesn't alter the fact that I can't allow von Wachtstein to try to smuggle him and his pal into Argentina.

Presuming of course that von Wachtstein pops to attention and says, "Yes, sir!" when I tell him he can't, which is about as likely as me being taken bodily into heaven.

And what am I going to do with the two suitcases in the back of the Horch?

"Mattingly, I can't believe that you just handed over to a German — a German who is still listed as an escapee from Fort Hunt — intelligence material of that importance. What the hell were you thinking?"

Well, turning the bags over to Major Harry Wallace and telling him to get on von Wachtstein's Constellation and personally hand them over to Cletus Frade in Buenos Aires would be an option.

Except that I need Harry to finish setting up the South German Industrial Development Organization in Pullach.

491

And I can't have Cronley take that over so that Major Harold Wallace can go to Argentina. He's a second lieutenant — a smart one, okay — but he just doesn't have the knowledge or experience to supervise the setting-up of Pullach. . . .

Jesus Christ, why didn't I think of this before?

Cronley takes the suitcases to Argentina!

"Why did you turn the suitcases over to a second lieutenant, Mattingly?"

"Because he was the only intelligence officer I had for the assignment."

Now all I have to do is keep the Condor pilot and von Wachtstein's other buddy off the Constellation. That shouldn't be hard. I'll tell von Wachtstein they'll have to wait until we can arrange passports for them.

Von Wachtstein came back into the kitchen, his arm around the shoulder of a short, muscular, blond man about his age and also wearing remnants of a Luftwaffe uniform.

"You remember Willi, Karl?"

"Of course. How are you, Grüner?"

"Alive," Willi said as they shook hands. "And a little confused. What's going on here? What was that uniform Hansel was wearing when he came here earlier?"

"That's my Mexican bus driver's uniform. If you play your cards right, we can probably get you — and of course Dieter — ones just like it in Buenos Aires."

What? Mattingly thought.

492

"Buenos Aires?" Dieter asked incredulously. "And how do we get to Argentina?"

"You get on my bus, and twenty-five, twenty-six hours later you're in Buenos Aires."

I've got to somehow stop this!

"So you are involved with that Argentine airplane," Dieter said. "What the hell is that all about?"

"Involved? I'll have you know I'm the pilot-in-command of that airplane. On which you will shortly — tomorrow morning — be flying to Buenos Aires."

"Just like that?" Dieter asked.

No!

"Not quite just like that, I'm afraid," Mattingly said. "It'll take a little time to get the documentation, passports, et cetera. Have you been through a De-Nazification Court?"

"We were never POWs," von und zu Aschenburg said. "We were both in Silesia when the war ended. If we'd entered a Russian POW cage, they would probably have sent us to Siberia. And we'd already been there and didn't want to go back."

"You were together in Silesia?" von Wachtstein asked.

"First in the fighter squadron and then in Volkssturm."

"And when you were run over by the Red Army you hid out?" Boltitz asked.

Von und zu Aschenburg nodded. "We're

still hiding out."

"Well, we'll work something out," Mattingly said. "It shouldn't take long, no more than a week or two."

But long enough to keep you off von Wacht-stein's Constellation tomorrow.

"Not necessary," von Wachtstein said. "I just happen to have both the passports and the *libretas de enrolamiento* of these Argentine gentlemen in my luggage. All I have to do is glue their photographs onto them."

Mattingly saw on von Wachtstein's face that he did, in fact, have passports and identity cards requiring only the addition of photographs for his friends.

Okay. I give up.

There's nothing I can do to stop von Wacht-stein from taking them with him tomorrow.

That means all I have to do between now and then is drive to Kloster Grünau, pick up Cronley, then get him and the two suitcases to Rhine-Main by oh-nine-hundred tomorrow.

That sounds fairly simple. So why does an experienced, senior intelligence officer such as myself think that I am somehow, in some way, going to royally fuck it up?

494

[FIVE]

Aeropuerto Coronel Jorge G. Frade
Morón, Buenos Aires Province, Argentina
1605 18 October 1945

"Jorge Frade, SAA Six One Six," Cletus Frade called from the cockpit of the Lodestar.

"Six One Six, Jorge Frade."

"Get General Martín on the radio," Frade ordered.

Martín's voice came over Frade's headset almost immediately, which told Frade that he was in the control tower.

"This is General Martín. Who is this?"

"Christopher Columbus. Who else could it possibly be?"

"My God, Cletus, are you never serious?" Martín asked. It was impossible to tell from his tone if he was amused or grossly annoyed.

"Right now, I'm as serious as I get."

"Is your Tío Juan with you?"

"He's in the back, wearing one of my father's suits and looking very nervous. I'm over Pilar, about five minutes out. What am I going to find when I land there?"

"A battalion of the Patricios Regiment and an ambulance."

"What's the ambulance for?"

"Your Tío Juan."

"He's not that badly injured. He doesn't need an ambulance."

495

"How badly injured is he?"

"Not badly enough to need an ambulance."

"President Farrell is waiting for him, for you and him, at the Argerich Military Hospital. The safest way to get him there is in an ambulance. Guarded by the Patricios, of course."

"General Martín," Perón's voice came over the earphones. "This is the vice president of the Argentine Republic speaking."

Startled, Clete looked over his shoulder. Perón was standing just inside the cockpit door and wearing a headset.

"Yes, sir?"

"I will of course meet el Presidente wherever he chooses," Perón announced. "But before I go to meet him, I have to go to my apartment for a uniform. And I am not going there, or to the military hospital, or anywhere, hiding in an ambulance. I will not give the bastards who are trying to kill me the satisfaction of suggesting that I'm afraid of them."

"Can I put my two cents in?" Cletus asked.

Perón looked at him in annoyance, considered the question, and then said, "Of course."

"The SAA guards at the airport are all ex-Húsares —"

"Known, I believe, as Frade's Private Army," Perón interrupted.

Frade nodded, then went on: "They can protect you as well as the Patricios. There are probably reporters from *El País* and *La Nación* at the gates to the airport right now trying to find out what's going on out here. If you try to leave — protected by a battalion, even a company, of the Patricios — you will be recognized and it will be all over Buenos Aires in an hour that the civil war you're worried about has started."

Perón considered this for a moment, then asked, "What are you suggesting?"

"There's always a couple of station wagons on the field. They take pilots home, pick them up, that sort of thing. We can have a couple meet the airplane when I park it. You and the Húsares we have with us get in, and we drive to your apartment. Which is where, by the way?"

"The sixteen hundred block of Arenales," Perón replied absently.

"And then when you're in uniform, we get back in the station wagons and take you — again without attracting attention — to the military hospital. Enrico knows how to sneak in the back way."

"I'm not going to sneak in or out of anywhere," Perón said.

"You'd be discreet, Tío Juan, not cowardly."

There was a long moment of silence, then Perón asked, "I presume you heard what Don Cletus said, General?"

"Yes, sir."

"Have the station wagons and the men he speaks of meet the airplane when we land."

"El Coronel —"

"That was an order, General, not a suggestion. Have the Patricios return to their barracks, where they will stand by in case they're needed."

"Yes, sir."

"We will meet you at the hospital, General," Perón said, and then ordered, "You may land now, Cletus."

[SIX]

Apartamento 5B
Arenales 1623
Buenos Aires, Argentina
1645 18 October 1945

"Thank God you're alive!" Señorita Evita Duarte said when Perón let himself into the apartment.

She ran to him and they embraced.

A moment later, she said: "My God, what happened to your face?"

And a moment later: "What are *they* doing here?"

The latter question was in reference to Don Cletus Frade and Suboficial Mayor Enrico Rodríguez. They had followed Perón into the apartment.

"Cletus, I don't believe you know my fiancée, Señorita Duarte. Darling, this is my godson, Cletus Frade."

"Actually, we've met," Cletus said, and the moment the words were out of his mouth, he thought, *Well, that was fucking stupid, Stupid!*

"I don't think so," she said icily, offering her cheek to be kissed. "I would remember."

Oh, but you do remember, don't you, señorita?

You probably even remember rubbing my crotch when you said you hoped we would meet again.

He smiled at her warmly.

"Whatever you say, señorita."

"I said," she flared, "that I have never met you." Then she turned to Perón. "I asked you, Juan Domingo, what this rude person is doing here."

"One," Perón said icily, "don't use that tone when talking to me. Two, Cletus is here (a) because I asked him to be here and (b) because he saved my life yesterday. Three, since he is going to play a large part in my life in the future, you had better learn to get along with him."

"You sonofabitch!" she screamed. "I'm going to make you president!"

Perón slapped her, hard enough to make her stagger backward until she encountered the wall, whereupon she slid down it. She started to cry.

Perón walked to her and stood over her, looking down.

"I don't know what is bothering you, Evita,

and I don't care. I don't have time for whatever it is right now. Now, either behave yourself or get the hell out of my apartment!"

He turned away from her, raised his voice, and called, "Rudy!"

"Here, Juan Domingo," Rodolfo Nulder replied from an inner doorway.

Nulder looks, Clete thought, *like a cheap copy of Juan Domingo Perón.*

There's something about him that is the opposite of confidence-inspiring.

Nulder walked to Perón, embraced him, and asked, "Your face?"

"As we took off from the airfield yesterday, the goddamned Horse Rifles fired machine guns at us. I was struck by a piece of broken window."

"But you're all right?" Nulder said.

Perón nodded and went on: "I bled quite a bit. Ruined an almost new uniform. Cletus had to give me a blood transfusion."

Nulder for the first time acknowledged Frade's presence.

"Don Cletus," he said.

What do I call this guy? He's a cashiered pervert.

My father threatened to kill him if he ever put foot on Estancia San Pedro y San Pablo again.

"Mi Coronel" is not an option.

Frade nodded wordlessly at Nulder.

Nulder turned to Juan Domingo and announced: "Fernando Lopez will bleed more when we stand him against a wall!"

"No one is going to stand Fernando Lopez or anyone else against a wall," Perón said.

"Trying to assassinate the vice president of the Argentine Republic is high treason in anyone's book, Juan Domingo. You have every right to have him shot. To have every one of the bastards involved shot."

"Where the hell have you been, Rudy?" Perón flared. "Didn't you listen to anything I said?"

Nulder didn't reply.

"This time, pay attention, Rudy, because this is the last time I'm going to tell you. The objective is for me to become president — peacefully, without a single shot being fired or making any more enemies than we already have. And the last thing we want to do is give anyone — our friends or our enemies — any excuse whatever to do anything that could result in civil war."

He turned and looked at Cletus and announced, "I will now change into a uniform."

Perón then walked across the room, opened a door next to where Evita was sitting on the floor with her back against the wall, her skirt pulled high above her knees, wiping tears from her eyes. He ignored her and went through the door.

He didn't even look at his beloved Evita, Clete thought.

All of my life I was taught, and believed, that

men don't hit women.

So why didn't I have the slightest inclination to rush to that poor woman — as I know I should have, both as an Eagle Scout and as a Marine officer — wrap her in my manly arms and tell my Tío Juan if he wanted to belt her again, he'd have to come through me?

Why don't I have the slightest inclination now to go to her and help her to her feet?

What the hell is happening with me?

All the questions became immediately moot as Evita suddenly leapt to her feet with surprising agility and followed Perón through the door and pushed it closed after her.

If she screams at him again, calls him a sonofabitch again, he's really liable to hurt her.

He walked quickly to the door.

Maybe just seeing me will be enough, and I won't have to hit him.

When he opened the door, Clete saw that Evita was in Perón's arms. She was running her fingers over the bandage on his face and referring to him as her "poor precious darling."

"I'll be with you shortly, Cletus," Perón announced.

Clete hurriedly closed the door and turned.

"I'll be a sonofabitch" he said, softly but aloud.

He glanced at Enrico, who quietly stood guard at the front door, then looked around the room and found Perón's cigar case. When

502

he opened it, it was empty.

"I'll be a sonofabitch," Clete said again.

"May I offer you a cigar, Don Cletus?" Nulder asked, extending his cigar case.

No, thanks, you perverted sonofabitch.

I don't want anything to do with you, including taking one of your fucking cigars.

"Yes, thank you. Very kind of you."

"Not at all."

When Clete had finished the ritual of cutting and then lighting the cigar, Nulder said, "That sort of thing happens from time to time."

When Perón came out of the bedroom five minutes later, he was in an immaculate uniform.

"Evita has a suggestion, Cletus, that I'd like your opinion of," Perón said.

"What's that?"

"I thought, Cletus," Evita said, "that if I put some of my makeup base on that dreadful bandage it would make it less conspicuous. What do you think?"

The first thing I think, from your tone of voice, is that somehow we've become pals.

"Well, I'm sure it would, but what's the point?"

"When we appear on the balcony of the Casa Rosada, the bandage might cause comment," Evita said.

What the hell is she talking about?

"When are you going to appear on the balcony of the Casa Rosada?"

"Just as soon as we have our chat with President Farrell," Perón said. "Evita says there are somewhere over two hundred thousand *descamisados* . . ."

"My shirtless ones," Evita said with quiet pride.

". . . in the Plaza de Mayo already, and that once she gives the word, which she will do as soon as you and I leave for the hospital to meet with Farrell, at least another hundred thousand will be there by the time we get to the Casa Rosada."

Evita smiled. "What do you think about my makeup base covering Juan Domingo's bandage, Cletus?"

I think it's an absolutely stupid idea!

But this is not the time to disturb the new, and fragile, peace between us.

"I think it's a wonderful idea," Clete said quickly, then asked, "Does President Farrell know you're going to speak from the Casa Rosada?"

"Of course he does. What I want to speak with him about is making sure he doesn't do anything foolish with Fernando Lopez and the others involved in the assassination plot."

"How are you going to get from the hospital to the Casa Rosada?" Clete asked. "Do you want me to take you in the station wagon?"

Perón considered that for a moment, and

then said thoughtfully, "No."

Good. Then after the meeting with Farrell, I can go home.

By now, Dorotea is climbing the walls wondering where the hell I am. And I don't even want to think what my grandfather is doing.

"I think two Ejército Argentino staff cars would be better," Perón went on. "Martín, President Farrell, and — presuming the sonofabitch is at the hospital — Fernando Lopez in the first, and you, Father Welner, and me in the second."

"Why do you want me to go to the Casa Rosada?"

Perón's face showed that he was surprised at what he considered a stupid question. But he answered it nevertheless.

"Because the people — especially Evita's *descamisados* — will see that the president is taking me to the Casa Rosada. The army will see that Lopez is not in a cell somewhere making his peace with God before getting shot. When they see Father Welner and you riding with me through the *descamisados,* the army and the people will all see that the Church is behind me and that the son of Argentina hero el Coronel Jorge G. Frade and I have made our peace. That there is unity, not the threat of civil war."

Goddamn it, he's got this all figured out.

"We should be going, Juan Domingo," Nulder said.

505

"You and Evita go in two cars," Perón ordered. "I don't want you to be seen with her. I don't want you to be seen at all."

"I understand, Juan Domingo," Nulder said.

[SEVEN]

Apartment 4-C
1044 Calle Talcahuano
Buenos Aires, Argentina
1835 18 October 1945

Señor Erich Richter — formerly SS-Sturmführer Erich Raschner — watched as Señor Ludwig Mannhoffer — formerly SS-Brigadeführer Ludwig Hoffmann — hung up the telelphone. Richter then waited patiently for Mannhoffer to collect his thoughts, then repeat what had just been discussed on the call.

Finally, he did.

"That was of course Schwartz reporting from the military hospital," Mannhoffer began. "From which two staff cars have just departed, suitably escorted by the police, for the Casa Rosada. Accompanying President Farrell are Colonel Perón . . ."

He stopped and corrected himself.

"Actually, what I should have said was 'Accompanying *Oberst Perón*' — as he is obviously in charge — are President Farrell,

506

General Martín, that priest, the Jesuit, what's his name?"

"Father Welner?" Richter suggested.

"And *Father Welner* and Oberst Lopez of the Horse Rifles Regiment. *And* Señor Cletus Frade. The latter two surprise me. I would have thought that Perón would have had Lopez shot out of hand, or at the very least have him locked up at Campo Mayo awaiting court-martial. And what is Frade doing there?"

"I have no idea, sir."

"I didn't think you would. That was a rhetorical question."

"Sorry, sir."

"Apparently, they are going to put a face of 'we're all friends, we all support Perón' in his little coup. We already know there are a quarter of a million people waiting at the Casa Rosada to hear Perón speak.

"What we don't know is where the colonel's paramour, Señorita Duarte, is. We do know that she and that deviate Nulder are responsible for the quarter-million shirtless ones, which is why Farrell is going along with Perón. So she may be expected to play an important role in this. There is even talk that Perón is so confident that he will have her at his side when he speaks.

"We don't know what role Frade will play in this. But he has just moved to the top of the list of candidates to be eliminated in order to make the point to Perón, the Argentine people, and of course our own that National Socialism — and its enforcement mechanism, the SS — is alive and functioning in Argentina.

"We could eliminate Nulder. That has a certain personal appeal, as I find him offensive. But who would care? Perón might be glad to be rid of him. After tonight, he doesn't need him as much as he did, if at all.

"We could eliminate Señorita Duarte. Perón might be glad to be rid of her, too. But he might be thinking with his crotch.

"That leaves Frade. Eliminating him would not only make our point, but also would remove an American with the ear of Perón from the scene."

He stopped, paused, and then looked at Richter.

"You may comment."

"I can't find a flaw in your reasoning, sir."

"All right. Get started on a plan, multiple plans, to eliminate Cletus Frade. And as soon as possible."

"Yes, sir."

■ ■ ■ ■ ■

IX

■ ■ ■ ■ ■

[ONE]

Rhine-Main Airfield
Frankfurt am Main, Germany
0835 19 October 1945

Colonel Robert Mattingly, Second Lieutenant James D. Cronley Jr., Technical Sergeant Abraham L. Tedworth, and Staff Sergeant Paul D. Miller were all crammed in Mattingly's Horch when *La Ciudad de Mar del Plata* taxied up to the terminal.

The car was filthy. Its passengers looked both tired and scruffy.

Mattingly and the sergeants had left Berlin just after noon the day before, headed directly for Kloster Grünau in Bavaria, a distance of approximately 360 miles. They paused only for fuel and coffee and bologna sandwiches at Quartermaster POL (for Petrol, Oil, and Lubricants) stations, and for roadside breaks for draining their bladders and taking turns at the wheel.

En route, they had been forced three times to pull off the autobahn after having been

511

caught by Military Police speed traps driving in excess — far in excess — of the rigidly enforced 35 m.p.h. speed limit. Once, at a speed trap south of Kassel, an MP sergeant, who appeared more impressed than indignant, told Mattingly that he had clocked him at 105 m.p.h., which was three times the limit.

The normal procedure called for the detention of both driver and vehicle until, in the case of enlisted men, the miscreant could be turned over to his first sergeant or, in the case of officers, an officer of superior grade from his unit.

The detention procedure was waived for Mattingly. He was a colonel; Rank Hath Its Privileges.

He and the Horch were released after he signed an acknowledgment that he had been speeding. A report detailing his misbehavior would be sent through channels to his commanding officer. The MP sergeant also told him that the violation, speeding, was automatically upgraded to reckless driving when the speeder was caught going ten miles over the 35 m.p.h. limit.

At Kloster Grünau, Mattingly raised Second Lieutenant James D. Cronley Jr. and First Sergeant Tiny Dunwiddie from their more or less innocent sleep. He told the latter he was going to have to hold down the fort for a couple of weeks as the former was going to Argentina.

He then proceeded to brief Lieutenant Cronley as to what was expected of him, including the means of protecting the two canvas suitcases that he was not to let out of his sight until he placed them into the hands of Lieutenant Colonel Frade.

They then drove the approximately 226 road miles from Kloster Grünau to the Rhine-Main airfield outside Frankfurt am Main, acquiring en route two more citations for far exceeding the speed limit.

The citations, Mattingly knew, were going to delight General Greene when they came down through channels and landed on his desk requiring that he reply as to what punitive action he had taken. Greene would salivate when he got the one reporting that Mattingly had been clocked at triple the speed limit and cited for reckless driving.

While there were a number of punitive possibilities the speeding could cause, ranging from a verbal reprimand to a court-martial, the most likely thing that could happen was that Mattingly would find himself standing at attention before Lieutenant General Seidel — the EUCOM intelligence officer and General Greene's boss.

Seidel would ask him what the hell the speeding was all about, and Mattingly would reply with the truth: *"I had to get an officer onto the Buenos Aires plane, sir. The weather*

513

precluded the use of a light airplane, so the only way I could do that in the time available was by car, and ignoring the speed limit. Sir."

It was possible — unlikely but possible — that General Seidel would give him a pass on that alone. He had worked if not for, then around, Seidel in London and Paris. And Seidel had raised no objections when he had — with, to be sure, the blessings of both I. D. White and David Bruce, head of OSS in London — been named chief of OSS in Germany.

More likely was the probability that Seidel would ask, *"What officer? Buenos Aires? Why?"*

Questions that Mattingly could not answer, which would annoy Seidel even more than his refusal to answer Greene's questions had annoyed Greene.

And that would see him standing before Ike's chief of staff, General "Beetle" Smith. Smith knew about OPERATION OST, so Mattingly could explain to him why he had acted as he had, but Smith was not likely to give him a pass. Eisenhower would have to be told of the problem.

The problem of course was not Colonel Robert Mattingly's five citations for reckless driving, but the compromise of OPERATION OST, which carried with it the absolutely unacceptable embarrassment of both Eisenhower and President Truman.

It was possible, once Mattingly told Eisenhower that the files he had sent to Argentina were the ones — the only ones — that, should they fall into the wrong hands, could embarrass the President, that Eisenhower would tell Seidel to back off, what was going on at Kloster Grünau was none of his business. Or bring Seidel into the picture — he was, after all, the EUCOM G-2 — and have him tell Greene to back off.

More likely, however, Eisenhower's reaction to the situation would be: "Shut down Operation Ost."

That order could mean what it implied: Shut the whole damn thing down, including the South German Industrial Development Organization in Pullach.

But more likely, Eisenhower would order that no more Gehlen people be allowed to go to Argentina, and to wait and see if shutting down Pullach would be necessary. Ike knew how important the intelligence was that would be coming from Pullach.

In either — in any — event, Colonel Robert Mattingly would have to go. When the rumors inevitably got out that the United States was not only complicit in permitting Nazis to escape to Argentina, but actively involved in getting them there, his name would come up.

If the speeding resulted in his appearing before Eisenhower, Mattingly had decided to propose that Major Harry Wallace be put in charge of the South German Industrial Development Organization and that he himself be immediately returned to the United States for separation from the service. Not released from active duty. Separated. He would resign his commission and go back to the University of the South.

If somehow they ran him down in Suwanee, he could credibly protest that the suggestion he was smuggling Nazis into Germany was absurd. He was an academic, not a spy. A professor of history and languages. He had been a technician — one of many — in the OSS. Nothing more. What he had been doing at Kloster Grünau was sorting through captured enemy records.

This would derail his plans to apply for a Regular Army commission and stay in the Army, and close forever the door to service in the New OSS — if there actually was going to be one.

But this scenario would protect the President, Eisenhower, and Gehlen's Germans in Argentina, and ensure that the flow of intelligence from OPERATION OST was not cut off.

It was a gloomy forecast for the future, but that was the way — the only way — the ball seemed to be bouncing.

As far as Second Lieutenant James D. Cronley Jr. was concerned, the future looked so bright he was afraid the other shoe would fall at any moment. Something would keep him from boarding the aircraft with Colonel Mattingly's two suitcases and flying off to be reunited with Elsa.

She had been in his thoughts constantly since Mattingly had told him he was going to Argentina. In just about all the mental images of Elsa that flooded his mind, she was wearing the see-through black brassiere and panties he had bought for her in the PX.

[Two]

Aboard SAA Flight 2231
Altitude 20,000 feet Above Luxembourg City
0945 19 October 1945
La Ciudad de Mar del Plata had been on the ground at Rhine-Main just long enough to top off its fuel tanks and load five passengers, plus brown paper sacks containing egg sandwiches and two large thermos jugs of coffee. The passengers were two priests and two nuns traveling on Vatican passports, and of course Second Lieutenant James D. Cronley Jr., who boarded last with two canvas suitcases.

Cronley had been seated by the steward at the very rear of the passenger compartment beside a plump and balding mustachioed man who began their relationship by demanding, "Why didn't you check those bags? They're going to be in the way all the way to

517

Buenos Aires."

"Sorry," Jimmy replied in his Texican Spanish, "I don't speak Spanish."

Fifteen minutes later, right after the shift in the roar of the engines told him they had reached cruising altitude, the steward came and announced, "Sorry, sir, but we must change your seat."

Jimmy, dragging the two canvas suitcases, followed the steward up the narrow aisle to the front part of the passenger compartment. It was curtained off from the rear.

The steward held open the curtain for Cronley, and then closed it after him when he had passed through.

Cronley found himself in an area made up of the foremost two rows of double seats and — beyond an open door — an area holding a small table on one side and a rack of radios on the other. He could see all the way into the cockpit.

Von Wachtstein — whom Jimmy thought of as Elsa's brother-in-law — was resting his rear end on the small table. In the seats were three men he didn't know.

"Hello, Cronley," von Wachtstein said in German. "I guess I should have told the steward to seat you up here, but I didn't. Sorry. Anyway, you're here." He turned to the crew. "Gentlemen, this is Lieutenant Cronley, who found our Elsa for us. His mother is a Strasbourger, which explains why

518

he speaks German like a Strasbourger." He turned back. "Colonel Frade calls you Jimmy. Any objections if I do?"

"No."

"Jimmy, these people" — he pointed to them as he named them — "are Karl Boltitz, Willi Grüner, and Dieter von und zu Aschenburg. Willi and I used to fly under Dieter when we were in the Luftwaffe. I just showed them around the cockpit, which I thought I had better do first, as otherwise they wouldn't have paid attention to what I have to say now.

"Jimmy," von Wachtstein went on, as Cronley went to each of the men and shook hands, "is on a mission that Colonel Mattingly tells me is none of my business. So we can't get into that. What we can get into — what I did not get into with Colonel Mattingly — is what's going on, and what may be going on in Argentina.

"The last time I saw Cletus Frade, who not only is my best friend, and Jimmy's sort of big brother, but used to be the OSS's man in Argentina —"

He interrupted himself.

"I'm getting ahead of myself," he said. "Okay, Jimmy. Question. Prefacing this with the announcement that not only would I trust my life to Willi and Dieter but have done so more times than I like to remember, what do you think Cletus's reaction would be if he heard I told them about Operation Ost?"

Before Cronley could begin to reply, von Wachtstein added: "Karl knows all about it."

"You're putting me on a hell of a spot," Jimmy said.

"In other words, you don't want to answer the question?"

"I don't, but I will. I think Cletus wouldn't like it, but would give you the benefit of the doubt, providing he knew your friends understand the rules."

"Which are?" Dieter von und zu Aschenburg asked.

"That if you run at the mouth to anyone — anyone at all — about what he tells you — or you learn in some other way — Cletus will kill you, and if he doesn't, I will."

"Oddly enough," von und zu Aschenburg said, thoughtfully, after a moment, "I think the lieutenant is perfectly serious."

"I am," Cronley said simply.

"Herr Oberstleutnant," Boltitz said, looking at Dieter, "if Hansel decides to tell you, and you — as Lieutenant Cronley puts it — 'run at the mouth,' and Cletus Frade doesn't kill you both, or the lieutenant here doesn't, I will."

"Understood, Herr Kapitän zur See," von und zu Aschenburg said.

"Understood, Herr Kapitän zur See," Willi Grüner said.

"What did they call you?" Jimmy asked.

"I was at one time a Kriegsmarine officer, a

kapitän zur see," Boltitz said.

"Well, the decision having been made," von Wachtstein said, "let's take the plunge. Dieter, does the name Generalmajor Reinhard Gehlen mean anything to you?"

"Abwehr Ost?"

Von Wachtstein nodded.

"Shortly before the war ended," von Wachtstein began, "Gehlen went to Allen Dulles of the OSS. . . ."

"How much of this do the Soviets know?" von und zu Aschenburg asked five minutes later.

"Precisely how much, no one knows. But something certainly," von Wachtstein replied. "We know they are sending the man who was running the KGB in Mexico to Argentina. We not only have to keep Operation Ost a secret from the Soviets but from the American people as well. The political damage to President Truman should it come out that he's been smuggling German officers — much less Nazis — out of Germany into Argentina is something that just can't be allowed to happen."

"And you're prepared to kill to do that?"

"We," Cronley explained, "are prepared to kill to keep the Soviets from laying their hands on the former Abwehr Ost officers and men and their families we haven't — yet — been able to get out of Eastern Europe and the Russian Zone of Germany."

"That was stupid of me. I should have thought of that," von und zu Aschenburg said. "That's who the KGB'll go after, especially the families. Good luck with that, Lieutenant."

"And now to the situation in Argentina," von Wachtstein said. "The last time I saw Cletus Frade he was taking off — in a hail of machine-gun fire — in a Lodestar from Oberst Jorge Frade airfield in Buenos Aires with Oberst Juan Domingo Perón aboard, trying to keep him from being assassinated.

"I don't know where he was headed, probably to Mendoza, where he has an estancia. But he may have gone the other way, across the River Plate to Uruguay. The head of the Argentine Bureau of Internal Security, General Martín . . ."

Relating the story of the attempted assassination of Perón and all the possible ramifications of that — what had happened at the airport, the scenarios of what they might find when they landed, and the scenarios to deal with those scenarios — took almost twenty minutes.

"We'll just have to see what happens when we get there," von Wachtstein said finally. "My problem with all of this is Cletus Frade's ability to get thrown down a latrine, only to emerge moments later puffing on one of his cigars, smiling, and smelling like a rose. I suppose I expect that to happen again now. And I know that's not smart." He paused, glanced at each man, then added, "No, I won't take any questions because I don't really have any answers."

He paused again.

"We're over France now. It's a little over a thousand nautical miles to Lisbon, where we'll take on fuel and have lunch. We cruise at just about three hundred knots, so we should be there in about three hours.

"From there we go to Dakar, Senegal, a distance of fifteen hundred nautical miles. That's five hours. There we have dinner, take on fuel, and head for Buenos Aires. It's thirty-eight hundred nautical miles, give or take —"

"You're going to fly nonstop Dakar–Buenos Aires?" von und zu Aschenburg asked incredulously.

"If we're lucky. Five hours into the flight, I'll get our position shooting the stars. That'll tell me if we can make Buenos Aires with available fuel. Sometimes we encounter really bad headwinds. If that happens, we'll go to either São Paulo or Belém, Brazil, and from there to Buenos Aires."

"At an altitude of sixty-five hundred meters, in a pressurized cabin, making three hundred knots," von und zu Aschenburg said in awe. "This is one hell of an airplane, Hansel!"

"Yeah, it is," von Wachtstein said.

"Peter," Boltitz said, "what are the chances of finding U-405?"

"What?" von Wachtstein asked, visibly confused.

"I learned something when I was in Norway, and later in Bremen," Boltitz said. "You remember hearing that before U-234 sailed from Narvik for Japan, her captain permitted a dozen of her crew to go ashore? I mean, not to sail with her."

"What's that got to do with U-405?" von Wachtstein asked.

"Bear with me, please, Peter. I ran down one, an old shipmate, Kurt Schrann, who had been the U-405's second engineer. I found him in Bremen. He told me there was a contingency plan. If, when U-234 reached the South Atlantic and they hadn't been able to take on the fuel they needed to reach Japan, they were to make for a location on the Argentine coast. It was a point south of Río Gallegas, near the Chilean-Argentina border just north of the Magellan Strait."

Von Wachtstein nodded. "And?"

"And there they were to put ashore their passengers and cargo, bury the cargo — which is not only crates of money and jewels, but that five hundred kilos of the nuclear whatever . . ."

"Five hundred *and sixty* kilos of *uranium oxide*," von Wachtstein furnished.

". . . that Clete was so concerned about.

The U-234 would then be scuttled, and the crew and the passengers were supposed to make their way to someplace, San Carlos —"

"San Carlos de Bariloche?" von Wachtstein offered.

"Right. Where there are some SS people who would take care of them. When things calmed down, they could go back and dig up the stuff they buried. That uranium oxide is apparently worth a lot of money."

"There are several large holes in that plan that I can see," von Wachtstein said. "For one thing, the area south of Río Gallegas — that whole area is the opposite of hospitable. For hundreds of kilometers there's nothing but ice and snow. Year-round. It's really part of the Antarctic. The waters close to shore are uncharted, which means getting in close enough to off-load anything would be next to impossible. And even if you managed to unload the cargo and bury it, how could you go back and find it later? In a week, it would be buried under new snow and ice."

"So you think I should forget this, Peter?"

"I probably will tell you just that, after you explain what this has to do with Willi von Dattenberg's U-405."

"Maybe they knew all about that ice and snow," Boltitz said. "That there was a possibility the crew wouldn't make it to San Carlos Whatever. What they did was put the coordinates of where the landing would take place in a sealed envelope and put that in U-405's safe."

"I can't believe that Willi wouldn't have said something," von Wachtstein said. "After Cletus gave him sixty seconds to forget his duty as an honorable Kriegsmarine officer and start talking or Cletus would shoot him and bury him on the Pampas, Willi was a fountain of information."

"All I thought, Peter, is that if we knew where Willi scuttled U-405, maybe we could send a diver down and get into his safe and get these coordinates. Since we don't want the Soviets to get their hands on that uranium oxide, the effort seems justified."

"Well, unless Willi burned the contents of his safe before he sailed into the Port Belgrano Navy Base at Punta Alta flying a black flag and surrendered — and now that I think about it, he almost certainly did . . ."

"He didn't scuttle U-405?"

Von Wachtstein shook his head.

"She was tied up between two old Argentine battleships, the *Rivadavia* and the *Moreno,* at Punta Alta, under the control of a vice admiral named Crater. He's a pal of Cletus's pal General Martín."

"So we can get the coordinates?" Boltitz asked.

"Very possibly . . . if Willi didn't burn them *and* if there is no civil war that has found Oberst Perón shot — as well as Cletus and

Martín and Crater for good measure."

Jesus! Cronley thought.

There's that goddamned other shoe I've been worried about dropping.

How am I going to get to be with Elsa now?

"Do you think that's likely? Clete getting shot?" Cronley asked.

"If the civil war they were worried about got started, I'd say the odds are fifty-fifty," von Wachtstein said.

"So why the hell are we going to Buenos Aires before we find out what's going on?" Jimmy asked.

Von Wachtstein chuckled.

"One day, my young friend, you may fall in love. And when you are in love you go to where your beloved is, even if that might get you shot. My wife and son are in Buenos Aires. Understand?"

[THREE]

4730 Avenida Libertador General San Martín
Buenos Aires, Argentina
1235 19 October 1945

"I think," Doña Dorotea Mallín de Frade said, tapping her fingers on a photograph that took up a third of the front page of *La Nacíon,* "that I'll see if I can't get *La Nacíon* to make me a large print of that. I'll frame it."

The photo was of the vice president of the

527

Argentine Republic, el Coronel Juan D. Perón, standing on the balcony of the Casa Rosada and addressing a crowd *La Nación* estimated at "more than 325,000 persons." On his immediate right was Señorita Evita Duarte, who was beaming. Standing to his immediate left was Don Cletus Frade, his arms folded across his chest, wearing an *I don't know what the hell I'm doing here* look on his face.

"Whatever for?" Doña Claudia Carzino-Cormano asked.

"It's an historic moment," Dorotea said.

"Indeed it is," Clete said. "But we're not going to frame a photograph of it."

"I was kidding, my darling."

"What we are going to do is have an oil portrait made from it. At least two meters tall. We'll hang it in the foyer. And before it, on a small table, there will be votive candles for the faithful to prayerfully light."

Marjorie Howell giggled.

"Don't let Father Whatsisname hear you say that, Clete," she said.

"Father *Welner's* in the picture," Clete said. "Behind Evita. He'll love it. We'll have the artist paint one of those glowing circles around his head."

Dorotea laughed.

"Why not?" she asked. "Over time it will become as well known as da Vinci's *The Last*

Supper."

"I think we are confusing poor Elsa," Claudia said.

"I never know when you're serious," Elsa von Wachtstein said.

She was sitting next to Willi von Dattenberg, who agreed.

"Either do I," he said. "The Argentine sense of humor . . ."

"Cletus is half-American," Claudia said.

"Only half, unfortunately," Cletus Marcus Howell said.

"Don't start up, Grandfather," Clete said.

"Or what?"

"I'll have the artist paint you into the picture, with one of those glowing circles over your head, and send a copy of it to the Dallas Petroleum Club. It'll look great in the lobby."

"They call those halos, Clete," Marjorie said. "Not 'glowing circles.' "

"No fooling?"

"No fooling. They go back to around four hundred and fifty B.C. The first pictures showed one over the head of Perseus as he killed Medusa."

"I'm awed. I guess I forgot they finally let you out of the eighth grade and into junior high."

Marjorie made a face.

"Then I guess you also forgot," she snapped, "to send that Browning over-and-under for graduating from Rice a year early and *summa cum laude*! I always suspected either Mom or Grandfather sent it. If you had sent me a shotgun, it would have been a Sears Roebuck economy special."

"God have mercy on the man who marries her," Clete said. "She's as bad as the old man."

"I'll take that as a compliment," Marjorie said.

"Both of you knock it off," Martha Howell ordered with a mother's authority.

Antonio, the butler, came to where Clete was sitting at the head of the dining table.

"El Coronel Perón is on the telephone for you, Don Cletus," he announced.

"Tell him Don Cletus is not at home, Antonio," Dorotea ordered.

"I did. He said it's very important, Señora."

"What the hell does he want?" Clete asked rhetorically. "Okay, Antonio, bring in the goddamned phone."

"Watch your mouth, Cletus," Martha Howell said.

Antonio brought in a telephone, plugged it in under the table, and handed him the receiver.

"Cletus, this is your godfather," Juan Domingo Perón announced.

"What can I do for you, Tío Juan?"

"I need a great favor from you, Cletus."

"Will this wait? I have a houseful of people."

"No. It won't."

530

"What kind of a favor?"

"I want you to meet me at the city hall in Junín."

"I'm not even sure where that is."

"In the north of the province. Take National Route 7. It's about two hundred sixty kilometers."

"What the hell's going on in Junín?"

"I'll tell you when you get here."

"You sound like you want me to come wherever the hell that is right now," Clete said incredulously. "I just told you I have a houseful of people."

"I do. Father Welner and General Martín will also be here."

"Martín's going to drive two hundred sixty kilometers to be there? For Christ's sake, he took a bullet in his leg. He's on crutches and painkillers. I was surprised the poor bastard didn't pass out on the Casa Rosada balcony last night."

"I told you to watch your mouth, Cletus," Martha said.

Frade glanced at her and made a face as Perón said, "Cletus, this is very important to me. Please."

"What's going on in Junín, for the second time?"

"I can't get into that on the telephone. I can only repeat that this is very important to me."

"And Welner and Martín are going to be there?"

"Yes, they are."

"Okay, I'll come. But this had really better be important."

"God bless you, Cletus. How soon can you leave?"

"Just as soon as I hang up and escape from my wife. You heard what I said about this better be important?"

He hung up and looked at Dorotea.

"My precious," she said, "did I just hear that you're going to walk out of here right now and drive two hundred sixty kilometers to Junín?"

"I don't believe it myself," Clete said.

"Darling, in that picturesque Texas — or is it Marine Corps? — phrase you so often use, 'In a pig's ass, you are!' "

"You tell him, Dorotea," Marjorie said.

"Marjorie, you keep out of this," Martha said.

"What the hell is the matter with you?" Dorotea demanded. "Why couldn't you just have told him no?"

"Sweetheart, I just don't know," Clete admitted.

"Well, call him back and tell him you're not going," Dorotea said.

"Call him back where?" Clete asked.

"Junín?" Marjorie said sarcastically.

"Where in Junín?" Clete challenged.

"What's going on there anyway?" Dorotea asked.

"I guess I'll find out when I get there," Clete said.

"You're not really going?" Martha asked.

"I have to. I said I would."

"Not alone you're not," Dorotea said.

"Dorotea and I are going with you," Marjorie said.

"Oh, come on," Clete said.

"Yes, thank you," Marjorie said. "I'd love to. I get to see Junín and meet your Uncle Juan."

"Out of the question," Clete said. "God only knows what's going on in Junín."

"Don Cletus," Enrico Rodríguez said, joining the discussion. "If we took two station wagons with Húsares, we'd be all right."

"Thanks a lot, Enrico," Frade said.

"Your call," Dorotea said. "Either we all go, or no one does."

[FOUR]

Plaza San Martín
Junín, Buenos Aires Province
1645 19 October 1945

Father Welner's Packard convertible was parked at the curb before the city hall, a not-too-imposing three-story turn-of-the-century masonry structure. Clete, at the wheel of the

533

Horch, followed the first Ford station wagon and pulled up alongside it. There were also a half-dozen cars, four of them official-looking but unmarked Mercedes sedans. At least one of them, Clete decided, probably belonged to General Martín.

Without orders, the ex-Húsares of Frade's Private Army spilled out of the two station wagons and, led by Enrico Rodríguez, entered the city hall.

Rodríguez came back out almost immediately. He was trailed by el Coronel Juan Domingo Perón, who was wearing a well-tailored suit and a fresh bandage on his cheek. Father Welner came out a moment later, and finally General Bernardo Martín, on crutches.

Perón marched up to the Horch as everyone got out of it.

"My dear Dorotea," Perón said. "I can't tell you how glad I am to see you. Thank you so very much for coming. Evita will be so pleased."

"Juan Domingo," Dorotea said — and nothing else.

"I don't have the privilege of this beautiful lady's acquaintance," Perón then said.

"This is my sister, Marjorie Howell," Clete said. "Marj, this is the vice president of the Argentine Republic, my godfather, Colonel Juan Domingo Perón."

"How can she be your sister?" Perón challenged.

"Actually, she's my cousin. But we were raised together, and I think of her as my sister."

"Of course," Perón said, and then announced, "Why don't we all go inside?"

"What happens when we do?" Clete asked.

"The ceremony, I'm told, will take about fifteen minutes," Perón said. "And afterward we'll have a small celebration."

"Of what?" Dorotea asked.

"The wedding, of course. Evita and I are to be married!"

He turned his smile on Marjorie.

"In Argentina, my dear young woman, the system is that there are two ceremonies. A civil ceremony, which takes care of all the administrative details, and then, later, a church ceremony. Today, this will be the civil ceremony."

Señorita Evita Duarte came out of the city hall and advanced on the crowd at the Horch with a smile. She had a bouquet of roses pinned to a tight-fitting silver lamé dress.

"My darling," Perón said, "Cletus brought Señora de Frade with him. And his cousin, from the United States, Señorita Marjorie Howell."

"Oh, Cletus," Evita gushed. "More family! How wonderful of you! I can't thank you enough!"

She kissed his cheek affectionately, and then went to Perón and hung tightly to his arm.

He beamed at her, then turned toward the city hall door, where two men Clete did not recognize were standing.

"Numenez," Perón ordered curtly. "You can see that my guests have arrived. Go get the mayor!"

There was a small room off the foyer of the city hall. It looked something like a courtroom, except there was no elevated desk or platform for a judge. There was a small wooden barrier separating the front part of the room from the rear.

In the room's front part were a lectern and three tables. Two of the tables had three chairs at each. The third table, with a pair of chairs, was in the center beside the lectern, and held some sort of register beside a pen-and-inkwell set. There was a large crucifix on the rear wall, and an Argentine flag to the left.

The rear of the room held a dozen rows of benches on each side. Six or eight people could be crowded onto each bench.

It wasn't hard to figure out that the room was the official place where civil marriages were performed.

But why, Clete wondered, *did we have to come way the hell out here for that?*

There must be ten, probably more than ten, places like this in Buenos Aires.

For that matter, Perón is vice president; he

536

could have summoned the proper officials to do their thing anywhere he wanted.

Perón ushered people into their proper places.

"Father," he said to Welner, "if you would be so good, you're at the right witness table with the general and Cletus. The ladies, I'm afraid, are going to have to use one of the benches."

There was a man in a business suit at the left witness table. He had risen to his feet when everyone entered the room. Perón now introduced him.

"Señor Duarte," Peron said, "this is my godson, Don Cletus Frade, and Señora de Frade, and Señorita Howell. Señor Duarte is Evita's uncle. He will give the bride away."

Señor Duarte offered his hand to Clete and said, with absolutely no sincerity, that he was delighted to make his acquaintance.

"I have a few words to say," Perón announced, "and I might as well say them while we are waiting for the mayor, in his own sweet time, to join us.

"When I became godfather to the firstborn of my best friend, el Coronel Jorge G. Frade, may he be resting in peace, I swore to almighty God that I would protect his life as I would my own.

"As things turned out, as some of you know, it was Cletus who protected my life as he would his own, and at great risk to his own life. I would not be standing here today were it not for his courage and loyalty. And more than that, were it not for the blood from his veins now flowing in mine.

"Christ taught us, 'Greater love has no one than this, that one lay down his life for his friends.' General Martín proved his love for me by doing just that on the airfield named for my beloved best friend, Jorge Frade, and almost lost it to protect my life, suffering grievous wounds in the process.

"So I can say that I am grateful to Almighty God that the two men who have proved their love for me are here with me today to witness my marriage to my beloved Evita."

Jesus H. Christ!

Does he believe that?

And/or does he expect us to believe it?

A middle-aged man in a business suit hurried into the room.

"I'm so glad you could find time in your busy schedule for me, Señor Alcalde," Perón said unpleasantly. He turned to the man he had spoken to before. "Numenez, get the others in here."

Clete wondered who Numenez was.

"The others" filed into the room from the foyer, where apparently they had been waiting. There were ten of them. They all looked like plainclothes policemen. Clete remembered Martín telling him that — in his role as secretary of Labor and Retirement Plans

538

— Perón had his own security service, run by Rodolfo Nulder.

And where the hell is randy ol' Rodolfo?

Eight of the men took seats on the benches. The other two — one of whom held an American Speed Graphic "Press" camera and the other a German 35mm Leica — remained standing. The man with the Leica started snapping pictures.

The mayor took his position behind the lectern, and after a moment signaled, somewhat nervously, to Perón that he was ready. Perón walked to the lectern and stood to the right of it. Evita walked to the man Perón had identified as her uncle and stood beside him.

"Father Welner," Perón called, "would you be good enough to bless us before we begin the ceremony?"

Welner started to raise his hand.

"Up here, if you would be so good, Father," Perón stopped him.

Clete thought he saw on the priest's face a moment's indecision before he smiled and walked to the lectern.

When he raised his hand this time, a flashbulb on the Speed Graphic went off, startling Clete.

Welner returned to the table and took his seat beside Clete and Martín.

"In the name of the Republic and Buenos Aires Province . . ." the mayor began.

From what Clete remembered of his own civil wedding ceremony — not much; for some reason he had been a bit distracted at the time — the civil ceremonies were apparently standard.

The mayor gave a little speech announcing they were gathered to witness the union of Juan Domingo Perón and Evita Duarte, told everybody how important marriage was to society in general and the Argentine Republic specifically, and then asked who was giving this woman to be married.

Señor Duarte led Señorita Duarte to the lectern and handed her over to Vice President Perón. Another flashbulb went off. Señor Duarte returned to his seat. When it was only Evita, Juan Domingo, and His Honor the Mayor at the lectern, another flashbulb went off.

"You may kiss your bride," the mayor announced.

Perón kissed Evita with all the enthusiasm he might have had if he had been kissing the mayor.

"And now, if the witnesses will come forward," the mayor said.

The man with the Speed Graphic used it three times, first as Clete, then Father Welner, and finally General Martín signed the register documents.

"I'll require two copies of that," Perón announced.

"Copies?" the mayor asked, confused. "There is only the original."

"Don't argue with me," Perón snapped. "Bring the forms to the hotel. My witnesses can sign them there."

Flashbulbs went off another three times as the Speed Graphic photographer captured for posterity the bride, the groom, and the three official witnesses to their wedding. The Leica photographer had meanwhile been snapping away steadily.

And for what besides posterity? Clete wondered.

What is my Tío Juan going to do with all these pictures?

What is the clever sonofabitch up to?

The bridal party marched to the Hotel Colón, where the missing Señor Nulder was waiting for them in the lobby.

"Everything is ready, Juan Domingo." He pointed to a door.

"Don't let them take your picture, Rudy," Perón replied.

"I understand, Juan Domingo."

Beyond the door to which Nulder had pointed was a room in which half a dozen bottles of champagne and a not very impressive array of hors d'oeuvres waited for them on a table.

Flashbulbs went off again as Perón toasted his bride with a champagne stem, and a half-dozen times as the witnesses were photographed with the bride and groom, separately and together.

The mayor appeared with two copies of the witness page.

Clete, Martín, and Father Welner signed both copies.

Perón examined both and then handed them to General Martín.

"When the boys show up for breakfast tomorrow at the Circulo Militar and the senior officers' mess at Campo Mayo, General, I want them to find one of these posted at the door. You will arrange that for me, won't you?"

"Certainly," Martín said.

"Okay. Well, while I hate leaving this charming company, duty calls. Thank you all for coming."

Thirty seconds later, the newlyweds were gone.

"What the hell was that all about?" Marjorie Howell inquired.

"True love," Clete began sarcastically. "One day you may —"

"Shut up, Cletus," Dorotea said.

He clapped both of his hands over his mouth.

Marjorie smiled. Father Welner shook his head in resignation.

"What that was, Marjorie," Dorotea went on, "was the brilliant manipulation by Juan Domingo Perón of three people — four, if you want to count me — who are not usually able to be manipulated by anyone."

"You want to explain that?" Marjorie asked.

"Yeah, honey," Clete said, smiling at Dorotea as he reached for a bottle of champagne. "Why don't you? I'm just a little confused by all this myself."

"So far as the army — the officer corps, army and navy — is concerned," Dorotea said, "they don't know what to expect of Perón after the assassination plot failed and his speech from the balcony of the Casa Rosada. So, he just told them, using these three as actors in a carefully staged little play.

"I would say that he extended the olive branch of peace, but the gesture was more like this."

She held her left hand out, fingers closed except for the center finger, which pointed upward.

"I can't believe my wife," Clete said in mock horror, "the mother of my children, a member of the altar guild of the Anglican Cathedral of Saint John the Baptist, has any idea what that gesture she's making means."

Marjorie chuckled.

"You told me on our wedding night, darling," Dorotea said. "The message of the copies of the wedding register he's having Bernardo pin to the doors of the senior officers' mess at Campo Mayo and the Circulo Militar dining room is: 'I just married that woman you don't like, so go screw yourselves.' And there's a second message: 'General Martín pinned these up because he works for me and does what I tell him to do.'

"And when the photographs of the wedding appear in *La Nacíon* and *El País,* there will be Father Welner blessing the wedding. The message there is: 'Don't think you can still complain to the Church about me marrying' — in my husband's words — 'a semi-hooker half my age because if Father Welner approves, you know that the Church does.' "

"I think you're grossly overestimating my reputation, Dorotea," the priest said. "As well as my influence."

"Hah!" Clete snorted.

"And the presence of my husband here today," Dorotea went on, "and last night on the balcony, tells them, 'Whatever you may have heard about Don Cletus throwing me out of el Coronel Frade's house on Libertador because he disapproved of me sleeping with teenaged girls . . .' "

"He was doing what?" Marjorie asked incredulously.

" '. . . is untrue. Or at least has been forgiven,' " Dorotea finished.

"He was doing what?" Marjorie asked again.

"What Mom thought Jimmy Cronley was doing with you," Clete said.

"You sonofabitch!" Marjorie exploded. "You know that never happened! The last person in the world I'd do something like that with is Jimmy Cronley. He's just a . . . shallow kid."

"Cletus, stop!" Dorotea said angrily.

"Not any longer. He's now an officer and a gentleman," Clete went on. "They even let him have a pistol. No cartridges, but a pistol. He wears it slung low, like John Wayne. All the fräuleins are dazzled."

"I don't see how you can stand to live with him," Marjorie said to Dorotea.

"It's not easy," Dorotea said.

"Quickly changing the subject," Clete said, "tell me, General Martín, your professional analysis of Dorotea's analysis of recent events."

"Actually, I thought it was quite accurate," Martín said.

Dorotea gave Clete the finger.

"There she goes again! Shocking! Did you ever hear, Bernardo, that the true test of another man's intelligence is how much he agrees with you?"

"You've mentioned that once or twice in the past, Cletus," Martín said, smiling.

"What I have been trying to figure out is

why he had to stage his little amateur theatrical here. He could just as easily have done everything in Buenos Aires."

"I think I can answer that," Father Welner said.

"Please do," Dorotea said.

"Señora Duarte de Perón was born not far from here, in a little village called Los Toldos," the priest said. "Her birth certificate says that she was born out of wedlock to a Señor Duarte — the manager of the estancia on which they lived — and a Señorita Ibarguren. As I understand it, Señor Duarte and Señorita Ibarguren lived together essentially as man and wife. They never married, as he was already married when he met Evita's mother. But Evita looked upon him as her father.

"He died when Evita was fifteen. His lawful wife inherited all his property — it wasn't much but she got all of it. And when Evita tried to attend her father's funeral here in Junín, the lawful wife refused to let her in the church, or be present at the Junín cemetery when he was buried. Evita moved to Buenos Aires the following year when she turned sixteen."

"So she returns to the site of her humiliation for her marriage to an army colonel," Marjorie said.

"An army colonel who will be the next president of Argentina," Welner said.

"I thought you priests were supposed to keep family secrets like this to yourselves," Clete said. "Why did you tell us this?"

"My God, Clete!" Dorotea protested.

"For one thing, it's public knowledge," Welner said. "More important, for another, we — the four of us — are going be dealing with Señora de Perón in the future. This afternoon, with her marriage to Juan Domingo, she became an important woman. The more that all of us know about her, the better."

"You knew about this, Bernardo?" Clete asked.

Martín nodded.

"And didn't tell me?"

"An oversight, Cletus. The subject just never came up."

"I wonder what the mattresses in this place are going to be like," Dorotea said.

"We're not staying," Clete said. "Hansel will be back from Germany in the morning. I want to be there."

"He can land without your advice."

"He's bringing with him the dossiers of those Nazis who von Dattenberg brought with him. The sooner Bernardo has that information, the better, and Bernardo will be too tired from nailing the wedding registry announcements to the mess hall doors to be at Jorge Frade."

[FIVE]

Aeropuerto Coronel Jorge G. Frade
Morón, Buenos Aires Province, Argentina
1100 20 October 1945

As the truck-mounted stairs were positioned at the passenger door of *La Ciudad de Mar del Plata,* men pushed a narrow set of stairs on wheels up to the cockpit door. As soon as it was in place, Cletus Frade quickly climbed it.

Hans-Peter von Wachtstein was getting out of the pilot's seat when Clete entered the cockpit.

They shook hands.

"We were getting a little worried, Hansel."

"We ran into a hell of a storm in the middle of the Atlantic, Cletus, and —"

Frade spotted Boltitz and interrupted him.

"Beth has been pawing the ground since nine o'clock. I thought we were going to have to pour a bucket of cold water on her."

"Very funny, Cletus," Boltitz said.

"Hansel, did Colonel Mattingly give you a package for me?" Frade asked.

"If you're talking about two canvas suitcases, he entrusted it to the care of Second Lieutenant Cronley," von Wachtstein said.

"What the hell is that supposed to mean?"

"Say, 'Welcome to Argentina, Jimmy,'

Clete," Cronley said from the radio compartment.

He was wearing an olive drab U.S. Army uniform with gold second lieutenant's bars and the crossed swords of cavalry on it — not the "civilian employee" blue triangles he had been wearing in Marburg an der Lahn. The jacket was unbuttoned, revealing a Colt Model 1911-A1 .45 ACP in a shoulder holster.

Why the pistol, Jimmy?

Who are you going to shoot on this airplane?

There were two other men in the radio compartment. The older of them looked vaguely familiar, but he couldn't come up with a name. He had never seen the younger one.

Who the hell are these guys?

"What the hell are you doing here, Jimmy?" Frade asked, wrapping his arms around Cronley.

"Colonel Mattingly said because I ate my spinach I could come out and play with the big boys. I guess our side won in the civil war, huh?"

"What and where did you hear about a civil war?"

"Peter said the last time he saw you, you were taking off from here in a Lodestar with the local dictator aboard and the bad guys shooting machine guns at you."

"Did von Wachtstein use that term, 'local

dictator'?" Clete asked, looking at Peter.

"No. He said it was a Colonel Peon."

"Perón," Frade said. "Colonel Juan Domingo *Perón.* I don't want you ever to say, or even think, 'local dictator' again. Got it?"

"Got it," Cronley said, smiling.

"Say, 'Aye, aye, sir.' That was an order."

"Begging the colonel's pardon, sir, the lieutenant is an Army officer. Army officers don't say 'aye, aye.' But, that out of the way, yes, sir. I understand."

Clete saw that all the Germans were amused. It was only with a major effort that he kept his temper under control.

If I stand Cronley tall and really let him have it, all that will accomplish is to really amuse the Germans.

How do I know these other two are German?

"Peter, who are these people?" Clete asked.

"Old comrades from the Luftwaffe," von Wachtstein said. "Willi Grüner and Dieter von und zu Aschenburg."

Frade's memory banks kicked in.

The older one used to fly Lufthansa Condors into here. That's why I recognize him.

The young one is who Peter went to flight school with and flew with in Spain.

And now that I think about it, von Whatever-his-name-is was their commanding officer.

So, what obviously has happened is that they somehow got together in Berlin, or Frankfurt, and he just loaded them on the plane.

550

Without of course asking me if that was okay.

And without considering it was putting Operation Ost at risk.

He felt his temper rise, and then got it under control as he wordlessly shook their hands.

Get off your high horse, Cletus.

You would have done exactly the same thing.

"Welcome to Argentina," he said. "Getting you off the airport may pose a problem. The man who handles things like that for us isn't here." He looked at Peter. "When they were shooting at me in the Lodestar, they managed to hit General Martín in the leg. He's on crutches."

"Is he going to be all right?" von Wachtstein asked.

"Yeah."

"And Colonel Peon?" von Wachtstein asked, smiling.

"You think that's funny, do you?"

"Colonel Peon is a good name for a dictator, wouldn't you say?"

"Colonel *Perón*'s fine. As a matter of fact, Colonel *Perón* and Señorita Evita Duarte were married yesterday. Martín, Father Welner, and I were the witnesses."

"He actually married her?"

"He actually married her. And ordered Bernardo to pin copies of the wedding register to the doors of the dining rooms at the Circulo Militar and the officers' club at Campo Mayo."

"I thought you said Bernardo was on crutches," von Wachtstein said.

"He was. He is. Enrico's here — he'll know how to get your friends past the immigration people."

"That's not going to be a problem. I went to Germany with Argentine passports and *libretas de enrolamiento* for Dieter and Willi in my pocket. Courtesy of Bernardo."

Frade nodded.

"Cletus," Boltitz then said, "I turned up something interesting about U-405 in Bremen. It is possible she made landfall in southern Argentina."

"How good is your information?"

"You heard that before she sailed from Narvik, some of her crew was allowed to leave?"

Frade nodded.

"I knew one of them, her second engineer, Kurt Schrann, when he was a simple seaman. We made five patrols together. I recommended him for a direct commission. I ran Kurt down in Bremen. He wouldn't lie to me. He said the coordinates for the landfall were also furnished, in code, to U-405. If von Dattenberg didn't burn the contents of his safe before he surrendered . . ."

"He didn't," Clete said simply. "Did Willi know about this document, whatever it is, with the coordinates?" He looked at von

Wachtstein. "Hansel, he damned sure didn't say anything."

"If Willi didn't say anything, he didn't know," von Wachtstein replied.

"He was the captain of U-405 and he didn't know?" Frade asked sarcastically.

"Where are the contents of U-405's safe?" Boltitz asked.

"Bernardo has them," Clete replied. "I was about to send them to Casa Montagna to see if someone there could find something of value."

"Clete, I think if we put together what I know — or think I know — with Willi and the contents of the safe . . ."

"Okay. I'll see what I can do to set that up," Clete said. "I'll call Martín from the passenger terminal and see how he wants to handle this."

He turned to Cronley.

"Do you know what's in those bags you brought?"

Cronley nodded.

"And, briefly, what would that be?"

"Well, in addition to thermite grenades —"

"Thermite grenades!" Frade interrupted.

"Right. Grenades, Hand, Thermite, M14 — one in each suitcase. I wouldn't tug on that nylon cord you see snaking out the side."

"Spare me your wit, Jimmy," Frade snapped.

"I'm not being funny, Cletus. You tug on

that cord and you can say good-bye not only
to what's in the suitcases but to your airplane."

*My God, he's serious! He has thermite gre-
nades in there.*

*And what the hell else? The dossiers I asked
for are not that important.*

*They're useful, but not important in a keep-
the-other-side-from-learning-what-they-say way.*

*With the exception that we got them from the
Gehlen people, there's no reason they should
be classified at all.*

"I asked you what's in those bags," Frade
said.

"You're putting me on a spot, Clete. Colonel Mattingly said I'm not supposed to tell
anyone but you. That was my last order and
I'm going to obey it."

"Your last order, goddamn it, Jimmy, is
from me. Tell me what's in the goddamn
suitcases."

"The way that works, Clete, and you know
it, is that an order remains valid until changed
by someone senior to the officer who issued
the original order. Mattingly is a full bull
colonel. You're a light bird."

"I would say, Lieutenant Colonel Frade,
that the lieutenant has you," von Wachtstein
said drily.

Frade took Cronley's arm and led him into
the passenger compartment. It was already
just about empty. Clete, arms crossed, impa-

554

tiently waited until it was entirely empty, then turned to Cronley.

"Why are you trying to make me look the fool in front of my friends?"

"I'm not doing that. Jesus, Clete!"

"Then what's going on?"

"Mattingly said, 'If Frade wants to tell his German and Argentine friends what I'm sending him, that's his business. But I'm not going to hand over this material to them, and neither are you. You're not even to tell them what's in the bags.' Or words to that effect."

"Okay, understood. So, what's in the bags?"

"Those dossiers you asked for of the Nazis who came ashore from U-405 —"

"Von Wachtstein and the others know all about that. What else is there that requires thermite grenades?"

"And the names of all the Gehlen people who are here. And all records of anything that connects the South German Industrial Development Organization to anything here. Mattingly thinks Grünau and Pullach are about to be raided."

"Raided? By who?"

Cronley told him everything that had happened at Kloster Grünau. And of Mattingly's session with General Greene. And of Mattingly's belief that Greene was about to raid Kloster Grünau, Pullach, and Mattingly's office in the I.G. Farben Building to see what he could find.

"So he got you the hell out of Dodge, huh?" Frade said when Cronley had finished.

"Me and the incriminating evidence."

"Major Habanzo — he is probably really a colonel, anyway, he's General Martín's Number Two in the Bureau of Internal Security — is in the passenger terminal. He'll know where to find Martín. While we're waiting to get in touch with him, we'll go to a house of mine downtown. Martín will probably come there, even if they have to carry him. He's a good man, Jimmy. Keep that in mind."

"Got it."

"Okay, let's do it. Where do you want to disarm the thermite grenades?"

"Why would I want to do that?"

"Because no one is going to try to get at those bags here, and it would be a shame to see all that stuff go up in smoke because there was some kind of accident."

Frade heard the sarcasm in his voice and hoped that it didn't go too far.

It went, instead, right over Cronley's head.

He's going to disarm those grenades when he decides it's safe to do so. Not when — or because — Colonel Frade tells him to.

And what Colonel Frade had better do is understand that his Little Brother Jimmy is really an Army officer now. And not your typical wet-behind-the-ears second lieutenant.

Mattingly put him in charge of Kloster Grünau. He certainly would have preferred to hand that

556

job to a thirty-year-old major. But he gave it to Jimmy and then entrusted to Jimmy's care documents that would, if they got out, embarrass the commander in chief, European Command, and the President of the United States.

Second lieutenants are not usually handed responsibilities like that.

Second Lieutenant Cronley made his decision: "I could do it right here. But if I screw up, there goes your airplane. What I'm going to do is get off the airplane and go fifty — better, a hundred — yards away and disarm the thermite there."

"I'll send Enrico with you."

"Who's he?"

"You saw him in Marburg. He's a retired Argentine sergeant major. Now he's my bodyguard."

"You need a bodyguard, Clete?"

Frade nodded. "I'm afraid so," he said, then added, "Bring the bags and follow me."

Clete led Jimmy through the passenger cabin — rather than back to the cockpit — and then down the passenger stairway. Enrico, who had been waiting at the foot of the crew steps, came over to them.

"You remember Subteniente Cronley, Sergeant Major?"

"*Sí*, Don Cletus. Your little brother." He smiled and thrust his hand at Cronley.

"Think of him, Suboficial Mayor, as subteniente."

557

Enrico looked surprised.

"*Sí, mi Coronel.*"

"In the subteniente's luggage, Sergeant Major," Frade went on, "are two thermite grenades. I want you to go with him out there and help disarm the grenades. And then take him to the terminal and load him and the bags in one of the station wagons."

"*Sí, mi Coronel.*"

Frade saw Boltitz and Hansel's old Luftwaffe buddies coming down the stairs and started to walk to the terminal.

Cletus Marcus Howell, Martha Howell, and Beth and Marjorie came out of the passenger terminal onto the tarmac.

"You better have a bucket of cold water ready, Martha," Clete said. "Beth's seen Karl Boltitz."

"You sonofabitch!" Beth said, as she started to run toward Boltitz.

"That's not funny, Cletus. You should be ashamed of yourself," Martha replied, but she couldn't stop from smiling.

"Who's the man in the American uniform?" Marjorie then asked. "Walking here with Enrico?"

"Not a man you'd be interested in, Marj. Just a shallow kid who works for me."

"If I didn't know better, I'd say he looks like Jimmy Cronley," Martha said.

"You do know better, Martha. And it looks

like you're going to need two buckets of ice water."

"Beth's right," Marj said. "You are a sonofabitch!"

"I can't believe my baby sister said that to me!"

"What's Jimmy doing here?" Martha asked.

"He heard Marj was here and hopped on the next plane."

"I mean, really," Martha said, and then stopped when she realized Cronley was now almost up to them.

"Hey, Miz Howell!" he greeted her.

"I know you well enough to get kissed, Jimmy," she said.

"Yes, ma'am," he said, and kissed her on the cheek.

"And you're Clete's grandfather, right?"

"The last time I saw you, you were in a Boy Scout uniform," the old man said.

"No, sir. I think it was in my A&M pinks and greens. And it was at Mr. Howell's funeral."

"So it was," the old man said.

Cronley turned to Marjorie.

"Hey, Squirt. How goes it?"

Frade smiled, thinking, *Well, the shallow boy just cut the sophisticated lady off at the knees, didn't he?*

Marjorie, face flushed, was literally speechless.

Major Habanzo walked up to them.

"Don Cletus, General Martín will want to know if . . . if what he was looking for was on the plane."

"It was. Major Habanzo, this is Subteniente Cronley, the . . . officer courier" — *Marjorie, put that "officer courier" in your pipe and smoke it* — "who brought it. And some other things that will be of interest to the general."

"Teniente," Habanzo said to Jimmy, and put out his hand.

Cronley saluted, and said, *"A sus órdenes, mi Mayor,"* before shaking it.

Marjie didn't miss any of that either.

"How do we get the general and this material together?" Frade asked.

"The general has suggested that, presuming what he hoped would be on the airplane was, that he could be at your Libertador house by the time you get there if I called him, and if that would be convenient."

"Call him, please," Frade said. "Martha, I'll have to ride with Jimmy in one of the station wagons."

"I was hoping he could ride with us. I want to ask him what he's been up to."

"No, you don't, Martha. Even if he could tell you, you don't want to know."

"You're serious, aren't you?"

Frade nodded.

"We'll see you at the house. Let's go, Jimmy."

[Six]

"Don Cletus, Captain von Dattenberg and Señora von Wachtstein are in the garage," Antonio the butler announced.

Jimmy Cronley looked up with interest.

"Well, that's everybody then," Frade said. "I'd say we should go in the library, but I suspect we're going to need this table."

Everyone was still seated around the enormous dining room table where they had just had lunch. Clete had decided to wait until von Dattenberg could drive in from Estancia San Pedro y San Pablo before getting into the business at hand, so that everybody would be present.

"Antonio, would you have someone clear the table, and bring coffee?"

"*Sí*, Don Cletus."

"Show Captain von Dattenberg in here, please, Antonio. Hold the lady in the foyer, where the other ladies and — I'm sorry, Grandfather — Señor Howell will join them."

"I'm going to sit in on this, Cletus," Dorotea announced.

"I think I will, too," the old man announced.

"Grandfather, don't blow a gasket, but

561

that's absolutely impossible."

"How did you ever get to be a colonel," the old man replied, "much less a senior intelligence officer, without learning that nothing is ever absolutely impossible?"

He reached into his inner pocket, came out with a small envelope, and tossed it onto the table in front of Clete.

Clete was surprised when he saw what was printed on the flap of the envelope and even more shocked when he saw what it contained:

The White House

Washington, D.C.
12 October 1945

Dear Colonel Frade:

I asked your grandfather to go down there to have a look around for me.
I have told him what you're all up to, and look forward to him telling me how well you're doing it.

Sincerely,
Harry S Truman

"Bernardo," Frade said, as he tossed the note to General Martín, "you've always wondered where I acquired my skill as an intelligence officer. Now I can tell you. It's in my genes. Say hello to my grandfather, Super Spy."

X

[ONE]

4730 Avenida Libertador General San Martín
Buenos Aires, Argentina
1347 20 October 1945

Martha Howell looked up from the Truman note and at her father-in-law.

"Dad, where the hell did you get this?"

"One of the President's Secret Service agents brought it to my apartment in the Hay-Adams."

"That's not what I was asking, and you know it."

"Oh, you mean, 'Why did Harry write it?' "

" 'Harry'?" she parroted incredulously. "You now call him Harry?"

"Well, not in public, of course. After all, Harry is the President."

"The last time I heard you mention his name, Dad, you used language I can't repeat in mixed company."

"I don't know where you got that," the old man replied. "Harry Truman is a fine man. A fellow Thirty-third Degree Mason, among other things."

"My God!" Martha said.

"Do you know what I'm talking about, General Martín?" the old man asked. "Free-masonry? Do they have that down here?"

"There are Masons here of course, Señor Howell," Martín replied. "Many of our founding fathers — José de San Martín, Manuel Belgrano, and Domingo Sarmiento, for example, all presidents of the Argentine Republic — were Masons."

"I didn't know that," the old man said. "I thought you were all Roman Catholics down here. No offense intended, Father Welner."

"Most of us are," Martín said.

"That's something else you're going to have to do, Cletus," the old man said. "And, for that matter, you, too, Jimmy. See about getting into the Masons. You're both old enough. I'm surprised your father, Jimmy, hasn't talked to you already."

"How the hell did we get on this subject?" Clete asked.

"Because he doesn't want to explain that letter, or whatever it is, from President Truman," Martha said.

"Nonsense," the old man said. "What happened was that Harry — excuse me, *President Truman* — and I were having a little Tennessee pick-me-up in my apartment and I happened to mention that I'd bought the Constellation and was coming down here, and he

566

said, that being the case, he wondered if I would do him a favor, and I said certainly. He is the President. How can you tell the President of the United States no?

"So he told me what you're doing down here —"

"What did he tell you we're doing down here?" Clete interrupted.

"What the hell do you think he told me? About keeping General Gehlen's people out of the hands of the goddamn Communists is what he told me. My God, Cletus!"

"I'll be a sonofabitch," Clete said.

"Watch your mouth, Cletus," Martha said. Then she had a second thought: "I never heard about any of this. Who is General Gehlen?"

"Harry also told me," the old man went on, "that you're looking for a German submarine, or submarines, that left Germany with uranium oxide aboard that he's afraid the Russians will get their hands on."

"I'm having trouble believing the President ran at the mouth like that," Clete said.

"Well, Harry knows I'm not exactly a Commie in the closet. That probably had something to do with it."

"And what exactly does the commander in chief want you to do for him here?" Clete asked.

"What he said, Cletus, is that while as far as he's concerned you've been doing a first-class job down here, you can't get away from the fact that you're pretty young to be a lieutenant colonel. He said that when he was your age, he was a captain."

"So?"

"What he said was that he would be more comfortable with this situation if someone a little older, a little more experienced, and with the wisdom that comes only with a lot of years . . ."

"I wonder who he had in mind?" Clete asked sarcastically.

". . . had a look at everything," the old man went on. "And, if needed, put a gentle hand on the tiller and got your boat back on the right course."

The door opened and Antonio announced, "Captain von Dattenberg, Don Cletus."

Jimmy snapped his head toward the door.

He saw a tall, slim, hawk-featured man in nice-looking civilian clothing that seemed just a little too large for him.

But he saw no Elsa.

Where is she?

And why did she come here with this sonofabitch?

"Come on in, Willi," Frade called. "The ladies are just leaving."

Frade waited until all the women but Dorotea had left.

Cronley kept his eyes on the door until it

was closed. He still didn't get a glimpse of Elsa.

Von Dattenberg saw Boltitz and walked quickly to him.

"I'm delighted to see you, Karl."

"And you, Willi."

They stiffly shook hands.

"Willi, this is Subteniente Cronley," Frade said. "I think you know everybody else."

Von Dattenberg advanced on Cronley and offered his hand.

"I don't think I've ever seen an American officer in uniform before, Lieutenant," he said in English.

"I speak German," Cronley said.

"His mother's from Strasbourg," the old man said. "That's where he got the German. My mother was from New Orleans, which means we can do this in French, Cajun, Spanish, or English. Any language but German. I don't want to miss anything."

"And this," Frade said, continuing in English, "is my grandfather."

Von Dattenberg shook his hand and said, "My honor, sir."

"My grandfather, Willi, has been sent by President Truman, who is very interested in the five hundred sixty kilograms of uranium oxide that was on U-234 when she sailed for Japan from Narvik."

"Your grandfather?" von Dattenberg said, surprised.

"Yeah, my grandfather," Clete replied. "What can you tell us?"

"The only thing I can tell you for certain is that I think uranium oxide being on U-234 is nothing more than a rumor."

"Karl," Clete said, "tell him."

"It's not a rumor, Willi. Did you know Kurt Schrann?"

Von Dattenberg nodded. "The fellow you had directly commissioned, right?"

"He was second engineer officer on U-234. He was among those who Kapitän Schneider . . ."

"Good man," von Dattenberg said.

". . . allowed to leave the boat in Narvik before they sailed. I ran Kurt down in Bremen. He wouldn't lie to me. He said the coordinates for the landfall were also furnished, in code, to U-405."

"Not to me," von Dattenberg said.

"Then why would this guy say that they were?" Clete asked.

"I don't know," von Dattenberg replied thoughtfully. "The only coded coordinates I had in my safe were the rendezvous coordinates."

"What are they?" Jimmy Cronley asked.

Von Dattenberg gave him an annoyed look.

Cronley interpreted it to mean: *Who the hell are you, Subteniente, to be asking questions?*

When von Dattenberg didn't reply immediately, Frade asked, not pleasantly, "Well, what are they?"

"During the war," von Dattenberg began, "we were following Admiral Doenitz's Wolfpack tactic, and when the Kriegsmarine learned of the location of an Allied convoy, we would receive orders by radio to rendezvous at a certain point —"

"You'd be ordered to rendezvous at Point A, or somesuch," Cronley interrupted. "I mean, they didn't radio you the actual coordinates, right?"

"The Atlantic Ocean, Subteniente, is enormous," von Dattenberg said.

"I think everyone knows that, Willi," Frade said unpleasantly. "Answer his question."

"Have I done something to offend you, Oberstleutnant Frade?" von Dattenberg asked.

"As a matter of fact," Frade said evenly, "I'm having a little trouble believing that the captain of a submarine would not know that he had been given a set of coded coordinates for something as important as U–234's Argentine landfall. And I've been wondering if you're back to that officer's honor bullshit."

"Take it easy, Clete," Cronley said. "Maybe he didn't know what they were."

"How could he not know?" Frade snapped.

"Because they didn't want him to know unless it was necessary."

Clete looked at Jimmy a long moment, then

turned to von Dattenberg.

"Answer Cronley's question, Willi. Now I forget what it was. . . ."

"I asked if the Kriegsmarine radioed the actual coordinates of a rendezvous point," Cronley said. "Or whether you got a message saying 'Rendezvous Four' or 'Rendezvous 219' or something like that."

"There were five sheets of rendezvous points," von Dattenberg said. "Twenty rendezvous points to a page, for a total of one hundred. As I was saying before, the Atlantic Ocean is enormous — we needed that many possible rendezvous sites."

"So the message said, in effect, 'Rendezvous Point 55'?" Cronley said.

"Actually, the messages were in three parts," von Dattenberg explained. "The first identified, by line number, the rendezvous point. For example, if it was Rendezvous Point 55, the first part of the message would be '3-15'. The '3' meaning page three of the five pages, and the '15' being the fifteenth set of coordinates on page three. The second part of the message would be a date and time block. That was an order to be at the rendezvous point no later than, say, seventeen hundred hours on the twentieth. In that case, the second part of the message would be 1700-20."

"And the third part?" Cronley said.

"The third part would be the code. Are you

familiar, Subteniente, with nautical map coordinates?"

"A little," Cronley said.

"You know that longitude and latitude are written — to pull one out of the air — S50.62795, W60.56676. That means 50 degrees, 62795 seconds south latitude and 60 degrees 56676 seconds west longitude. That would be in the South Atlantic, several hundred miles north of the Falkland Islands."

"Okay," Cronley said.

"The code would read '5258.' That would be an instruction to change the south latitude to S52 and the west longitude to W62. That would be a point — if I can still do this in my head — about one hundred miles southwest of the Falklands."

"Do you remember, Kapitän," Cronley asked, "getting one of these lists of rendezvous points just before you sailed from Narvik?"

Von Dattenberg nodded. "You think the landfall coordinates are on that list?"

"Did you turn it over to General Martín?" Cronley asked.

"Yes."

"But, Jimmy, what good would it do?" Frade asked. "There was never a message about it. We don't have any idea which of the one hundred rendezvous points it would be, and we don't have the third part of the message, the code."

"We do it backwards," Cronley said.

"What the hell does that mean?" Frade demanded.

"On the airplane," Cronley explained, "when I first heard anything about any of this, Kapitän Boltitz said —"

"Karl, please, Jimmy," Boltitz said. "We're all friends here."

That was for you, Cletus, Cronley thought.

For as much as accusing von Dattenberg of being a liar.

Was that on purpose? Or does Clete have a burr under his saddle about von Dattenberg?

"Thanks, Karl," Cronley said. "Okay, you said the guy in Bremen told you the landfall was just north of the Magellan Strait. We know pretty well where that is, what its coordinates are."

"Yeah," von Dattenberg said thoughtfully. "Subteniente, you're thinking of the seconds, am I correct?"

Cronley nodded. "We need charts of that area, good charts —"

"And of course the list of rendezvous points," von Dattenberg said. He looked at Frade. "Can we get them here?"

"The list of rendezvous points from U-405 is in my safe at the Edificio Libertador," General Martín said.

"With the charts from U-405?" von Dattenberg asked.

Martín nodded.

"Can we get them here?" Cronley asked.

Martín got out of his chair and, moving carefully without aid of his crutches, walked to a sideboard. He picked up the telephone and dialed a number.

"General," Cronley called as Martín waited for someone to answer. "Your — the Argentine army's — maps of the area also would be helpful."

Martín nodded.

They listened to the one-sided conversation.

"You are supposed to answer before the third ring," Martín said sternly, and then before a reply could be made, went on: "Write this down. Go to the Topographic Service and get every map, in every scale, they have on the coast from Río Gallegos down to San Sebastian Bay . . .

"Yes, I know that's going to be a lot of maps . . .

"If they ask what we want them for, tell them it's a matter of national security . . .

"*Madre de Dios!* If I don't tell you what I want them for, Major, then you can truthfully tell them you have no idea what the chief of the Bureau of Internal Security wants them for, only that he has the authority to demand them immediately and is doing so . . .

"And while they are collecting the maps, go to the safe and take out all the documents we

575

have from U–405 . . .

"Yes, all of them . . .

"And when you have them all, bring them to Don Cletus Frade's house on Libertador . . .

"Yes, the one across from the racetrack . . .

"I know you'll need a truck. I don't care if it takes three trucks. Just do it. And make sure the truck, or trucks, are guarded. By our people . . .

"How large a guard detail? You're a major. You figure that out."

He slammed the handset into the base and turned to Major Habanzo.

"That was Marinelli," he said, and then asked rhetorically, "How did that idiot ever get assigned to BIS?"

"Calm down, Bernardo," Frade said. "What might have been off-loaded from U–234 — operative word 'might' — is the stuff from which they make atomic bombs, not an actual atomic bomb. There's not going to be a mushroom cloud from an atomic explosion in the Strait of Magellan."

Martín snapped his head to face Frade.

"Cletus," he said icily, "I am not going to permit anything — *anything* — connected with atomic bombs to be brought into Argentina, whether it's a bomb or 'the stuff from which they make atomic bombs.' "

"Okay, I can understand that, Bernardo. But why don't you take a couple of deep breaths, count to twenty, and calm down? I don't know what Cronley is talking about and I don't think you do either."

"I think Cronley is suggesting that he has a method to determine the landfall of U-234, and I think that Kapitän von Dattenberg agrees with him. Am I wrong, Subteniente?"

"Let me answer for the subteniente, General," von Dattenberg said. "He has a theory that will be difficult — almost impossible — to explain — at least quickly — without having both the suitable charts — maps — and the list of rendezvous sites in hand. I suggest that we wait until we have them. There is no need for any hasty actions."

Martín, Frade thought, *is about to jump all over him. He just about lost it a moment ago.*

I never saw him lose control — or almost lose it, and almost losing control is like being a little bit pregnant — like that before.

I wonder why he's so excited about the uranium oxide?

Jesus, Stupid! You know why!

In real life, unlike the movies, people don't take a bullet in the upper leg and then take an aspirin, or a drink, and then forget about it. God only knows how much morphine he's been taking.

It's surprising he makes any sense at all.

"Why don't we go upstairs and watch the races — they just started — while we wait?" Dorotea said.

"What?" Martín snapped.

His face clearly showed both confusion — *What the hell is she talking about, "races"?* — and annoyance — *Why is this female inserting herself into this?*

Doña Dorotea flashed him a warm smile.

"While we're waiting for your people to bring the maps and the list of rendezvous points, Bernardo," she said.

Oh, Jesus! Clete thought, waiting for Martín's reaction.

When it came, it wasn't what Clete expected.

"I think that's a splendid idea," Martín said. "All we're doing until the maps and list of rendezvous points arrive is spinning our wheels. And, frankly, I'm a little tired. I can't imagine why. A few minutes' rest is probably just what I need."

[Two]

Jimmy Cronley really didn't know what to think about Clete's "house," except that it wasn't exactly a house. It was enormous, certainly a lot bigger than the house in Midland where Clete had grown up, and, for that matter, far larger and more impressive than Cletus Marcus Howell's house on Saint Charles Avenue in New Orleans, which, after he'd gone there with Clete when he was twelve or thirteen, was what he thought of when he heard the word "mansion."

This place looked more like a library, or a museum, or maybe a city hall or a courthouse than it did a house in which real people actually lived. The stone and iron fence around it looked more substantial than the one the United States government had built around the gold vault at Fort Knox.

Neither did Jimmy know what to really think about Clete's wife. The first thing he had thought when he met Dorotea at the airport was that Clete finally had been snagged by one of the long line of long-legged blondes to whom Clete had been attracted — and vice versa — as far back as Jimmy could remember.

This long-legged blonde was different from the others, somehow. It wasn't just the British accent, although that was somehow erotic and probably appealed to Clete at least as much as it did to him.

The first hint he had that Dorotea was something special was when she announced in the dining room that she was going to sit in on the meeting. Clete had accepted that announcement without question — while at the same time trying to throw out the old man.

Jimmy had decided that was because she was Clete's wife — you can't throw your wife out of her own dining room — but changed that opinion during the discussion of the

579

landfall. He saw by her face that she wasn't just politely listening. She was interested.

And more than interested: Jimmy had the feeling that Dorotea knew where he was going with the discussion as soon as von Dattenberg did. Which meant before Colonel Cletus did. Clete still didn't have a clue.

And then when the Argentine general was right on the edge of losing it, she put that fire out by suggesting they "go upstairs and watch the races."

Jimmy had no idea what she was talking about, but whatever it was had calmed the general.

Everybody in the dining room filed out into the enormous foyer of the mansion and headed toward a wide stairway — divided at the top — leading to the upper floors. Clete and Dorotea walked behind General Martín, who was having a hard time with his crutches. Jimmy fell in line behind them.

As Jimmy wondered how the hell the general was going to get up the stairway on his crutches, the general hobbled to the left of the staircase. When Jimmy got there, he saw what he thought of as an old-fashioned elevator.

First, what looked like an ordinary closet door had been pulled open. Exposed was the elevator door itself, sort of a fence that opened and closed like an accordion.

Clete reached around General Martín and folded open the accordion fence door.

General Martín carefully hobbled inside the elevator.

Clete literally bowed Dorotea into the elevator, then got on himself.

There was barely room for all of them on the elevator.

"I'm surprised you don't know this, Jimmy," Frade announced. "Generals and field grade officers, plus of course beautiful women, get to ride. Second lieutenants climb the stairs. Three flights up. Good luck, Lieutenant, and Godspeed!"

Dorotea and the general laughed. Clete closed the door, there came a *clank,* and the elevator began to rise.

[THREE]

Apartment 4-C
1044 Calle Talcahuano
Buenos Aires, Argentina
1405 20 October 1945

Konrad Fassbinder answered the telephone on the second ring.

"Hola?" he said, listened, and then said, "Wait there."

Then he put the handset in the cradle and turned to Ludwig Mannhoffer.

"The messenger is at the opera, Herr Mannhoffer. At the ticket booth."

"That being the case, I suggest you go get the message," Mannhoffer said. "Richter, you go with him and make sure that he's not being followed."

"Jawohl, Herr Mannhoffer," Erich Richter said, and gestured for Fassbinder to go to the door.

Fassbinder returned five minutes later. And a minute after that Richter came into the apartment.

"He was not followed," Richter announced.

"As far as you could tell," Mannhoffer said. "Well, let me have it, Fassbinder."

Fassbinder handed him a large sealed envelope. Mannhoffer put it on the kitchen table and opened it. When he did so, there came a harsh odor of chemicals.

"I hate that smell," Mannhoffer said.

The envelope contained a sheaf of what photographers called "immediate proofs." They were photographic prints made as quickly as possible — as soon as the developed film was out of the tank, dried, and fed to an automatic advancing device in an enlarger. The prints most times were not "fixed" well, or at all, which caused them to fade more quickly than those properly processed.

But they did provide a quick view of what the photographer had caught on film, and that was what Mannhoffer wanted as soon as possible — and had paid a great deal of money to get.

These immediate proofs showed passengers disembarking the South American Airways Constellation *La Ciudad de Mar del Plata* after its arrival a little more than two hours earlier at Aeropuerto El Coronel Jorge G. Frade at the conclusion of its final leg from Berlin.

Mannhoffer didn't *know* of course where the photographer had been when he took the pictures. But he had been in the Sicherheitsdienst of the SS long enough to make a good guess. He had somehow managed to set up his cameras — almost certainly Leica CIIs — on tripods on the roof of Hangar Two. The Leicas had spring-driven film-advance mechanisms and film magazines that held 120 35mm frames, rather than the normal magazine that contained twenty-four.

Once the cameras had been focused on the stairways leading to the passenger and cockpit doors, all the photographer had to do was push their shutter release button and he had his series of images being snapped.

And it was immediately apparent to Mannhoffer that these pictures were worth every *centavo* he was paying for them. Within thirty seconds, he had decided that it was going to be necessary to start eliminating people now, tomorrow, rather than when it would be more convenient or safer.

583

In addition to the traitorous former Major Hans-Peter von Wachtstein, whom Mannhoffer expected to see, there was von Wachtstein's traitorous friend, former Kapitän zur See Karl Boltitz, walking down the stairway with two other Germans whom Mannhoffer absolutely didn't expect to see: former Oberstleutnant Dieter von und zu Aschenburg and former Major Wilhelm Grüner of the Luftwaffe.

Both had obviously betrayed their solemn oath of loyalty to the Führer and were now happily in the employ of the *gottverdammt* Americans.

Just, Mannhoffer thought disgustedly, as Fregattenkapitän Wilhelm von Dattenberg had proven to be a traitor. Instead of scuttling U-405 as ordered, von Dattenberg had surrendered the U-boat to the Armada Argentina. Which meant — although the Armada Argentina was too stupid to know it — that the landfall coordinates for U-234 were not destroyed but in their hands.

And then the immediate proof photos showed an American officer, armed, climbing down the stairwell with two suitcases, whereupon he and the suitcases fell under the protection of General Martín and Frade's Private Army.

And then there were photos that showed everybody had gone to Frade's house across from the racetrack. Whatever they had gone there for, he knew that it was not to watch the races.

Mannhoffer looked up from the photographs.

"Fassbinder," he ordered, "I want you to contact our man at Jorge Frade, and tell him that I want to know what's going on at Frade's house as soon as it happens."

"I believe he's already got the mansion under surveillance, Herr Mannhoffer. There are the photos of it —"

"We know they are there, but not what they are doing there! So, get in a taxi and go to Avenida Libertador, find whoever it is we have doing the surveilling, find out what he's learned, and report back to me."

"Jawohl, Herr Mannhoffer."

"Well, don't just stand there. Get moving!"

As soon as the door had closed behind Fassbinder, Mannhoffer motioned for Richter to join him.

"Erich, you have heard, I'm sure, that the more people who know a secret, the more quickly it stops being a secret."

"Yes, sir."

"For that reason, until now, I have not told you that both SS-Brigadeführer Gerhard Körtig and SS-Oberführer Horst Lang are here in Argentina."

Richter's surprise was evident on his face.

"They came aboard U-234," Mannhoffer said.

"U-234 made it here?"

Mannhoffer nodded.

"There's a good deal I have to tell you," Mannhoffer said. "But first go to the telephone kiosk in the Café Colón. Call this number . . ."

He wrote a number on a piece of paper.

"Memorize that, and then burn it," he ordered.

"Jawohl, Herr Mannhoffer."

"Either Lang or Körtig will answer. They are . . . not in Buenos Aires. Whoever answers, ask for Señor Kramer. Tell Señor Kramer that you're Señor Schmidt and that you're sorry but you can't have dinner with him today. Perhaps next week. Got it?"

Richter looked at the number and nodded.

"That will get them both here as soon as possible, Erich. Which should take three hours, perhaps a little less."

"Jawohl, Herr Mannhoffer."

[FOUR]

4730 Avenida Libertador General San Martín
Buenos Aires, Argentina
1415 20 October 1945

Still wondering what kind of races could be held in what had to be the mansion's attic, Jimmy finally reached the top of the third flight of stairs, which ended facing a door.

He pushed it open and found himself at the off-the-street end of a cavernous room that stretched across the entire floor. Huge doors opened onto a large balcony.

Everyone who had been at lunch was in the room, plus servants and nannies. There were also an infant and a little boy who Jimmy decided were Clete and Dorotea's kids.

And Elsa.

She was standing, with von Dattenberg, at the far end of the room, on the balcony.

She was wearing a dress — a pale blue dress, a real dress — not an insignia-less WAC officer's uniform skirt.

She was even more beautiful than Jimmy remembered.

As he watched, von Dattenberg touched her arm and nodded toward Jimmy, as if to say, "There he is."

Elsa looked, and then smiled brightly at him.

Too brightly.

He knew from that moment that he was not going to spend the rest of his life with Elsa von Wachtstein.

I'm probably not even going to have dinner with her.

Not that I would want to anyway.

If you make a horse's ass of yourself with somebody, you want to get away from them, not have dinner.

Von Dattenberg put his hand on Elsa's arm

and led her across the room to him.

"I understand you know each other," von Dattenberg said.

"Jimmy," Elsa said, "what a pleasant surprise. Willi just told me that you were here."

Surprise, sure. Pleasant? I don't think so.

I think the last person in the world you wanted to see here, Baroness, was Second Lieutenant James D. Cronley Jr.

She kissed his cheek with all the passion of a Sunday school teacher kissing one of her students.

"And here I am," Jimmy said.

"I didn't expect to see you here."

I never would have guessed from that dazzling smile.

"Well, life is full of surprises, isn't it?"

"What are you doing here?" Elsa asked.

"I don't think he can tell you," von Dattenberg said.

"Oh."

"Elsa told me how kind you were to her in Marburg, Jimmy," von Dattenberg said.

"I was just doing my duty, Willi."

I'm an Aggie, Willi. A graduate of Texas A&M.

It is a matter of pride with us Aggies that we never turn down a drink or a piece of ass.

"I got the impression that it went beyond that," von Dattenberg said. "I know she's really grateful."

And she damn sure should be.

It's a pity she's not Catherine the Great of

Russia — who is probably, come to think of it, a distant cousin of the baroness. Catherine was known to reward lieutenants of the Household Cavalry for sexual services rendered.

She made some colonels and a few — for outstanding stud service — she made dukes.

For my stud service — God knows Elsa the Great found no fault with it — I should now be Colonel James Cronley, the Grand Duke of Marburg.

Elsa would not look at him.

"I hate to break up this touching reunion," Frade said at his ear, "but General Martín thinks we should get you out of that uniform, and he's right."

Jimmy turned to Clete. "How are we going to do that?"

"We're going in there," Frade said, pointing at a door.

"And I'm going with you," Martha Howell said, as she walked up to them. "To make sure he gives you something nice. What's your trouser size, Jimmy?"

"Waist thirty, length thirty-six," Cronley said. He turned back to Elsa. "Maybe we'll bump into each other again while I'm here."

"That would be nice," Elsa said.

[FIVE]

"What is this place? It looks like a clothing store," Cronley said.

"This was my father's wardrobe. He was something of a clotheshorse," Clete replied.

"What about shoes? What's your shoe size, Jimmy?" Martha asked.

"Ten and a half D."

"What size does that convert to down here, Cletus?" Martha asked.

"I have no idea, but it's moot. El Coronel didn't go to shoe stores. He had shoemakers come here. Or had his shoes made in London. But they fit me, and back in the days when I went to shoe stores like the common people, I was a ten and a half. And in the Marine Corps my trouser size was thirty, thirty-seven. You seem to have grown, little brother."

"Pick out a jacket, Jimmy," Martha ordered. "We'll start with that."

"Which jacket do I get, Clete?"

"Any one your greedy little heart desires. There's plenty of them. El Coronel ordered them three at a time."

"You're kidding," Martha said.

"No, I'm not. One went to Estancia San Pedro y San Pablo, one went in here, and one went to Casa Montagna. I've been passing out those latter ones to the Good Gehlens."

"You haven't told me about the . . . Good Gehlens," Martha said.

"I'm still making up my mind whether I will or not," Frade said.

There were more suits than Jimmy could

count hanging in the wardrobe, and on the other side as many sport coats. He found one — a tweed jacket with suede leather patches at the elbows — that he really liked. He held it out for Clete to see. When Clete gave him a thumbs-up, he took it from its hanger.

Jimmy tossed the jacket on a red leather upholstered bolster in the center of the room, unbuttoned his Ike jacket, and tossed that on the bolster. Then he slipped out of his shoulder holster.

"What's that for?" Marjorie asked.

Jimmy hadn't seen her come into the room.

"He needs it, Squirt," Clete said. "Leave it at that."

"Needs it for what? And don't call me Squirt."

"Why does he need it, Cletus?" Martha asked.

"If he needs a gun, what about you?" Marjorie challenged. "I don't see you wearing a shoulder holster like Edward G. Robinson in a gangster movie."

"She used to be such a sweet little girl," Clete said.

"Answer her question," Martha said. "And my questions. It's time for that."

"I don't usually carry a pistol because Enrico and his riot gun are ten steps away ninety percent of the time. And because Dorotea carries a revolver in her purse. And because . . ."

He pushed aside the suits hanging close to the door and pulled out a Thompson submachine gun.

"Okay?"

"Tell me about this General Gehlen," Martha said.

"Shouldn't we get Beth in here?" Marjorie asked. "Shouldn't she hear this, too?"

"Not necessary," Clete said. "Karl has already told her."

"You told Beth — or told Karl he could tell Beth — and didn't tell me?" Martha asked.

"I told Karl he could tell Beth because I knew he would anyway," Clete said. "If you haven't noticed, they're pretty close."

Martha ignored the sarcasm.

"And didn't tell me?" Martha pursued.

Clete didn't reply directly.

"Jimmy, pick out enough clothing for a week," he ordered. "Shoes, socks, shirts, ties — everything. Take it all in the dressing room" — he pointed to a door — "and try it on. Try everything on. And after you've done that, put on one set of civvies and put the rest on that" — he pointed to the bolster — "and I'll rustle up a valise for it."

"Am I going somewhere?"

Again, Clete didn't reply directly. "And, while you're doing that, I'll explain to the ladies what's going on."

He jerked his thumb in a *get moving* gesture.

[Six]

Jimmy backed out of the dressing room into the wardrobe, his arms full of his new clothing. He was wearing some of it, the tweed jacket with suede elbow patches, a white dress shirt, a striped silk tie, gray flannel trousers, and a pair of what looked like new loafers. The shoes had surprised him — he'd thought loafers were purely American. These, which had belonged to Clete's Argentine father, were English. Stamped on the leather inside was *Joseph Cheaney & Sons London.*

All the clothing — even the shirt and shoes — *almost* fit, which also had surprised him. It was a little loose, but it fit. To judge by that, Clete was only slightly larger than he was, which was a little surprising as he had always thought of Clete as being "bigger."

He dropped the armful of clothing on the bolster and turned around. Mrs. Howell and Clete were no longer in the wardrobe.

But Marjorie was. She was holding the Thompson submachine gun.

"Jesus, Squirt, be careful with that!"

"I took the magazine out," she said, and held the weapon up to show him that she had. "I've never fired one of these."

"It would knock you on your . . . *keister.*"

"Says the expert."

"As a matter of fact, I fired expert with the Thompson."

593

"Wow!" she said sarcastically.

Now is not the time to get into a scrap with her.

Never argue with a female holding a Tommy gun.

He struck a pose he thought was like that of a model.

"Well, what do you think?"

Marjorie put the magazine back in the Thompson and then put the weapon back where Clete kept it behind the clothes.

"You look," she said, "like a high school sophomore wearing your big brother's clothes about to go on a big date where you will try to seduce a cheerleader."

"Thank you very much."

"Worse, you're still acting like a high school sophomore."

"What the hell is that supposed to mean?"

"I saw the way you looked at her, and I saw the way she looked at you. You better hope my mother didn't."

"Your mother didn't what?"

"See the way you were looking at Frau von Wachtstein."

"How was I looking at Frau von Wachtstein?"

"The way you looked at Miss Schenck."

"At who?"

"Miss Schenck. The librarian. Don't try to tell me you've forgotten her."

"No, I haven't forgotten her," Jimmy admitted, as he remembered.

"The year you got yourself expelled from Saint Mark's and came home to Midland . . ."

"I remember that, too."

". . . you followed that poor woman around like a suckling calf," Marjorie, who was just warming up, went on.

"Poor woman? Where'd you get that?"

"She was just out of college. The first job she ever had was in the library. And there is this gawky fourteen-year-old with pimples hanging around the library after school every day —"

"I did not."

"Yes, you did. You used to stand beside a bookcase and look at her through it."

After a moment, he said, "How the hell did you know that?"

"Because I was a gawky thirteen-year-old with a crush on you. I used to hang around the library after school every day watching you watch Miss Schenck."

"Jesus H. Christ!"

"But then I grew up. And, apparently, you haven't. I told you, I saw the way you were looking at Frau von Wachtstein, and the way she was looking at you."

"How was she looking at me?"

"As if she was terrified you were going to embarrass her by saying or doing something stupid. Or that people would see that suckling-calf look on your stupid face and wonder what she'd done to encourage you."

"You don't know what you're talking about
—"

He stopped mid-sentence.

Frade had come back into the wardrobe.

"What have I interrupted here?" he asked.

"Nothing," they both said, on top of each other.

"Yeah. Like hell!"

He let that sink in a moment, and then went on: "The maps and the list of rendezvous points are here. Let's go, Jimmy."

[SEVEN]

"Lieutenant, the floor — or at least the table — is yours," Frade said. "This had better not be a waste of everybody's time."

Sitting around the table were General Martín, Cletus Marcus Howell, Clete, Dorotea, von Wachtstein, von Dattenberg, Major Habanzo, and Boltitz.

Clete's pissed about something, Jimmy thought.

God knows what, but what I have to do is kiss his ass, not antagonize him.

"Sir," Jimmy said politely, "I hope this won't be a waste of anybody's time."

"Okay then, hotshot," Frade said. "Explain how you've broken the Kriegsmarine Code."

"Sir, I already have part of it. All I have to do is fill in the blanks."

"Start from scratch. I'm a little slow, and I don't think I'm the only one who is."

"From scratch, sir?"

"From scratch, Lieutenant."

"Yes, sir. Positions are given in east and west longitude, which means either east or west of Greenwich, England. They are also given in north and south longitude, which means north or south of the equator. They're written like this."

He held up a page from the list of rendezvous points that had been removed from the U-405 safe so that everybody around the table could see it. It was a simple document.

Rubber-stamped in red at the top and bottom of the page was GEHEIMST ("Top Secret"). The page had columns of blocks, and in the blocks were numbers giving a position — for example, *S54.62785, W68.42647.* There were twenty such blocks on the page.

"Sir, there are five pages like this, a total of one hundred position blocks, one of which is the intended landfall of U-234," Cronley said.

"Hidden by a code which we don't have," Frade said.

"Let him finish, Cletus!" General Martín ordered.

Frade impatiently gestured, *Well, go on . . .*

Cronley nodded as he thought, *What the hell did I do?*

What the hell's bothering Clete?

He continued: "Hidden by a code we don't

have, but I don't think we need. What's missing on this list is the *correct* longitude and latitude numbers. S54, for south longitude, for example, and W68, for west latitude, are dummy figures — they don't mean anything.

"But the rest of *one* of those one hundred blocks, the five digits after the big number are right on the money. . . . The first two are called minutes and seconds. One minute means one-sixtieth of a degree, and one second means one-sixtieth of a minute. I have no idea what the last three digits are called, but they break down the same way."

"I'm not following you," Frade said coldly. "Are you sure you know what you're talking about?"

"I think I'm starting to," Martín said thoughtfully. "Go on."

"Yes, sir. Sir, if you add the correct figures for south longitude and west latitude to one of those blocks, you'll have the intended landfall, probably within a hundred meters. *Maybe* two hundred meters. But close. I'm sure the Germans, what with being German, plotted it very carefully."

"And all we have to do is connect the correct longitude and latitude in degrees with the minutes and seconds in one of the coded blocks, correct?" Martín said.

"Yes, sir."

"And how do we know the correct longitude and latitude is in fact correct?" Clete asked sarcastically.

Up yours, Clete!

"We already have it. If Karl's friend in Bremen was telling him the truth."

"I'm sure he was," Boltitz said.

"The landfall is somewhere around here, at the mouth of the Magellan Strait," Jimmy said, putting his finger on the map. "And the map should give us the correct longitude and latitude."

Clete looked at the map, then at Jimmy.

After a long moment, he announced: "If you're right about this, I will publicly admit you're a lot smarter than you look. How the hell did you figure this out?"

It's a simple problem in logic, Colonel, sir, which posed no problem for me once I gave it a little thought, Colonel, sir.

"Sir, it's the way Gehlen's people set up rendezvous points in Russia for their agents. On the Steppes."

"And how do you know that?" Frade asked.

"Sir, at Kloster Grünau I got pretty close to a Gehlen officer, Ludwig Mannberg. He used to be a colonel. He showed me how it worked."

"And why are you so sure this former *colonel* isn't pulling your chain, *Lieutenant*?" Frade asked.

How are you so sure Boltitz's guy in Bremen isn't pulling his chain?

And I didn't hear you ask him about that.

"Sir, I believe Oberst Mannberg can be trusted."

And you better trust Oberst Mannberg, too.

He's the source of the dossiers on the Nazis that von Dattenberg brought here.

"That doesn't answer my question," Frade said.

"Well, sir, his mother is a Strasbourgerin, like mine. Sons of Strasbourgerins don't lie to each other."

"Spare me your wiseass wit."

"Yes, sir. Sorry, sir."

"Okay, wiseass, put your theory to the test. What does the map say?"

"I hope this is the one with the lowest scale," Cronley said, looking for the legend. "Or is it the largest? The one that shows the finest details. And frankly, I really wish I had German maps."

"Those are the next best thing to German maps," General Martín said proudly. "The Wehrmacht sent their army map people here to teach the Ejército Argentino military map-making. But there's one in that stack that may be just what you're looking for."

Martín went through the stack of maps, selected one, and spread it out on the table.

There was no sign of civilization on the map in the area just north of the mouth of the Magellan Strait and the international border — south of which was Chilean territory — except Argentine National Route 3 and an unnamed, unpaved road to the east of it.

Route 3 was sixty kilometers from the coast. The unnamed, unpaved road ran off Route 3 parallel to the coast, about thirty kilometers from it to a dot on the map identified as Estancia Condor.

Jimmy wondered what could possibly be grown on an estancia so isolated and so close to Antarctica but decided this wasn't the time to ask.

From the estancia the unnamed road went a few kilometers farther south, until it was close to the international border, went toward the coast parallel to the border for twenty kilometers or so, and then turned northeast until it reached a point maybe eight kilometers from the coast. After that, it turned just about dead south and continued south until it reached the border, then due east until it reached the coast, where it made a final dead south turn until it ended right at the coast.

Jimmy put his finger on the map there and looked at Willi von Dattenberg.

"Too close, I think," Jimmy said.

"Too obvious," von Dattenberg agreed. "And there would be vessels headed for the Magellan Strait."

"But here," Jimmy said, laying his finger on the coast dead east of where the unnamed road came closest before turning south.

"See what you come up with," von Dattenberg said.

Jimmy located lines on the map identifying south latitude, then one in particular.

"See if you can find in south latitude point zero five something," Jimmy ordered.

Von Dattenberg went down the row of positions on page one and found nothing. He said so, and then went down the row of positions on page two, found nothing, said so again, and turned to page three. Near the bottom of page three, he stopped moving his finger.

"I have a decimal zero five three nine nine," he said.

"And the longitude?" Jimmy asked, very softly.

"Decimal six three zero eight eight."

"Bingo," Jimmy said. He put his finger on the map. "Right in here."

"You're telling me you found it?" Martín asked softly, as Frade asked incredulously, sarcastically, on top of him, "You're telling me you found it?"

"In my judgment, General," von Dattenberg said, looking from the map back to the sheet, "Lieutenant Cronley has established the landfall ordered for U-234 at 52.05399 degrees south latitude, 58.63088 degrees west longitude."

He looked to where Jimmy pointed on the map.

"Right there," he said.

"Operative phrase 'the landfall *ordered* for

U-234,' " Frade said. "We don't know that the submarine even got through the English Channel, much less here."

"In that case, I'd like proof that it didn't," General Martín said. "How do we get that?"

"Bernardo," Frade said, "you know as well as I do that proving a negative is just about impossible."

"Is my opinion welcome?" von Dattenberg asked.

"Let's have it," Frade said.

"Despite what I said before — I've had a little time to rethink it — I would suggest you proceed on the premise that U-234 did make it here and to the landfall Cronley has come up with."

"What made you change your mind?" Frade asked.

"I was following the scenario that U-234 was trying to go to Japan. There is another credible scenario — two others. I suggest that Kapitän Schneider, who had as much experience coming here and unloading cargo and personnel as I do, knew before sailing from Narvik that he couldn't make Japan and decided on his own to come here directly. Or that the Kriegsmarine, knowing that the SS order to go to Japan was impossible to obey, quietly told Schneider he was to ignore it, or perhaps just that he was authorized, once under way, to decide that for himself."

"You think he made it here, in other

words?" Martín asked.

"Either here or to South Africa," von Dattenberg said. "What I'm suggesting, General, is that it would be worth the effort to see if he did come here."

"Put yourself in this guy's shoes, Willi," Frade said. "What's his name?"

"Schneider, Alois Schneider."

"Put yourself in Schneider's shoes. You're commanding U-234 and decide there's no way you can make it to Japan. Then what?"

"Then I would come here."

"And then what? Just unload everything in the middle of nowhere?"

"I see where you're going," von Dattenberg said. "He would have to have help from shore. He would be running very low on fuel and rations. He was probably — almost certainly — under orders to scuttle the boat, as was I.

"My orders were to scuttle U-405 'on the high seas no closer than twenty-four hours full surface speed sailing time from discharge point,' and his probably were the same. And Alois would be no more willing — less willing — to load his crew onto rubber boats on the high seas that close to the Antarctic than I was to scuttle U-405 under similar, if less hazardous, conditions."

"What you're saying," Martín asked, "is that if he did make this landfall and discharged his cargo — (a) that he could not do so without assistance from the shore, and (b) that if he scuttled his submarine, it would be close enough to shore so that his crew could make it safely to shore?"

"There's no question he'd have to have people onshore," Frade said. "He just couldn't put his crew ashore in the middle of nowhere."

"What are you thinking, Cletus?" Martín asked.

"The Tenth Mountain Regiment. Argentina's own SS Regiment."

"*Sí,*" Martín agreed.

"May I ask what that is?" Jimmy asked.

Martín held up his index finger in a *be patient* gesture.

"They have the equipment to operate in snow and ice," Martín said.

"And experience in surreptitiously unloading submarines," Frade picked up, then asked, "Who replaced el Coronel Schmidt?"

"After you shot him, you mean?" Martín answered. "El Coronel Edmundo Wattersly. But after Wattersly had the regiment under control, President Farrell brought him back to Buenos Aires."

"Who took his place?"

"President Farrell sent me to San Martín de los Andes to make sure he could rely on the regiment in the future," Martín said.

"That Wattersly had cleaned it up, you mean?" Frade asked.

Martín nodded. "And he had. And I told the president he had, and he brought Wattersly back to Buenos Aires."

"And gave the regiment to who?"

"El Coronel Juan Torrez, Don Cletus," Major Habanzo furnished. "A good man. Who cleaned up the regiment further."

"I'm sorry to hear that," Frade said.

"Excuse me?" Habanzo asked.

"I was hoping there'd be some officers left who could tell us if the regiment took one of its famous road marches down south."

"Probably not," Martín said. "But I'll bet there are soldiers who would know, and I would be surprised if Suboficial Mayor Rodríguez, Retired, would have trouble finding them."

"What did Wattersly — or el Coronel Torrez — do with the Tenth's suboficial mayor, Martinez?" Clete asked.

"After you shot Schmidt, you mean?"

Frade nodded.

"Nothing. We all knew how helpful he'd been after you shot Schmidt," Martín said. "That he took the regiment back to San Martín de los Andes."

"Bernardo," Frade said, "Martinez and Enrico are old buddies. Martinez tipped us off when the Tenth Mountain was headed to shoot up my place in Tandil."

"Well, getting Rodríguez together with Martinez would seem the solution to that problem," Martín said. "But there are others."

"May I ask a question?" Cronley asked.

Frade made a face, then considered the request a moment and nodded.

"How hard would it be to send people down there? I mean, maybe they could find some sign that a submarine had landed. From what I've heard, there's absolutely nothing down there for hundreds of miles except this farm, or whatever it is."

"Estancia Condor," Major Habanzo furnished.

"What the hell does Estancia Condor grow?" Cronley asked. "If it's all ice and snow down there?"

"I think it started, years and years ago, as a whaling station," Martín said. "I don't really know what I'm talking about, but I think I heard somewhere that it's still sort of a *frigorifico* for seals. I mean, they kill the seals on the water, or the shore, and process the meat there."

"There are people at this place?" Frade asked.

"A few people and a detachment of soldiers to operate the radio relay station and service the lighthouses," Habanzo said.

"And they have reported no sighting of a submarine? Or even anything out of the ordinary?" Frade asked.

"Nothing," Martín said. "And isn't that

interesting?"

"Possible scenarios?" Frade asked. "Anyone?"

There was no response.

"Then let's see what we have," Martín said. "Let's start with 'Mountain Troops' being something of a misnomer. We think of the Tenth repelling a Chilean invasion of Argentina in the Andes. And that was their original mission. And they are trained and equipped to fight in the Andes, which means, most of the year, in ice and snow —"

"Which is what we have in the landfall," Frade interjected.

Martín nodded. "So to whom would the Edificio Libertador turn if some military action — and operating a radio relay station qualifies as a military action — was necessary in that area of Argentina? The regiment equipped to operate in frigid conditions."

Martín thought for a moment, then finished: "So, for the sake of argument, let us presume the operators of the radio relay station on Estancia Condor are from the Signals Company of the Tenth Mountain."

"Which would have given German submarines a radio contact," Habanzo offered.

"And given the Tenth Mountain an excuse to regularly dispatch truck convoys down there to supply their troops at Estancia Condor," Frade put in.

"And who would think to search trucks

returning from a supply mission?" Martín asked rhetorically.

"I don't suppose there's an airstrip on the estancia?" von Wachtstein asked. "Or, for that matter, anywhere down there where it would be useful to us?"

"No, I don't think there is," Martín said.

"If there was," Habanzo said, "the aircraft that periodically fly over the coast would have seen it."

"It's kind of hard to hide an airstrip," Frade said.

"Tangential scenario," Martín said. "If you were a Tenth Mountain officer, either a senior officer or maybe a major or even a captain, who knew about something involving a German submarine down there, what would you have done with the Signals people on the estancia after Colonel Schmidt was shot, and el Coronel Wattersly was en route with his broom to clean things up?"

"Left them there," Cronley said. "This Wattersly didn't know about U-234, and as long as those Signal Corps guys were on ice down there — how's that for a metaphor? — it was not going to come out by mistake."

Martín shook his index finger approvingly at Cronley.

"God, Bernardo, don't encourage him," Frade said. "He's been enough of a wiseass."

Is Clete going to ream me again? Jimmy thought.

"He's right about what he just said, Cletus," Martín said. "We're going to have to get someone — Habanzo, maybe — down to Estancia Condor to see what he can find out."

"But do it without my Tío Juan hearing about it," Frade said. "We don't know what he knows about U-234, and he's liable to tell you — on general principles — to back off."

"You think he might know about U-234?"

"I don't know," Clete said. "I do know that he and Schmidt were pals for a long time."

"Then we'll have to get Habanzo down there quickly," Martín said.

"Do they have Piper Cubs down here?" Cronley asked.

The question silenced everybody as everybody looked at Cronley.

"Piper Cubs?" Frade then asked incredulously.

Oh, shit, Jimmy thought. *Here it comes.*
But what the hell . . .

"Yeah, Piper Cubs. J-3s. Or something like them."

Frade glanced at Martín and said, "See what the hell you started by encouraging him?" then looked at Jimmy and added coldly, "Overwhelming curiosity causes me to ask: Why do you want, at this moment in time, to know if there are Piper Cubs, J-3s, down here?"

Fuck you, Clete.

"Sir, are there Cubs or not?" Cronley asked.

"Yes, there are. As a matter of fact, I have six of them. Why do you ask?"

"Take the wings off one — better, off two — load them on a flatbed trailer and send them down to Estancia Condor."

"To use, I presume, to look for signs of a submarine having landed?" Frade asked sarcastically.

"Yeah."

"You heard what General Martín said. There's nothing down there but ice and snow. You can't fly a Cub in those conditions."

"You know better than that," Cronley said.

"What did you say?" Frade snapped.

"I said you know better than that."

"I do? Tell me, hotshot, how do you know what I know?"

"Get off my back, Clete."

"What did you say?"

"Back off, Clete. I'm right on the edge of telling you to go fuck yourself."

"Stand to attention, Lieutenant!"

"Okay," Jimmy said, not moving except to give Clete the finger. "Go fuck yourself, *Colonel.*"

Frade leapt to his feet.

"I ordered you to come to attention!"

"And I didn't. So now what?"

"And apologize to my wife for that obscenity!" Frade shouted.

"That I'll do," Cronley said. "Sorry, Dorotea."

"I've heard the word before," Dorotea said, and then added, "Sit down, Cletus."

"What did you say?" he asked incredulously.

"I said sit down," Dorotea said. "And be grateful these people know this childish behavior is between you as brothers, not officers."

He looked at her but said nothing.

"You heard her, Cletus," Cletus Marcus Howell said. "Sit down!"

Cletus slowly took his seat.

The old man was not through.

"And get off Jimmy's back, Cletus," he went on. "I don't know and don't care what set this off between you, but I do know that if it wasn't for Jimmy, none of us would be sitting here. He's earned the right to be heard." He let that sink in, then said, "What's on your mind, Jimmy?"

"No," Dorotea said. "Let's clear this up right now. Otherwise it'll fester. What has Jimmy done, Cletus?"

Clete glared at Jimmy. "He knows."

"I don't have a clue."

"The hell you don't."

"What has he done, Cletus?" Dorotea asked again, her tone exasperated.

"Okay, but you asked. He's been in Argentina — what? — maybe five hours. And I walk into the wardrobe and he's hitting on Marjorie."

"That's bullshit!" Jimmy exploded.

612

"She told you that, Cletus?" Dorotea asked.

"She didn't have to. You should have seen her face. His face. It was written all over both of them."

Dorotea laughed out loud.

"Cletus Frade," she proclaimed, "protector of the family virgin!"

"Goddamn it, it's not funny!"

"Absurd is what it is," she said, her tone now disgusted. "And, more important, none of your business, Cletus. She's not twelve years old."

"I did not hit on Marjie," Jimmy announced righteously. "My God, he's out of his mind."

"And people who live in glass houses should not throw stones," Dorotea said. "Especially about other people chasing virgins."

"Meaning what?"

"I don't think, my darling, that you really want me to explain that in the hearing of all your friends, do you?"

She turned to Cronley.

"You were saying something, Jimmy, about Cletus knowing better than that. Better than what?"

Jimmy looked at Clete. Clete gave him the finger.

Jimmy returned the gesture with both hands.

He then said, "Years ago, Clete and I flew his father's Cub up to Rapid City, South

Dakota, to shoot pheasant. We landed on a dirt road near the farmer's house. You can do that in a Cub. We hunted, went to bed, and during the night there was an early snowstorm. Eight, ten inches of snow — it was up over the Cub's wheels. I figured we'd be stuck there for at least a week. But Clete went out on the road with a pickup truck and drove back and forth and packed the snow. . . ."

"I remember," Clete said. "And you're suggesting we could do that at Estancia Condor?"

Frade was now smiling. Jimmy smiled back.

"I think it's worth a shot. We flew away from Rapid City, didn't we?"

"Cletus," von Wachtstein said. "We already have an airplane that's better suited to arctic conditions than a Piper Cub, and someone with a hell of a lot of experience doing that."

"You're volunteering to go to Estancia Condor?" Frade replied.

"I was thinking about Willi Grüner."

"Your old Luftwaffe buddy?"

"My old Luftwaffe buddy. He's got a lot of experience flying, and not only in the Storch — on the Eastern Front in near-arctic conditions."

"I don't know, Hansel," Frade said.

"Would this man be willing to help?" General Martín said. "And I have to ask this, too: Can he be trusted?"

"I'm sure he would help, General," von

Wachtstein said. "And I trust him completely."

"Where is he now?" Martín asked.

"Upstairs," von Wachtstein said, then smiled and added: "He and Dieter von und zu Aschenburg — the other man for whom you were so kind to provide identity documents — are consoling my sister-in-law in the absence of von Dattenberg."

"Very funny, Peter," von Dattenberg said.

Jimmy saw his face.

What he's pissed about is not that von Wachtstein is teasing him.

He's pissed because the other two Krauts are making passes at Elsa, which means he thinks she's his girl.

Well, it apparently didn't take Elsa the Great very long at all to replace the American stud with a German one.

Or two German studs.

"Go get him, please, Hansel," Frade ordered. "Actually, get both of them in here."

And — what the hell — bring Elsa, too.

We can have a party!

"Dieter, Willi," von Wachtstein said, "this is General Martín, through whose good offices you have your identity documents. General, my former commanding officer, Dieter von und zu Aschenburg, and my old friend Willi Grüner."

"I am very grateful to you, sir," von und zu

615

Aschenburg said.

"I have always been impressed with your flying skill, Señor Aschenburg," Martín said, "as well as your personal courage. When Peter came to me about bringing you to Argentina, I had no problem at all bending a rule here and a regulation there. I have no doubt that you will make a fine Argentine citizen."

"Thank you, sir."

"Señor Grüner's situation," Martín went on, "unfortunately did not lend itself — *does not* lend itself — to my making a quick decision."

"Sir?" Willi Grüner asked, confused.

"Please let me finish, Señor Grüner. And Colonel Frade, I would be most grateful if you would keep any thoughts you might have on this subject to yourself until I'm finished. Actually, I'm going to have to insist on that."

"*A su órdenes, mi General,*" Frade said, jovially sarcastic.

"Like your brother, Cletus," Martín said, "I have had just about all of your sarcasm that I'm going to take. Just sit there and shut up."

"Or leave the room," Cletus Marcus Howell added. "I don't know what the hell is the matter with you, but like everybody else, I've had enough of it."

Frade appeared on the edge of saying something but didn't.

Martín waited ten seconds, which seemed longer, and then started.

"I knew your father, Señor Grüner," he said, "and a good deal about him. I detested him for a number of reasons, ones general and specific. Generally — this should surprise no one — because he was not only a *coronel* — an *oberst* — in the Sicherheitsdienst of the Schutzstaffel but was very good at what the SD-SS did. Which here in Argentina meant the corruption of our officer and diplomatic corps and the murder of anyone who got in your father's way."

"General, my father is dead," Willi Grüner said.

"Do not interrupt me again, please, Señor Grüner," Martín said evenly, then went on: "And, specifically, I hated him because he ordered the assassination of an officer who was a dear friend and destined to be president of the Argentine Republic.

"I refer of course to late el Coronel Jorge G. Frade. Cletus's father. Your father also tried on several occasions to assassinate Cletus. The most memorable of those occurred in this house. In the room we just left on the top floor, Cletus killed two of the murderers hired by your father, but not before they had slit the throat of the housekeeper, a middle-aged woman, in the kitchen."

My God, Jimmy realized, genuinely shocked, *this is all true.*

"You said a moment, ago, Señor Grüner,

that your father is dead. Are you aware of the circumstances of his death?"

"I have heard —"

Martín held up his hand to silence Grüner.

"Permit me to tell you the circumstances, Señor Grüner. I think it important that you know them. Your father was shot on the beach of Samborombón Bay. He was engaged at the time in the off-loading from an ostensibly neutral merchant ship crates of currency and other valuables. These were to purchase sanctuary here in Argentina for senior Nazi officials once they lost the war. The vessel was also intending to smuggle into Argentina a detachment of SS officers and other ranks to guard the vast valuables.

"While assisting in this smuggling operation, your father was shot in the head by a retired Argentine army sergeant major in defiance of his orders from then-Major Frade to observe only and take no action. Sergeant Major Enrico Rodríguez was aware of your father's role in the attempted assassination here of Cletus Frade, and the brutal murder of the housekeeper. She was his sister. Rodríguez was also aware of your father's role in the assassination of el Coronel Frade. He had been at Colonel Frade's side — as he had been for twenty years during their active duty — when the assassination took place. He had been so seriously wounded himself that the assassins presumed him dead. El

Colonel Frade's death was caused by a twelve-bore shotgun loaded with double-aught buckshot fired twice into his face —"

"Good God! I never heard that!" Cletus Marcus Howell exclaimed. "In the face? Cletus, you never told me that!"

Cletus looked at him and said, "Now it's your turn to just sit there and shut up, Grandfather. Let's see where Bernardo is going with this."

As if he had heard neither, Martín went on: "The assassins were never arrested. Your father, Señor Grüner — as I said, he was very good at what he did — arranged for them to be murdered when they arrived in Paraguay expecting to be paid the second half of their fee. 'Dead men tell no tales,' it is said.

"And there are other examples of your father's ruthlessness. But those should suffice.

"We have a saying in Spanish — and, if I'm not mistaken, there's one in German as well — to the effect that the apple never drops far from the tree. . . ."

Willi nodded.

" 'Der Apfel fällt nicht weit vom Stamm,' " he quoted softly. "I thought that's what this was going to be about."

"And now that you know, Señor Grüner, your reaction?"

"I hope you didn't expect me to apologize for my father. I didn't order the assassination of Cletus's father, or hire anyone to kill Cletus. He was an SS-SD officer. I think he saw what he did as his duty. I think — and I don't offer this as an extenuation for his behavior, but possibly an explanation for it — that that obscene personal oath of loyalty to Adolf Hitler had a lot to do with it."

When Martín didn't reply immediately, Grüner asked, "Do you know what I'm talking about, General? That holy oath of personal loyalty?"

Martín nodded. "Didn't you yourself take it?"

"Hansel and I took it, and so did Dieter" — he nodded toward von und zu Aschenburg — "when we were with the Condor Legion in Spain. Hansel and I thought it was one more example of Nazi nonsense."

He paused.

"I never knew," he went on, his tone suggesting that he wondered why he had never considered it, "and he certainly never said anything about it, how Dieter, who was then our squadron commander, thought about it."

It was more a question than a statement, and von und zu Aschenburg answered it.

"I was ordered, General, as squadron commander, to administer that oath to those under my command. It never entered my mind to refuse that order. But I never felt bound by it."

"I did," von Dattenberg said. "It wasn't

until I came here that I realized it was, as somebody just said, obscene."

"Willi," Boltitz said, "as a U-boat commander, did you ever surface and machine-gun the sailors in the lifeboats of vessels you had just sunk?"

"You know better than that, Karl!" von Dattenberg said.

"The first time either of us, as honorable officers, refused to do that, we broke our holy oath of personal loyalty to the Führer. . . ."

"I really would like to have a lengthy discussion about this subject," Martín said. "But we're pressed for time and have to deal with the basic questions."

"Which are?" Cletus Marcus Howell said, admitting his confusion.

"Will Señor Grüner be willing to risk his life in the service of the Argentine Republic? His new country —"

"Doing what, General?" Willi asked.

"Anything we ask you," Martín said.

"Yes," Grüner said.

"Why?"

It took Grüner a long time to put his thoughts into words.

"Because it's the only country I have, and I don't want it taken over by either Nazis or Communists."

"That's not the answer I expected," Martín said.

"What did you expect me to say?"

"I don't know, but it wasn't that. Now the second question. And this one is for you, Cletus, as both the son of your father and as Lieutenant Colonel Frade of the OSS: Can we trust him, the son of the man who ordered the killing of your father?"

Frade stood. For a long moment, he couldn't find his voice.

Finally he did, and it all came out in a burst: "Stupid fucking question, Bernardo. Of course we can."

There was an awkward moment's silence before Martín matter-of-factly broke it.

"Señor Grüner, Lieutenant Cronley and von Dattenberg have determined what they believe is the landfall U-234 made. It's at the southern tip of Argentina, close to the Strait of Magellan. In other words, the weather conditions there are much like those of the Antarctic, or Russia in the worst of winters. If we were to truck an airplane down there —"

"What kind of an airplane?" Grüner interrupted.

"A Storch, Willi," von Wachtstein furnished.

"Could you somehow make a landing strip and operate from it?"

"Sure," Grüner said without hesitation, and turned to von Wachtstein. "Hansel, where the hell did you get a Storch?"

"It is a long story for later," von Wachtstein said.

"May I volunteer for this operation?" von und zu Aschenburg asked.

"Yeah," Frade answered, "but we old men are going to have to fly the transports and miss out on the fun." He turned to Martín. "When do we start?"

"This is your area of expertise, but I would suggest that getting the Storch down to Estancia Condor should head the list of priorities. It's going to be at least a three-day drive to get it there. And where are we going to get a flatbed truck on short notice?"

"There's several at the airport," Frade offered. "The contractor building the second runway brought his earthmovers on them. No reason one or more can't be pressed into the service of the Argentine Republic."

"Next important question," Martín said. "Maybe the most important of all. How do we keep people — in particular, el Coronel Perón — from learning what we're doing?"

"Why don't we ask Dorotea?" Frade asked. "She seems to have an answer for everything."

"And more often than not it's the right one," Dorotea said, smiling. "Now, that's the last of your sarcasm, agreed?"

"Yes, ma'am."

XI

[ONE]

Apartment 4-C
1044 Calle Talcahuano
Buenos Aires, Argentina
2125 20 October 1945

Former SS-Brigadeführer Gerhard Körtig, a fifty-year-old, short, plump, ruddy-faced Bavarian, wheezed as he got out of the taxi in front of the Colón Opera House. He was wearing a well-tailored suit and carrying a shiny leather briefcase.

He walked to a news kiosk just across an alley from the opera house and picked up a copy of *La Nacíon.* He dropped coins on the stack of newspapers, then opened his copy to the classified advertisements section.

Looking over it, he saw Konrad Fassbinder puffing on a cigar as he leaned on the wall of the opera house. He knew that Fassbinder had seen him, too, but there was no indication of this — not even a discreet nod — by either of them.

Körtig returned his attention to the newspaper for perhaps thirty seconds. Then he folded it and stuck it under his arm.

A bus pulled to the curb where he stood. The third passenger to get off was former SS-Oberführer Horst Lang, a tall, slim, fair-skinned Prussian. He was also wearing a well-tailored suit and carrying a briefcase.

The two exchanged no sign of recognition.

Lang started down the alley and was soon out of sight. Körtig could see no indication of any kind that Lang had been followed. Körtig started down the alley. If anyone was following him, Fassbinder would see.

When the wheezing Körtig reached the end of the alley, he saw that Lang was halfway down the path through the park across the street and almost on Calle Talcahuano.

Körtig thought, *The bastard should have walked slower.*

Körtig waited for the traffic light to change, then crossed the street and entered the small park. At the far side of it, there was opportunity for him to glance over his shoulder. Fassbinder was crossing the street between the opera house and the park.

Körtig sat on a bench along the path through the park. He opened his *La Nacíon.* Fassbinder walked past him a minute or so later. As far as Körtig could see, no one was following, or watching, Fassbinder.

Lang was now on Calle Talcahuano approaching number 1044. Fassbinder walked past him, then entered 1044. Lang followed.

Körtig waited until he had time to really make sure that he was neither being followed nor under observation, then stood up, tucked *La Nación* under his arm again, and walked quickly out of the park, crossed Calle Talcahuano, and entered 1044.

Neither Fassbinder nor Lang was in sight, and the door from the foyer was closed.

Körtig took a penknife from his vest pocket, slipped it into the lock, depressed the spring-loaded stop, and pushed the door open. The interior corridor was empty. He could hear the whine of the elevator, and as he walked up to its door, it came down to the foyer.

He slid the accordion door open, got on the elevator, and rode it to the fourth floor.

When he stepped into the foyer there, the door to 4-C opened, and he walked to it and entered.

As soon as the door closed behind him, former SS-Brigadeführer Ludwig Hoffmann offered Körtig his hand.

"This had better be important, Ludwig," Körtig said.

Mannhoffer led everyone to the dining room table. He picked up the thick envelope of photograph proofs.

"I think you both should take a careful look at these," he said.

"What are they?" Gerhard Körtig said.

629

"Pictures of people getting off the SAA flight from Berlin this morning."

Körtig sat and took them from the envelope. He examined the first one carefully but without expression, then handed it to Horst Lang.

"I was hoping that von und zu Aschenburg had died in the East," Lang said, after examining it. "I heard that he had been shot down."

"We should have eliminated him in 1944, when his relationship with Canaris became known," Mannhoffer said.

"Became *suspected*, Ludwig," Körtig said. "There was never any proof, was there? And in 1944, Canaris wasn't suspected of anything, was he? No one dreamed he would betray the Führer."

"I would say we have it now. The both of them betrayed their oath," Lang said.

"And Canaris was hung as a traitor. Von und zu Aschenburg apparently escaped punishment," Körtig said. He paused and waved one of the proofs. "Who is this? He looks familiar."

"Kapitän Wilhelm Grüner," Mannhoffer said.

"Karl-Heinz's son?"

"That's him."

"What's he doing on that plane? And with von und zu Aschenburg?"

"That's one of the things we have to talk about."

"Ah, von Wachtstein," Körtig said, turning to another proof. "We know how seriously he took his oath to the Führer, don't we? He and his despicable father."

He turned to the next proof.

"And yet another. Kapitän zur See Karl Boltitz. What is this, Ludwig, a convention of traitors?"

"I think it's more than that," Mannhoffer said.

"And who is this man? This young American officer?"

"I don't have his name. I think he's an officer courier."

"Carrying what, from whom, and to whom?" Körtig asked.

"I should have more information shortly, but right now I don't know. I would hazard the guess that he's bringing material from General Gehlen to Oberstleutnant Frade. And that would mean to General Martín as well."

"You haven't told me why this — how should I say? — *gaggle* of traitors has alarmed you to the point that you called this meeting."

"Indulge me a moment, Gerhard," Mannhoffer said. "Tell me the latest on U-234."

"There is, I am happy to say, not much to report."

"I went down there last week with the supply truck," Lang offered, "and the sailors taking their turn on the boat. We are actually increasing the fuel aboard — not by much, to be sure — but we no longer have to worry about them running out of fuel, as we were originally. Morale is surprisingly high. Boredom of course is a problem. The chief of the boat actually asked me if I could bring two or three ladies of the evening with me on the next trip."

"Was he serious?" Mannhoffer asked.

"Perfectly. He said that he had never been so far from a *Dirnenviertel* in his life. Or for so long."

Everybody laughed at the mental picture of the sexually frustrated sailor desperate for a red-light district.

"If Kapitän Schneider wasn't such a prude, I'd consider it," Körtig said.

"He is a prude, isn't he?" Mannhoffer asked rhetorically.

"A devout *Evangelische* prude. The worst kind," Lang said.

"Maybe we should be grateful for that," Körtig said. "Alois Schneider takes his vow of personal loyalty to the Führer very seriously. He's not going to wind up on Oberstleutnant Frade's payroll."

"He's still in Villa General Belgrano?" Mannhoffer asked.

"With his brother," Lang said, "who was

one of Langsdorf's protégés on the *Graf Spee*. He was second gunnery officer."

"I think you told me that," Mannhoffer said.

"I don't think I told you the brother has now decided he wants to be a farmer," Lang said.

"Meaning what?"

"Meaning, Ludwig, that he's married to an Argentine woman, has a son, and another in the oven, and has decided that raising cattle with her father offers a more promising future than being repatriated to the fatherland."

"He doesn't have any choice about that, does he?"

"I would not be surprised if he disappeared before they can load him on a ship, and that the Argentines wouldn't look very hard for him."

"How could he get a *libreta de enrolamiento*?" Mannhoffer asked.

"If we have one, I wouldn't be surprised if he already has one," Lang said simply. "Nor would I be surprised if he hasn't been working on his brother to make a new life for himself here."

"That's a problem down the road, possibly," Mannhoffer said. "We have more immediate problems to deal with."

"We're finally getting to that, are we?" Körtig said.

"How are negotiations going with the new

Russian?"

"The *new* Russian?" Lang parroted.

"Gerhard, why am I getting the idea that you two are not sharing everything with me?" Mannhoffer said. "That would be unwise."

"What do you think I'm not telling you?" Körtig asked.

"The answer to what I just asked: how negotiations are going with the new Russian."

"Oh, you mean Pavel Egorov," Lang offered.

"If that's his name. The one the Kremlin sent here from Mexico City."

"Well, for obvious reasons," Körtig said, "neither Lang nor I have met him personally. I don't think he even knows our names."

"Never underestimate the NKVD. He probably knows everybody's name. He just doesn't know, for the moment, where to find us."

"You asked how the negotiations are going," Körtig said, a bit impatiently. "Moreno, of the Banco Suisse Creditanstalt, tells me that they are willing to meet our price —"

"One hundred million U.S. dollars?"

Körtig nodded. "Deposited in the Banco Suisse Creditanstalt in Johannesburg. But with certain conditions. First, that we provide them with a fifty-kilogram sample of the uranium oxide so they can test it to make sure of what they're getting."

"All they would need to make sure it is what we say is a cupful, not fifty kilograms."

"I raised that objection through Moreno. They replied that if we have fifty kilos of the stuff, that would tend to suggest we have, and will give them, the rest — the other five hundred and ten kilos."

"And how will the transfer be accomplished?" Mannhoffer asked.

"The U-234 will rendezvous with a Russian freighter at a to-be-determined point in the South Atlantic, somewhere south of the Falkland Islands —"

"Whereupon," Mannhoffer interrupted, "fifty NKVD agents, or that many Marines, will board U-234, kill every German aboard, take the uranium oxide, and then sink the U-234."

"Now, Ludwig, you're beginning to annoy me. Did you really think I wouldn't think of that?"

"And?"

"When U-234 sails for the rendezvous point, Pavel Egorov will be aboard. If anything goes wrong, your favorite new Russian will be eliminated. He will remain on U-234 until she comes back to Argentina. When Moreno tells us the money is safely in our account in South Africa, Egorov will be freed."

"How do you know you can trust Moreno?"

"Because I have told him if he betrays us in any way, we will kill him and all members of his family."

Mannhoffer considered everything he had been told, but said nothing.

"Does that answer your concerns, Ludwig?"

"I have a few others," Mannhoffer said.

"Let's have them."

"How much time do the Russians want to test the uranium oxide we give them for that purpose?"

"I've looked carefully into that, too. What they told Moreno they intend to do is break the fifty kilos down into small packets. They will then be taken in luggage to Rio de Janeiro. There is a Soviet embassy there. The uranium oxide will then be sent via diplomatic pouch to Moscow. The Americans are now offering flying boat service between London and Rio."

"The entire fifty kilos?"

"I don't think they're going to send it all. You were right, Ludwig, that they only need a cupful or whatever to test it."

"And did they say how long it would take to get a report back?"

"Three weeks to a month."

"During which time they can look for and probably find U-234," Mannhoffer said. "And once they find it . . ."

"I don't think we have to worry about that."

". . . if they can send a freighter to a rendezvous point near the Falkland Islands, they can send it — with those fifty NKVD agents or Marines aboard —"

"You're not listening to me, Ludwig," Körtig interrupted. "There's no way they could
find U-234."

"Gerhard, the landfall coordinates were in
the safe of U-405 when that *gottverdammt*
von Dattenberg surrendered it to the Argentines."

"Encoded," Körtig said. "The coordinates
were encoded among other coordinates. Von
Dattenberg didn't even know he had them.
And even if they suspected U-234 made it to
Argentina — and I don't think they do —
but even if they knew she was down there
somewhere, they could never find her."

"Ludwig," Lang offered, "I have trouble
finding the damn U-boat when I go down
there. And I know exactly where she is. She
blends into the landscape — seascape? —
because she's painted white — a sort of gray-
ish white — and she's covered with white
camouflage nets. You can't see her, you have
no suggestion there's anything there until you
get within a couple of hundred meters."

"Could she be seen from the air?"

"Not if the airplane was flying any higher
than two or three hundred meters. She is
covered with white camouflage netting. I just
told you that."

"For the sake of argument, Horst — indulge
me — could she be seen from a slow, low-
flying — say, one-fifty- or two-hundred-meter
— aircraft?"

637

"If Santa Claus was flying overhead in his sleigh — and looking carefully — *maybe.*"

Mannhoffer ignored the sarcasm. "What if the aircraft was a Piper Cub or, say, a Storch? Flown by a pilot with extensive experience in flying in arctic conditions in Russia? Could he see the U-234, camouflage netting or no camouflage netting?"

"He probably could. But that's a hell of a stretch, Ludwig."

"What if I told you that flatbed trucks carrying a Piper Cub, a Storch, and a bulldozer capable of carving out an airfield, plus a fuel truck with twelve thousand liters of fuel, and two army trucks — one carrying twenty heavily armed soldiers and the other rations, heavy weapons, and ammunition — are about to leave, if they haven't already left, Aeropuerto Frade for an undisclosed destination in the south of the country?"

"My God!" Körtig exclaimed.

"They've got a Storch?" Lang asked incredulously. "Where did they get a Storch?"

"I have no idea," Mannhoffer said. "But Frade has one. It's painted bright red. And now he's got a pilot skilled in arctic operations — former Major Wilhelm Grüner — to fly it."

"His father must be spinning in his grave," Lang said.

"Let's not get excited," Körtig said. "They

638

don't know where U-234 is. How could they?"

"They broke the coded rendezvous points?" Mannhoffer said. "There's a number of possibilities there."

"Such as?"

"One that comes immediately to mind —"

"Let's accept, for the sake of argument," Körtig said, "that they know that U-234 made it here, and have a general idea where she lies. How are they going to find it?"

"With the Storch, obviously."

"All right, let's go down that path. If the Storch doesn't make it down there, ergo, they can't find U-234. How can we arrange that? Get some of the Tenth Mountain people already down there at Estancia Condor to set up a roadblock, something like that?"

"You're pissing into the wind, Gerhard. Never underestimate the enemy," Mannhoffer said.

"Meaning what?"

"Meaning General Martín is way ahead of you. You remember me telling you that for quaint and mysterious resaons of their own, the deputy head of the BIS, Habanzo, usually wears civilian clothing? And that when he does deign to wear a uniform, it is that of a major?"

"But he's actually an *oberst*? So what?"

"The convoy headed south will be led by a staff car, with Habanzo riding regally in the backseat, wearing his colonel's uniform. The only people who would dare to question a colonel of the BIS — much less stop or turn around a convoy he is leading — would be either Perón or Farrell. BIS *de jure* answers only to President Farrell, although just about everybody *de facto* answers to Oberst Perón."

"Well, obviously, we can't go to Farrell to rein in Martín. And if we go to Perón, we'll have to tell him what's going on."

"And he would demand a small percentage — possibly fifty percent — of what the Russians will pay us," Lang said. "Or — and I think he's perfectly capable of this — he'd send the Armada Argentina to seize U-234 and sell the uranium oxide to the Russians himself."

"So what do we do?" Körtig said.

"I presume I have the floor?" Mannhoffer asked, and when both Lang and Körtig nodded, began: "I have not only given this a good deal of thought, but have discussed it in some detail with Fassbinder and Richter. All of this of course before this current problem presented itself, which of course has changed everything."

"I have no idea what you're talking about," Körtig said.

"At first, the intuitive thing to do — lay low, bide our time, make no waves, et cetera — seemed to make sense. But then I realized that we — the people in this room — are all that's left of National Socialism. Our superiors are either dead or locked up awaiting trial. There will be no more submarines from Germany, no more funds with which we can cause National Socialism to rise, using Himmler's phrase, 'phoenixlike from the ashes.' Either we do it, or it doesn't get done."

"So we do it. What's the problem?" Lang asked.

"We'll have that hundred million dollars from the Russians," Körtig said. "That should help."

"The problem is there is no state. The Germans here have nothing to which they owe their allegiance. To put a point on that, no state of which they are afraid. If we, for example, decided to call a demonstration to protest the trials of Goering and the others in Nuremberg, I'm afraid a large number of our countrymen might decide they'd rather not participate, and all of them, I'm sure, would ask, 'Just who are these people issuing these orders? Where do they get their authority?' "

"I'm not saying I agree with you," Körtig said, "but for the sake of argument, what should we do in your judgment?"

"*Das Deutschesvolk* cheerfully and enthusiastically obeyed der Führer for two reasons. One, he was a spellbinding orator. Two, they knew if they didn't, they'd have to deal with the SS."

"That's cynicism."

"Whatever it is, it's true, and you know it."

"What's your point, Ludwig?"

"If we are serious about keeping National Socialism alive, we are going to need the support of the German people here in Argentina and in Paraguay and Uruguay, and we're not going to get that unless they respect the state."

"You mean, are afraid of the SS?"

"Precisely."

"And how are you going to do that when we have no more than a hundred or so SS people?"

"They don't know how many people we have," Mannhoffer said. "But they believe that the SS, like they do, must stay out of the public eye. All we have to do is convince them not only is the SS larger than it happens to be, but it is inflicting punishment on those disloyal to National Socialism."

"Explain that," Lang said.

"They know what's going on in this country. They know, for a specific example, that von Wachtstein was a traitor to the Third Reich all the time he was serving as air attaché in the embassy. And that he is now married into one of the better families and flying an airliner. That he not only got away with his treason, but has been rewarded for it. And they have concluded, with reason, that the SS has been unable to do anything about it."

"So you're saying we should do something about it? Eliminate von Wachtstein?"

"What I want to do is build an image of the SS in the public's imagination as a secret organization — a *large* secret organization — dedicated to the maintenance of National Socialist principles. Now, try to follow my reasoning. We eliminate von Wachtstein. No one will *know* who did it. But they will wonder: 'Who did this and why?' And they will conclude, wondering why it took them so long to understand, that the Sicherheitsdienst of the SS is alive, well, and as dangerous as ever. And here."

"You may be onto something, Ludwig," Körtig said. "First, von Wachtstein. And then Boltitz . . ."

"And of course von Dattenberg, who surrendered U-405 to the Argentines," Lang chipped in.

"And most important, Don Cletus Frade," Mannhoffer said. "His elimination will send a message not only to das Deutschesvolk, but to Juan Domingo Perón."

"I don't like that," Körtig said. "Frade was standing beside him on the balcony of the Casa Rosada. Perón looks on him almost as a son."

"We can argue about that later," Mannhoffer said. "Right now, the first thing we do is get Kapitän Schneider and the rest of U-234's crew back down there with enough diesel fuel so that they can move the U-boat a hundred kilometers away. The second thing we do is get enough SS men down there — thirty, thirty-five troopers — to eliminate the problem there, and —"

"Exactly what does 'eliminate the problem' mean?" Lang asked.

"When our men are finished, Colonel Habanzo, Major Grüner, the Storch, the fuel truck — everybody and everything that *gottverdammt* Martín sent down there — will have disappeared from the face of the earth."

"I thought you wanted to eliminate von Wachtstein and Boltitz?"

"And von Dattenberg. But right now I don't know where they are — or are going to be by the time we can form another SS Kommando unit — so where and when that will happen will depend on where they are. If they're in Brazil or, for that matter, in the United States, terminating them will have to go on the back burner for a while."

"The United States?" Lang asked.

"My man at the airport says they're preparing the American Constellation for flight. They don't know where it's going —"

" 'The American Constellation'?" Körtig parroted.

"Frade's grandfather's, the Howell Petroleum Corporation airplane. A good possibility is that Frade is getting the women and the children out of Argentina until the submarine business is over. Sending them to the United States on his grandfather's airplane would be a simple way to do that."

"It would also get the grandfather out of the way," Lang said.

"I should — we should — have more information fairly soon. The trouble is that I have only two people at the airport. One of them has to leave the airport and go to a telephone kiosk ten kilometers away to call me here."

"Isn't there a public telephone at the airport?"

"There is. Actually there's three. And the women who operate that kiosk — and listen to every conversation — work for the BIS. As I was saying, the one who does make the calls is terrified of being caught at it."

"Why? What could the BIS do to him?"

"The BIS, nothing. But my man believes that some ex-Húsares corporal in Frade's Private Army would take him out onto the Pampas, slit his throat with his *cuchillo criollo,* and leave him there for the condors to eat."

"With his what?" Lang asked.

"His gaucho's knife. It's a great big thing," Mannhoffer explained, as he held his hands eighteen inches apart to show the length of a *cuchillo criollo* blade. "They carry them in the back, stuck in their wide leather belts."

"Frade is that ruthless?" Körtig asked. There was a certain tone of professional admiration in his voice.

"Frade is," he said, turning to Körtig. "But that wouldn't happen if they caught him talking to me on the telephone. They would turn him over to the BIS, who would professionally interrogate him and then lock him up until this is over. I've often thought the one major weakness of the BIS is a certain lack of ruthlessness. My point here is that my man at the airport *believes* he would get his throat cut. What people believe is what counts, not the truth. What we have to do is convince the Deutschesvolk that the SS is here, strong, and prepared to be as ruthless as we ever were in Germany."

"So where do we start?" Körtig asked.

"How'd you get to Buenos Aires?" Mannhoffer asked.

"By auto. Separately. We put them in garages. Separately. Mine's in Recoleta."

"Well, I suggest that one of you get back in one of them and head for Villa General Belgrano. Get Schneider and the rest of his crew back to U-234. Making sure Frade doesn't get the uranium oxide is the highest priority, and the way to ensure that is to move the U-234."

"You go, Lang," Körtig said. "I'll stay here a little longer — at least until we find out what Frade is up to at the airport."

[Two]

Cletus Frade was alone in his office with, of course, the ever-present Enrico Rodríguez. He was waiting impatiently for the crew of his grandfather's Constellation to show up. Sparing no expense, the old man had put them up in the Alvear Palace.

That was in keeping with Cletus Marcus Howell's philosophy of treating employees, which Clete had heard perhaps a hundred times since he was a child: *"Find the best people, pay them one hundred twenty-five percent of what they would be making anywhere else, and stay out of their way when they're doing what you've told them to do."*

In this case he didn't have to find the best people. When Howard Hughes sent the Connie to New Orleans, it was a given that the crew was first class. All the old man had to do was offer them a twenty-five percent pay increase to get them to change employers.

When he thought about that, Clete decided Howard, knowing what the old man was likely to do now that he owned the Connie and needed a crew for it, had sent him a good

— but not necessarily the best — crew.

It didn't matter. The crew was first class. As good as, and almost certainly more experienced than, any SAA crew.

When the crew finally showed up and filed into his office, Clete was glad that he was not wearing his SAA captain's uniform.

Jimmy was right, he thought, *the SAA uniform does make me look like a Mexican bus driver.*

I would have given these guys a laugh, and that's the last thing I can afford to do with them.

The men who came into his office were wearing, not surprisingly, American-style flight crew uniforms. That was to say, they all had blue tunics with gold wings pinned to them. There were two captains, one taller and one older, each wearing four gold stripes on their cuffs. And there were four first officers, with three stripes on their sleeves. One or two of the first officers, Clete guessed, were the flight engineers. It was wise to have flight engineers who were qualified pilots.

And there were four men with a single gold stripe. One of them — the one wearing wings, Clete guessed — was the radio operator. That meant the other three, who were not wearing pilot's wings, were stewards.

"My name is Cletus Frade," he began. "I guess you've heard Mr. Howell is my grandfather. I'm with South American Airways. I'm sorry to get you out here on such short notice, but it couldn't be helped. I'll tell you as much as I can — which won't be much — starting with the fact that we need my grandfather's airplane. I can't tell you why, but I can tell you that you would not want to be involved. And you won't be.

"As soon as you leave here, a Lodestar will fly you all to Rio de Janeiro, Brazil, where you have first-class reservations at a hotel — I don't know which one, but it'll be a good one — until we can get you on one of Juan Trippe's Panagra flying boats. . . ."

He became aware that both of the captains and one of the first officers were smiling ear to ear.

"Did I say something funny?" Clete demanded. "Or is there a piece of spinach stuck in my teeth? My fly open? What?"

"Sir," the older of the captains said, "could Captain Ford and myself have a moment of your time in private? I think that would probably make things a little easier all around."

Frade nodded. "Would the rest of your crew mind stepping into the outer office for a moment?"

"Outside, please, people," Captain Ford ordered. "This probably won't take long."

Everybody but the two captains filed out of the office. Captain Ford closed the door after them.

"Okay," Clete said. "What's on your mind?"

Captain Ford took a small envelope from his tunic pocket and handed it to Frade, who opened it and read it.

The White House

Washington, D.C.
12 October 1945

To Whom It May Concern:

Commander Anthony C. Armstrong, USN, and Commander Richard W. Ford, USN, are engaged in carrying out a confidential mission for me which they are not at liberty to discuss.

    All U.S. Government installations and activities are directed to provide them with any and all support they deem necessary to carry out their mission.

Harry S Truman

"I will be damned," Clete said.

"I'm Ford," the tall captain said, "and this ugly old man is Commander Tony Armstrong, USN. You really don't remember ever seeing either of us, sir?"

Clete shook his head.

"But you do remember having been on what is now *your grandfather's* Flying Brothel?" Armstrong asked.

" 'Tempelhof approach control, this is Navy 7077 . . .' " Commander Ford recited.

"Jesus!" Clete said, as he put together the pieces.

"And then we flew you — and Boltitz and von Wachtstein and those two German kids — from Berlin to Brazil," Armstrong said, "to Val de Cans U.S. Air Force Base."

"The . . . Flying Brothel . . . then had U.S. Navy markings, and the pilots were Navy officers," Clete remembered, out loud.

"Under orders never to talk to their passengers," Ford said. "Nice to see you again, Colonel."

"Are you going to tell me what's going on?" Clete asked.

"Yeah," Ford said. "I guess we're going to have to. The reason we were flying Navy 7077 — the Brothel — was because we worked for Admiral Souers. . . ."

"Doing what?"

"This is classified Top Secret–Presidential, Colonel Frade. Got it?"

"Got it."

"Whatever the President asked him to do."

"Like what, for example?"

"You're not cleared for that, generally, but, for example, picking up a jarhead light bird in New Orleans and flying him to Berlin because the President wanted to talk to him. Getting the picture?"

"Got it," Clete, vividly recalling that surprise trip and secret meeting with Truman, replied with a chuckle.

"Apparently," Ford went on, "the President told the admiral that your grandfather had bought the Flying Brothel from Howard Hughes, and Hughes was going to provide a crew from Lockheed to fly it down here for him. The President said the Lockheed crew was likely to see things he'd rather they not see, so why not send those nice guys who do flying jobs for the admiral — who knew how to fly the Brothel and how to keep their mouths shut — instead. And here we are."

"Does my grandfather know about this?"

Both men shook their heads.

"But the admiral told me," Ford said, "to tell you that you could tell him if you thought it was a good idea."

"Anything else?"

"Cutting to the chase," Armstrong said, "we are under orders to render any service Lieutenant Colonel Frade may ask of us."

"So please don't send us to Rio to catch a slow boat to China — a slow-flying boat to Miami — Colonel," Ford said. "It looks like the fun here is just about to start."

"What about the rest of your crew?" Frade asked. "How much do they know? How much can they be told?"

"They're all assigned to the Naval Office of the President — we are, too, by the way — and all of them have all the exotic security clearances. I have complete trust in them."

This is not what I expected, Clete decided.

But as my beloved grandfather is wont to say, "Don't complain, just play whatever cards the dealer gives you."

"I've got a couple of Top Secret–Presidential operations going here," Clete said. "One of them you don't really have to know about, but I'm going to tell you a little about it. You two only. Don't share this with the rest of your crew. Understood?"

"Understood."

"Just before the war ended, the German general Gehlen, who was in charge of Abwehr Ost — Russian intelligence — went to . . ."

"Yeah, I can see why President Truman wouldn't want that to come out," Armstrong said, when Clete had finished.

"Is that what he wanted to talk to you about in Berlin?" Ford asked.

Frade nodded.

"What I'm doing with that is holding down the fort, all by my lonesome, until the President can set up a replacement for the OSS."

"Under Admiral Souers," Armstrong said. "He told us — Dick and me only — about that. They're going to call it the Central Agency for Intelligence."

"Central Intelligence Agency," Ford corrected him.

Frade nodded, then said, "The second operation — it just came up — is something damned near as important. Just before the

653

war ended, the Germans dispatched a submarine, U-234, ostensible destination Japan. Onboard were a couple of very senior SS officers, some German nuclear physicists, and five hundred sixty kilograms — about three-quarters of a ton — of uranium oxide."

"Jesus Christ!" Armstrong said. "I heard the Germans had a nuclear program but . . ."

"They were trying to hand it to the Japs, right?" Ford asked.

"It looks that way," Frade said.

"What's the connection here?" Armstrong asked.

"We have some reliable intelligence that U-234 came to Argentina, and yesterday we think — operative word 'think' — we learned where it made landfall. Very close to the Strait of Magellan."

"That's almost in the Antarctic, isn't it?" Armstrong asked. "A lot of ice-covered rock?"

Frade nodded.

"You think it's just sitting down there?" Ford asked dubiously.

"Personally, I think it unloaded its cargo and then was scuttled. But I don't *know* that. What we're going to do is look for any signs of a landing, and go from there. Play it by ear."

"How are you going to look for it? On snowshoes?" Ford asked.

"With an airplane," Frade said. "You ever hear of a Fieseler Storch?"

"I've seen pictures, but I've never actually seen one," Ford said.

Armstrong shook his head.

"We have one. Great airplane. They stall at about thirty knots. That ought to be slow enough to have a good look. And the guy flying it has lots of experience in Russia."

"How are you going to get it down there? Refuel it? Where's it going to land?"

"A convoy with a Storch, a Piper Cub, a bulldozer, a tanker truck with twelve thousand liters of Avgas, and some soldiers to protect it left here about thirty minutes ago. It'll take them three or four days to get there. It'll take another day to put the wings back on the airplanes, and for the dozer to hack out an airstrip."

"Where does the Flying Brothel fit into all this?" Armstrong asked.

"I'm an optimist," Frade said. "Thirty minutes into his first flight, Willi Grüner — he went to flight school with von Wachtstein, and they flew Luftwaffe fighters together — is going to look out the window of the Storch and see an arrow and a sign in the snow that says *Uranium Oxide Buried Here*."

Both Ford and Armstrong chuckled.

"And, so now that I have it, what do I do with the uranium oxide?" Frade asked, and immediately answered his own question. "I send it to the States. . . ."

"In the Brothel," Ford interjected.

Frade nodded.

"Radioactivity?" Ford asked. "We arrive in the States — plane and crew — glowing brightly?"

"I don't know, but it seems to me the Germans would have to have figured out how to deal with it. It took that submarine at least a month to get here from Norway."

"Where can the Brothel land down there in all that ice and snow?" Armstrong asked.

"I doubt it can. But I've got a Lodestar that I can probably put on the ground and get in the air again. And then fly to Mendoza and rendezvous with the Brothel, which has been waiting patiently in Santiago, Chile, for the message to go to Mendoza."

"I hate to piss on your parade, Colonel," Armstrong said.

"Please do. I tend to get carried away with boyish enthusiasm."

"Let's say your man in the Storch finds the uranium oxide. Frankly, that seems unlikely, but let's say he does. How are you going to get word to Santiago?"

"Are you familiar with the Collins Radio Corporation's Model 7.2 transceiver?"

"Yeah."

"Two of them are in the convoy I mentioned. They call that 'redundancy.' That means in case one breaks, you've got another."

"But that's fixed station equipment."

656

"Not our 7.2s," Frade said, just a little smugly.

"Yours are portable?"

"Not only portable but they work in airplanes. I've got one in my Lodestar, and if you can put the Brothel on the ground in Mendoza without breaking it, my whiz-bang commo man, Sergeant Siggie Stein, will put one in the Brothel. So you can get the message, o ye of little faith, that I have the uranium oxide and it's time for you to leave scenic Santiago and pick it up in Mendoza. Or maybe even at the mouth of the Magellan Strait."

Commander Armstrong shook his head in disbelief.

"And, forgive me for being of so little faith, but what are you going to do if your guy can't find it in Antarctica?"

"I thought you might ask about Plan B," Frade said. "Did you happen to notice as you passed through downstairs a nice-looking young man with two suitcases? He was probably looking lustfully at my baby sister."

Both nodded.

"Well, I can understand why," Ford said.

Frade gave him a withering look and went on: "He's Second Lieutenant James D. Cronley Junior, Cavalry, USA, detailed to what used to be OSS in Europe. Those suitcases — brought from Germany yesterday — are full of, among other things, dossiers of high-level Nazis we're looking for. Karl Boltitz — he's the tall blond one downstairs looking lustfully at my *older* baby sister — used to be the naval attaché at the German embassy. He just brought from Germany the manifest of U-234, including the names of the Nazis aboard we didn't have until just now.

"General Martín, who heads BIS, is going to Mendoza with us. He is bringing along his two experts in charge of 'where are the Nazis hiding?' Between them and the Gehlen officers who specialized in keeping an eye on the SS, we're going to see if we can find these guys and, when we do, ask them, more or less politely, 'Hey, Asshole, where's the uranium oxide?' "

"I'm just a simple sailor . . ." Armstrong said.

Clete snorted.

". . . but I don't understand the urgency in getting the uranium oxide. It's not an atom bomb, just the stuff from which they make the stuff that goes into atomic bombs. Right?"

"Did I mention that the Russians are sending — maybe that should be 'have sent' — a guy down here by the name of Pavel Egorov? He was the NKVD's man in Mexico City."

"No, actually you didn't," Armstrong said. "But I can understand why an unimportant detail like that might easily slip through the cracks."

Clete gave him the finger.

"So when do we go to work?" Armstrong asked.

"As soon as we leave here," Clete said. "Would it hurt your Navy ego if I flew in the right seat of the Brothel in case you have trouble finding Mendoza?"

"Not if you promise not to touch any of the switches, levers, or the yoke."

"You have my Naval Aviator's word of honor, Commander, and we both know how much that's worth."

"Well, then, I guess we can get started. After you answer two questions."

"Shoot."

"Who is the gentleman sitting by the door with the riot gun?"

"He is my friend Enrico Rodríguez. You may call him *suboficial mayor* — that means sergeant major."

"And what does he do with the riot gun?"

"When someone says something unkind or disrespectful to me, he puts a round in the chamber. That is a warning not to do it again. I give a pass the first time. The second time, however, *Bang!*"

"Fascinating. Second question: You don't happen to have a third baby sister, do you? She doesn't have to be anything special since Ford is still a bachelor at twenty-nine and can't afford to be choosy."

Very softly, Clete ordered, *"Ponga un cartucho en la recámara, Enrico."*

It was Spanish for "Put a round in the chamber, Enrico."

Enrico did so.

The chambering of a round in a Remington Model 10 shotgun was accomplished by pushing a metal button that was on the side of the receiver. This caused the spring-loaded bolt to slam forward, pushing the shotgun shell into the chamber. This caused a distinct — some would say menacing — metallic *Clunk!*

"Nice try, jarhead, but no brass ring," Commander Armstrong said, then switched to perfect Spanish: "You wouldn't shoot a nice old sailor like me, would you, *Suboficial Mayor?*"

Enrico smiled and shook his head.

"I only shoot people who don't like Don Cletus, señor. I can tell you like him and he likes you."

Frade grunted — but he was smiling.

"Shall we get our little show on the road, Colonel Don Cletus?" Armstrong asked.

[THREE]

When they came down the stairway from the second floor of the passenger terminal, Cletus Marcus Howell was waiting for them outside the VIP Lounge.

"I'd like a word with you, Captain Armstrong, and you, too, Captain Ford, if you'd be so kind," the old man said, waving them into the VIP Lounge.

The two captains and Clete marched into the room. The old man followed, then closed the door.

"Captain Ford, I think you'd better show him the letter —" Clete began.

"My God, Cletus, I haven't even opened my mouth and you're interrupting me."

"Sorry, Grandfather."

"Believe it or not, gentlemen," the old man said, "my son raised Cletus to show more respect to his elders than he's showing now."

"Yes, sir," Armstrong said.

"By now I presume that he's told you we're going to need the Flying Brothel for purposes we cannot share with you, that your services will not be required for that, and that we're going to fly you to Rio de Janeiro on the first leg of your trip to New Orleans."

No one said a word.

"Well, has he?" the old man demanded.

"Yes, sir," Ford and Armstrong said, in chorus.

"I want to assure you this is in no way a suggestion that you are inadequate in any way," the old man went on. "When I get to the States, I am going to get on the phone to Howard Hughes, tell him how pleased I have been with your services, and ask him how angry he's going to be when I offer all of you employment at one hundred twenty-five

661

percent of whatever he's paying you."

"You'd better show him the letter —" Clete repeated.

"Shut up, Cletus!" the old man snapped. "I'm not through!"

"Yes, sir."

"In the meantime, vis-à-vis Rio, I am going to send the manager of the Hotel Astoria Palace a telegram telling him to put you up in the best accommodations he has until it's time for you to board one of that goddamn Juan Trippe's flying boats to take you to Miami.

"I think you'll like the Astoria Palace. It's on the Copacabana Beach. The best rooms provide clear views of the beach, on which some of the most beautiful women in the world go swimming in bathing suits no larger than postage stamps. Spectacular!"

He paused, grinning broadly.

"Well, how does that sound, gentlemen?"

"They're not going to Rio," Clete said.

"What did you say?"

"Show him the letter," Clete said.

Armstrong handed the old man the President's letter.

The old man read it.

"This proves my point that you can never trust a goddamn Democrat!" the old man exploded. "That sonofabitch never told me about this!"

"But the President of the United States and

662

commander in chief of its armed forces did tell Commander Armstrong that I had his permission, at my discretion, to tell you about it, which I just did," Clete said.

The old man glared at him for a moment.

"I was carried away by surprise," he said finally. "You'll please forgive that outburst. The President of the United States and commander in chief of its armed forces is, like myself, a Thirty-third Degree Mason. We Master Masons never lie to each other. I'm sure ol' Harry had good reasons to keep it quiet that the crew was OSS."

"There is no OSS, Grandfather," Clete said. "Ol' Harry put it out of business some time ago."

"Then who the hell do you work for?"

"I guess you could say ol' Harry," Clete said. "I thought he told you."

"I think it could be fairly said that we are ol' Harry's secret weapon," Armstrong said.

The old man snorted, then asked, "So, what are you two wiseasses going to do now, as President Truman's secret weapon?"

"Well," Clete said, "first we're going to load all the civilians on the Flying Brothel — civilians being defined as the women and children and you, Grandfather — and ol' Tony and ol' Dick here and I are going to fly it to Mendoza."

"What's in Mendoza?"

Frade ignored the question.

"The men who aren't civilians will fly to Mendoza in my red Lodestar and one Lodestar chartered from SAA by the Bureau of Internal Security. These men will include some of General Martín's specialists in tracking Nazis who have sneaked into the country." He looked between the captains, and added, "This was the plan before my horny little brother broke the Kriegsmarine code and found the U-234's landfall."

" 'Horny little brother'?" Ford parroted.

"He wasn't off the plane from Germany four hours before he started hitting on my little sister."

"Did I hear that right?" Armstrong asked. "Your little brother hit on your little sister?"

"You're goddamned right he did," Clete said indignantly.

"Jimmy Cronley," the old man clarified, "is not really his little brother, and his little sister Marjie is not really his sister."

"Well, I must say I'm relieved to hear that," Armstrong said.

"Marjie is my cousin. We were raised together. I think of her as my baby sister," Clete said.

"May I ask where this Cronley fellow fits into this fascinating genealogy?" Ford asked.

"He lived next door to me in Midland, Texas."

"And what's he doing here? You said he broke the Kriegsmarine code? What code is that?" Armstrong asked.

"The Kriegsmarine furnished U-boat commanders with a list of one hundred rendezvous points. Coded, of course. One of them was the intended landfall of U-234. Just take my word for it, the horny little bastard broke it."

"He's a crypto expert?" Ford asked.

"He's a goddamn second lieutenant. I don't think he can spell 'cryptographic,' much less knows what it means. He was in the CIC solely because he speaks German. Then he found von Wachtstein's sister-in-law in a line of refugees in Germany. Then the OSS, scraping the bottom of the barrel, got him out of the CIC and into the OSS just before they put us out of business. They made him OIC of the detachment guarding General Gehlen. His qualifications for that job were that he was an officer and they didn't have any other officers.

"Then the CIC stumbled onto the Gehlen camp, and Jimmy wouldn't let them in. As a matter of fact, he blew a hole in the engine block of the colonel-who-was-trying-to-get-in's staff car with a .50 caliber machine gun. That kept the colonel out for the moment, but with a burning desire to come back and get in.

"The guy in charge, a really smart bird colonel, realizing the CIC colonel was going to come back, wisely got my horny little

665

brother and any paperwork that could compromise Operation Ost out of Dodge by load-
ing him on the next SAA Connie leaving
Frankfurt. The one that arrived this morning."

"And since he's been here," Ford said, "he
broke the Kriegsmarine code and made a
pass at your baby sister? I can't wait to meet
this guy. He sounds like Errol Flynn."

"He'll be, not counting us, the only non-
civilian on the Flying Brothel to Mendoza.
I'll see that he sits as far away from my baby
sister as possible. Which brings us back to
Mendoza. Karl Boltitz brought us the names
of the senior Nazi officers aboard the U-234.
General Martín's experts are going to see if
they can find out where they are. If they do,
we'll ask them about U-234.

"An Argentine regiment, the Tenth Mountain, was until recently commanded by an
Argentine colonel named Schmidt, who was
more of a Nazi than Adolf Hitler."

" 'Was' commanded?" Ford asked.

"He met an untimely death," Frade said.
"But while he was alive, the Tenth Mountain
helped unload German subs coming here
secretly. We're pretty sure if the U-234 did
land here, the Tenth was involved. The officers still with the regiment probably —
almost certainly — won't want to talk about
submarines. But Enrico here and the Tenth's
sergeant major are old buddies, and we can

probably learn something from him. First thing tomorrow morning, we'll fly Enrico down to the Tenth's regimental barracks in San Martín de los Andes in a Húsares de Pueyrredón Piper Cub."

Ford's eyebrows went up. "What the hell are the Húsares . . . *What* did you say?"

"The Húsares de Pueyrredón. My father's — and Enrico's — old regiment. We have sort of a special arrangement with them."

"And what makes you think, Colonel, that the regimental commander . . ."

"El Coronel Hans Klausberger," Frade furnished.

". . . who took over when the old one, Schmidt, met his untimely death — and how did that happen, by the way?"

Frade did not answer.

"Don Cletus shot him," Enrico furnished matter-of-factly.

Ford's eyebrows rose again. He didn't respond to that, but went on, paraphrasing his original question, ". . . The new regimental commander's going to let Enrico snoop around his regiment? That seems unlikely."

"We'll get General Martín to send a BIS agent with him," Frade said. "BIS officers can ask anybody they want anything."

"Okay."

Clete nodded. "Now, while everybody is boarding the Flying Brothel, why don't we go check the weather?"

[FOUR]

Second Lieutenant James D. Cronley Jr. stood, alone, at the foot of the narrow ladder leading upward toward the Lockheed Constellation with *Howell Petroleum Corporation* lettered on its fuselage. He had with him not only the two large canvas suitcases he'd brought from Kloster Grünau, but a third one, an enormous saddle leather object once the property of el Coronel Frade. This held all the clothing he'd been told to take from the wardrobe, plus the last-minute addition of some really heavy cold-weather gear.

Enrico — who had brought the third case to him — told him that after el Coronel had read about the American admiral Richard Byrd successfully exploring Antarctica, he had ordered from the United States cold-weather gear identical to that Byrd had worn, with an eye to equipping the Húsares de Pueyrredón with it. He thought that the Húsares might have to fight the Chileans, either in the Andes or at the southern tip of South America.

Enrico also had told him that Don Cletus had said, in effect, "You'd might as well put a set of that stuff for me in the bag Cronley will take. That way I won't have to worry about it."

Jimmy looked up at the airplane.

If I try to carry just one of these up that god-

damn steep and narrow stairway, I'm going to bust my ass.

Trying to carry all three would be tantamount to suicide.

He was just about to put his fingers in his mouth and see if a shrill whistle would summon assistance from within the aircraft or, for that matter, from anywhere in Argentina, when Marjorie Howell walked up to him.

"What are you doing?" she said. "Waiting for a bus?"

"Very funny."

"Can I help with the bags?"

"I don't think so. They're heavy as hell."

"And I'm a big strong girl."

She then tried to pick up one of the bags and failed.

"But not that strong," she said. "What's in there, bricks?"

Before he could respond, she asked another question: "Jimmy, where do you think Clete picked up the nutty notion that we could possibly be interested . . . *that way* . . . in each other?"

He was about to reply when he realized she was standing so close to him that he felt and smelled her breath as she spoke.

With a mind of its own, his head bent.

And he kissed her.

Just a light brushing of his lips against hers. But undeniably a kiss.

Here's where you get whacked with her

purse, you damned fool!

"I will be damned," Marjie said softly, then raised her face to his and kissed him.

"Jesus Christ, Marjie," Jimmy said, almost inaudibly.

"I've got to think about this," she said, and quickly started up the stairs.

Halfway up, she had to stop and start back down. Two men in flight crew uniforms were coming down the stairs. The stairs were so narrow that squeezing past them would have been impossible.

When everybody was on the ground, one of the men said, "We'll get the bags, sir."

They picked one up.

Marjie then looked up at Jimmy and said, "Now that I've thought it over, I like it."

When he started to lower his head to hers, she said, "Not now. Clete's standing in the airplane door."

[FIVE]

Apartment 4-C
1044 Calle Talcahuano
Buenos Aires, Argentina
0020 21 October 1945

"Very well," Ludwig Mannhoffer said into the telephone receiver. "Now get back to the airport and see what else might develop. Call me at whatever hour if something significant,

670

I repeat, significant happens. Otherwise, call me about half past eight."

He broke the connection then, put the receiver in its base, and turned to Körtig.

"Gerhard, I think we can now get some sleep. I think, based on that last report, that everything of interest to us at Aeropuerto Coronel Frade has happened."

"Specifically?"

"Well, the convoy with the Storch left several hours ago — we knew that. Kramer just reported that the three aircraft — the big Lockheed —"

"The Constellation?" Körtig asked.

"The four-engine Constellation," Mannhoffer confirmed, "and the two smaller — two-engine — Lockheeds, the red Lodestar and a South American Airways Lodestar, have all taken off, all fully loaded."

"Tell me about the red Lodestar. What's that all about?"

"There's a story going around — I don't know how true it is — that it was a gift from the American President, Roosevelt, to Oberst Frade. Anyway, now it's Oberstleutnant Frade's personal airplane."

"It must be nice to be rich enough to have your own personal airliner," Körtig said.

"Well, if we can conclude the deal about the uranium oxide, I think you could consider getting your own airliner."

"That's an interesting thought, indeed,"

Körtig said, then asked, "We don't really know where these airplanes are headed, do we?"

"We know the Lodestars are going to Mendoza. The Constellation may be headed for Brazil or the United States — its passengers include all the women and children. They may be being taken out of Argentina for their protection. But I think it, too, is headed to Mendoza. That mountaintop fortress of his is as good a place to protect people as one can find."

"Why did he build a mountaintop fortress, do you suppose?"

"Now, understand I'm getting this second- and thirdhand. Oberst Klausberger, who now commands the Tenth Mountain Regiment, told me that Oberst Schmidt, who commanded the regiment before Frade shot him —"

"Frade's father, or the one we're dealing with?"

"Ours. Klausberger told me that Schmidt told him it didn't start out to be a fortress. The original house was built by an uncle of Oberst Frade as sort of a love nest to go with the vineyard. His name was Guillermo Frade. The place and the vineyard are known as Estancia Don Guillermo. It's great wine, incidentally. The Don Guillermo Cabernet Sauvignon is marvelous! Anyway, Guillermo was apparently a hell of a gambler. He almost lost the estancia betting on the wrong horse. His father got him out of trouble, but took the estancia and the house across from the racetrack away from him and gave it to his other son — 'our' Frade's father. He had just married and so built a magnificent house on the mountain. Then she died, and he never went back. But the place was used to stage that coup d'état in 1942. They cached arms there, held secret meetings, that sort of thing. Frade was then commanding the Húsares de Pueyrredón and he put them to work fortifying the place. He went so far as to blast a runway out of the mountain that those little American planes — Cubs? — could use."

"*Piper* Cubs. They can't hold a candle to a Storch of course, but the Americans used them successfully to direct artillery fire, that sort of thing."

"That's the plane he built a runway for. Then, after Oberst Grüner sent the colonel to whatever Valhalla the Argentines use, and the son took over, he fortified and expanded the place even more. He's got all of General Gehlen's people living up there now."

"What are we going to do about Gehlen?"

"We'll cross that bridge when we're finished crossing the one we're on," Mannhoffer said. "Anyway, Klausberger told me Schmidt told him that he had reconnoitered the place with the idea of taking it and maybe killing Frade in the process. Schmidt decided it couldn't be taken without an unacceptable loss of troops."

"Then how are we going to eliminate Frade and the traitors?"

"It's forty kilometers from the airport to the estancia. Most of that is curving roads through the foothills of the Andes. We find out when one of their little convoys is carrying Frade and at least two of the others to or from the airport, and we shoot up the convoy from such point as you select in the next couple of days with Oberst Klausberger's expert assistance.

"Which means I suggest we go to bed. Your train to San Martín de los Andes leaves the Retiro station at five past eight. And you don't want to oversleep and miss it, do you?"

"No, I really don't. I have to tell you, Ludwig, I'm actually looking forward to this operation."

XII

[ONE]

During the descent and approach to the airfield, Second Lieutenant James D. Cronley Jr., Cavalry, AUS, looking through the small window high in the navigation compartment, had enjoyed a spectacular view of the snow-capped Andes Mountains bathed in the light of a nearly full moon. But now, with the Constellation on the ground, he could see almost nothing out the window.

Cronley knew that Cletus Frade had put him in the navigation compartment because that provided the greatest distance between him and Marjie, whom Clete had seated in the far rear of the passenger compartment.

Jimmy had spent most of the flight thinking of her, mostly of the touch of her lips against his but also wondering if she knew that their airplane had been dubbed the Flying Brothel by the President of the United States and

677

wondering what she thought about that.

And Jimmy wondered if Enrico Rodríguez, who sat on the navigation room's other stool, was there to keep him away from Marjie or whether that stool was the only place Clete could find for the old soldier to sit.

After the aircraft engines had shut down, the door between the cockpit and the navigation compartment opened. Clete Frade appeared in it and, using his index finger, beckoned Jimmy out of the navigation room.

In the cockpit, Jimmy saw two new men with Clete. They were crowded in the space immediately behind the pilot's and co-pilot's seats. The men wore civilian clothing. Both also had .45 ACP Model 1911-A1 pistols in shoulder holsters — making no effort to conceal them.

"Max, Siggie, this is Second Lieutenant Cronley," Frade said. "Jimmy, Major Maxwell Ashton and Master Sergeant Sigfried Stein."

The three wordlessly shook hands.

"Jimmy, take your bags," Clete then ordered, pointing to the aircraft crew door, "and put them in the back of one of the station wagons."

Jimmy went to the door and saw the narrow stairway — not much more than a ladder — and the line of vehicles beside the airplane.

At the head of the line was a Ford pickup.

It had been converted to a small stake-bed truck. It was painted a darker shade of olive brown than U.S. Army vehicles were painted, but it was obviously an Army truck. There were half a dozen soldiers sitting on rack seats in the bed, and two more leaning against the pickup's front fender. Most of them were armed with bolt-action rifles — *probably Mausers,* Jimmy decided — but there were at least three armed with Thompson submachine guns.

Immediately behind the pickup was a Mercedes-Benz sedan painted olive brown and with a soldier leaning against its fender. Behind that was a custom-bodied 1940 Lincoln Continental, then three 1941 Ford wood-sided station wagons, and finally another stake-bed pickup, this one painted dark blue. In its bed were half a dozen men armed primarily with Thompsons.

"There's no way I can carry those bags down that narrow ladder," Jimmy announced.

"Then toss them down," Frade suggested.

"If I did that, they would burst," Jimmy argued reasonably.

"Then when everybody is out of the passenger compartment, take them down the passenger stairway."

Jimmy nodded. "Much better idea, Clete."

Frade turned to Stein.

"Siggie, why don't you take a quick look and see if the 7.2 will fit in there?"

Stein went into the navigation compartment and quickly reported, "The rack installation is identical to the SAA Connies. I can get a 7.2 in here, and up and running, in a couple of hours."

"When can you start?"

"Right now, if you want."

"I want. We need to get this plane out of here and to Santiago as quickly as we can."

"Santiago?" Ashton said. "Why Chile?"

"Are you also going to put a SIGABA in here?" Stein asked.

Frade ignored Ashton's question and responded to Stein by asking, "How many do we have left?"

"There's one here — plus a spare — and another at the airport. I hope you brought it."

"Dammit! It slipped my mind," Clete said bitterly, then added sarcastically, "I must have had other things on my mind."

"Which our beloved commander, Sergeant Stein," Ashton said, "will tell us all about soon. Won't you, Colonel?"

Clete looked at him but didn't respond.

"What the hell is going on, Clete?" Ashton pursued.

"We think we found where U-234, the sub with the uranium oxide, made landfall here," Frade said.

"No fooling?" Ashton said, his surprise showing.

"Way down south," Frade said. "Near the mouth of the Strait of Magellan."

"And you're going to try to grab it?" Ashton asked. "The uranium oxide?"

"That's the idea."

"How the hell did you find U-234?" Stein asked.

"Okay, that's the last question until we get to the estancia," Frade said. "Von Dattenberg had the landfall coordinates all the time in his safe on U-405. He didn't know he had them, and they were of course in the Kriegsmarine code. Boltitz learned about that in Germany."

"And Karl got his hands on the Kriegsmarine code?" Ashton asked.

Frade looked at Cronley.

"No," Frade said.

"Then Karl must have broken it."

"No," Frade said. "Karl didn't have a clue how to break the code."

"Then what?"

Frade pointed at Cronley and, smiling, said, "Sometimes second lieutenants aren't as dumb as legend has it. As hard as it is to believe, Jimmy broke it. And now — I meant it about that being the last question until we get to the estancia and I can bring everybody up to speed at once — let's get everybody off the plane and up to Casa Montagna."

If I didn't know better, Cronley thought, *I*

might think Clete just said something nice to me.

And with a smile.

[Two]

Estancia Don Guillermo
Km 40.4, Provincial Route 60
Mendoza Province, Argentina
0510 21 October 1945

Jimmy carefully watched as the station wagon in which he, three armed men, and his luggage had ridden from the airport came to a stop in front of a large house on the mountaintop. Floodlights lit the immediate area. Jimmy saw one of the other station wagons in their caravan now pulling away and several muscular servants, of both genders, carrying luggage into the house.

The luggage, Jimmy decided, belonged to the women, the babies, and Cletus Marcus Howell.

When two of the armed men in the station wagon opened the rear door and put Jimmy's suitcases on the ground, he thought he would be next. Somebody would come out of the house, take care of the luggage, and show him where breakfast was going to be served.

That didn't happen.

The men got back in the station wagon and drove off. And the floodlights that had illuminated the unloading point went out.

Jimmy was left with his three suitcases in the moonlit dark.

He would have tried to carry them into the house himself, but he didn't feel up to that, and he didn't know where to carry them to.

He sat down on the saddle leather case holding his new wardrobe and the Admiral Byrd Antarctic clothing and waited to see what would happen next. He yawned.

Five minutes later, Cletus Frade appeared.

"What the hell are you doing out here?" he demanded. "I've been looking all over for you."

"Since I can't carry these goddamned suitcases by myself, I've been thinking of putting on an Admiral Byrd suit and catching some shut-eye."

Frade ignored that.

"We have to talk, Jimmy."

"About what?"

"In Buenos Aires, just before we took off, Martha jumped all over me for what I thought about you and the Squirt. She said my imagination is wildly out of control."

"You don't say?"

"And, now that I've thought it over, she's right."

"You don't say?"

"So I apologize."

"Not necessary."

"What do you mean by that?"

683

"You were right all along, Clete. The truth of the matter is that the Squirt and I are madly in love. We're even thinking of eloping."

Frade laughed.

"That's absurd! Fuck you, Jimmy. I'm trying to make amends."

"Is that why you left me out here in the dark?"

"That just happened. It wasn't on purpose."

"You don't say?"

"Goddammit! Stop saying 'You don't say.' "

"Whatever you say, Colonel."

"I'll tell you what's going to happen now," Frade said. "I'm going to go in the house and get somebody to deal with your luggage. The canvas cases might as well go to the BOQ, where we'll work on the dossiers. My father's case goes to your room in the house. As soon as the people come out for the luggage, you go into the house. Third door on the left off the foyer is the dining room. Get yourself some breakfast."

"Okay."

"And I really would be grateful, Jimmy, if you accepted my apology."

"Accepted."

"Thank you."

"You're welcome."

Frade went back into the house.

Sixty seconds later, three sturdy women came out. They picked up the luggage with no apparent effort and started off with it.

Jimmy walked to the house.

Just inside, Marjie was waiting for him in the dark foyer.

"Hi," she said, a little shyly, and kissed him, a little shyly.

"We're going to have to work on that," Jimmy said. "I'm sure we'll get better with a little practice."

She shook her head and said, "What did Clete want?"

"Your mother made him apologize for the evil thoughts he had about us."

"Really? He actually apologized? What did you say?"

"I told him no apology was necessary. He was right. You and I are madly in love and thinking of eloping."

"You didn't!"

"I did. But I had the feeling he didn't believe me."

"Oh, Jimmy," she said, laughing. "You'd better pray he didn't!"

Then she kissed him again, this time not quite as shyly as before.

[THREE]

When Clete led Cletus Marcus Howell, Captain Alfredo Garcia, Second Lieutenant James D. Cronley Jr., Doña Dorotea Mallín de Frade, and Enrico Rodríguez into the room, four men were already seated at the long table reserved for the senior "Good Gehlen" former officers. One was Major Maxwell Ashton III. The other three were Germans. All of them stood.

"Sorry to get everybody up so early," Frade said, "but we have a hell of a lot to do, and the sooner we get started, the better. So, first things first —"

"Excuse me," Cletus Marcus Howell said. "I don't believe I know these gentlemen."

"Sorry," Clete said. "Gentlemen, this is my grandfather, Cletus Marcus Howell, who is with us not in that role but as the representative of President Truman. And this is Lieutenant Cronley, who is the officer courier who brought us all that from Kloster Grünau."

Frade then pointed to the stacks of documents already taken from the canvas suitcases and spread out on the table.

686

He went on: "And, Grandfather, these are the senior officers of the operation here."

He pointed to the two men seated at the side of the table.

"That's Alois Strübel and Wilhelm Frogger."

Then he pointed to the tall, hawk-featured man in his mid-thirties standing at the head of the table.

"And that is the senior man of Operation Ost, Otto Niedermeyer."

Lieutenant Colonel Cletus Frade had known former Oberstleutnant Wilhelm Frogger the longest — having met him after first having Frogger's parents forced upon him.

In July of 1943, Milton Leibermann, the "legal attaché" — the euphemism for FBI agent — of the U.S. embassy, who had been forbidden by FBI Director J. Edgar Hoover to have any contact with OSS agents in Argentina, nevertheless called Frade. He and Frade — who regarded as asinine the OSS's order not to have any contact with FBI agents in Argentina — had started sharing intelligence with one another almost from the day they'd met. And they had become friends.

Leibermann told Frade that he had a Wilhelm Frogger and wife, Else, cached in his apartment. Frogger, the commercial attaché of the German embassy, had been ordered home to Germany. Fearing for a number of reasons that meant he was headed for a *konzentrationslager* and/or a painful death, Frogger fled with his wife to Leibermann's apartment.

Leibermann told Frade he had to get the Froggers to safety. Frade moved them to a small house on an estancia he owned in Tandil, turning them over to Sergeant Siggie Stein for interrogation.

Almost as soon as they got to Tandil, Frau Frogger, a dedicated Nazi, changed her mind. She announced that she was going to return to the embassy and place herself under the orders of the Führer. Frade thought she was crazy.

And then an attempt to either get the Froggers back or kill them was mounted by a detachment of SS troopers and a company of the Tenth Mountain Regiment. Warned of the operation by the regiment's sergeant major — an old comrade of Enrico Rodríguez — Frade's Private Army was ready for them.

After removing the Froggers from their hideout, and watching the Tenth Mountain reduce the house to rubble with heavy machine-gun fire and then drive away, the ex–Húsares de Pueyrredón eliminated the SS troops who had stayed behind to make sure that the Froggers were dead. They buried the bodies in unmarked graves on the Pampas.

The question then had become what to do with the Froggers.

And that problem was greatly compounded by Frau Frogger, now manifesting symptoms of total insanity.

Enrico Rodríguez suggested that she be taken to "the vineyard in Mendoza." Until that moment, Clete had been only vaguely aware that among the properties he had inherited from his father was the vineyard called Estancia Don Guillermo.

When Clete asked the old soldier what he was talking about, Enrico told him that when Clete's aunt lost her mind after her son's death in Stalingrad, she had been taken to the vineyard and placed in the care of the Little Sisters of Saint Pilar. Part of the house had been converted to sort of a one-bed psychiatric hospital — and that seemed ideal for the crazy Nazi woman.

When Clete asked Enrico why he had never heard any of this, the old soldier replied, "Because you never asked, Don Cletus."

The next step in the Frogger saga occurred when President Franklin Roosevelt became annoyed with Juan Trippe, the president of Pan American–Grace (Panagra) Airways, for his close relationship with aviator Charles A. Lindbergh. A national hero, Medal of Honor recipient "Lucky Lindy" was also a vocal critic of the President and his policies. FDR decided to punish Trippe by giving him a little competition. He authorized the sale of twenty-four Lockheed Lodestar twin-engine transports — ones the Air Corps had no need for — to a new airline, South American Airways, starting up in Argentina.

The managing director of the new airline, Señor Cletus Frade, flew to Los Angeles to take delivery of the first of the Lodestars at the Lockheed plant. There, Colonel A. F. Graham, deputy OSS director for the Western Hemisphere, told Frade that the reason the OSS was starting an airline in Argentina was because FDR ordered it, the subject not open for debate.

When Clete reported on Wilhelm Frogger and his problems therewith — Frade said that he didn't know how far he could trust the Kraut, and that the wife was mad as a March hare — the name "Frogger" rang a bell with Graham.

Two days later, a Lockheed Constellation piloted by Howard Hughes left California with Frade and Graham aboard. Ostensibly, Hughes thought a familiarization flight with SAA's managing director might result in future sales of the brand-new advanced aircraft. Hughes even checked out Frade on the Constellation's peculiarities and allowed him to make half a dozen touch-and-go landings. But their secret destination had been the Senior German Officer Prisoner of War Detention Facility at Camp Clinton, Mississippi.

Camp Clinton held Oberstleutnant Wilhelm Frogger, the sole surviving son of Wilhelm and Else Frogger. He had been captured while serving with the Afrikakorps. More important, before he had been captured he had served as the contact between Field Marshall Erwin Rommel and Colonel Count Claus von Stauffenberg.

Von Stauffenberg was planning to kill Adolf Hitler.

It was shortly thereafter announced that Oberstleutnant Frogger had escaped from Camp Clinton. He was believed to be trying to get to Mexico, from where he would return to Germany. FBI Director Hoover promised President Roosevelt that the full resources of the FBI would be called into motion to recapture the escaped Nazi.

By the time the last of the more than two hundred FBI agents had made it to the Mexican border to prevent Frogger's escape, he was in Argentina, flown there by Frade in one of the Lockheed Lodestars painted in the South American Airways color scheme.

The first time that Frade had ever seen Niedermeyer and Strübel was some time later, as they boarded one of SAA's Constellations in Frankfurt. Traveling on Vatican passports, the Germans had been wearing the brown robes and the sandals of Franciscan monks.

Frau Niedermeyer and Frau Strübel also had been on that flight, and wearing the white robes of the Order of the Little Sisters of the Poor. And the three Niedermeyer children carried Vatican passports identifying them as orphans on their way to Argentina to be placed in the care of distant relatives.

Frade had been told Obersturmbannführer Alois Strübel had been sent by General Gehlen to determine whether the Americans would — or could — make good on their promise to keep the officers of the Gehlen Organization and their families out of the hands of the Russians. Hauptscharführer (Sergeant Major) Niedermeyer had been sent along to help.

That had been a relatively long time ago — just over two years — and neither Strübel nor Niedermeyer any longer dressed like Franciscan friars or, for that matter, much like Germans. Today, Strübel and Frogger were both wearing well-tailored business suits, appropriate to people engaged in the wine trade, their new cover. And Niedermeyer was more spectacularly dressed. He wore a tweed sport coat with leather elbow patches much like the one that Jimmy Cronley had inherited from Clete Frade's father. Niedermeyer also had on riding breeches, highly polished riding boots, and a pale yellow silk shirt, and knotted around his neck was a foulard. He could easily pass for a successful *estanciero,* and that, in fact, was what he had become.

In their first serious meeting — after Niedermeyer had confessed to being General Gehlen's Number Three and a lieutenant colonel, and had sent word to Gehlen that it would be safe to start sending Abwehr Ost officers, non-coms, and their families into the care of the Americans — the question came up of how to pay for establishing new homes and lives for what eventually would be about a hundred "Good Gehlen" families and one-quarter that many "Nazi Gehlen" families.

It had already been agreed between General Gehlen and Allen W. Dulles that once the Germans got to Argentina, the Americans — in other words, Frade — would continue to pay their Wehrmacht/SS salaries, including family allowances. They would be paid what their American counterparts would be paid — except, Dulles said, not paid extra, as Americans were, for service outside their home country.

Dulles arranged for the OSS to send a million dollars in cash to Clete via the American embassy for this purpose, and promised to send more, as needed. Clete knew the million dollars wouldn't last long and he didn't think that additional money would be sent. Dulles knew that Clete had inherited his father's enormous wealth, and knew that Frade would continue to pay the Gehlens should it be decided that additional funds could not be sent because of the likelihood the wrong people would find out about it and ask questions that couldn't be answered about why millions of dollars were being sent to Argentina.

Dulles expecting Frade to support the operation out of his own pocket wasn't fair to Frade, of course. But it reminded Frade that someone had once observed, "All's fair in love and war."

Yet Frade had managed to come up with the money, more or less painlessly.

In April 1943, Major Hans-Peter von Wachtstein, then the assistant military attaché for air at the German embassy, had tipped off Clete to the German plan to smuggle ashore a shipment of valuables — not further described — and approximately forty members of the SS from an ostensibly neutral Spanish merchant steamer.

The illicit landing on the shore of Samborombón Bay would be under the supervision of Oberst Grüner, the military attaché, his deputy, Standartenführer Goltz, and Major von Wachtstein.

Frade had been delighted. Once he had smoking-gun photographs of Grüner, Goltz, and von Wachtstein smuggling, he would deliver them to the U.S. ambassador, who would immediately hand them to the Argentine foreign minister as he registered a formal complaint with the Argentine foreign ministry.

Although the Argentine government tilted heavily toward the Third Reich, they would not be able to ignore this outrageous breach of their sovereignty and neutrality. The Germans would be embarrassed, and the Spaniards could no longer righteously proclaim their own neutrality.

Maxwell Ashton III, then a captain, was dispatched to the beach with two Leica cameras. Clete sent Enrico with him to serve as scout and bodyguard.

On the beach, as Ashton snapped away, Oberst Grüner's forehead came to be in the crosshairs of the Zeiss 4× telescopic sight mounted on what had been el Coronel Frade's favorite 7mm Mauser hunting rifle. Enrico then blew Grüner's brains out, turned the rifle on Standartenführer Goltz and blew his brains out, and then emptied the magazine on the SS men on the beach, being careful not to shoot Major von Wachtstein.

Clete understood why Enrico had done what he had — Enrico knew Grüner had hired the assassins who had murdered Clete's father and Enrico's sister — but he was nonetheless furious with the old soldier for ruining his planned diplomatic triumph.

The old soldier was unrepentant.

He waited until Clete had stopped screaming at him, then gave him a huge, heavy leather box.

"I brought this from the beach, Don Cletus.

I thought you should have it."

Clete was so furious that he didn't even look in the box for three days.

When he finally opened it, it took him twenty minutes to count the $32,500,000 in brand-new U.S. one-hundred-dollar bills it contained. They were still in the packing in which they had come from the Federal Reserve Bank in New York.

Frade had a pretty good idea whose cash it was. It was money intended for someone very high in the Nazi hierarchy — perhaps Himmler or Goering, someone at that level — to buy refuge in Argentina once the Thousand-Year Reich came tumbling down around them.

He quickly realized that while it might have been Himmler's or Goering's money, that was no longer true. It was now his.

But what to do with it?

He knew if he told Allen Dulles, then the OSS, always short of money, would send an airplane to take it away.

Clete put the money in his father's safe and allowed it to just slip his mind to mention it to Dulles.

When the million dollars Dulles had sent him to fund OPERATION OST ran out — even more quickly than Clete thought it would; he had spent almost $500,000 buying a small hotel in Rosario to discreetly house the arriving Gehlens until other arrangements could be made for them — he had to dip into the $32.5 million.

The next step had been to make loans from it so the Gehlens could buy houses or apartments and go into businesses of one kind or another. Niedermeyer had talked him out of just making grants; if the Gehlens knew they would have to repay the loans, he said, they would have a real interest in making their new businesses successful.

He himself, Niedermeyer said, would be interested in buying a farm on which he could raise cattle and horses "even before this is all over."

Clete was not as naïve as he suspected Niedermeyer and the other Gehlens thought he was. He wondered, for example, what he would do if any of them, including Niedermeyer, didn't repay the money they were borrowing. It was certainly a possibility that Niedermeyer recognized a cash cow when he saw one.

And he wondered why Niedermeyer had asked him for a pistol. Who did he think he was going to have to shoot in Mendoza? But he gave him the benefit of the doubt and provided a Ballester-Molina .45 ACP pistol from the cache of arms in the basement of Casa Montagna.

Within a week, quite by accident, Niedermeyer literally bumped into SS-Brigadeführer Ritter Manfred von Deitzberg in the men's room of the Edelweiss Hotel in San Carlos de Bariloche. Von Deitzberg was first deputy adjutant to Reichsführer-SS Heinrich Himmler.

Both had been in San Carlos de Bariloche for the same purpose, to acquire real estate to house Germans for whom the Fatherland was about to be no longer hospitable. Von Deitzberg had come secretly by submarine to Argentina to implement OPERATION PHOENIX, which would see the senior Nazi leadership find sanctuary in Argentina, and start the process by which National Socialism would rise, phoenix-like, from the ashes of the Thousand-Year Reich.

The SS had no idea of the deal struck between General Gehlen and Allen W. Dulles, and if von Deitzberg learned of it, everyone connected with Abwehr Ost still in Germany and Russia — and most of its personnel were still there in the spring of 1943 — would be arrested, tortured, and executed.

Niedermeyer the next day told Clete of the encounter, and that he had taken the only action appropriate to the situation: He had used the Ballester-Molina .45 to eliminate SS-Brigadeführer von Deitzberg. He said he was sure he was "gone" as he had shot him twice in the face. And, no, he added, the police were not looking for him.

"Like you, Colonel," Niedermeyer had said, "I'm a professional."

After that, Clete had felt much safer in trusting Niedermeyer and had turned over to him just about all of the responsibility for dealing with both the Good Gehlens and the Nazi Gehlens. And when Niedermeyer asked to borrow three-quarters of a million dollars to purchase the estancia he had seen near San Carlos de Bariloche, Clete handed him packages of crisp new one-hundred-dollar bills two days later.

Clete had also dipped into "the money in the safe" for other purposes. For example, he had built the building everyone called The BOQ with it, and used it to fortify the mountaintop, and paid and equipped his private army of ex–Húsares de Pueyrredón. They, after all, were working for the OSS, not for Estancia San Pedro y San Pablo.

"Now that everyone knows everybody else," Frade said, "with your kind permission I will continue. Was all that protection at the airport and that convoy here necessary? All those Thompsons scared the hell out of the women."

"This woman was curious, my darling," Dorotea said, "not on the edge of hysteria."

"Okay. Then it scared hell out of me," Clete said. "Was it necessary?"

"We've been under increased surveillance, Clete . . ." Major Ashton began.

"By whom?"

"Well, the only way we can learn that is by asking them," Niedermeyer said. "And if we do that, they'll know we know they're snooping. We thought we'd ask you first before we grab — or dispose of — one or more of them."

"We suspect, of course," Frogger said, "that it's people from the Tenth Mountain. And, letting my imagination run wild, I thought there was at least a possibility that whoever it is might be thinking of attacking our people while they're on the road between here and the airport."

"I can't imagine who they might want to do that to," Clete said sarcastically. He turned to Captain Garcia. "Alfredo, how angry do you think General Martín would be if he heard I told these people you're actually Teniente Coronel Garcia and the Number Three at BIS?"

"Livid," Garcia said, shaking his head and smiling.

"Then I guess I'd better not tell them, huh? We know none of them can keep a secret. So tell me, *Captain* Garcia, what you would do about these people who are spying on us with an eye to ambushing us?"

"First, I would find out who they are," Garcia said.

"And how would you do that?"

"I'd arrange for the Gendarmería Nacional to make a random patrol where they were last seen. The *gendarmería* can question the Ejército — the Policía Federal can't."

"And you have acquaintances in the *gendarmerie*, right?"

"Don Cletus, I'd rather wait until the general gets here," Garcia said.

"Martín is coming here?" Niedermeyer asked, surprised. "I'd have thought he'd be in the hospital."

"There's an SAA Lodestar with Martín and a bunch of his BIS people en route here now," Frade said. "He had some things to take care of in Buenos Aires. And von Wachtstein is bringing with him Boltitz, von Dattenberg —"

"Willi von Dattenberg?" Niedermeyer said.

Frade nodded, and went on: "And as many of my people who can fit in my Lodestar. One or both of them should be landing within the next thirty minutes or so. So we can wait, Alfredo, until he gets here before we call the gendarmes."

"The gendarmes are going to be far more receptive to a request from General Martín than they would be to one from Captain Garcia," Garcia said.

"Understood," Frade said.

"Whatever is going on seems very interesting," Niedermeyer said. "Starting with why is von Dattenberg coming here? I would have thought he'd be confined somewhere, or at the very least have been interned with the

Graf Spee survivors at Villa General Belgrano."

"He was in Villa General Belgrano," Frade said, stopped, and after a moment went on: "You're not going to like this answer, Otto."

"Well, that would certainly be a first for us, wouldn't it, Cletus?" Niedermeyer replied, lightly sarcastic.

"And it will probably piss off Frogger, Strübel, von Wachtstein, Boltitz, and my wife, as well."

"I can't believe you would do that," Niedermeyer said drily.

"I asked General Martín to arrange for von Dattenberg to escape from Villa General Belgrano and he did so."

Niedermeyer's eyebrows rose. "Why? I mean why did you want him released? Or permitted to escape?"

"Which was it?" Frogger said.

Frade grunted. "As that ancient Chinaman said, 'Keep your friends close, and your enemies closer.' I got von Dattenberg out of Villa General Belgrano and am bringing him here because I don't trust the sonofabitch. I want to keep an eye on him."

"Sun Tzu?" Niedermeyer asked. "That Chinaman?"

"That's the guy. Either him or Confucius."

"Correct me if I'm wrong, but didn't Sun Tzu also say, 'Even though you are competent, appear to be incompetent. Though effective, appear to be ineffective'?"

"I think it was that other famous Chinese philosopher, One Hung Low, who said what you just said."

Cronley laughed.

After a moment, Martín and Ashton shook their heads and chuckled, and Dorotea said, "My God, Cletus!"

"I was simply going to observe," Niedermeyer said, smiling, "that most of us — all of us, come to think about it — have learned that is your very successful modus operandi."

"Why don't you trust Willi?" Dorotea challenged.

"I think he still feels bound by that damn oath of personal loyalty he took to Hitler," Clete said. "When I first confronted him at Estancia San Pedro y San Pablo, he started talking only after he realized I wasn't kidding when I told him his choice was either talk or get shot."

"That's all?"

"He started to talk, and I started to think he'd seen the light. But then that rendezvous point business came up. I'm having a hard time believing he didn't know all along that he had it in his safe. It's bullshit. He was captain — and he knew what he had in his safe."

"Well, I think you're wrong," Dorotea said.

"Sweetheart, just because he and Hansel's sister-in-law are holding hands and staring soulfully into each other's eyes doesn't make him a good guy."

Cronley looked at Clete.

No, Jimmy thought, *but it does make him probably Number Three Hundred and Seven on the list of Elsa the Great's Lengthy List of Lovers.*

And then Jimmy had a flood of disquieting thoughts:

Jesus, what if Marjie knew there was more between Elsa and me than me — what did she say? — "looking at her like a lovesick calf"?

Would she be angry, pissed, disgusted, jealous — what?

Do I care?

And what the hell am I doing with the Squirt?

So far nothing. At least nothing serious.

And that's where it stops.

Marjie is too nice a girl to get involved with someone who fucked his brains out with someone like Elsa.

Not to mention doing the same thing with that Hungarian redhead in that whorehouse Sergeant Freddy Hessinger got us into in Munich.

And what did Tiny Dunwiddie have to say about that? That I obviously have a natural talent for that sort of recreation. . . .

You really ought to be ashamed of yourself, you oversexed whoremonger.

The Squirt is like a sister.

Even Mom was always saying the Squirt was the daughter she never had.

And — for Christ's sake! — you used to go to Sunday school with her!

Well, it stops right here!

Cronley heard Niedermeyer as he said, "Clete, none of us" — he gestured around the table at Strübel, Frogger, and Ashton — "know what you're talking about. What rendezvous points?"

Clete pointed to Jimmy.

"He found the point where we think U-234 made landfall. That's what all this is about."

"And Willi helped him find it," Dorotea said. "You know that."

"Willi helped only when he realized Jimmy didn't need any help," Clete countered.

"U-234 made it to Argentina?" Strübel asked, visibly surprised.

Frade nodded. He began: "This is where we are. . . ."

Frade was halfway through the briefing when the telephone rang. Dorotea answered it and reported that both aircraft had landed in Mendoza, and that all aboard were now headed for Casa Montagna.

[FOUR]

When General de Brigada Martín lurched into the room on his crutches, Frade saw that it would not be necessary to ask his permission to seek the assistance of the Gendarmería Nacional. He had with him Inspector General Santiago Nervo, who commanded the Gendarmería Nacional, and his deputy, Subinspector General Pedro Nolasco.

And von Wachtstein and Boltitz and von Dattenberg.

Shit! I should have thought Hansel would bring von Dattenberg in here.

I don't want him to learn any more about what's going on than I have to.

But if I throw him out, he'll know it's because I don't trust him.

"I know who you are, you ugly gringo!" General Nervo cried happily as he went to Frade. "I saw your picture on the front page of *La Nacíon*. You were standing on the balcony of the Casa Rosada beside our beloved Coronel Juan Domingo Perón as he waved at the idiots."

He picked Frade off his feet in a bear hug.

706

"Have you been a good boy, Cletus, or are you fomenting revolution again?"

"What I want to know, Santiago, is why you shot Bernardo," Frade said.

"I had no choice. He was saying unkind things about dear Juan Domingo," Nervo said, as he finally let Frade loose. "I can only hope he's learned his lesson."

Frade then said: "Grandfather, this is Inspector General Santiago Nervo, of the Gendarmería Nacional. Santiago, Cletus Marcus Howell and Subteniente Cronley."

"Why do I think you and my grandson, General, are a dangerous combination?" the old man asked.

"Perhaps Father Welner told you?" Nervo asked.

"Where is the wily Jesuit, by the way?" Frade said.

"He'll be on the afternoon flight," Martín said.

"Okay," Nervo said, "enough of the social niceties. What's going on here?"

"Well, to begin —" Frade began.

"No, Cletus," Nervo interrupted. "In my classroom — I thought you knew this — you have to raise your hand and get my permission to speak."

"Sorry," Frade said, shaking his head and chuckling.

Nervo pointed to Cronley.

"If you raise your hand, Subteniente," he

said, "then I will call on you."

"I'll pass, thank you just the same," Jimmy said.

"According to the cripple-on-crutches sitting there, Subteniente," Nervo said, "you started all this. You're the one responsible for getting him all excited. So you tell Pedro and me what's going on. Either that, or go stand in the corner."

Cronley smiled, then shrugged. "Okay. We think we have found where U-234, the sub with the uranium oxide, made landfall . . ."

"And that's about it?" Nervo asked, when Cronley had finished.

"Except that Señor Niedermeyer says he thinks we're being surveilled, probably by the Tenth Mountain Regiment or Division, or whatever it is."

"I hadn't heard that," Nervo said. "We'll get to that in a minute. First, I'd like to say that General Martín has finally said something I now can agree with."

"And what would that be?" Martín challenged.

"That Subteniente Cronley is sort of a junior version of Teniente Coronel Frade. In other words, he's a lot smarter than he looks. I thought that was a pretty good summation. So, what I am going to do now is in no way a reflection on him."

"What are you going to do now?" the old

man asked.

"Be the devil's advocate," Nervo said. "When I say something negative, feel free to refute me. Okay? Remember to raise your hand and wait to be recognized.

"One. We *think* we know where this submarine U-234 may have landed. But we have no proof."

Martín raised his hand.

Cronley was surprised. *I thought Nervo was just being a smart-ass with that childish hand-raising business.*

Nervo nodded at Martín, who said, "When Boltitz brought us the names of the two senior Nazis known to be aboard U-234 — SS-Oberführer Horst Lang and SS-Brigadeführer Gerhard Körtig — I was familiar with the names. I knew the Interior Ministry had issued, at the request of former Teniente Coronel Rudy Nulder, *libretas de enrolamiento* to both of them, oddly enough in their own names. And I knew they were both living in Rosario, in apartments arranged for them by the Bishop of Rosario, Salvador Lombardi.

"So we know, Santiago, that U-234 did make landfall here. We don't know that took place where Subteniente Cronley believes it did. But let me go on with this a moment, I believe it's cogent.

"We know that Perón and Lombardi are

709

close. But we don't know if Perón knows these two came off U-234, or whether he thinks they came here by other means. What I'm saying is that Nulder may have arranged for the *libretas* as a routine courtesy to Lombardi and doesn't know of the U-234 connection. That offers the possibility that Perón doesn't know about U-234. The *possibility* that he doesn't.

"Yesterday, both Lang and Körtig came to Buenos Aires to an apartment at 1044 Calle Talcahuan, near the Colón Opera House. The apartment . . ."

Frogger, recognizing the address, blurted, "My parents' apartment?"

Martín nodded and went on: ". . . was owned by the German embassy. Señor Frogger and his wife were housed there. After they defected, the embassy retained ownership of course until the end of the war. Then something very interesting happened. Several weeks before the German surrender, the first secretary of the German embassy, Anton von Gradny-Sawz, offered to defect to the BIS. I wondered what he was up to and accepted the defection. I got nothing of value from him before the surrender occurred, but then I learned what he was up to.

"It seems — for reasons I admit I don't understand — that the Allies are not treating Ostmark, the name the Germans gave to Austria after it was annexed, as still part of

Germany. They have decided that Austria was liberated, not conquered, and is again a sovereign nation."

"I'll be goddamned," Frade said softly. "Some of the worst Nazis were Austrians. Allen Dulles told me that seventy to eighty percent of SS officers were Austrians."

"That's a little high, Cletus," Alois Strübel said. "More than half, but not seventy to eighty percent."

"I will defer to your greater knowledge of the subject, Herr SS-Obersturmbannführer," Frade said, somewhat sarcastically.

Strübel replied with an American hand gesture he had learned from Frade. He held his balled fist, center finger extended, out to him.

"If I may continue?" Martín asked impatiently.

"Sorry," Strübel and Frade said over one another.

"At the moment, there are two occupation authorities," Martín went on. "One for Germany and, wholly separate from that, one for Austria. Gradny-Sawz got in touch with the British ambassador here, whom he knew. He told the ambassador that he had defected to the Argentines before the war ended and that he now would like to make himself again of service to the country of his birth, Austria.

"The British ambassador, who is not too bright, called me to see if Anton had in fact defected. When I told him he had, he contacted the British element of the Allied Occupational Authority in Vienna and told them he had found just the man to handle Austrian diplomatic affairs in Argentina until diplomats could be sent from Vienna.

"Then the ambassador went to the Foreign Ministry and asked them to release the apartment on Calle Talcahuano to Gradny-Sawz, who needed a place to live now that he was going to be handling Austrian affairs. They agreed.

"When I heard about this, I was curious, because I knew Gradny-Sawz was living in an apartment he owned in Belgrano. By then it was too late to install surveillance devices in the apartment on Talcahuano, but I kept an eye on it.

"The day after the apartment was turned over to Gradny-Sawz, a man we'd been keeping an eye on, one of the Nazis who'd come here on one of the first submarines, whom I knew to be SS-Sturmführer Erich Raschner, started to use the apartment to meet other people.

"Rudy Nulder had arranged a *libreta* for him in the name of Erich Richter. After seeing who went to the apartment to meet Richter, in particular Señor José Moreno of Banco Suisse Creditanstalt S.A., I started to believe that it was all connected with what these people called the 'Special Fund.'

"I think everybody here knows this is the money they extorted from both our Jews and North American Jews to ransom their relatives out of the concentration camps in Germany. That operation differs from Operation Phoenix in that the beneficiaries of the latter are all senior SS officers. It has been in some disarray since SS-Brigadeführer Ritter Manfred von Deitzberg — after taking control of all its assets in Uruguay — met his untimely death in the men's room of the Edelweiss Hotel in San Carlos de Bariloche."

Cronley saw the look exchanged between Niedermeyer and Frade and wondered what it meant.

"I had to adjust my thinking, however," Martín went on, "when another senior SS officer, Brigadeführer Ludwig Hoffmann . . ."

"Whom I brought here," von Dattenberg offered.

Martín nodded and went on: ". . . for whom Rudy Nulder had arranged a *libreta* identifying him as Ludwig Mannhoffer, first showed up at the apartment. He was joined there yesterday by SS-Brigadeführer Gerhard Körtig and SS-Oberführer Horst Lang.

"Last night, Lang drove to Villa General Belgrano, from which at three A.M., in a hastily assembled convoy, he set out with Kapitän Schneider and members of the crew of U-234 for an unknown destination, which is more than likely either Estancia Condor or perhaps even the U-234 itself.

"Körtig has a reservation for a drawing room on the *Bariloche Special,* which is scheduled to depart the Retiro Station at six-fifty this morning." He looked at his watch. "In other words, about fifteen minutes ago. He has a ticket all the way to San Carlos de Bariloche, but the train stops at San Martín de los Andes at five twenty-five before it gets to San Carlos.

"I confess I don't know the significance of all this — the significance of *any* of this — as Cletus says, 'Unless there's an application for it, intelligence is useless' — but for the moment it's all I have and I thought it might be useful and that I should put it on the table."

For a moment, there was silence.

Doña Dorotea broke it.

"My God, Bernardo," she said in awe. "It's *all* you have?"

Then Niedermeyer said, "*Might* be useful? Amazing. Absolutely amazing!"

Then he began to applaud loudly and was quickly joined by the others.

"Bernardo, you've really been earning your pay, haven't you?" Nervo said.

Martín flushed.

"That's very kind," he said. "But your applause should be directed to my staff, especially to Captain Garcia here. He and his men spent the long nights surveilling these people, not me."

"Professed modesty will not work for you, Bernardo," Frade said. "People of genius, such as you and me, simply cannot hide it."

"Throw your crutch at him, Bernardo," Dorotea said.

"Well, now that we know, thanks to Bernardo," Nervo said, "just about everything about everything — where do we go from here?"

"To what we don't know," Frade said. "Who's surveilling us?"

"Pedro," Nervo ordered, "find out."

Nolasco nodded, stood, mimed using a telephone, and was directed to one on a sideboard.

"Are we sure there's not a tap on that line?" Frade asked.

"I will use it knowing that's a real possibility, Don Cletus."

"No offense, Pedro."

"None taken, Don Cletus. General, when I have these people, should I bring them here?"

"No. Take them to the gendarmerie barracks in Mendoza. Charge them with unlawful trespass. Have one of the people we brought with us — one of the smarter ones — conduct the interrogation. And get a description of the Nazi bastard on the train, and get it to both the station in San Martín and the station in Bariloche before the train gets there. I want to keep an eye on him."

"I can do better than a description, General," Niedermeyer said. "Cronley brought our dossier on him from Germany. With photos. Give me an hour and I can have prints made."

"That would be helpful," Nervo said. "May I ask a question?"

"Certainly."

"Abwehr Ost maintained dossiers on people like this?"

"Abwehr Ost did not. General Gehlen did. Actually, his Number Two, Coronel Mannberg, and I did. General Gehlen said it was our duty to protect Germany from all of its enemies."

"Interesting," Nervo said, and then went on: "Now that we have a little more probably irrelevant intelligence from Bernardo, let me go back to being the devil's advocate. I think we're all agreed that U-234 did make a landing here. Now what's most important about that?"

"The uranium oxide," Frade said.

"And what's the worst-case scenario involving the uranium oxide?"

"That the Russians get their hands on it," Frade answered.

"And how would that happen?"

"The Russian NKVD guy from Mexico . . ." Frade began.

"Egorov," Cronley furnished. "Pavel Egorov."

". . . comes here with a suitcase full of

money and buys it from whoever has it. 'Whoever' just might include Juan Domingo Perón."

"Egorov's here," Martín announced, "legally accredited to the Argentine Republic as the new chief of the Soviet Trade Mission, replacing Oleg Fedoseev, who is staying on for an indefinite period until Egorov has his feet on the ground. But no suitcase full of money."

"Why not?" Frade said.

"Simple answer, you can't get fifty million dollars or a hundred million dollars or — and I really heard this figure — one hundred fifty million dollars in a suitcase."

"More sophisticated answer?" Frade asked.

"The sale, or the transfer, whatever you want to call it, is not going to take place in Argentina," Martín said. "Think about it, Cletus. There's supposed to be five hundred sixty kilos of the uranium — that's a little over half a ton. Even if Egorov had it in the Trade Mission right now, what would he do with it? How would he get it out of Argentina? And let's say Mannhoffer — or Körtig or Lang — either separately or together, had the hundred or the hundred fifty million dollars Egorov paid them. What would they do with it? Put it under the mattress? They know we'd be looking for signs of sudden wealth. If a transfer takes place, neither the ore nor the cash will be actually involved here.

"The most credible scenario is that the ore will be moved from wherever it is now to a Russian ship on the high seas, and the money — which will never have been in Argentina at all — will be transferred, probably through the Banco Suisse Creditanstalt, to an account or accounts in South Africa or Switzerland."

"Then how would the uranium oxide get from where it is now to rendezvous with a Soviet ship on the high seas?"

"On U-234," Martín said. "I don't think U-234 has been scuttled."

Frade nodded thoughtfully. "Don't let this go to your head, Bernardo, but that's the most credible scenario I've heard so far."

"I thought so," Martín said, "when I heard it from von Dattenberg on the way here this morning."

Damn it!

I give a five-minute speech on why I don't trust that sonofabitch, then Martín marches him in here, offers a scenario I declare is the best one I've heard, then says he got it from von Dattenberg.

"From von Dattenberg?" Frade asked softly.

"Cletus," von Dattenberg said, "earlier on you told me to put myself in Alois Schneider's shoes. . . ."

I don't recall giving you permission to address me by my Christian name.

Oh, Christ. Yes, I did . . .

"I remember," Frade said.

718

"And I did. But that first attempt resulted in only changing my mind about whether U-234 made landfall in Argentina or not. But when I thought about what Alois would do about the uranium oxide —"

"You referred to Schneider by his first name just now. That implies you're close."

"Very close," von Dattenberg said. "All of us who served aboard U-boats are sort of a brotherhood. But Alois and I were even closer than —"

"Were . . . or are?"

"*Are.* I should have said that."

"Why?"

"Because we are alive, Colonel Frade — the U-boat service had a casualty rate approaching seventy-five percent — and because both of us made a number of special missions here. Only a few of us were selected, time and again, for that duty."

Now he's back to addressing me by rank?

"By 'special missions,' " Frade said, "you mean smuggling missions?"

"Yes. That's what I meant."

"Where do you think U-234 is right now?" Frade asked.

"Very probably where Cronley thinks it is. If not there, then tied up somewhere close — within one hundred kilometers of there. I can't think of any reason for Schneider to be taken from Villa General Belgrano except to do something with the boat."

"Like what?"

"Move her. Or perhaps take her to sea. She's been down there long enough for her to take on fuel and provisions."

"Have you any suggestion how we should deal with your scenario?" Frade asked.

"Yes, I do, Colonel. Get me down there somehow so I can help Major Grüner look for her from his Storch."

Why does he want to go down there?

"What could you do to help him? That he can't do himself?" Frade asked.

"General Martín says he can get me nautical charts of the area — Argentine charts would be better than the ones I had on U-450 — and from them I could make a better guess, I suggest, than could Grüner about where she might lie, and where she might be moving to."

What is it the lawyers say?

"Never ask a question unless you're sure what the answer will be."

How the hell can I argue with what he said?

This is not the time to ask him, "How do I know that if you find the sub you won't live up to your sacred oath to der Führer by doing whatever you can to let him know we're onto him?

"Or that if you do see the sub, and Grüner doesn't, that you'll just keep your mouth shut?"

"That makes sense to me," Nervo said.

"And to me," Frade said. "But the only way

720

we can get von Dattenberg down there — unless we put him in a car right now, and he drives down there — is in the Lodestar, and we won't know if we can do that until we hear from Grüner. His convoy — the flatbed trucks carrying the Cub, Storch, and bull-dozer, and the Army trucks with soldiers, heavy arms, food, and fuel — left Aeropuerto Frade yesterday afternoon. They aren't even halfway there. And once they do get there, we don't know how long it will take them to grade a suitable runway. So we're going to have to wait for that."

"When you're thinking of sending people down there, Cletus," the old man offered, "you're going to have to give some thought — presuming of course you find and seize either the submarine with the uranium oxide aboard or the uranium oxide where it is be-ing kept on land — to who will take legal possession of it."

"I don't follow you, Grandfather."

"Both the Argentines — General Martín and the BIS, or the Argentine army —"

"The Ejército Argentino," Clete furnished without thinking.

"Thank you ever so much, Cletus," the old man said, icily sarcastic. "I'll write that on my shirt cuff so I won't forget it again. If I may continue?"

"Sorry."

Where the hell did this come from?

And where the hell is he going with it?

"Both the Ejército Argentino and the U.S. Army and Navy — and I suppose the Royal Army and every other ally — have the right to seize the uranium oxide and, for that matter, the submarine itself, as property of the defeated enemy. In the same way as you acquired the Storch.

"As I understand that, a military attaché from our embassy seized the Storch in the name of the United States from an Argentine national, one Don Cletus Frade, in whose possession — illegal possession — it was."

"What do you mean, 'illegal possession'?" Clete protested.

"Von Wachtstein had no right to give you that airplane, which was the property of the German embassy," the old man said. "Isn't that right, General Martín?"

"Yes, it is," Martín said. "The polite fiction at the time was that I believed von Wachtstein had crashed it into the River Plate, taking Boltitz with him."

"Is there a point to this?" Clete asked.

"Oh, yes," the old man said. "A very important point."

Why do I think I just asked another question without knowing what the answer would be?

"Now, if General Martín seizes the uranium oxide, which he has every right to do, he would have to inform General Farrell and Coronel Perón. Is that right, General?"

"Yes, it is."

"And we don't want either of them — in particular Coronel Perón — to know about that, do we?"

"No," Clete said. "We do not."

"So that means the uranium oxide will have to be seized by an officer of one of the armed forces of the United States."

"Cletus Frade, Lieutenant Colonel, U.S. Marine Corps, at your service. Okay?"

The old man shook his head. "Not okay. Don Cletus Frade is in Argentina as his birthright. He is an Argentine."

"I'm also a serving officer of the USMC."

"*That* Cletus Frade, Colonel Frade, is in this country illegally. Am I right, General?"

"You're right, Señor Howell."

"Okay," Clete said. "Then Maxwell."

He pointed to Major Maxwell Ashton III.

"No. For the same reason. He's here illegally, as are all your OSS comrades. How about the military attaché who seized the Storch for you? Is he available?"

Frade exhaled audibly.

"No. For one thing, the American ambassador told me I was not to have any contact with the embassy at all. For another, I don't want him or anyone in the embassy to know anything about U-234 or the uranium oxide."

"Jesus Christ," Jimmy Cronley breathed as he realized the significance of what was being said.

Frade looked at him, then suddenly announced, "Anticipating this line of discussion, Grandfather, I have already equipped Lieutenant Cronley with Antarctic cold-weather gear identical to that worn by Admiral Byrd so that he can go down south and seize U-234 and the uranium oxide in comfort."

Silence greeted this announcement and lasted thirty seconds before Nervo laughed out loud.

"You got them all, gringo. You even had me — for fifteen seconds or so — thinking, *Goddamn, ol' Clete really is a genius.*"

"Me, too, and I live with him and know better," Dorotea said.

"I smell a rat here," Clete said. "Why do I think my beloved grandfather didn't come up with this seizure idea all by himself?"

"That cruel and unfounded accusation hurts me deeply," the old man said. "Although I will admit that Harry — excuse me, *President Truman* — touched on the subject of the seizure of enemy assets briefly while we were having our little pick-me-up, and then, on my way down here, when it came out that Commander Ford is also an attorney —"

"*Also* an attorney?" Clete challenged.

"I have that privilege," the old man said. "I thought you knew. Anyway, Commander Ford and I discussed it at some length."

724

If I ask him if he's really a lawyer, I won't like his answer.

He probably graduated from the University of Texas Law School magna cum laude.

"So, what do we do now?" Nervo asked.

"We wait to hear from Grüner," Frade said. "And we send Enrico and Colonel Garcia to San Martín de los Andes. And we wait to see who's been surveilling us and why."

"Does that mean I'm going down there to help Grüner find the *U-boot*?" von Dattenberg asked.

"That's what it means," Frade said.

XIII

[ONE]

Estancia Don Guillermo
Km 40.4, Provincial Route 60
Mendoza Province, Argentina
0935 21 October 1945

Just before walking out of the officers' mess, Clete had solved Jimmy Cronley's immediate problem — *I really don't want to see the Squirt right now,* Jimmy had thought, *not until I do better at figuring that situation out than I have so far* — by pointing to the stacks of paper on the table and ordering, "You better stay here and try to help straighten that mess out."

"That mess" was the stacks of files Colonel Manning had stuffed into the bags at Kloster Grünau, Manning's selection criteria being, *If it could possibly compromise Operation Ost, send it to Argentina.*

The bags had been carried into the officers' mess while Cronley was having breakfast. Niedermeyer, Strübel, and Frogger had gone into — pawed through — the documents looking for dossiers. They had stopped doing that when the meeting had begun, but had gone back to it as soon as the meeting was over.

Jimmy realized he had not been very useful — the documents were, after all, Abwehr Ost files, and they knew more about them than he did — but being there kept him from having to see Marjie, and that was the priority.

The only solution to the Marjie problem he could think of was to get Clete to send him back to Bavaria, dodging Marjie until he could get on the plane. But that had been blown out of the water when Mr. Howell had seen him appointed as Official Seizer of Uranium Oxide in the Name of the United States Government.

The only honorable solution he could think of now was to allow himself to freeze to death at the mouth of the Strait of Magellan. Freezing to death was supposed to be painless.

There was the sound of an aircraft engine. A familiar sound.

That's a Franklin! So that has to be a Piper Cub.

A single sixty-five-horsepower Franklin 4AC-176-B2 four-cylinder engine powered the Piper J-3 aircraft.

What's going on?

"That must be the puddle jumpers from the Húsares de Pueyrredón," Strübel said. "You ought to take a look at that, Cronley. It's something to see."

Cronley went outside in time to see the first of two Piper Cubs in Ejército Argentino markings making a slow approach to the mountaintop.

It touched down and ended its landing roll about fifty yards from where Cronley stood. Clete was waiting there with Enrico and Captain Garcia, whose uniform now carried the insignia of a lieutenant colonel. Garcia quickly got into the Cub, which then turned around, taxied to the end of the "runway" — which also served as the front lawn of the big house — and took off.

The second Piper began its approach.

Cronley now saw, standing in front of the big house, Martha Howell, Beth Howell, and Empress Elsa the Great von Wachtstein. They also apparently had been told that watching the Pipers land and take off was something they should see. Reasoning that if Beth and her mother were there, Marjie would not be far away, Cronley quickly retreated to the safety of the BOQ.

He took one step inside the building when someone grabbed his arm.

"We're going to have to stop meeting this way," Marjie said. "People will talk."

She raised her face to be kissed.

Jimmy grabbed her arms and held her away.

"What we're going to have to do, Squirt, is stop this nonsense."

"What?"

"I'm not a nice guy."

"I guess I've known that for — what? — sixteen, seventeen years."

"I mean, really not nice. If you knew, you wouldn't be —"

"Knew what?"

He looked over her shoulder and out the door where Martha, Beth, and Elsa were watching Enrico Rodríguez get into the second Piper Cub.

He nodded toward them.

"I did more with her than follow her around like a lovesick calf," Jimmy said.

Marjie turned to see what his nod was pointing out.

When she turned to look at him, her face showed that she had taken his meaning.

"And there's more you don't know about me," he proclaimed. "Worse than that."

"What could be worse than that?"

"You really want me to tell you?"

Her reply to that was nonverbal.

She struck his face. Not with an open hand, a slap, against his cheek — but with her fist balled. She hit him square in the nose, with sufficient force to both daze him and cause his eyes to water.

When he could see again, he saw that his right hand — which in a reflex action he had brought to his face — was bloody.

And when he looked away from his hand, he saw that Marjie was gone.

He looked out the door but couldn't see her.

He fished out his handkerchief — with some difficulty, as his bloody hand was at his face and he had to use his unbloodied left to get to his right hip pocket — and held it against his nose, and leaned against the wall just inside the door.

He had been there about five minutes, long enough to decide that, all things considered, a bloody nose was a fair price to pay for being able to end the business with Marjie — and then to wonder who the hell had taught her to punch as she had.

He was about to push himself off the wall, find a men's room, wash off the blood, and return to help Niedermeyer and the others with the documents he'd brought from Kloster Grünau when Cletus Frade came through the door.

Oh, God! Marjie was probably crying, and he saw her, and now he's come to settle with me for whatever I did to make his baby sister cry!

"Jesus Christ!" Frade exclaimed when he saw the bloody handkerchief, then asked, sarcastically, "What did you do, walk into a door?"

Jimmy decided that that seemed an obviously better thing to confess to than the truth.

"That's exactly what I did," Jimmy said, pointing at the door.

"You have to be careful, Jimmy. You can

really hurt yourself that way. You sure you're all right?"

"I'm fine. A little bloody, but . . . What's up?"

"I'm going to take von und zu A to the airport and shoot some touch-and-gos in the Lodestar. I thought you might want to come along."

Who the hell is von und zu A?

Oh . . . the guy who used to fly transports here from Germany.

Oberstleutnant Dieter von und zu Aschenburg.

"Why?"

"Why are we going to shoot touch-and-gos, or why am I asking you along?"

"Both."

"We may need von und zu A to fly down south. He's got a lot of experience in flying in Arctic — *Antarctic* — conditions like that, and I have zero such experience."

"North Dakota doesn't count?"

"That was a Cub in North Dakota. A Cub is not a Lodestar. And North Dakota is not the mouth of the Magellan Strait."

"Okay."

"And the reason I'm asking if you want to ride along — I may even let you shoot a couple of touch-and-gos — is because I'm still trying to make amends."

"For what you thought about the Squirt and me?"

734

"Right."

"Thanks, I'd like to go along."

There were two Ford station wagons parked in front of the BOQ. Former Oberstleutnant Dieter von und zu Aschenburg was in the front passenger seat of one. There were six men, all armed, in the second.

Clete got behind the wheel of the first station wagon and Jimmy got in the back. There was a Thompson submachine gun on the seat.

As they were moving slowly down the steep and narrow road from the mountaintop, von und zu Aschenburg turned in the seat and offered his hand to Jimmy.

Dieter began: "The colonel —"

"I asked you to call me Clete," Frade interrupted.

"— *Clete* tells me he taught you how to fly," Dieter went on.

"That he did. And when my father found out, I was grounded for thirty days."

"Grounded?"

"No movies, no radio, no bicycle, nothing but school and looking at the ceiling in my room. For a month."

Clete laughed. "They were pissed, weren't they? Possibly because you had just turned fourteen."

"Clete also told me you got pretty good at it."

"Clete never told me that."

"I was wondering why you didn't follow him into the Corps of Marines as a pilot."

"I wondered about that, too," Clete said, glancing over his shoulder.

"You really want to know?" Jimmy asked.

Clete, looking forward again, nodded. "Yeah."

Jimmy turned to Dieter and said, "Clete joined the Boy Scouts. When I was old enough, I joined the Boy Scouts. He got to be an Eagle Scout. I got to be an Eagle Scout. He went away to school, and the next year I went away to the same school."

"Saint Mark's," Clete offered, "from which you got the boot."

"Because I got caught running the poker game you taught me how to run," Jimmy said, looking at Clete. He looked back at Dieter and went on: "Then Clete went to A&M —"

"To what?"

"Texas Agricultural and Mechanical University," Clete furnished.

"So I went to A&M. Then Clete dropped out and went to play tennis at Tulane and then into the Marine Corps and became a Naval Aviator. And then the Marine recruiters showed up at College Station — my clue to follow him into the Marine Corps and become a Naval Aviator."

"And?" Clete said.

"I had an epiphany. It was time for me to

stop following Cletus."

"No kidding?" Clete said.

"No kidding."

"Then why didn't you go in the Air Corps?"

"Two reasons. One, that would have been following you as a pilot."

"But you are a pilot. You've had a commercial ticket and an instrument ticket since you were eighteen."

"And a multi-engine ticket and fifty hours as pilot-in-command of my father's Beechcraft Model 18. And while I was doing that, I had another epiphany."

"Which was?" Clete said.

"It was just about the time the Marines were trying to recruit me. I was home from College Station for the weekend. Dad had some people at the ranch who had to go back to Dallas. He said, 'We'll have Jimmy fly us there in the Beech.' And they said, 'Oh, is your son a pilot?' or words to that effect, to which Dad replied, bursting with pride, 'Oh, yes. He soloed just after he turned fourteen. He's one hell of a pilot' or words to that effect.

"So there I was, at the end of Twenty-two at Midland Airport, with my father and my mother and three of his pals and their wives in the back, and the tower says, 'Beech Six Four Four, you are cleared for takeoff.' And I put my hand on the throttles and said, 'Six Four Four rolling' — and then had my epiphany."

"Which was?"

" 'What the fuck am I doing here, about to take eight people into the air? I'm a lousy pilot and I know it. I don't even like flying. My stomach knots every time I put my hand on the throttle quadrant. The only reason I'm flying is so that I can be like Cletus. And being like Cletus is not a good enough reason to risk my life, not to mention other people's lives.'

"So I went in the Army, not the Marine Corps, and when I was in Officer Basic School and they came and said, 'We see you've got twelve hundred hours and an instrument ticket and a multi-engine ticket. So as soon as you finish here, we're going to make you an Army aviator, a liaison pilot,' I said, 'No, thank you just the same, I'll drive a tank.' "

"You're serious, aren't you?" Clete asked.

"Yeah."

"I'm sorry, Jimmy," Clete said, his tone sincere.

"And then they found out that Dad and General Donovan were World War One buddies, and sent me to the Counterintelligence Corps."

"I'm sorry, Jimmy," Clete repeated.

"Don't be. If I hadn't been drafted into the CIC, I wouldn't be here about to seize a half-ton of uranium oxide and maybe a German

738

submarine for the U.S. government."

He exhaled audibly and added, "Thus making the world safe for democracy and Mom's apple pie."

Clete chuckled. "I guess this means you don't want to shoot touch-and-gos in my Lodestar."

"You don't understand, Clete. I'm happy to shoot touch-and-gos in your Lodestar, providing you're sitting in the left seat. What I *don't* like to do — what I've stopped doing — is flying by my lonesome."

Dieter von und zu Aschenburg grunted.

"I knew others like you," he said, nodding. "Both fighter pilots. One in France, and a second in the East."

"How'd you find out about them?" Jimmy said.

"They told me. I guess you've heard that fighter pilots drink more than they should."

"What happened to them?" Jimmy pursued.

"They didn't have a choice, Jimmy, so they continued flying until they went down."

Jimmy met his eyes, and thought, *Meaning of course that you — and probably Clete, too — think I'm a coward for not following Clete into the Marines and the cockpit of a fighter.*

Well, maybe I am. That's what it looks like.

Why the hell did I open this bag of worms?

"If you 'turned in your wings' in the Luftwaffe," von und zu Aschenburg went on, "you were assigned to a penal battalion. You went to the front as a rifleman, and you stayed there until you were killed. If you were wounded, when you got out of the hospital, you went back to the penal battalion. The people I'm talking about knew this, so they kept flying."

Jimmy shook his head.

"What I'm saying, Jimmy, is they didn't have a choice. Be glad you did."

"Even if it brings my yellow streak out in the open?"

"I don't think you're a coward, and I don't think Clete does, either. Trying to stay alive isn't cowardice. It's common sense. Be glad you had the choice — and the courage to make it. Walking into suicide isn't bravery . . . it's stupidity."

"Hey! Hey!" Clete said, suddenly and excitedly. "Look at this!"

They looked where he was pointing.

On the road ahead, half a dozen gendarmes armed with Mauser submachine guns were leading at least that many men — dressed in military field clothing, their hands locked at the back of their necks — toward a canvas-roofed gendarmerie truck.

"I would hazard the guess those are the people who have been surveilling us," Clete said. "After we shoot our touch-and-gos, we'll stop by the gendarmerie barracks in Mendoza and see what the gendarmes have found out about who they are. Five-to-one they're from the Tenth Mountain, but you never know."

[Two]

As they drove onto the airport, the Howell Petroleum Corporation Constellation was just lifting off. It flashed over them, retracted its landing gear, and went into a steep climb.

Clete Frade's first reaction to this was to tell Dieter von und zu Aschenburg and Jimmy Cronley that the first problem in flying from Mendoza to Santiago de Chile was picking up enough altitude to get over the Andes.

"It's not a problem in a Connie," he said. "But when we started SAA with Lodestars, I was going to call it ATAA — Around and Through the Andes Airlines — because the Lodestars can't make enough altitude to get over some of the mountains."

Then he had a second thought, and said it aloud: "They should have been out of here before this. Siggie must have had trouble installing the Collins 7.2."

They found Master Sergeant Siggie Stein in Hangar Two, and he apologized for taking so long to install the Collins radio.

741

"That happens, Colonel," he said.

"Well, they're on their way to Santiago," Frade said. "What are you doing in here?"

Stein pointed to a Lodestar painted in the SAA color scheme.

"That's not working, either. The plane's more badly shot up than we thought."

Cronley realized that the Lodestar was the one in which Frade had flown Perón from Buenos Aires. When he looked closer he saw bullet holes in the fuselage.

"The mechanics were able to fix the hydraulics," Stein explained, "and there was no damage to the engines. But the radios — you have zero radios. . . ."

"They were working when I landed," Frade protested.

"They aren't now, Colonel," Stein said. "And they can't replace the shot-out windows or patch the bullet holes here. That'll have to be done in Buenos Aires, which means that this is going to have to be flown there, which means, since it doesn't have any navigation equipment — except for a magnetic compass — that it will have to be shepherded there by another airplane — another Lodestar — that does have working navigation equipment."

"But it is flyable?"

"The mechanics say so, but there's been no pilots to give it a test hop, so the answer to your question is 'probably.' "

"Well, there's one way to find out," Frade

said. "Get a tractor to drag it outside and call for the fuel truck."

Frade turned to von und zu Aschenburg and asked, "Do you say 'kill two birds with one stone' in German? As in 'combine test flight with touch-and-gos'?"

"*Zwei Fliegen mit einer Klappe schlagen,*" Dieter said.

"The German phrase that comes to my mind," Jimmy said, "is *drei Piloten mit einem Flugzeug schlagen.*"

" 'Kill three pilots with one airplane'?" Dieter translated. "I like that."

"For Christ's sake, Dieter, don't encourage him," Frade said, laughing.

After the tractor had pulled the Lodestar from the hangar, and it had its tanks topped off, Clete conducted the walk-around while Jimmy and Dieter got to see the bullet holes in the fuselage close up.

When they boarded, Jimmy got to see the holes again as he followed Clete and Dieter up the aisle toward the cockpit. And he saw where the shot-out window had been. It now was covered with a plywood patch. He also saw that the upholstery on the seat and the carpet under the seat were stained, and wondered what that was.

And then understood that he was looking at a bloodstain.

That's where Perón was sitting.

If he lost that much blood, he damn near died.

And when they were talking about General Martín getting shot, they said it was possible, even likely, that he had been hit by the same machine gun that had "shot up Clete in the Lodestar."

And then he had another epiphany, a frightening one.

They really are trying to kill people around here.

And I am one of the people that someone is going to try to kill.

Why didn't I understand that before?

Did I think the Thompson on the seat of the station wagon just now — or, for that matter, the one Clete keeps in his wardrobe back in Buenos Aires — was there to shoot beer bottles?

And everybody here — except Mrs. Howell, Marjie, and Beth — has been shot at before.

What are you going to do, Jimmy Cronley, when someone takes a shot at you — which is probably going to happen in the next forty-eight hours?

You know you're a coward. Otherwise you would have followed Clete into the Marine Corps. Dieter was just being a nice guy when he said trying to stay alive isn't cowardice.

So, what the hell are you going to do?

"Get your ass up here," Clete shouted from the cockpit. "I don't want to have to do this cockpit orientation twice."

Jimmy hurried up the aisle and sat on the jump seat behind the pilot's and co-pilot's seats. When Frade had finished explaining the functions of all the switches and levers, he said, "And this is how we start the engines. Pay attention."

I will pay attention because I'm here and have no choice.

But it will be a cold day in hell before I start the engines on this airplane alone.

Or any other airplane.

Three hours later, as Cronley brought the Lodestar to the end of its landing roll, Frade said, "Well, Jimmy, that last landing wasn't especially awful. Another ten hours or so of my expert instruction and I might be tempted to sign you off on this airplane."

Wasn't he listening in the station wagon?

Or was he listening and pretending that didn't happen?

I can't let it go.

"Clete, I will fly your airplane anywhere in the world — except maybe to the mouth of the Magellan Strait — just as long as you're sitting right there in the left seat. Weren't you listening before?"

Frade met his eyes for a long moment and then said, "Yeah, I was listening. I was trying to talk you out of what you said."

"Don't."

After another long moment, Frade said,

"Okay. Your call. But I think you're wrong. Now park the airplane and then we'll go see what the gendarmes found out."

[THREE]

"Why do I think General Nervo is here?" Cletus Frade said, pointing to a glistening black 1942 Buick Roadmaster sitting in front of a large NO PARKING! sign by the front door of the building. A small Argentine flag flew from a mast on the right front fender and a small Gendarmería Nacional flag was similarly mounted on the left front fender.

"You're just guessing that's his car," Jimmy Cronley said, playing along. "There must be . . . I don't know . . . a hundred, maybe more, cars just like that around."

When they got inside the building, Frade, von und zu Aschenburg, and Cronley were shown into the office of the commander of the Mendoza District of the Gendarmería.

General Santiago Nervo was sitting at the commander's desk, and the commander, a gendarmerie comandante — major — was sitting backward on a folding chair. Both of them were looking through a plate glass window into a small room.

746

In the room, Subinspector General Pedro Nolasco and a pleasant-appearing young man were sitting at a metal table to which the young man was attached with handcuffs.

"Say hello to Comandante Sanchez," Nervo greeted them.

"I know Don Cletus, of course," Raul Sanchez said.

"Comandante," Frade said, and they shook hands.

"Do you remember, Raul," Nervo asked, "when the Germans, during the war, were flying that four-engined airplane here from Europe? The Condor?"

"Of course."

"The pilot was this gentleman," Nervo said, "Dieter von und zu Aschenburg, who came here to give Don Cletus flying lessons."

Sanchez smiled.

"And this young man, James Cronley, is another gringo," Nervo said. "A very unusual young man."

"How is that, my general?" Sanchez asked.

"He is a *subteniente* who not only can find his ass with only one hand, but without assistance."

"I can only hope, *Teniente*," Sanchez said, smiling at Cronley, "that Don Cletus has warned you about General Nervo."

Nervo looked at Cronley.

"How did the flying lesson go?" he asked.

"If I give them just a little more training,"

Jimmy said, "I think the both of them could be permitted to fly short distances without supervision."

Nervo and Sanchez laughed.

"What's going on in there?" Frade asked, pointing at the window.

"The young fellow is Captain Guillermo O'Reilley of the Tenth Mountain," Nervo said. "We know that because he told us. He also told us the gendarmerie has no right to ask him what he's doing while he is on official business of the Ejército Argentino, much less a right to detain him. But that's all he's told us."

"Is he right about you not having such authority?" Frade asked.

"No, he's not. And he knows he's not. I suspect he's one of the brighter young officers in the Tenth, which makes me suspect that he was told to say what he's been saying by a senior officer of the Tenth — possibly even by el Coronel Hans Klausberger himself — should the gendarmerie catch him at what he was doing."

"Which was?" Jimmy asked.

"Surveilling Casa Montagna," Nervo said. "And also Provincial Route 60, probably with the purpose of finding the best place from which they could shoot up cars and trucks moving to and from Mendoza."

"Hoping to shoot who?"

"Well, I'd say Don Cletus is high on that

list, and probably any of the Good Gehlens, as I suspect they are regarded as traitors by a number of people."

"What would they get out of killing Clete?" Jimmy asked. "Or any of the Good Gehlens?"

"I don't know, Jimmy. They have to know that Juan Domingo would be really furious. He would have been furious before Clete took him off Isla Martín García and brought him here, a little bloody but alive. After that happened —"

"What are you going to do with this guy?" Clete interrupted, nodding toward Captain O'Reilley. "And the others? How many were there?"

"Two *tenientes,* six sergeants, and a corporal. I have placed them all under arrest. And I've been sitting here wondering how effective it would be if I put the corporal — he's about as old as Jimmy — in there with Nolasco and Captain O'Reilley, then announced to O'Reilley that unless he tells us everything we want to know, we will cut off the corporal's fingers one at a time with bolt cutters. That would force O'Reilley to consider what an officer's moral obligations to his enlisted soldiers are."

"Jesus Christ!" Clete said. "You can't be serious —"

Nervo put up his hand to stop him, and grinned.

"Everyone will please notice that Cletus

was the only one who fell for that. What I really have been thinking is that the smart thing to do is nothing while we wait for one or both of two things to happen. One, they send people looking for Captain O'Reilley and his men, and we lock them up. And we keep doing that until we get a *teniente coronel* or better in our bag."

"That's a thought," Clete said.

"And the other is wait until Garcia and Rodríguez return from San Martín de los Andes — the Tenth's barracks — and hear what they have to say. I am open to suggestion, Don Cletus."

"I leave the entire matter in your capable hands, General," Clete said.

"You're only saying that because you don't have any better ideas."

"True. And now my friends and I will return to Casa Montagna and pull some corks. We have earned that. You're coming for dinner?"

"I promised our Jesuit to meet his plane and take him up there."

"Then we'll see you later."

[FOUR]

Mother Superior came into the reception area. The white coat she wore over her habit was heavily bloodstained and so was the surgical mask hanging loosely around her neck.

"I don't know if it was your intention, Cletus, but they're all dead," she announced.

She turned to Second Lieutenant James D. Cronley Jr., pointed to the Thompson he held with the butt resting on his hip, and said, "You can put that down, young man. You're not going to need it here."

"All dead?" Cletus repeated.

"All of those nine men . . . the ones in the black overalls," she amplified. "Plus one of your Húsares."

"And the others?"

"Your German friend — Dieter? I think you said Dieter was his name — as you saw, he was hit twice, once in the side." She demonstrated by stabbing at her body with a finger. "And again in the upper right leg." She demonstrated that again with her finger. "There is considerable muscle damage, but he will live. The second of your Húsares did

751

considerable damage — compound fractures in both areas — to his right arm and wrist when, according to him, he was getting out of his station wagon and slipped."

"Can I see Dieter?" Frade asked.

"If you want to wait several hours until he recovers from the anesthesia," Mother Superior said. "But I suggest you go to Casa Montagna and show Dorotea you're all right. I don't think she believed me when I told her that you were."

"Why did you tell her anything, for Christ's sake?"

"Spare me your blasphemy, please. To answer your question: because I knew word of this would quickly reach the estancia, and I didn't want her to come down here."

She turned to Cronley again.

"I asked you to put that down."

"Sling the Thompson, Jimmy," Frade ordered. "It's over."

"Sorry," Cronley said.

He turned the submachine gun so that he could check that the safety was on. Because the Thompson fired from an open bolt, he could see that there was a round in the drum magazine, waiting for the bolt to be rammed into the chamber, whereupon the fixed firing pin on the bolt would strike the primer in the cartridge case. This would cause the weapon not only to fire, but to continue firing as long as the trigger was depressed and there were cartridges in the fifty-round drum magazine.

He saw that the little arrow on the side of the receiver pointed to "F" — for Fire — which meant the safety was not on. The Thompson had been ready to fire all along.

What the hell is the matter with me?

I know better than that.

He removed the fifty-round drum magazine from the Thompson, eased the bolt forward onto the empty chamber, reinstalled the magazine, and then slung the weapon on his shoulder.

I'm dazed, that's what's the matter with me.

What the hell happened?

The last thing I remember was being on my knees in the backseat, so that I could rest my arms on the back of the front seat.

I remember seeing Kilometer Marker 29, and that I was listening to Clete and Dieter talking.

About what? What the hell were they talking about?

And then the windshield blew up.

Windshields. Both of them. The one in front of Clete and the one in front of Dieter.

And Dieter grunted.

And Clete said, "Oh, shit!"

And he slammed on the brakes and started to turn hard left.

Then the station wagon with Clete's guys slammed into our rear end, spinning us around.

And then we stopped moving, and I realized

we were half on our side in a ditch.

And I grabbed the Thompson and opened the door and got out and fell in the ditch.

And then I was running through some kind of a field — a cornfield.

How did I get into that field?

Where did I think I was going?

And then I saw the truck and the bad guys — four, five, six of them — in black coveralls running to it.

And they saw me and shot at me.

With Schmeisser submachine guns.

And I shot back.

Somehow I remembered what that old sergeant had taught me at Fort Knox: Just tap the trigger to get off two or three rounds; if you squeeze the trigger, you won't be able to hold your aim, and the muzzle will climb and you'll be shooting at the clouds.

He made me practice until I could do it automatically.

So either I remembered, or it was a Pavlovian reflex or something.

I took down four of the bastards who were shooting at me.

I remember counting the shots, feeling the recoil, hearing the rounds go off.

One Two. One Two Three. One Two. One Two Three.

And I was about to take down another of the bastards but all of a sudden he stopped running and fell forward on his face. And so did the guy next to him.

And then I saw the Húsares, three of them, and realized they had taken down the last two.

Then the truck started to move and two of the Húsares ran to it and fired into the cab and the truck stopped.

One of the Húsares jumped on the running board and pulled the driver out onto the ground. He had to be dead; I could see into his skull.

Clete came running up, his .45 in his hand.

"No wonder I couldn't find my goddamn Thompson!" he yelled at me.

"Mi Coronel," another Húsare said, "your brother killed four of the Nazi bastards with the Thompson."

Clete looked at me and said, "Does that truck run?"

Not "Good for you!" or "Good job!"

Just "Does that truck run?"

"Sí, Don Cletus," the Húsare said.

"You stay here," Clete then said, pointing at two of the Húsares. "Search the bodies, collect weapons. Antonio broke his arm. We have to get him and my German friend to the hospital." He pointed to a third Húsare. "You get in the back of the truck. You can bring it back out here. Keep your eyes open. There may be more of the bastards out there."

Then he turned to me.

"Get in the truck. In the front."

I remember that there was blood all over the inside of the truck cab, and some bloody white stuff stuck to the windshield that had to be brain tissue.

I remember that I had to press against the door so that I wouldn't be sitting in the pool of blood on the seat.

And I remember that the Húsare with the broken arm screamed with pain when they loaded him in the truck.

And that Dieter's face was white, that he was unconscious, and I thought maybe he was dead — until he groaned.

And I remember starting down the road . . . but that's all I remember until just now when this nun, or whatever she is — Mother Superior? The head nun? — walked out here.

"Thank you, Mother," Clete said.

"This is how God wants me to spend my life, Cletus. No thanks is required. Now get out of here."

She went back into the interior of the hospital.

"The question now becomes, Jimmy," Frade said, "how do we go home? We don't have any wheels."

"While you were taking a leak, a gendarmerie sergeant came in here. He said whenever we're ready, he'll take us to Casa Montagna."

When they went outside, three gendarmerie pickup trucks — loaded with gendarmes — and General Nervo's 1942 Buick Roadmaster were waiting for them.

"Sergeant, we can ride in one of the trucks," Clete said to Nervo's driver. "Send General Nervo's car back to him with my respects."

"With respect, Don Cletus," the sergeant replied, "General Nervo said that if you give me any trouble about using his car, I am to cut off your fingers with this."

He held up a massive bolt cutter.

Clete and Jimmy got in the backseat of the Buick.

When they passed Kilometer Marker 29, there was no sign of the shot-up and wrecked station wagons nor any other sign that anything extraordinary had happened there.

[FIVE]

Estancia Don Guillermo
Km 40.4, Provincial Route 60
Mendoza Province, Argentina
1805 21 October 1945

A large delegation of people was waiting for them when the Buick pulled up to Casa Montagna.

"The Family" — Doña Dorotea, holding Master Jorge Howell Frade by the hand; Martha Howell, holding Cletus Howell Frade Jr. in her arms; Beth and Marjorie Howell; and patriarch Cletus Marcus Howell — stood in front. Perhaps twenty Germans, Argentines,

757

and Americans stood in a half circle behind them.

Clete climbed out of the backseat of the Buick, then Jimmy followed.

"Good evening," Clete said.

"Is that all you have to say, my darling?" Doña Dorotea asked, somewhat coldly.

"Well, Jimmy and I were sort of expecting a brass band. You know, playing" — he sang — " 'the eyes of Texas are upon you . . .' "

"Oh, damn you, Cletus," Doña Dorotea said as she went to her husband. They embraced.

Martha Howell handed the baby to Marjie and went to Jimmy.

"You get a hug, too, sweetheart," she said, and embraced him. "You all right?"

"I'm fine, thank you, Miz Howell," he said.

Marjie, holding the baby, was looking at him.

Not at me. Into me.

"The other hero and I require liquid sustenance," Clete then announced. "Why don't we all go in the bar?"

"So we took Dieter and Antonio to the hospital," Clete said, finishing his after-action report as he held up an empty bottle of Don Guillermo Cabernet Sauvignon '40 to indicate another was required. "Mother Superior says they're both going to be all right, but neither — especially Dieter — is going to get

758

out of bed for a while."

"I should have been with you, Don Cletus," Enrico said.

"We could have used your riot gun, that's for sure," Clete said. "What did you learn in San Martín de los Andes?"

"Excuse me," Cletus Marcus Howell said. "Where was Jimmy when all this was going on? I must have missed something."

Jimmy shook his head at Clete to ask — tell — him to leave his role out of the narrative.

The request was denied.

"By the time I was able to crawl out of the station wagon," Clete answered, "Jimmy had stolen my Thompson and was chasing the bad guys through a cornfield. By the time we caught up with them, he'd put four of the bad guys down."

"By himself?" Marjie asked.

"Yeah, Squirt, by himself," Clete said. "He really gets a gold star to take home to Mommy."

"Speaking of that," Jimmy said, aware that Marjie's eyes were again looking at him. *Into him.* "There's no reason my mother has to hear any of this, is there?"

"Well, I certainly won't tell her," Martha said. "And neither will Beth and Marjie."

"That won't work, Martha," the old man said. "Not only do Jimmy's folks have a right to know something like this happened, but not telling them is tantamount to lying, and I won't be party to that."

Martha considered that for a moment.

"You're right, Dad. And it would eventually come out anyway." She turned to Jimmy. "And your dad is entitled to be proud of you, sweetheart."

"Getting back to what you learned in San Martín, Enrico?" Clete asked.

"Suboficial Martinez told me something interesting, Don Cletus," the old soldier reported. "He said the worst Nazi in the Tenth Mountain is an Irisher."

"An *Irishman*," Colonel Garcia corrected him. "Captain Guillermo O'Reilley . . ."

"Now that is interesting," Frade said.

". . . who hates all things British and, by extension, American," Garcia finished. He then asked, "Why interesting, Cletus?"

"I saw Captain O'Reilley earlier today," Clete replied. "Nolasco had him handcuffed to a table in the gendarmerie barracks asking him why he and his men were so interested in Estancia Guillermo and the people going back and forth to it."

"Presumably, that was before you were attacked?" General Martín asked.

Frade nodded.

"After Rodríguez told me what his friend told him about O'Reilley," Colonel Garcia said, "I asked to see him. El Coronel Klausberger told me that O'Reilley was on a training exercise in the Andes and would not be back until Sunday, if then."

"That raises the question: Did Klausberger know what O'Reilley was up to?" Martín said. "Or was O'Reilley working on his own? Or for someone else? If so, who?"

"Bernardo," Frade said, "Nervo thinks O'Reilley — who kept insisting that the gendarmes had no authority over him and his men, and demanded that they be released — is confident that someone with power is covering his ass. He refused to answer Nolasco's questions."

"What's Nervo going to do with him? And where is Nervo, by the way?"

"The last I heard he was going to see if whoever sent O'Reilley snooping was going to send someone looking for him," Frade said. "When we left them, he said that after he picked up Father Welner, he would come up here for dinner. Welner was at the hospital, deciding what to do with the bodies."

"No identification on them, I presume?" Martín asked.

"None," Frade replied. "The coveralls they were wearing were Argentine. They all had Schmeissers, but that doesn't prove they were SS. It doesn't even prove they were German."

Martín went off on a tangent: "When do you expect to hear from the convoy you sent to Estancia Condor?"

"Not until they get there. Making en route reports would involve stopping to set up the

761

Collins and the SIGABA — that'd take an hour, at least — and the information we need is that they're at Estancia Condor, not where they are on a road in Patagonia."

"So when do you expect to hear from them?"

"Probably not until the morning, if then."

"So we have to wait for that."

"Everything depends on that," Frade said. "By morning, too, with a little luck, Dieter — von und zu Aschenburg — should be awake enough to make sense of what Grüner has learned about landing airplanes down there."

"So we have to wait," Martín repeated. "It has been my experience over the years that Inspector General Nervo does not take kindly to suggestions from me. Nevertheless, I'm going to make one: that as soon as he gets his car back, he put the Irish Nazi into it and bring him here. Maybe Captain O'Reilley will answer questions put to him by an Ejército Argentino *general de brigada*." He turned to Garcia. "See if you can get him on the phone."

Two minutes later, Coronel Garcia put the handset of the telephone back in the base, and with a smile reported on his conversation with Inspector General Nervo.

"The general tells me he is, as usual, two steps in front of General Martín. At the moment, Captain O'Reilley is being given a tour of Mendoza in a gendarmerie convoy, with their sirens screaming and lights flashing. He is sitting strapped to a chair in the bed of a gendarmerie pickup truck. General Nervo wants to make sure that whoever Klausberger has in Mendoza reporting to him learns that the gendarmerie has O'Reilley. When the tour of the city is over, the convoy will pick up Nervo and Nolasco and bring them here — with O'Reilley still strapped in the chair in the back of the truck in case Klausberger has other people watching Route 60."

"Nervo seems pretty sure that Klausberger is the villain," Frade said.

"So am I," Martín said. "What I would really like to do is get Captain O'Reilley to admit (a) that he knew about the shooters who tried to kill our Cletus, (b) that he knew they were SS, and (c) — or maybe (c) and (d) — that not only did Klausberger know, but he issued the order. We could go to President Farrell and el Coronel Perón with that.

"The attempt on our Cletus's life is going to infuriate Perón, as he will see it as an attack — another attack — on him. And while Farrell and Perón are dealing with el Coronel Klausberger, we can quietly deal with what has to be done in the South."

"Yeah," Clete said thoughtfully.

"I think I could be of service in that regard,"

von Dattenberg said. "If there was some way I could get down there."

"Oddly enough," Frade said, "I was just thinking about that."

"And?"

"When I make up my mind, you'll be the first to know. Or maybe the second. Or third . . ."

There was laughter.

". . . But right now," Frade went on, "having just had a whiff of myself, I'm going to have a shower."

[SIX]

Jimmy Cronley had been in his room not quite a minute — just enough time for him to take off his jacket — when Cletus Frade came in without knocking.

"I decided I might as well tell you this now," Clete said, "to give you time to get used to it."

"Used to what?"

"Dieter obviously can't fly, so you're probably going to have to."

"No."

"Yeah, Jimmy."

"Fly what?"

"Maybe the Cub down south. Maybe one of the Lodestars. It depends on how this develops."

"No."

"Yes. I mean it. Get used to it. You don't have a choice. Think it through and you'll see I'm right."

Frade turned and walked out of the room.

"Shit," Jimmy said aloud.

He started again to undress. He had his shoes and necktie off and was unbuttoning his shirt when the door opened again.

"Now what?" he snarled, then raised his eyes and saw it was Marjie.

"Jesus Christ!" he said.

"No. Not even the Virgin Mary."

"What the hell do you want?"

"I thought you could use a little tenderness."

"Marjie, get out of here."

"Relax. Clete didn't see me come in."

When he didn't reply to that, she added, "Not that I really care."

"What the hell is that supposed to mean?"

"There's something I think I should tell you."

"Like what?"

"Like when we first got word that you'd been attacked, but nobody knew what happened to you. My reaction to that."

"Which was?"

" 'Oh, my God, he's dead and I never got to tell him I love him. That I've always loved him.' "

"Weren't you listening when I told you about Elsa? And the other things I've done?"

"Okay. Let's get that out of the way. If you ever do something like that again, or even think about doing something like that again, I'll cut off your dingus and feed it to the hogs."

"You never had hogs on your spread, Squirt, and we never had them on ours. So how do you know that hogs would eat it?"

"Maybe with mustard? Or sauerkraut?"

"You're crazy. Absolutely bonkers."

"I think you're supposed to be crazy if you're in love," Marjie said, and then asked, "Aren't you going to kiss me?"

He did so.

When they broke apart, he said, "Jesus H. Christ, Marjie!"

"My God, you stink! What have you been doing, eating garlic?"

"That's the smell of terror. I get it when I'm flying airplanes — and when people shoot at me."

"Go take a shower," she ordered. "Right now. I'll wait."

He tried to kiss her again. She avoided him.

"And so will that have to wait," she said.

Jimmy had just finished soaping his armpits for the fourth time and was wondering what was the best way to go back into the bedroom — *With a towel around my waist? Or maybe I could open the door a crack, stick my hand out, say my underwear is in the top drawer of the*

766

dresser and would she please hand it to me?
— when the glass door of the shower opened
and Marjie joined him.

"I got tired of waiting," she said.

She was naked.

"I wondered if that was true," Marjie said
about six minutes later.

"You wondered if what was true?"

"They say that when a man takes a virgin
to bed, afterward there's blood on the sheets."

She pointed and he looked and there was
indeed a bloody stain.

"Did I hurt you?"

She shook her head and kissed him as she
ran her fingertips down his face.

"No, but thank you for asking."

And then she had a second thought: "I've
got to get out of here."

She slipped out of bed and trotted to the
bathroom.

When she came out, she was in her underwear, and thirty seconds after that had her
skirt and sweater on and was slipping her feet
into her loafers.

She went to the door, and turned.

"Wait a couple of minutes," she said, blew
him a kiss, and then went through the door.

Well, she seems to have taken this in stride.

*Won't people be able to tell, just looking at
us?*

Jesus Christ, I didn't use a rubber!

What if I made her pregnant?

You hear all the time about pregnant girls who did it just once.

He swung his feet out of bed. As he did, he saw the bloodstain.

Maybe if I left my razor and shaving cream on the sheet the maid will think I cut myself shaving.

[SEVEN]

When Jimmy went in the dining room, Father Welner was there. When the priest saw Jimmy, he quickly stood and went to him.

"Let me have a minute, my son," Welner said, and took Jimmy's arm and led him out a door into a corridor.

"I heard what happened. Are you all right, my son?"

"Yes, sir. They missed."

"I mean, all right about taking the lives of those four men. Are you disturbed about that?"

"Jesus Christ! They were shooting at me. What was I supposed to do?" He paused. "Sorry about the language."

"You feel you had no choice, is that what you're saying?"

"Yes, sir."

"Then I'm sure God will understand. Bless you, my son."

"Thank you, Father."

■ ■ ■ ■

When Jimmy went back in the dining room, Martha Howell waved him to an empty seat at the table beside her. Marjie was sitting next to the empty seat.

"Are you okay, Jimmy?" Martha Howell asked when he had taken the seat.

"Yes, ma'am, I'm fine."

"We were wondering what happened to you. You were gone a long time. I was getting worried."

"I'm fine, Miz Howell."

"Good," she said, and patted his hand.

Jimmy felt the sole of Marjie's foot running up and down his calf.

When he looked at her, she smiled.

"Are you hungry?" she asked innocently. "For some reason, I'm starved."

There was a pinging noise.

Jimmy looked at the head of the table. Cletus was tapping his knife on a wine bottle.

When he thought he had everyone's attention, he said, "General Nervo just sent word from the barrier at the foot of the hill. He wants everybody to be on the veranda when his convoy arrives here. I figure that will be in about five or so minutes."

"What's that all about, my darling?" Doña Dorotea asked.

"I have no idea, my love. But I treat him

the way I treat you. When he asks me to do something, I give him the benefit of the doubt and do it."

The first vehicle to appear was a gendarmerie Ford pickup truck carrying a half-dozen heavily armed gendarmes. Second in line was General Nervo's Buick Roadmaster.

I guess they met on Route 60, Frade thought, *and Nervo reclaimed it.*

The third vehicle in line was another gendarmerie pickup. Strapped to a chair in the bed was Captain Guillermo O'Reilley. Three more gendarmerie pickups followed it.

"What's that all about?" Father Welner said. "I don't care what that fellow has done, he should not be humiliated that way."

"I think his humiliation is what General Nervo wants, Father," General Martín said.

The convoy stopped with the pickup carrying Captain O'Reilley directly in front of the steps to the Casa Montagna veranda, and the Buick just in front of it.

Captain O'Reilley, who could move nothing but his head, quickly examined the two dozen or so people on the veranda, and then looked straight ahead.

Nervo's driver opened the rear door of the Buick. Nervo and Nolasco got out. They walked onto the veranda, greeting first Father Welner, then moving to the women, then everybody else and finally Clete, Jimmy, Mar-

770

tín, and Garcia.

The two gendarmerie officers greeted each of them effusively.

The entire process took perhaps three minutes but it seemed longer. Finally, Nervo pointed to Captain O'Reilley.

"That's one of yours, General," he said to Martín. "He said that as an army officer he's not required to answer questions posed by the gendarmerie."

"That's the chap you caught spying on us?"

"That's him."

"Get him out of there," Martín ordered. "Perhaps he'll tell me what you want to know."

Nervo gestured to two gendarmes, who then jumped into the bed of the truck, unstrapped O'Reilley, and walked him to the end of the bed and lowered him onto the ground.

Martín gestured for him to approach.

He began to do so, in tiny steps.

"Why are you walking that way?" Martín asked.

"They've tied my boot laces together," O'Reilley proclaimed indignantly.

"Standard gendarmerie procedure, General," Nolasco said. "You can't run very fast when your boot laces are tied together."

"I suppose that's so," Martín said.

O'Reilley finally came close to Martín and came to attention.

"You've forgotten how to report, Captain?" Martín asked.

O'Reilley saluted.

"Captain O'Reilley, Guillermo, Tenth Mountain, *mi General.*"

"You recognize me, then?" Martín asked. "I'm not in uniform. Who do you think I am?"

"*Mi General,* you are General de Brigada Bernardo Martín."

"And my assignment?"

"*Mi General,* you are chief of the Bureau of Internal Security."

"What happened to your cap, Captain?" Martín asked, pointing to O'Reilley's head.

"It blew off in the truck, *mi General.*"

"Perhaps you should have put it on more carefully. An officer should always be in proper uniform. What were you doing in the back of the truck, Captain?"

"The gendarmes put me there," O'Reilley said indignantly. "*Mi General,* may I have a word with you in private?"

Martín considered that a moment.

"Why not?" he said finally. "Put him back in the truck and take him to the officers' mess."

O'Reilley saluted again and started to shuffle back to the truck. Nervo gestured to two gendarmes, who then caught up with O'Reilley, picked him up, carried him to the pickup, lowered the tailgate, and sat him in

772

the bed, with his feet dangling.

When the truck was halfway across the lawn and O'Reilley out of earshot, Frade asked, "What are you up to, Bernardo?"

"To quote you, 'I'm playing this by ear,' " Martín said. "Garcia, have you got that copy of *La Nacíon*?"

"In my room," Garcia said.

"Please get it and then join us in the mess," Martín said. " 'Us' being Generals Nolasco and Nervo, plus Don Cletus . . . and Subteniente Cronley and Father Welner, now that I think about it."

"You sure you want to walk — hobble — all the way over there on your crutches?" Frade asked.

"Think about it, Cletus," Martín said. "Only a cretin would want to. One does what one must."

He began lurching across the lawn, and the others followed.

[EIGHT]

Captain O'Reilley had been installed in a chair facing the "senior officers" table in the mess.

If that table wasn't loaded with the stuff I brought from Kloster Grünau, Cronley thought, *it would look like this room had been set up for a court-martial.*

All that's missing is an American flag, a Bible,

and the Manual for Courts-Martial 1928.
   And a couple of MPs.

When Martín waved everybody into chairs at the table, Jimmy started to put the material in stacks.

O'Reilley stood.

"With respect, *mi General,* I asked for a moment of your time in private."

"I remember," Martín said. "Perhaps a little later. You may stand if you wish, but you have my permission to sit."

O'Reilley sat down.

"Frankly, O'Reilley, you puzzle me," Martín then said. "I really can't understand how an officer like you, with a fine record and a career to look forward to, got involved in something shameful like this."

"With respect, *mi General,* I don't know what you're talking about."

"The next time you lie to me, Captain," Martín said conversationally, "one of General Nervo's gendarmes will smash your left hand with his truncheon. If you're unwilling to tell me the truth, it would behoove you to say nothing."

He let that sink in for a moment.

"Is this the first time you've actually seen Don Cletus, O'Reilley?"

"No, sir."

"You saw him while surveilling Casa Montagna? Or perhaps as he went up and down Route 60?"

For a long moment it looked as if O'Reilley wasn't going to reply, but then, as if he had carefully composed his reply before uttering it, he said, "I saw Don Cletus on several occasions while carrying out my lawful orders to report on any suspicious activity I saw here."

"Lawful orders from el Coronel Klausberger, you mean?"

This time O'Reilley didn't reply.

"Who else could issue an order like that but el Coronel Klausberger?" Martín asked. "Or did this 'lawful order' come from someone else? And if so, whom?"

It took a long time for O'Reilley to consider the answer he finally gave.

"Yes, sir. I was ordered to surveille Casa Montagna by el Coronel Klausberger."

"And did el Coronel Klausberger order you to protect the SS men as they looked for, and ultimately found, a spot along Route 60 from which they could attack Don Cletus?"

O'Reilley didn't reply.

"If I were in your shoes, O'Reilley, faced with the choice between lying and betraying your commander, I wouldn't have answered that question either," Martín said, almost kindly.

"May I suggest, General," Frade said, "that you tell the captain that in the failed attempt on my life, all of the SS men involved died?"

"Don Cletus speaks the truth, Captain

O'Reilley," Martín said. "But I suggest it would not be wise for you to heave a sigh of relief because dead men tell no tales and thus you can't be tied to them. We should know their identities shortly, in a matter of days."

Again there was no response from O'Reilley.

"Cronley," Martín said, "tell the captain how we are going to identify the SS men who tried to assassinate you and Don Cletus earlier today."

How the hell am I going to do that?

He looked at Martín, who directed him with his eyes to the stack of dossiers Cronley was still in the process of straightening.

"Yes, sir," Jimmy said. "Actually it's quite simple."

And I will explain how simple once I figure it out.

"We have dossiers, like these," Jimmy said, holding one up.

"Who is 'we'?" O'Reilley blurted.

"The U.S. Army," Jimmy answered.

"Señor Cronley is Don Cletus's liaison officer with the U.S. Army in Germany," Martín clarified.

"He's an American officer?" O'Reilley asked incredulously.

"Yes, I am," Jimmy said. "We captured all the records of the SS, all their dossiers like this. They include photographs and fingerprints. Now as I understand how this is going to work, General Nervo's people have photographed the people we killed and taken their fingerprints. The photographs and prints will be sent as priority cargo on SAA to Germany, where they will be matched with the SS dossiers. I think we'll have answers in less than a week, and certainly in ten days."

Jimmy looked at O'Reilley and decided, to his genuine surprise, that O'Reilley wasn't questioning anything he had said.

"Thank you," Martín said. "So, O'Reilley, these dead men will tell tales."

O'Reilley didn't reply.

"What I don't understand, O'Reilley," Martín said reasonably, "is why el Coronel Klausberger wanted to kill Don Cletus. He must know who he is."

"I am afraid I do not know what that means, *mi General.*"

"Well, he's one of el Coronel Perón's closest advisers. You don't know that? I'm sure Klausberger does."

"Sir, with respect, I find that very hard to believe," O'Reilley said.

"Garcia, you don't happen to have that copy of *La Nación,* do you?" Martín asked. "Did you throw it away?"

"Let me check my briefcase, *mi General.* But I'm almost sure I threw it away."

After a twenty-second search, Garcia said, "Well, I'll be damned, here it is!"

He handed the newspaper to Martín, who held it up to O'Reilley.

"Recognize anybody standing with President Farrell and el Coronel Perón, Captain? On the balcony of Casa Rosada? How about Father Welner? Maybe Don Cletus?"

O'Reilley's genuine shock was visible on his face.

"Why do you think, Captain O'Reilley, that el Coronel Klausberger wants Don Cletus dead — and el Coronel Perón, too? Were you aware an attempt was made on el Coronel Perón's life?"

"And your life, General," Frade offered. "Attempts that nearly succeeded."

"I can't imagine why he would want to do that," Martín went on. "But it's clearly not in the best interests of our beloved Argentine Republic."

"It looks to me, Captain," Frade said, "that Colonel Klausberger has made a fool of you, appealing to your patriotism and your officer's Code of Honor."

O'Reilley looked at him and after a long moment asked, plaintively, "What can I do now?"

"You can go to President Farrell, my son," Father Welner said, "and to el Coronel Perón and make a clean breast of everything. Perhaps they will be able to find it in their hearts to forgive you."

"How would I do that?" O'Reilley asked.

"If you're sure that's what you want to do, we'll fly you to Buenos Aires tonight," Martín said. "Father Welner will go with you."

O'Reilley nodded solemnly.

"It's clearly my duty, *mi General,*" he said.

[NINE]

The interrogators went from the officers' mess to the bar in Casa Montagna.

Cletus Marcus Howell, Doña Dorotea, Martha Howell, Marjie, Beth, Alicia von Wachtstein, Elsa von Wachtstein, Karl Boltitz, and Willi von Dattenberg were sitting in small armchairs around a huge, circular table.

Jimmy saw that Marjie was looking curiously at Elsa.

To judge her reaction to me coming into the room?

Hans-Peter von Wachtstein was behind the bar, opening a bottle of wine.

"Yes, barkeep, I will have a little of that," Frade said. "You won't."

"I won't? Why?"

"How much have you had so far?" Frade said.

"Why do I think you have a reason for asking?"

"Because you have a suspicious nature," Frade said. "But I'll give you a hint: Jimmy doesn't get any either."

"We're going flying? Tonight?"

"Congratulations! You have just won the cement bicycle and an all-expenses-paid tour

779

of downtown Mendoza."

"I presume," Cletus Marcus Howell said, "that when you're through being clever, you will tell us what happened to the guy in the truck."

"Certainly," Clete replied. "After an absolutely brilliant interrogation by General Martín . . ."

"Yes, it was," General Nervo agreed. "He should really consider a career in intelligence."

"Or maybe becoming a Jesuit," Clete said. "They're always trying to get people to confess their sins."

"I don't know if he could handle that," Nervo said. "The obedience and poverty that goes with it, maybe. But the chastity?"

"Oh, for Christ's sake!" Cletus Marcus Howell exploded.

"You both will go to hell for such mockery," Father Welner said.

"Sorry," Clete said. "As I was saying, Captain O'Reilley fessed up. More important, he's going to confess all — all including that the villain behind the surveillance of Casa Montagna and the ambush on Route 60 is el Coronel Hans Klausberger. And more important than that, he's going to tell my Tío Juan all about it just as soon as we can get him to Buenos Aires. Him and our Jesuit."

"Tonight?" Doña Dorotea asked.

"Just as soon as we can round up half a

dozen Húsares to go with them."

"And the purpose of telling Colonel Perón is . . . ?" the old man asked.

"To keep his attention away from what we're doing down south until after we do it."

"And why is Jimmy going along?" Marjie asked.

"This is Argentina, Squirt," Clete said, "where women are not allowed to ask questions."

"Screw you, Cletus," Marjie said.

"*This* woman, Cletus," Martha began, paused, then said, "My God! I can't believe you — either of you — said what you did. But this woman asks questions wherever she damned well pleases. Cletus, why is Jimmy flying, not you?"

"Because if I go to Buenos Aires, I'll have to deal with my Tío Juan. And because Jimmy needs the practice."

"Practice for what?" Marjie asked.

Clete didn't have to answer the question. Enrico Rodríguez came into the bar.

"The men are in the station wagons, Don Cletus."

"Let's go, guys," Clete ordered.

"Hansel will need a change of clothes," Doña Alicia said.

"No, he won't," Clete said. "As soon as he unloads and arranges for one — or, better, two — SAA Lodestars to come here, he'll be coming back."

"Why more airplanes?" the old man asked.

"I have a hunch we're going to need them down south," Clete said.

Doña Alicia, Doña Dorotea, and Martha Howell went out onto the veranda to see their men off with a kiss.

So did Marjie.

"Hey, Mom," Marjie said. "Watch me piss Clete off!"

"What did you say?"

Marjie walked quickly to Jimmy, grabbed his ears, pulled his face to hers, kissed him wetly on the mouth, and said, "Have a nice flight, Jimmy!"

"I'll be a sonofabitch!" Clete said. "The Squirt is nuts!"

"Yeah," Marjie said.

XIV

[ONE]

El Plumerillo Airfield
Mendoza, Mendoza Province, Argentina
0810 22 October 1945

As the red Lodestar reached the end of its landing roll, Second Lieutenant James D. Cronley Jr., who was sitting in the left seat, turned to Hans-Peter von Wachtstein, who was sitting in the right seat, and announced, "Well, Hansel, as Clete likes to say, it would seem that we have cheated death again."

"One, you are not Cletus. And, two, I don't recall giving you permission to call me Hansel," von Wachtstein said with a smile. "But that aside, that was a nice landing. Not as smooth as one of my own, of course, but just as smooth as Cletus ever makes. What's this business about you hating to fly?"

"I hate to fly *alone*," Jimmy said, turning the Lodestar onto the taxiway. "I *refuse* to fly alone. But as long as I have someone like you sitting in the other seat, I'm Lucky Charlie Lindbergh."

"What's that all about?"

"Very simple. I acknowledge my cowardice."

Von Wachtstein shook his head, and then, pointing, said, "There they are."

Cletus Frade and Enrico Rodríguez were standing in front of one of the hangars.

Eighteen ex–Húsares de Pueyrredón, wearing SAA security uniforms and carrying a variety of weapons — mostly Thompsons — and canvas bags, got off the Lodestar. They formed ranks as automatically as if they were still on active duty with the Húsares de Pueyrredón. Von Wachtstein and Cronley disembarked last.

One of the SAA security men saluted Clete, and said, *"Mi Coronel."*

Clete returned the salute.

"Welcome to Mendoza," he called out. "Suboficial Mayor Rodríguez has breakfast for you in the hangar. Bread and water. No wine."

There were the expected chuckles from the group.

The man who had saluted Clete went to Enrico, hugged him, then motioned for the others to follow him into the hangar.

"Are the other planes far behind?" Cletus asked Jimmy and Hansel. "How many of them are there?"

Jimmy shook his head.

"Zero. Zilch. Zip. In other words, none."

"What the hell?"

"There were no available aircraft, Cletus," von Wachtstein said. "Half a dozen were down for maintenance until this afternoon, and the others were all scheduled. And since they weren't going to be needed, Martín's pilots — the ones who are BIS — took the day off. The only way we could have gotten one Lodestar, much less two, was to cancel a scheduled flight or flights — and they weren't about to do that without a reason, and I didn't think you would want us to give one."

"Damn, that's bad news," Clete said. "Okay, let's have all the bad news. What about Welner, O'Reilley, and my Tío Juan?"

Von Wachtstein looked at his watch.

"They have been together for the last ten minutes."

"Where?"

"Perón's apartment on Arenales. Jimmy said we didn't know (a) where he would be going to work — the Casa Rosada, the Edificio Libertador, or the Labor Ministry — and (b) if we could get into any of those places with your guys."

"How do you know he was in his apartment?"

"Jimmy's idea. We went into the lobby and used the house phone —"

"At two o'clock in the morning?" Clete interrupted.

Jimmy grinned.

"Actually, oh-two-thirty, Clete. I called, acting like an angry neighbor, and told him to turn down the volume on his radio. Your Tío Juan blew his cork. It was him, all right. So we left Father Welner, O'Reilley, and your guys there, then went back to Jorge Frade and got in the red Lodestar. At oh-eight-hundred, they knocked on his door."

"The concierge let them in?"

"It's hard to say no to a priest, Clete," Jimmy said. "Even more so if he has six guys with Thompsons standing behind him. The concierge and Perón's security detail — two guys — were very cooperative. They knew who Welner is."

"How's Dieter?" von Wachtstein asked.

"We're going to see him after I show you the bad news from Estancia Condor," Frade said, and motioned for them to go in the hangar.

The hangar was crowded with soldiers. Too many to count, but Jimmy guessed about forty. Plus of course the eighteen ex–Húsares de Pueyrredón they had brought from Buenos Aires.

"General Martin," Frade explained drily, "was able to persuade the commanding officer of the Húsares de Pueyrredón that the BIS needed half a squadron of troopers for an unspecified classified mission."

Master Sergeant Sigfried Stein was sitting at a table on which he had set up a Collins 7.2 and a SIGABA. The SIGABA's electric typewriter was clattering.

"More from down there, Siggie?" Frade asked.

"No. But I thought a printout would be more useful than the tape."

He pointed to the coiled strip of paper, which was the first product of an incoming message.

The typewriter stopped clattering.

Stein took two sheets of paper from the machine and handed them to Frade, who handed them to von Wachtstein.

"Read over his shoulder, Jimmy," Frade said. "Or take the tape."

Cronley, who knew what a pain in the ass reading from the narrow, fragile tape was, looked over von Wachtstein's shoulder. Frade picked up the tape and started to read it again.

SUBJECT: SITUATION REPORT 0705
22 OCT 1945

TO: GENERAL DE BRIGADE B. MAR-
TIN, BIS

1. AS OF 0615 22 OCT THE UN-
DERSIGNED HAS ASSUMED
CONTROL OF ESTANCIO
CONDOR AND THE RADIO RE-
LAY STATION HEREON.

2. IT WAS NECESSARY TO PLACE
UNDER ARREST ONE (1) CAP-
TAIN, TWO (2) LIEUTENANTS
AND SIX (6) OTHER RANKS
OF THE 10TH MOUNTAIN
REGIMENT SIGNALS COM-
PANY PLUS TWO (2) LIEUTEN-
ANTS AND TWENTY-FOUR
(24) OTHER RANKS OF THE
10TH MOUNTAIN SERVING AS
A PROTECTIVE DETACH-
MENT HERE INASMUCH AS
THEY REFUSED TO AC-
KNOWLEDGE THE AUTHOR-
ITY OF THE UNDERSIGNED.

3. THE 10TH MOUNTAIN CAP-
TAIN, AFTER INTERROGA-
TION, TOLD THE UNDER-
SIGNED THAT EL CORONEL
KLAUSBERGER HAD TELE-

PHONED HIM AT APPROXI-
MATELY 2300 HOURS 21 OC-
TOBER TO ALERT HIM TO
THE POSSIBILITY THAT UN-
AUTHORIZED PERSONNEL
WERE LIKELY TO APPEAR AT
ESTANCIO CONDOR WITHIN
THE NEXT DAY OR TWO,
WHEREUPON HE WAS TO
PLACE THEM UNDER AR-
REST AND REPORT THE
EVENT TO HIM. KLAUS-
BERGER ALSO STATED THAT
REINFORCEMENTS ARE ON
THE WAY BUT DID NOT
STATE THE STRENGTH OF
SUCH REINFORCEMENTS
OR WHEN THEY CAN BE EX-
PECTED.

4. THIS DIFFICULT SITUATION
IS EXACERBATED BY OUR
STRENGTH, WHICH IS NOW
THIRTEEN (13) ARMED CIVIL-
IANS, ALL FORMER MEMBERS
OF THE HÚSARES DE PUEY-
RREDÓN AND SIX (6) UN-
ARMED AND UNTRAINED
MECHANICS AND DRIVERS,
ALL EMPLOYEES OF SAA. THE
LATTER HAVE NOW BEEN

ARMED WITH WEAPONS SEIZED FROM 10TH MOUNTAIN PERSONNEL BUT THEIR ABILITY TO USE THEM EFFECTIVELY IS AT BEST QUESTIONABLE.

5. ON THE MARCH HERE THE UNDERSIGNED AGAIN ENCOUNTERED RESISTANCE TO MY AUTHORITY WHEN ATTEMPTING TO RESERVE THE AVIATION FUEL STOCKS AT THE TRELEW NAVAL AIRFIELD.

6. TO ENSURE THAT THE AVIATION FUEL STOCKS WOULD BE AVAILABLE AND TO PREVENT THE NAVY PERSONNEL OF THE TRELEW AIRFIELD FROM NOTIFYING THEIR HIGHER HEADQUARTERS OF OUR PRESENCE (AND OUR REQUISITION OF FUEL) IT WAS DEEMED NECESSARY TO BOTH SHUT DOWN THE TELEPHONE AND RADIO COMMUNICATION AT THE FIELD AND TO CONFINE THE NAVY PERSONNEL TO THE BASE. TO ACCOMPLISH THAT

IT WAS NECESSARY TO LEAVE THE HÚSARES DE PUEYRREDÓN MILITARY DETACHMENT OF ONE (1) SENIOR SERGEANT AND SIX (6) OTHER RANKS AT TRELEW. THE SHUTDOWN OF COMMUNICATIONS WILL PREVENT BOTH YOU AND THE UNDERSIGNED FROM CONTACTING THE SERGEANT IN CHARGE.

7. SENOR GRÜNER STATES THAT HE CAN HAVE THE STORCH AIRCRAFT READY FOR FLIGHT BY 0800 AND THE PIPER CUB READY BY 1000. HE FURTHER STATES THAT BOTH AIRCRAFT CAN BE OPERATED FROM THE TERRAIN HERE. IT IS NOTED THAT GRÜNER IS THE ONLY PILOT HERE AND HE HAS NEVER FLOWN A CUB, ALTHOUGH HE FEELS HE CAN DO SO.

8. GRÜNER FURTHER STATES THAT THE TERRAIN HERE IS SIMILAR TO THAT HE ENCOUNTERED IN RUSSIA --

THAT IS, WHILE THE ICE CAP THEREON WILL SUPPORT BOTH THE STORCH AND THE CUB IN LANDING AND TAKEOFF OPERATIONS AND PROBABLY -- EMPHASIS PROBABLY -- SUPPORT LANDING AND TAKEOFF OF LODESTAR AIRCRAFT, IT IS PROBABLE -- EMPHASIS PROBABLE -- THAT ONCE STOPPED THE WEIGHT OF LODESTAR AIRCRAFT WILL CAUSE IT TO BREAK THROUGH THE ICE CAP, THEREBY RENDERING IT IMMOBILE.

9. DIRECTION REQUESTED.

RESPECTFULLY SUBMITTED.

CARLOS HABANZO

CORONEL, BIS

"My God!" von Wachtstein said.

"Well, if Nervo wanted to see what this Klausberger character was going to do when he learned that O'Reilley had been bagged, I think he succeeded," Jimmy said. "How soon can he get his reinforcements to Estancia

Condor?"

"I don't know exactly," Clete said, "but they can get there quicker than we can get these guys down there by road. San Martín de los Andes is a lot closer to Estancia Condor than we are." He paused and shook his head. "Even before we got this, my plan was to fly our reinforcements to Trelew, and move them by truck to the estancia. Then you showed up with the wonderful news that there will be no more Lodestars."

"What are you going to do, Clete?" Jimmy asked.

"Following the famous Cletus Frade theory that it's better to do something, anything, when you don't have any idea at all what to do, I'm going to have the Húsares and my people start preparing for a road march. Find some trucks, fuel cans, food, et cetera. Then, as soon as we get back from seeing Dieter, you and Hansel are going to fly the Húsares captain and a dozen guys to Trelew, and play it by ear."

[Two]

The Hospital of the Little Sisters of Saint Pilar
Mendoza, Mendoza Province, Argentina
0850 22 October 1945
Dieter von und zu Aschenburg was propped up in the hospital bed when Mother Superior

came in his room followed by Clete, Hans, and Jimmy.

"You have five minutes with him," she announced. "Then I'm going to give him something for his pain."

"You haven't given him anything yet?" Frade blurted.

"He said he was going to wait until he heard from you, Cletus. I now understand why you're all such good friends. You're all crazy."

"What do we hear from Willi?" Dieter asked.

Clete handed him the printout from the SI-GABA.

"And there's more good news," Clete said, when he'd finished reading it. "We don't have any airplanes to reinforce Habanzo."

"What are you going to do?" Dieter asked.

Frade told him.

"My God!" Dieter said.

"Dieter," Jimmy said, "tell me about the landing and takeoff rolls in snow and ice like that. Would a Lodestar break through the ice cap the moment it stopped rolling?"

"Probably not," Dieter said. "You'd probably have a couple of minutes before the ice cracked."

"Now the takeoff. For the sake of argument, a Lodestar is sitting someplace where it won't, hasn't, crashed through the ice."

"Where are you going with this, Jimmy?"

796

Frade asked, half curious and half annoyed.

The look changed to pure annoyance when Jimmy held up his hand to silence him and went on: "And suppose the Lodestar could move a couple of meters, maybe four or five meters" — he looked at Clete — "off the plywood, or similar substance, timbers, et cetera, on which it has been sitting. Would it then be going fast enough so that it wouldn't crash through the ice and could begin its takeoff roll?"

Von und zu Aschenburg considered the question a long moment before replying.

"If the Lodestar was sitting on the 'plywood, or similar substance, timbers, et cetera' and the 'plywood, or similar substance, timbers, et cetera' was at the threshold of the runway, you probably could."

Cronley knew he was being mocked and smiled.

"You don't have a runway," Frade said.

"I'd be willing to give that a shot," von Wachtstein said.

"Silence, please," Jimmy said. "I'm having one of my epiphanies, and it's not quite complete."

"Oh, Jesus Christ," Clete said, in disgust.

"Okay, epiphany complete," Jimmy said, perhaps a minute later. He turned to von Wachtstein. "No, Hansel, as much as I would like to see you, rather than me, trying, you will be otherwise occupied."

"Doing what?" von Wachtstein asked.

"Flying the red Lodestar. Pay attention. What do we need at Estancia Condor? Primarily, someone to seize that atomic crap in the name of the United States government, and we have already decided that has to be me.

"We also need somebody to fly the Piper Cub to help find the submarine and said atomic crap supposedly aboard. Which I can do.

"We also need reinforcements for Colonel Habanzo as the Apaches are about to attack his wagon train and will scalp everybody.

"So here's the plan. We load as many of the real Húsares as will fit into Clete's red Lodestar, and as many of Clete's guys as will fit into the shot-up, no-radio-or-navigation-equipment SAA Lodestar. Hansel, flying the red Lodestar, will lead me in the Lodestar with no radio or nav equipment to Trelew, which is important as I never heard that name until about thirty minutes ago and have no idea where it is.

"At Trelew, we unload the real Húsares. We unload ten of Clete's people from the shot-up Lodestar and replace them with a like number of real Húsares. We refuel the aircraft, and Hansel leads me to Estancia Condor, where . . . I will crash and burn trying to land where my common sense tells me I shouldn't be landing."

Von und zu Aschenburg laughed.

"There will be no monument to my heroism," Jimmy went on, "as the Russians will arrive the next day, seize the uranium oxide, and use it to make atomic bombs with which *they* will make New York City, Buenos Aires, and Midland, Texas, disappear in mushroom-shaped nuclear clouds — all of which will clearly be my fault."

Von und zu Aschenburg laughed again.

"Stop being a comedian, for God's sake," he said. "Every time I laugh, it hurts."

"That does it," Mother Superior said from the door. "Everybody out!"

Jimmy looked at Clete.

"Well, Colonel, sir?"

"You'll have to take von Dattenberg with you," Frade said. "I have a gut feeling he'll be useful."

"Jimmy," Dieter said, "the trick is to make a very gradual descent as slow as you can, so there's no heavy shock to the ice cap. Glide it in like a feather."

"Got it. Thank you."

"Why do I think you'd rather go to a penal battalion?" Dieter asked.

"Because you're perceptive?"

Von und zu Aschenburg laughed and then put his hand on the bandage on his side.

"Goddamn it! I told you to stop!"

"And I said everybody out!" Mother Superior snapped.

[Three]

Three station wagons drove onto the tarmac and stopped between the red and shot-up SAA Lodestars.

Willi von Dattenberg got out of the middle station wagon. And so did Elsa von Wacht-stein.

Well, I guess the new girlfriend came to see him off, Clete thought.

If you think about it, it's sort of nice — her being a widow and all, and a friend of the family — that they've hit it off like that.

Von Dattenberg went to the rear of the station wagon and started to pull out the heavy case holding the Admiral Byrd cold-weather gear. Security guards rushed to help him load it into the SAA Lodestar.

And then Martha Howell got out of the station wagon.

And I guess she came to see Jimmy off.

Well, why not? He's always been like another son to her.

And then Miss Marjorie Howell got out of the station wagon.

What the hell is she doing here?

"Squirt," Clete called. "What the hell do you think you're doing here?"

800

"What the hell does it look like, you sonof-abitch?" Marjie replied.

She quickly scanned the tarmac and found Jimmy Cronley, who had just about finished his walk-around inspection of the SAA Lodestar.

She went up to him.

"You sonofabitch! You really were going to leave without saying good-bye."

She kicked him in the shin and, when he bent over, she slapped his face.

Clete stood with Martha Howell, watching the scene.

"What is that, true love?" he said.

"Shut up, Cletus," Martha Howell replied.

After a moment, she then said, "Well, I'd say that's what it looks like, wouldn't you?"

Marjie and Jimmy were now clutching each other tightly.

"I'll be a sonofabitch," Clete said.

"Yes, and you do that so well," Martha said.

Marjie and Jimmy broke apart, kissed, then he limped to the rear door of the SAA Lodestar, climbed aboard, and the door swung shut behind him.

When Jimmy got to the cockpit, von Dattenberg was strapping himself into the co-pilot's seat.

"Cletus said I should sit here," he announced. "To be of what help I can."

"That's known as the blind leading the

blind," Jimmy said as he got into the pilot's seat. "Don't touch anything!"

When Jimmy's face appeared in the cockpit window, Clete ran to where Marjie stood in front of the left engine nacelle. He led her back to Martha.

They watched as the whine of the engine starter came and the left engine began to turn, emitting smoke and a burst of flame before finally smoothing down.

Hans-Peter had the red Lodestar already taxiing off the tarmac.

As Jimmy hurried to follow, he started the right engine of the SAA Lodestar.

The red Lodestar turned onto the runway from the taxiway and immediately made its takeoff roll. The SAA Lodestar then turned onto the runway — and stopped.

As Jimmy stood on the brakes and ran up the throttles, he looked at von Dattenberg.

"See that lever with the wheel?" he said, pointing as the aircraft began vibrating heavily. "When we're in the air and I call out 'gear,' pull back on it, and then when that green light lights up, tell me. Got it?"

"Got it," von Dattenberg said, nodding and giving him a *thumbs-up* gesture.

Jimmy looked out the windscreen and saw the red Lodestar getting smaller as the aircraft quickly gained altitude.

He quietly wondered aloud, "What the fuck am I doing?"

Then he shoved the throttles to TAKEOFF POWER and released the brakes.

Marjie shrugged out of her mother's embrace and watched as the airplanes took off.

She turned to Clete.

"Jimmy's airplane is full of bullet holes!" she accused. "There's even plywood over one of the windows!"

Clete nodded. "And there's no navigation equipment except a magnetic compass. But it's airworthy. We flew it yesterday. Jimmy, too. He'll be all right, Squirt."

She threw herself into his arms and sobbed.

"Oh, Clete, I love him so much!"

"Really? I never would have guessed anything like that."

She pushed herself away from him and looked up at his face.

Then she laughed.

"Would you, Martha?" Clete added.

"I would never have guessed. I thought she was smoking those funny cigarettes."

"Well, now I know where not to go when I need a little sympathy," Marjie said, but she was smiling.

Clete put his arm around her shoulder and led her to the station wagon.

[Four]

Cronley shot three touch-and-gos on the Trelew runway, practicing what Dieter von und zu Aschenburg had told him was the trick to land on snow and ice. There was neither snow nor ice on the Trelew airfield, which made Cronley curious.

The fourth time he touched down, he completed the landing roll and turned onto a taxiway. When he'd reached the terminal tarmac, he stopped the SAA Lodestar beside the red Lodestar, and shut it down.

"Well, Kapitän von Dattenberg," he said, in German, "it looks as if I have once again cheated death."

Von Dattenberg's face showed surprise, even shock, at the remark, but didn't respond.

"As Cletus Frade taught me when he taught me how to fly, 'Any landing you can walk away from is a good one.' "

"I thought those were very good landings," von Dattenberg said.

"You don't have much of a sense of humor, do you?"

"I suppose I don't."

Hans-Peter von Wachtstein, accompanied by two men in army uniforms, Thompsons

804

slung from their shoulders, approached the airplane.

"I hope those guys are the Húsares de Pueyrredón who Oberst Habanzo left here," Jimmy said. "And that Hansel is not under arrest. Otherwise, we're going to find ourselves in a cell somewhere, or standing against a wall."

The joke went right past von Dattenberg.

"Who else could they be?" von Dattenberg asked, and then, after realization came, said, "Elsa — Frau von Wachtstein — told me you have a strange sense of humor."

"Did she really?"

And what else did Elsa the Great tell you about me?

Jimmy unfastened his shoulder harness and got out of the pilot's seat.

"Well, if we're going to get shot, let's get it over."

When Jimmy Cronley opened the door, Hans-Peter von Wachtstein was standing beside the two Húsares.

"The sergeant here," von Wachtstein said in German, "was so glad to see the Húsares de Pueyrredón captain on my plane that I thought he was going to cry."

"How so?" Cronley said.

"There's seven Húsares, including him, and about fifty Armada Argentina people. He was sure it was only a matter of time until the navy people remembered where they had put the ammo for their weapons and retook the base."

" 'Remembered where they had put their ammo?' " Cronley parroted.

"No kidding. When the Húsares sergeant disarmed the guards, only the commanding officer had a loaded gun, a pistol. None of the sailors had ammo in their rifles —"

"Where is the Húsares captain now?" von Dattenberg asked.

"He said he was going to try to convince the navy commander — he's a corvette captain — that by the authority vested in him by the Húsares de Pueyrredón colonel, he is authorized to requisition the fuel for our aircraft."

"And if this fellow says no?"

"That's a problem, Willi," von Wachtstein admitted.

"We have the weapons," Cronley reasoned.

"But we don't want to use them," von Wachtstein countered. "You don't want Perón to ask 'What exactly was your little brother doing in Trelew, Cletus, when he declared war on the Armada Argentina?' And sooner or later, probably sooner, one of these navy guys is going to realize nobody's watching him — and we don't have enough people to watch all of them all of the time — and go over the fence, go into the town of Trelew, and get on the telephone."

Cronley nodded.

Von Wachtstein went on: "And, for the sake of argument, let's say that you can put that Lodestar on the ground tomorrow —"

"On the ice, you mean?" Cronley interrupted.

Von Wachtstein nodded.

"On that subject, where is all this ice and snow I keep hearing about? There's none here."

"It starts about one hundred kilometers south of here," von Dattenberg offered. "And from that point southward, that's all there is."

"How do you know that?" Cronley challenged.

"That's what the charts I had on U-405 showed," von Dattenberg answered.

"If I may continue, gentlemen?" von Wachtstein said. "If you can land that Lodestar on the ice and snow at Estancia Condor tomorrow . . ."

"That presumes we can find Estancia Condor," Cronley said.

Von Wachtstein ignored him. ". . . without either bending it, or having it sink through the ice cap. And that presuming you and Willi Grüner can find U-234, and that the crew of U-234 gives you the uranium oxide because they like your smile, and that you can somehow get it from where you find the U-234 back to where you have parked your Lodestar, which has miraculously not broken through the ice cap, and that you manage to take off, you will have only enough fuel to make it back here. Not enough to fly to Mendoza to meet Señor Howell's Constellation."

He let that sink in, then finished with: "In other words, we are going to need more co-operation from the navy than we're liable to get by pointing guns at them."

Cronley didn't say anything for a moment, then said, "You didn't mention how I'm supposed to find my way back here with only a magnetic compass, but it's not important. I'm a second lieutenant, after all, and thus able to easily deal with those minor problems."

"Unless your modesty gets in your way," von Wachtstein said.

"But the . . . *diplomatic* problems of dealing with the navy is something else. Let me give it a moment's thought."

A long moment later, he said, "Eureka!"

"Eureka?" von Wachtstein said.

"That means 'the sudden, unexpected realization of the solution to a problem,' " Cronley said. "You might want to write that down."

"After I hear what it is, I might do just that," von Wachtstein replied.

"What General Martín did to convince that Tenth Mountain captain that he was on the wrong side of this was show him the picture on the front page of *La Nacíon* of Cletus standing next to Perón on the balcony of the Casa Rosada."

"So?"

"We tell the corvette captain we are on a confidential mission that Clete is running for Perón, and the proof of that is you're flying Clete's personal red Lodestar."

After a moment, von Wachtstein grinned and nodded.

"That might be just crazy enough to work. And you just happen to have a copy of *La Nacíon,* right?"

"No. But I wouldn't be surprised if there was one in the air force officers' club."

"And if there's not?"

"Then you're going to have to think of something else. That was my best shot at a solution to this dilemma."

After a moment, von Wachtstein said, thoughtfully, "You know, that's really not such a bad idea. And in the absence of anything else, I think we should try it."

When they got to the Officers' Club, the Húsares de Pueyrredón captain and the navy corvette captain were sharing a bottle of wine.

"Gentlemen," the Húsares de Pueyrredón captain announced, "may I introduce my cousin, Corvette Captain Raphael Aguirre? Rafe, this is Captain von Wachtstein of South American Airways, and Señores von Dattenberg and Cronley, who are on the staff of Don Cletus Frade."

"An honor, gentlemen," Corvette Captain Aguirre said, offering each of them his hand. "José has been telling me about your mission."

"I hope he hasn't told you things he should not have told you," von Wachtstein said sternly.

"Captain," Aguirre said, "my lips are sealed."

Von Wachtstein met his eyes for a long moment, then said, "Because he has told you whatever he has, and because you and José are family, I will tell you — with the understanding that it will go no further — what I can."

"I understand, sir."

"Did José tell you that an attempt was made to assassinate el Coronel Perón?" von Wachtstein asked.

"No, sir. José said there were difficulties, difficulties he could not share with me."

Cronley thought: *That's twice this guy has called Hansel "sir."*

That's a good sign . . .

"There was also an attempt on the life of General de Brigada Martín of BIS," von Wachtstein went on. "Both attempts failed, but unfortunately el Coronel Perón and General Martín were wounded, General Martín rather seriously."

"Who did it?" Aguirre asked.

"We have reason to believe that certain members of the Tenth Mountain are attempting a coup d'état."

"Do you know who?"

"No. We won't know until we catch them. When they realized that Martín and Perón were still alive, they ran."

"And you're chasing them?" he asked, but it was more of a statement than a question.

Von Wachtstein nodded.

"The delicate thing here, Captain, is that President Farrell and el Coronel Perón don't want the story to get out. They believe that it would be best for the country if this thing were dealt with quietly. Now, we know, or we think we know, where these traitors are headed."

"And you're going there to arrest them?"

Again, his question came out as a statement.

"You've noticed, I'm sure, that we're flying Don Cletus's personal airplane and an SAA aircraft. We took that from the maintenance hangar still bearing the bullet holes that were put in it during the assassination attempt. We wanted to get it out of Buenos Aires before the press saw it and started asking questions. And of course the whereabouts of Don Cletus's airplane is no one's business but Don Cletus's."

"Sir, how can I help?" Aguirre asked.

"In two ways, Captain, both equally important. First of course is refueling our aircraft now and when we return. Second, make absolutely sure that none of your men do anything that would tip these people that we're here. Our plan is to be where they're going when they get there."

"Where is that?"

"We absolutely cannot take the risk of them hearing there are people here headed where they're headed. I'm sure you understand."

"Perfectly."

"You can keep all of your men on the base until this is all over?"

"Absolutely. You have my word of honor, sir."

Von Wachtstein solemnly shook Corvette Captain Aguirre's hand.

Okay, Cronley thought. *He's swallowed everything Hansel told him.*

For now.

But what's he going to think in ten minutes, in an hour, when he's had time to think it over?

The answer came ten minutes later, when von Dattenberg turned up a copy of *La Nación* and announced, "Oh, here's a picture of Don Cletus with el Coronel Perón on the balcony of the Casa Rosada."

As Corvette Captain Aguirre examined the photograph, he said, "I had the privilege of meeting Don Cletus's father, el Coronel Jorge

Frade, when my father and I visited José at the regiment, shortly after José had joined the Húsares de Pueyrredón as a subteniente. My father was a great admirer of el Coronel Frade; he was hoping he would become president."

Well, Cronley thought, *we seem to have Corvette Captain Raphael Aguirre — and thus the whole situation here — under control.*

What is that?

"God rewards the virtuous" or "God takes care of fools and drunks"?

Whichever, let's hope it holds.

Odds are that any moment this mission will turn into a colossal clusterfuck . . .

[FIVE]

Almirante Marcos A. Zar Airfield
Trelew, Chubut Province (Patagonia), Argentina
0650 23 October 1945

The red Lodestar was at the end of the runway, with the SAA Lodestar on the taxiway next to it, when the engines of the red Lodestar stopped.

"Oh, shit!" Jimmy Cronley said.

He thought, *And so the colossal clusterfuck has begun . . .*

"What's going on?" Willi von Dattenberg asked.

"Whatever it is, it's not good."

813

When the door of the red Lodestar opened a moment later, von Wachtstein came through it and headed for the SAA Lodestar.

Cronley shut down his engines. Then he started to undo the harness of the pilot's seat. Before he could stand up, von Wachtstein appeared in the cockpit.

"I can't pick up the signal from the Collins 7.2," von Wachtstein said.

"What does that mean?" von Dattenberg asked.

"The plan is for us to home in on a signal from Estancia Condor," von Wachtstein explained. "We told them to start transmitting at six-thirty."

"How did you do that?"

"There's a Collins in Clete's airplane."

"But now you can't hear them?"

"No. It's a different kind of a signal, a directional signal, different frequency, intended to work with the RDF — Radio Direction Finder system."

"And you're too far from Estancia Condor for this other kind of transmission to be heard?"

"Either that, or the signal is being interfered with by some hills — mountains, really — that my map shows are between us and there. What I'm going to do is take off, climb to two thousand meters and see if I can get it there."

"And if you can't?" Cronley said.

"Then I will land and we'll discuss what we can do. If I get a signal, I'll make a pass over the field, and then you take off."

Cronley nodded, and von Wachtstein turned to go back to the red Lodestar.

"Willi," Cronley said, "if you're a religious man this would be a good time to start praying."

"Now," Cronley said as the red Lodestar broke ground.

"Excuse me?" von Dattenberg asked.

"Now is the time to start praying."

"Would you laugh if I told you that's just what I've been doing?"

"Really?"

" 'God, please let me live through this so that Elsa and I can start our new life.' "

"No. I won't laugh."

"You're not praying that God will allow you to return to Cletus's sister?"

Cronley didn't reply.

"I saw the two of you saying good-bye."

Cronley didn't reply immediately. Then, after a long moment, he said, "I don't like asking God for favors. What I will do, if everything works, is say, 'Thank you very much, God.' "

"Interesting."

Ten minutes later, the red Lodestar appeared approaching the runway.

When Cronley saw that both its landing gear and the flaps were retracted, he reached for the starboard engine priming lever.

"Starting Number One," he announced, and a minute later announced, "Starting Number Two."

The red Lodestar flashed overhead, then began a climbing turn to the right.

Cronley moved the Lodestar onto the runway and lined up with the center. He put his right hand on the throttle quadrant and advanced the throttles to TAKEOFF POWER.

"What the fuck am I doing here?" he again wondered aloud.

The Lodestar began accelerating.

Dear God, he prayed silently, *please get me safely back to the Squirt.*

[SIX]

Estancia Condor
National Route 3
Santa Cruz Province, Argentina
1105 23 October 1945

Von Dattenberg had been right. About fifty kilometers south of Trelew, patches of white appeared on the ground, and by the time they were one hundred kilometers south of the airfield snow covered the ground. Even the highway — Route 3 — was covered and hard to make out.

When a collection of buildings that could be nothing else but Estancia Condor appeared on the horizon, the fuel gauges indicated a little more than half was still available. As Cronley began his descent, he decided that was enough fuel for him to make a couple of low-level passes over the runway.

All I have to do now is find the damn runway.

On his first pass over the estancia, Jimmy saw the Storch and a Piper Cub parked one behind the other just outside the complex of buildings and, maybe twenty-five hundred feet away, a bulldozer and a pickup truck parked one behind the other facing the airplanes. There was also a crude windsock showing that steady winds were blowing westward over the "runway," which ran north-south between the aircraft and bulldozer.

That's not going to get any better, he decided, *no matter how many times I fly over it.*

He made a descending turn, slow and wide, and lined up with the bulldozer.

He lowered his flaps.

"Put the gear down, please, Herr Ko-pilot," Cronley ordered. "And call out our speed."

Von Dattenberg dropped the gear.

"One-ten," he called. "One hundred . . . Ninety . . . Eighty-five . . ."

The Lodestar had now dropped so low that for a terrifying two seconds Cronley thought he wasn't going to get over the bulldozer and the pickup. But a second after that he touched down.

He chopped the throttles, then fought hard against — and won over — his Pavlovian reflex to apply the brakes. Any application of the brakes was likely to cause the tires to skid or the gear to break through the ice.

Or both.

The Lodestar slowed almost to a stop as he approached the Storch and the Cub.

He applied just enough throttle to keep moving.

Willi Grüner was now in front of him, giving him hand signals where to go.

The rumble of the landing gear changed.

Grüner made a frantic *Stop!* gesture with his left hand held palm outward. His right hand simultaneously made a cutting motion across his throat with the right, gesturing *Cut the engines!*

Cronley slammed on the brakes and pulled the throttle levers to idle.

The Lodestar stopped.

Grüner, smiling, gave him a thumbs-up.

Cronley shut down the engines and suddenly realized that he was sweating. He slid open the side cockpit window and felt an immediate blast of icy air.

He closed the window as quickly as he had opened it.

He looked at von Dattenberg, and said, "God must have heard you. You're shaking and look a little pale, but we're still alive."

"I suspect He heard us both."

Colonel Carlos Habanzo and Wilhelm Grüner were waiting for Cronley and von Dattenberg when they came through the door of the Lodestar.

Cronley saw the airplane had stopped on some kind of a wooden structure, and after a moment he realized what it was: the wall of a building.

"What did you do, tear down a building?" he greeted them.

"Actually, two buildings," Grüner answered. "You're sitting on two walls. The other two are down there by the bulldozer. The roof is over there."

He pointed.

"I thought Don Cletus would be coming," Habanzo said in obvious disappointment.

Shall I go back and get him? Cronley thought but did not say. His mouth ran away with him anyway. "I'm expendable, Colonel. Cletus is not."

That earned him a dirty look.

Grüner picked up on that and quickly asked, "You brought your cold-weather gear?"

Cronley nodded. "It's in the airplane."

"You're going to need it. If there's a heater in the Cub, I couldn't find how to turn it on."

"You test-flew it after you put the wings on?"

"No. I've never flown one. I decided to wait for you."

"Well, let me take a piss and have some lunch, and then I'll give it a test hop."

"Better yet, why don't we kill two birds with one stone?"

Where have I heard that before?

"What two birds?"

"We get in both airplanes, and fly to the coast and make a couple of test runs, different altitudes, different speeds, et cetera, which shouldn't take more than an hour, and then we come back here and, over lunch, talk over how we'll search after lunch."

Jimmy didn't like it but couldn't find the words to say why.

"Would it be all right if I took my piss first?"

"Take it here, on the wall." He pointed at the material under the Lodestar. "And watch. It's very interesting. It freezes just about as soon as it hits the ground."

"I gather we don't have air-to-air radios?"

"If we do, I don't know to turn them on," Grüner said. "Clete made changes to the Storch communications panel. American stuff I've never seen before. Have a look."

After seeing that his Little Yellow Stream did indeed freeze just about the instant it hit the wall, Jimmy went to the Storch. By the time he managed to get into the cockpit he regretted not putting on his Admiral Byrd gear before doing so. He was chilled and began shivering.

But he found what he was hoping to find: A selection switch that offered several choices.

It's a switch unlike any other on the panel, and labeled in English, which clearly suggests it's Siggie Stein's handiwork.

One selection was labeled AG, which had to mean Air-to-Ground. Another read AA, which meant Air-to-Air. And a third reading COL.

That has to mean the pilot of the Storch has the ability to communicate with the Collins.

He pointed them out and explained them to Grüner and then got out of the Storch and went to the Lodestar. With some difficulty, he got the Admiral Byrd Antarctic cold-weather gear out of its bag, and then himself into the bulky gear.

The Thompson was also in the bag, and after a moment's thought he picked it up before he left the airplane. There he slung it over his shoulder, whereupon the canvas strap immediately slipped off. He slung it again and it slipped off again.

It needs a button or something on the shoulder to keep the strap on.

Von Dattenberg went into the airplane and put on a set of the gear.

There's no way both of us — maybe either of us — can get into the Cub wearing this stuff.

He said so when von Dattenberg came out of the Lodestar.

"I'll take him in the Storch," Grüner said, "and give him a quick course in aerial observation while you are determining whether or not your wings are going to stay on."

Cronley went to the Cub, put the Thompson in the backseat, and then, with less difficulty than he expected, got in. A man wearing SAA coveralls came to him and said that they had been running the engine for a couple of minutes every hour.

"To keep the oil from turning to rock again," he explained. "We had a hell of a hard time starting it the first time. But it should start fine now."

The engine caught on the fourth spin of the propeller, but took a long time to warm up. Cronley wondered if Grüner was having the same kind of trouble.

He found a small commo panel, with the same selector switch he had found in the Storch. He found the microphone and earphones and learned that he could wear the earphones or the hood that came with the Admiral Byrd gear — but not both at the same time.

He moved the switch to AA and pressed the TRANSMIT button.

"Can you hear me, Willi?"

There was no response.

When he looked at the Storch he saw why.

Willi did not have the earphones on.

Finally, Grüner looked at him, saw him pointing to his ears, and put the earphones on.

"This is working?" his voice came clearly over Jimmy's earphones.

"Five by five."

"What?"

"Five by five" apparently is not what the Luftwaffe says when one pilot wants to tell another that he's receiving his radio transmission "loud and clear."

"Loud and clear, Willi."

"You, also. Why don't you go first?" Grüner asked, but Cronley understood it as an order. "Head due east at two hundred fifty meters. I'll fly off your left wing at three hundred. Maybe we can find some kind of a landmark on the shore to help us find our way back here."

"Understand due east at two hundred fifty meters," Cronley responded. "The Mighty Cub is rolling."

He advanced the throttle.

If there was something special I should know about taking off, he would have said something.

Or would he have?

I don't know what the fuck I am doing here.

I'm insane.

And flying solo.

Shit . . .

He lifted the tail wheel, and then edged

back on the stick.

The Mighty Cub went airborne.

[Seven]

South Latitude 41.205 degrees,
West Longitude 65.114 degrees
The Atlantic Ocean Coast of Santa Cruz Prov-
ince, Argentina
1210 23 October 1945

If they had been flying at, say, thirty-five hundred feet and making ninety knots or better, they almost certainly wouldn't have seen it.

Or if they were actively looking for it, they probably wouldn't have seen it, either.

But what they were doing was pulling out of a forty-five-knot dive — the third dive, each one increasingly deeper, in the last forty minutes — at fifteen hundred feet (the Storch following at 1,750) to see if the wings on the Mighty Cub would stay on.

From the first dive, Cronley figured if the wings failed, he might survive the crash that would follow, and Grüner could safely put down the Storch on what looked like a reasonably level field and give him a ride back to Estancia Condor.

Presuming, of course, that Grüner and von Dattenberg could get close enough to the flaming wreckage of the Mighty Cub and pull

Cronley's battered body therefrom.

And then the Mighty Cub came out of the third dive, its wings still on.

And then Cronley leveled off — and there it was.

I'll be damned!

He wasn't looking down at U-234.

It was right in front of him.

Oh, shit!

If I can't pull up enough to get over that white camouflage net, or whatever the hell that is, I'm going to fly right into the sonofabitch!

He cleared the camouflage net by a good ten — maybe fifteen — feet and picked up a little more altitude.

"I guess you saw what I saw?" Cronley then said into his microphone.

"Yeah, but in the end you missed," Grüner replied.

"So, what do we do now?"

"I think we have lost the element of surprise," von Dattenberg said. "And you saw all those, several hundred, twenty-five-liter fuel cans?"

"I saw them," Cronley said. "By the trucks that had to bring them."

"And they weren't neatly stacked; they were tossed aside," von Dattenberg said. "The fuel they contained has to now be in U-234's tanks, suggesting she can go to sea to move elsewhere, or to rendezvous with a Russian ship somewhere."

"So, what do we do now?" Cronley repeated.

"We land and see if Willi and I can talk some sense to Alois."

"You want to land? Christ, there's fifty of them and three of us. And who the hell is Alois?"

"Her skipper, Alois Schneider. We're old friends."

"You can stay airborne if you want," Grüner said. "That would make more sense, anyway. But von Dattenberg is right: Unless we can somehow stop it, U-234 is going to leave here, maybe within the hour."

The Storch landed first. By the time it had, Cronley decided that he could do nothing useful staying in the air except notify Colonel Habanzo where they had located U-234, and that she appeared to be about to set sail.

Then he pushed the nose of the Cub down and landed.

He saw that Grüner and von Dattenberg were out of the Storch and walking toward the submarine, and that a group of people — a large group, most of the men carrying Schmeisser submachine guns — were walking toward them.

He got out of the Cub and took the Thompson from the backseat.

I don't think that either Grüner or von Dattenberg has any kind of a weapon.

826

I guess that makes me Wyatt Earp, or maybe Gary Cooper in High Noon.

When the Thompson again slid off the shoulder of his jacket, he decided to carry it with the butt against his hip.

And then he moved the lever to FIRE and racked back the bolt.

He trotted as fast as he could through the snow to catch up with Grüner and von Dattenberg.

He heard a crunching noise and looked around. The left gear of the Storch had broken through the ice. The airplane was now sitting crookedly.

Damn it!

When he looked at von Dattenberg and Grüner walking toward the U-boat, he now saw that the large group from the submarine was being led by four men in the black uniforms of the SS. The one in front, the only one without a Schmeisser, was wearing a black, ankle-length leather overcoat.

What the hell is that all about?

That's not cold-weather gear.

He had an epiphany.

That's to impress the sailors on the submarine! To dazzle them with the all-powerful SS!

Another man caught up with the SS.

"*Wie geht's, Alois?*" von Dattenberg asked.

"What are you doing here, Willi?" Schneider asked.

"I'll do the questioning!" the man in the black leather overcoat snapped.

"I'm here, Willi and I are here, to keep you from making a very serious mistake," von Dattenberg said.

"I said I will ask the questions!" the man in the black overcoat again snapped.

"You must be Lang," Cronley suddenly heard himself saying in German. "*Former* Sturmbannführer Horst Lang."

Where the hell is this coming from? Cronley thought.

"I am *SS-Oberführer* Horst Lang," Lang corrected him furiously. "And who are you?"

"*Former SS-Brigadeführer* Gerhard Körtig told us all about you, Señor Lang," Cronley went on, uncowed, "when we arrested him this morning as he got off the train in Bariloche."

"And you are . . . ?" Lang demanded arrogantly.

"My name is Cronley. I'm a special agent of the Counterintelligence Corps, U.S. Army, on detached service with the Argentine Bureau of Internal Security. You are all under arrest. Tell your men to drop their weapons and put their hands up."

"Willi?" Schneider asked, incredulously.

"He is who he says," von Dattenberg said. "Do what he says, Alois. Please."

They locked eyes.

"The war's over, Alois," von Dattenberg added.

Schneider glanced at Lang, then looked at von Dattenberg — and nodded. He started to turn to his sailors . . .

"Kill him!" Lang suddenly shouted. "Kill that *gottverdammt* American!"

"Nein," Schneider said.

"I said kill him! That is an order!" Lang screamed, almost hysterically.

Schneider made a *Put down your weapons* gesture to his men.

They did.

The SS men looked confused. They neither put down nor raised their weapons.

Lang fumbled as he quickly started to take a pistol from the pocket of his black leather overcoat. He had it almost out when there came a three-round burst from the Thompson.

Lang crumpled silently to the ground.

The SS men watched in shock as the snow around Lang became crimson stained.

They looked back at Cronley. He was gesturing with the muzzle of the Thompson for the SS men to drop their Schmeissers.

"Schnell!" Schneider ordered.

After a long moment, they did so.

Cronley gestured with the muzzle for the SS to raise their hands. They complied.

"What happens now?" Schneider asked.

"I think this is where I throw up," Cronley

said in English. "I've already pissed in my pants."

"Excuse me?" Willi Grüner asked. "I don't speak English."

Von Dattenberg, who spoke English, laughed.

"I can't believe anybody swallowed all that BIS bullshit," Cronley said. "I don't even know where it all came from."

"Wherever it came from it was the right thing to do," von Dattenberg said. "Now I know why Elsa told me you really are an unusual young man."

Cronley looked at Schneider, then at von Dattenberg.

"You trust this guy, right?" Cronley asked, still in English.

"Absolutely," von Dattenberg said.

Cronley switched to German.

"Captain, you have onboard half a ton of uranium oxide. I want it loaded on one of those trucks . . ."

He pointed.

"Excuse me," Schneider then said in perfect British-accented English. "You speak German very well — like a Strasbourger, as a matter of fact — but if you would be more comfortable speaking English . . ."

ABOUT THE AUTHORS

W.E.B. Griffin is the author of six bestselling series: The Corps, Brotherhood of War, Badge of Honor, Men at War, Honor Bound, and Presidential Agent. He has been invested into the orders of St. George of the U.S. Armor Association and St. Michael of the Army Aviation Association of America, and is a life member of the U.S. Special Operations Association; Gaston-Lee Post 5660, Veterans of Foreign Wars; the American Legion, China Post #1 in Exile; the Police Chiefs Association of Southeastern Pennsylvania, Southern New Jersey, and the State of Delaware; the National Rifle Association; the Office of Strategic Services (OSS) Society; and the Flat Earth Society (Pensacola, Florida, and Buenos Aires, Argentina, chapters). He is an honorary life member of the U.S. Army Otter-Caribou Association, the U.S. Army Special Forces Association, the U.S. Marine Raider Association, and the USMC Combat

Correspondents Association. Griffin lives in Alabama and Argentina.

William E. Butterworth IV has been an editor and writer for more than twenty-five years, and has worked closely with his father for a decade on the editing and writing of the Griffin books. He is coauthor of the bestselling novels *The Spymasters, The Saboteurs, The Double Agents, Death and Honor, The Traffickers, The Honor of Spies, The Vigilantes, The Outlaws, Victory and Honor,* and *Covert Warriors.* He is a member of the Sons of the American Legion, China Post #1 in Exile, and of the Office of Strategic Services (OSS) Society; and a life member of the National Rifle Association and the Texas Rifle Association. He lives in Texas.